"I NEVER BACK DOWN FROM A CHALLENGE"

He stepped closer until their bodies nearly touched.

"Is that what I am?" she asked.

"One I could easily win." His voice turned low and husky. "If I choose to stick around with a woman, I always leave her well satisfied."

"But we're not talking about another woman. We're talking about me."

"Exactly."

"So exactly what is it I want?" she demanded.

"Something I figure you've needed badly for a long time."

And then he did the unthinkable. And the irresistible. His mouth took hers in a kiss that drove the air from Dallas's lungs . . .

WILD FLOWER

DONNA STEPHENS

AVON BOOKS NEW YORK

WILD FLOWER is an original publication of Avon Books. This work has never before appeared in book form. This work is a novel. Any similarity to actual persons or events is purely coincidental.

AVON BOOKS
A division of
The Hearst Corporation
1350 Avenue of the Americas
New York, New York 10019

Inside cover author photo by Martha Weaver
Published by arrangement with the author
Library of Congress Catalog Card Number: 94-94079
ISBN: 0-380-77577-8

First Avon Books Printing: September 1994

Printed in the U.S.A.

RA 10 9 8 7 6 5 4 3 2 1

To Alice Orr, my agent, who took
me under her wing when I needed her most.

To my sister, Paula, and my
nieces, Natalie and Allie, I love you all.

WILD FLOWER

Chapter 1

April 1876

Instinct, raw and potent, took over, and Dallas O'Neal, steadying her grip on the lines, urged the four-horse team to breakneck speed over the rugged terrain. Sweat ran in rivulets down her face, neck, and sides, forming dark patches under the arms of the cotton shirt she wore. The dust, churned up by drumming hooves and steel-rimmed wheels, gritted against her teeth and stung her cheeks and eyes. But she couldn't cover her face with her bandanna, and under no circumstances could she loosen her hold on the lines.

"How many?" she asked her brother, who rode shotgun beside her.

"Six," Waco bit out. "Strung out single file."

"How close?"

Waco levered a shell into the firing chamber of his rifle with one efficient motion, cocking the repeater with a snap of his wrist.

"Half mile to our right and about a hundred

yards to our rear." His tense posture and expression revealed his readiness for the running fight to come.

Dallas looked over her shoulder at the outlaws. The riders were gaining ground, angling toward the stage—almost within shooting range.

Grim possibilities weighed on Dallas. Thoughts of the stage line's two-month string of robberies and problems flashed across her mind. She had too much at stake to give up without a fight. And fight, she would. She clenched her jaw in determination. She'd eluded them twice before.

Only five more miles till they were home, Dallas thought. They *had* to reach the waylay station. Everything depended on the stagecoach. Her job. Her family's welfare. Everything!

Dallas shifted her gaze from the road to the lathered team. The horses' nostrils flared from exertion, their ears twitched nervously, their manes and tails whipped in the breeze. The vibration of the seat told Dallas that the speed of the stage had passed the point of dangerous—to critical. An unexpected rut or hole could throw the coach out of control.

The outlaws were coming up on the stage's rear right side, giving them the advantage of shooting right-handed. So as not to ride on the roof and expose himself to every shot, Waco would have to twist around and fire behind his back to his left.

Suddenly, above the clamor of the careening stage, Dallas heard a shot behind her, followed by a second and a third. She spoke to her team, with practiced, firm movements through the lines, to check the frightened horses as best she could.

From inside the coach came the piercing screams of the three women passengers. Dallas clenched her teeth at their hysterics.

She forced herself to think. Clearly. Calmly. As Waco raised his rifle and turned on the driver's seat, Dallas realized what she must do.

"I can shoot left-handed," she shouted above the din of the thundering team and speeding stage, and trailing gunfire.

Brother and sister had worked together long enough not to question each other in times of crisis. Waco took the lines, and Dallas took the rifle.

Turning, she leveled the repeater, aimed, and snapped off a shot. A horse and rider went down in a cloud of dust. Reflexively she ducked as return fire erupted and bullets slammed into the stage.

Waiting a heartbeat, she raised the gun and fired again. Her shot missed. Her next shot dropped a second outlaw.

The acrid smell of gunpowder blended with the pungent smell of sweat and anxiety as Dallas emptied the rifle. Spent shells littered the coach. A third gunman fell from his horse in a spasm of pain.

Dallas kept firing, quickly levering bullets into the firing chamber without recoil. She was determined in her shooting. But so were the outlaws. Bullets whined through the air. One thudded into the side of the coach and sent bits of splintered wood flying.

The three remaining outlaws changed tactics and fanned out. One rider moved to the right. The second horseman dropped to the rear. The third bandit approached from the left.

Suddenly the coach bucked and swayed. A chuckhole. Damn. Dallas grabbed the side railing. Gunshots came from the rear. More came from the left. Instinctively she rose, twisted to the right, and fired.

Dallas heard her brother cry out. Waco! She jerked her head around to look at him. Her breath became a hard knot in her throat. His hand! Dear Lord, no, she thought frantically.

She tried to fight off the desperate panic as she lowered her gaze. . . . There on the ground, between the last pair of racing horses, trailed the lines.

Waco ripped the bandanna from his neck and wrapped it around his left hand. The stage hit several bumps and shimmied, knocking Waco, and his injured hand, against the side railing.

Cursing, Waco pulled his revolver from his holster. "I'll cover you."

She reacted without thinking, without considering the possible consequences, without considering anything beyond the fact that she had to get those traces.

Dallas moved cautiously, yet quickly, to the edge of the seat. She had to climb over the edge of the box and onto the hounds that secured the coach tongue to the frame. From there, she had a chance of reaching the lines.

Suddenly Dallas sensed a new danger. She jerked her head around. Another man rode hard at an angle to intercept the stage before the flat expanse of terrain ended.

She reached for the discarded rifle, braced herself, and fired. Her shot went high, but the bullet passed close enough to force the rider to stretch out low over his mount's neck. To Dallas's dismay, the outlaw didn't slow his horse's stride.

Time seemed to stop—seconds passed into numbing minutes—as the outlaw spurred his horse closer to the runaway team. He leaned toward one leader and reached for the harness.

Before she could get a second shot off, Dallas realized the rider was too close to the front runners to be sure she wouldn't hit one of the horses. Her love for her horses caused Dallas to hesitate, giving the outlaw the time he needed to grab the lead trace and pull.

She held her breath and waited, rifle stock snug against her shoulder, cheek touching metal warm from use.

As soon as he moved . . .

She never got the chance, for suddenly Waco yelled, "Don't shoot!"

"What?" she hollered over her shoulder, the man still within her sights.

"He's not one of them. The last one turned back. It's over."

"Are you sure?"

"Yes."

Dallas cut her eyes back to the stranger. He slowed the team to a halt, reined his horse in a half circle, and headed toward the stage.

Her eyes widened at the sight of the dust-covered stranger astride the lathered blue roan. The man was dressed entirely in black, from his boots to the hat pulled low over his eyes. Dallas noticed the way he wore his gun belt, low on his lean hips, and his holster, strapped to his muscular thigh, as if they were a natural part of him.

As if trouble followed—or lurked ahead of—him.

This man might not be an outlaw, but he looked as dangerous as one.

She lightly fingered the rifle trigger. She wasn't going to take any chances until she knew his intentions.

He maneuvered his sweat-darkened horse alongside the stage and gazed up at her. Her insides coiled tightly. She had never seen a more intimidating man. Crackling vitality, unmistakable and unsettling, radiated from his tall, muscular frame.

"Just what in hell did you think you were doing?" he asked in a tight voice that challenged her.

His haughty, demanding tone scraped her already raw nerves. Hell! She knew a great deal about hell. She'd just been through it! And she didn't care for the way his gaze traveled, slowly and insultingly, over her. Although she had never seen this man before, she saw what was coming—trouble, plain and simple.

She should have shot him.

"I might ask you the same thing," she said, putting down the rifle.

Her gaze, glowing green with warning, met his, smoldering blue with daring.

"You're the one who's got some explaining to do. I was trying to save your neck. I take being shot at real personal." He lifted a black brow. "And I'm not one to forget an injury or insult. Even from a woman who dresses like a man."

Tension shimmered in the air like heat waves on a hot day.

His bold stare fired her anger, and Dallas snapped, "I don't care how you take it. Or if you remember it until your dying day. Or if you approve of the way I dress." Her chin jutted at a stubborn angle. "I don't make it a habit of explaining myself to anyone, including you."

"It's just like a woman not to think before acting. Why shoot at a man who tries to help you?"

Her back stiffened. His insult to her intelligence cut Dallas to the core. "When I've got outlaws chasing me, and I can't tell one from the other, I don't stop to ask questions."

The rigid set to his jaw betrayed his own irritation. "You always so friendly?"

A few choice names—all of which would have made a churchgoing woman blush—flitted through her mind. She didn't cotton to this man, and she intended to put him in his place.

"Only with people I like," she said.

He leaned forward and folded his arms atop the pommel of his saddle. "I believe it's customary for a person to say thank you when someone saves her life." His voice was low and unhurried.

Dallas hated his unflappable air. She'd like nothing better than to put a kink in his tail. "I suppose most people would be grateful, but I'm not most people."

The stranger dismounted and looked up at her. "I can see that. But you could try being appreciative."

"All I have to do is say thanks?"

"Unless you can think of another way to show your gratitude."

Waco tensed beside her, and Dallas cast him a look that warned him not to interfere.

The stranger's insolent manner kindled her anger anew. "I can think of some places you could go, but you wouldn't like them."

"Can't find it in yourself to be obliged?"

"To you? No. I can take care of myself."

He had the temerity to laugh. "Didn't look that way to me."

Dallas saw red.

Waco cleared his throat, grimacing from the effort. "I'll check on our passengers." He glanced at the stranger, then to his sister, and held up his hand, a wry smile on his face despite his painful injury. "Maybe one of the ladies could see to my hand." He disappeared over the side of the stage.

Dallas recognized Waco's look. He didn't want to be around when the fireworks started. How well her brother knew her prideful temper.

Yet, despite her anger, she felt irritatingly aware of the stranger's sharp, clearly drawn features visible beneath the brim of his hat. She also felt the piercing, hypnotic intensity of his blue gaze—reflecting a poise and hidden strength that flashed a message to her: Beware.

His raw masculinity unnerved her, while at the same time, it stirred something inside her, something deliciously forbidden, something she had never felt before. Her womanly instincts whispered to her that this man possessed a dark passion that would burn her if she dared to touch him.

The man was more frightening than any previous danger she had faced.

Her thoughts broke like a thunderstorm. He was frustrating, egotistical . . . and handsome.

Anger was easier—and safer—to feel than the peculiar, unfamiliar emotions this man roused within her. Mentally she rose to the menacing challenge that he had laid down. She'd be damned if she'd allow this stranger to intimidate her.

She had wasted enough time already. She needed to get the stage under way. Intent on fetching the lines, Dallas began to climb down from the driver's seat. As she made her descent, she looked at him. Unsettled, she missed the small metal footpad with her foot and tumbled from the stage . . .

. . . into the stranger's arms.

He couldn't stop the forward momentum of Dallas's weight as she fell against him. They hit the ground. His arms locked about her waist, with him taking the brunt of the fall.

Neither moved for several seconds.

Dallas lay breathless, stunned. She slowly opened her eyes and found herself staring into his penetrating gaze. She was lying atop his hard-knit body, her slender legs tangled intimately with his muscular ones. Her mouth was perilously close to his, and she felt his warm, moist breath against her face. Musky leather and horse sweat and his own masculine scent assaulted her senses.

She felt the buckles of his belt and gun belt press intimately into her stomach. She felt the heat of his body penetrate the cotton of her pants and shirt, making her all too aware of his gender. Their harsh breathing and rapid heartbeats mingled.

Realizing the awkward position she was in, Dallas fought her embarrassment the only way she knew how—with anger. "Let go of me!"

He chuckled, a low, humorless rumble from deep inside his chest. "You never do say thank you."

"I didn't ask for your help."

"What was I supposed to do, let you fall and break your neck?"

"Just get your hands off me." Dallas squirmed within his hold, inadvertently rubbing her breasts across his chest.

"For God's sake, stop wiggling," the stranger said thickly.

He released his hold. She rolled off him and scrambled to her feet. Her breathing came fast and sporadic, and her pulse raced. She gulped air, trying to restore order to her chaotic senses.

Dallas lashed out in outrage and mortification. "If you've got something to say, then say it," she said tersely. "Otherwise, I've got work to do."

"And just what is that?"

"Driving this stage, if it's any of your business."

"And if it were my business, I'd want to know what a woman's doing driving a stagecoach."

Her pride had been scalded too often, by arrogant men who thought a woman incapable of doing a man's job, to let that one go. "The same as a man!"

"Really?" His inflection clearly stated his disapproval. The glint in his eyes reinforced the sentiment.

Now she was certain she should have shot him!

She still might if he didn't wipe that smug expression off his face.

"Yes. And I drive it bette
drew a burning breath. "Wo
anything, if given the opportu
gant, overbearing men like you
them that chance."

"And what would you do if give ...ce?"

She felt his mood shift from irri...ion to mild curiosity. She didn't like—or want—his interest.

"I'd do exactly what I do now. I don't need a man to take care of me. I can think for myself." Strong conviction underscored her words. "No man is going to tell me what to do."

"Never?"

Exasperation blew through her. "Never!"

"What would happen if one did?"

"He'd find out quick enough that I don't take to obeying orders."

"I'd be interested to see you up against a man who didn't allow a woman to dictate to him."

"Sorry to disappoint you, but no man is going to get the better of me."

"Hmm." An odd light entered his eyes. "I wonder what would happen if you ever met a man who had patience enough to tame you."

Dallas squared her shoulders. "That man hasn't been born yet."

He gave a dry chuckle, as if enjoying some private joke at her expense. Ohh! The nerve of the man!

"It's been a pleasure, ma'am." He mockingly touched the brim of his hat. "Maybe our paths will cross again one day."

"When hell freezes over."

"You know what they say about Texas weather." He gave her a half smile. "Stand around long and it'll change." He mounted his horse, ...ed the blue roan around, and rode away.

Incensed by his distasteful, cocksure attitude, his typical male narrow-mindedness, and the funny feelings churning inside her stomach, she glared at his retreating back, with her hands curled into fists at her sides.

She never wanted to lay eyes on that man again!

Suddenly the impact of the recent events returned with a vengeance. Needing time to gather her scattered wits, Dallas walked to a mesquite tree and sat down. Her body shook as she contemplated what could have happened to her. Or Waco. Or her passengers.

She hugged her middle, trying to gain some control over her shaking limbs. This feeling of helplessness went against her grain. She had stubbornly searched and fought for her independence, and she prided herself on her ability to maintain that hard-won self-sufficiency. Well, she thought, in the span of a single afternoon she had allowed herself to be ambushed by outlaws and manhandled by a stranger. So much for taking care of herself!

The measured tread of horse hooves and the rattle of wheels kept Dallas company on the return trip.

Spring was one of her favorite seasons. She loved to ride across the landscape and see the profusion of wildflowers erupting in glorious shades of bluebonnet blue, Indian paintbrush orange, wine-cup red, lazy Susan yellow, and primrose pink. Young shoots of grass painted the sloping hills in vivid, living shades of green.

Normally she enjoyed the familiar feel of leather between her fingers. Smooth and dark from use. The smell, tangy from sweat.

But not now.

Dallas thought of the tall stranger with bold blue eyes. Her cheeks burned.

She cursed the misfortune of coming across such a disagreeable man. He filled her mind with unsettling thoughts and her body with peculiar, unfamiliar feelings.

The feeling of being stripped of her natural defenses by his dark looks and heated touch left Dallas shaken. She pushed the disconcerting thoughts to the back of her mind.

She lived her life independent from other people's opinions and expectations. Especially men. Besides, what did she care if most people disapproved of her? She had grown accustomed to receiving strange looks and hearing talk behind her back, from passengers and townspeople, because she worked and dressed like a man. Well, it suited her just fine that people kept their distance. She had more important things to worry about than idle gossip. She didn't enjoy the company of most women, and she couldn't abide their ridiculous games of chasing men. She was more comfortable driving the stage, or riding horseback, than she would ever be wearing skirts.

But her independence had forced her to make sacrifices along the way. In moments of honesty, she admitted to herself that, although her days were bright and filled with satisfaction, her nights were sometimes dark and tortured with longing. Being in the compelling stranger's arms had only reinforced that nameless yearning.

The sun rode low on the western horizon when the stage rolled into the waylay station.

To say Dallas was in a foul mood would be an understatement. To say the arrogant stranger had nothing to do with her irritation would be a downright lie.

Home was a two-story wooden structure, with porches edged by railings on both levels, running the length of the house front. A weathered picket fence enclosed the yard, where a stately, ancient Spanish oak grew. Some feet away and to the left rear of the main house sat the barn with a large corral. Behind the barn was a smaller bunkhouse.

The three women passengers filed out of the stage and made their way inside the station house as two stock handlers unhitched the tired team and led the horses away to be rubbed down and fed.

Tired and hungry, and still in the grip of her black mood, Dallas retrieved the mail and payroll bags and climbed down from the box. She knew she wasn't fit company for anyone and decided she'd slip into the kitchen to eat alone.

Miguel, a longtime friend and worker, greeted Dallas, his bearded, middle-aged face wreathed in smiles. "It's good that you're home." His compassionate eyes took in her appearance. "You look tired, *niña*."

She managed a smile. "I am."

Usually Miguel could brighten her dark moods, but she didn't think even he could help her at the moment. Loyal and dependable, Miguel steadied her in a way that no one else could. When her parents had died of the fever, the elderly Mexican had become like a father to her. He shared his knowledge of people with Dallas. It wasn't always easy, but he helped her to understand. And he gave her unconditional love, not expecting her to be anyone other than herself. She returned that love.

Miguel walked to the stage and fingered the bullet marks that marred the painted wood. His expression grew somber as a faraway look entered his eyes.

"The Old Ones warned me of this," he said.

Dallas knew he meant the spirits with which he communicated. Since he had nearly died of fever when young, Miguel had been blessed— or cursed—depending on how one might perceive his special talents—with the gift of prophecy and the art of healing. He had instilled in her a healthy respect for the world beyond her knowledge.

Dallas's lips thinned. "The outlaws are becoming bolder and the robberies are occurring more often. We were lucky this time."

"I must see to Waco, but are you all right?"

"I just have a bad case of nerves."

For more than one reason, she thought.

A reason who had dark looks and spellbinding eyes.

Her nerves were stretched as tight as newly strung barbed wire. And just as jagged.

"If you like, I will make you a special cup of tea to help you sleep tonight."

Dallas smiled her appreciation, then her facial features tightened. "If you had sensed the danger, why didn't you warn me? Waco might not have been hurt if I'd known what to expect."

"Did you not come back alive?"

"Well, yes."

"The Old Ones' warning does not mean you must not face dangers and your fears. They have protected you and Waco well." Patience flowed in his voice. "You know, *niña,* that you cannot run from what must be. There are lessons to be learned."

Normally Dallas didn't question Miguel or his messages, but she wasn't in the best frame of mind at the moment. The fact that her brother had been shot only served to worsen her already vile mood.

"I don't see how Waco's getting shot teaches anything," she said tersely.

"Perhaps there is something you must do alone." His coffee-bean brown eyes darkened. "Or perhaps you must remove one thing to make room for another. Sometimes the Old Ones make choices for us, to prod us along our path."

"The Old Ones are certainly being vague tonight."

Suddenly a gust of wind knocked her hat from her head and blew loose tendrils of blond hair about her face.

"They laugh with you, but do not question their messages or show them less respect than they deserve. They are here to help us all. Those who listen and learn will be greatly rewarded."

Dallas felt contrite. "I'm sorry. I'm letting my bad mood affect me more than I should."

"It'll get worse before it gets better. But have heart, *niña,* it will pass into something of much happiness."

"Now, what's that supposed to mean?" she asked.

Miguel shrugged and smiled. "I've said enough. Go in and have your supper. I must see to your brother's hand."

Dallas hugged him affectionately. "You old bandit. I don't always understand what you mean, but I couldn't do without you."

She tossed the mail and payroll bags over her shoulder and walked with weary steps to the house. It was good to be home. This station was the one place where she felt she belonged, completely and without reservation.

Once she was inside, Dallas's gaze roamed over the familiar interior of the place she'd called home for the past ten years. She loved every crack, every creaking floorboard, every aging wooden plank. Plain, comfortable homemade furniture filled the rooms, except for pieces that her parents had brought from Tennessee in '42 when they seized the opportunity to own their own place and migrated to Texas. The downstairs consisted of a parlor, a dining room, the kitchen, and a covered back porch. A hallway bisected the house, with a staircase to the right, leading to the second floor. All the bedrooms were upstairs.

The aroma of meat and vegetables simmering was a welcoming one, and Dallas inhaled in anticipation. Her oldest sister, Abilene, was the best cook this side of San Antonio.

With a lighter step, Dallas passed the passenger dining room to the left of the stairs. From the open doorway she heard voices, clinking dishes, and scraping utensils.

Her sisters' familiar voices and laughter filtered down the hall to her. She smiled. They certainly were having a good time. After today, Lord knew she needed one.

She turned the corner and entered the kitchen, intent on having some fluffy biscuits, dripping with butter and clover honey. Her thoughts and her steps skidded to a halt as her gaze fell on the room's inhabitants. She dropped the bags she carried.

The smile died on her lips, and she stared in wide-eyed disbelief. No! It couldn't be! Not him!

From a distance, Abbey's voice broke through her shock. "Dallas, you're back. Come meet the new line boss, Trey Conner."

Chapter 2

"*You!*" Dallas said with a soft explosion of air.

Her gaze locked with the arresting blue eyes that had hauntingly plagued her thoughts. The very eyes that she had cursed every mile of her return run.

She paled, then blushed hotly from her neck to the tips of her ears as anger swept through her. Her fatigue evaporated. What kind of game had he been playing with her this afternoon, and what game did he play now?

Briefly her mind registered the difference in his appearance. His strongly carved jaw and cheeks were freshly shaved. His long, thick black hair hung in damp waves untidily about his collar. The corners of his mouth turned up slightly in an amused smile. The combined effect made him seem, to Dallas, more dangerous than before. She told herself that anger, not attraction, made her pulse throb at the base of her throat.

It would seem everyone in the room was having a grand time. But her.

Well, he may have washed and changed clothes, but that didn't sweeten the scent of the skunk underneath.

She moved closer to where he sat at the end of the table. "What are you doing here?" She clenched her teeth so hard that her jaw hurt.

"Just what your sister said."

"I want to hear it from you." A command underlined her words.

His eyes flashed briefly. "I don't take orders. I give them."

"I've run this station for the last three years."

"As of two hours ago, you don't anymore."

Dallas balled her hands into fists. "We don't need a new boss." She wanted to say that she didn't need him.

"I represent the new company owners." Sarcasm dripped from his words. "And since you're doing such a good job handling the outlaws, you won't mind if I at least pretend to do the job I'm paid to do."

Dallas gritted her teeth. "Probably overpaid."

His mouth curled into a humorless imitation of a smile. "Depends on what you get for your money."

"Where's your authority?" She smiled tightly. "Not that I don't trust you."

Conner produced a letter from his shirt pocket. "Right here."

He handed her the letter, and she unfolded the paper and read the contents. A frown tugged at her mouth. He was Trey Conner, the new line boss, with authority to do whatever he wanted.

She had heard talk of the line being sold, hoped the rumor wasn't true, yet dreaded that it was.

She took a deep breath. Well, she'd always been one to look trouble straight in the eye. She saw no reason to blink now.

She thrust the letter back at him, sensing Conner was a man who took control slowly, but surely. "Why didn't you tell me who you were?"

"You didn't ask," he replied smoothly.

His blue eyes bored deeply into hers, mercilessly, as if he probed her thoughts.

She gave him a go-to-hell look.

He gave her a crooked smile. Message received.

At the end of the table, Abbey sat with her smooth brow furrowed in bewilderment as she pushed curling wisps of blond hair away from her face. "Do you two know each other?" She looked at Conner with her large green eyes.

"We met earlier today," he said. "We had a very interesting conversation. Miss O'Neal told me quite a lot about herself."

Dallas went cold, then hot, as her mind reviewed every impassioned word she had said to him. And every passion he had made her feel. Did he intend to force those words down her throat until she choked on humility?

"Didn't you, Miss O'Neal?" His smile broadened.

"Call us by our first names," Tyler, the youngest sister, said in her distinctively rough voice. Much like Dallas, she had a quick temper and a unique way of expressing herself. "We're all Miss O'Neal. Except Waco, of course." She laughed.

"How did all of you get such unusual names?" Conner asked.

Abbey's pleasant voice drifted across the table.

"For each of the towns we were born in, except when it came time for Tyler and Waco to be born. Ma was in Tyler, having the babies, and Pa was in Waco, working. Since they're twins, it was quite convenient."

Conner regarded Dallas, his eyes glittering with challenge. "I want to talk to you after supper."

"Seems to me, we've said enough already."

"Don't make this harder on yourself by prolonging the inevitable."

Before Dallas could say anything, Abbey, always levelheaded, always the placater, said gently yet firmly, "Wash up, Dallas. Food's getting cold."

Wordlessly Dallas trudged from the room to the back porch and washed her face, neck, and arms. She dried herself and returned in time to hear the flowing conversation.

"Where are you from, Mr. Conner?" Abbey asked.

"Fort Worth."

Abbey poured herself a glass of milk. "You have family there?"

Dallas waited anxiously.

"Only my stepfather and mother." He turned his penetrating gaze on Dallas. "I'm not married."

The varmint! He could read her mind.

Dallas didn't realize she had been holding her breath until she exhaled softly. She regarded him, wondering what kind of emotions and ambitions drove this man.

He was certainly adept at hiding his feelings. Too good. The fact that she couldn't figure him out was irritating to her.

"How long you figure on staying on as line boss?" Waco interjected.

"As long as it takes to rid the line of trouble."

"What happened?" Abbey asked as she passed a steaming bowl of greens.

"There were six of them," Waco said, gingerly resting his bandaged hand in a shoulder sling. "Came out of nowhere. Luckily, we were on a good stretch of road." He looked first at Dallas, then at Trey Conner. "It was also lucky that Mr. Conner came to help."

"Call me Trey," Conner said, wiping his mouth on his napkin.

His deep, rich voice eroded the layers of indifference Dallas had built, exposing her attraction to him. Panic crept around the edges of her mind. She didn't want to find him appealing. She didn't want to find him interesting.

But she did.

Her attraction to Trey Conner irritated the blue blazes out of her. She knew she couldn't sit here a second longer.

She stood. "I'm going for a swim." Turning on her heel, she left.

She grabbed a towel, a bar of homemade soap, and a change of clothing from a chest of drawers near the back door. Then she headed for the creek below the main house.

She needed a swim to cool off. She needed to get as far away from Trey Conner as she possibly could.

Dallas clutched the bar of soap until she thought it would ooze out between her fingers.

This had turned out to be one hell of a day. And she had the feeling that it wasn't over.

At the creek she unbraided her single plait of thick hair and stripped off her clothes, boots, and socks. She sat on the bank, her bare bottom tickled by grass, and inched into the water. The cold water caused her to gasp. Taking a deep breath, she dove under. Surfacing with a toss of her wet mane, she smoothed the strands away from her face, her teeth chattering.

She wasted no time in lathering first her hair, then her body. Sighing, she felt the grime lift from her body, and along with it, her frustration. The cleansing served as a balm for her bruised body and spirit.

Dallas dressed, braided her hair, then retraced her path to the station, drawing her steps out. She didn't care to talk to Trey Conner.

Not ready for the impending confrontation with Conner, she detoured to the barn. She often went there when she wanted to be alone and think.

She stepped inside and eased the door shut behind her. She breathed deeply. Instantly the familiar, reassuring smells of hay, leather, and horses assailed her. The warm, musky air wrapped around her, making her feel safe and secure.

She strolled down the row of stalls until she heard a noise nearby. She stopped and looked over the shoulder-high wall of the next stall. Something unexplainable drew Dallas closer to the compartment, and she peered around the half wall.

The fading rays of the sun filtered through the

weathered planks of the barn, and small shafts of dust-sprinkled light danced about Trey Conner's dark head.

He was hunkered down beside his horse, rubbing the blue roan's legs with liniment. He spoke in a soft, soothing tone, his movements as gentle as his voice.

She watched his hands move with slow, easy motions. They were fascinating and sensual with their long, tapered fingers tanned by the sun. How well she remembered those hands on her.

Driving for the line over the past three years, she had seen a great many men, in various shapes and dispositions. But she had never been aware of such untamed, stark masculinity. Raw strength. Seasoned virility.

"You looking for me?" Conner rose and ran his hand over his horse's sleek rump.

Walking from the stall, he drew a bandanna from his pocket and wiped his hands. His own spicy scent blended with the sharp smell of liniment and musty air of the barn to create a strangely appealing combination.

She found herself staring into his hard blue eyes. His gaze held hers. A woman could lose herself in those eyes, could be led astray by his deep, rich voice, by the raw power that simmered behind Conner's civilized veneer.

Seconds ticked by silently. The air was thick with tension, unspoken thoughts, labored heartbeats.

She was immobilized by a strange, frightening excitement that knotted her stomach and set her heart to pounding. The primal current running between them made her go weak.

He shouldn't be that close to her. She knew it, yet she couldn't retreat.

She was that lost woman. . . .

Abruptly she broke off the thought. Well, she wasn't just any woman. She supposed any woman foolish, or crazy, enough to get mixed up with Trey Conner deserved what she got.

She, however, had no intention of becoming involved with such an impossible, rude man.

Dallas raised her stubborn chin. "You said you wanted to talk to me."

"That's right. There are going to be some changes around here—"

"You can't fire me!"

"Listen to me," Conner said tightly.

"No, you listen to me," Dallas shot back. "I've driven this stage for the past three years and done a damned good job of it. The former owners had no complaints. You shouldn't either." Her chest heaved.

"Driving a stage isn't a job for a woman."

"Only if she's not capable of doing it."

"I've already decided."

"You haven't given me a chance."

"A chance for what?" A tic developed in his cheek. "I've seen enough."

"What you saw today was out of my control."

"Exactly."

"I can't believe this!"

"I don't care if you believe it or not, so long as you understand it."

"What? Your dislike of women?"

His mouth lifted in a hint of a smile. "Oh, I like women all right—in their proper places."

"Proper places being at the feet of men?"

"That's not exactly where I had in mind."

Dallas snapped her mouth shut with a click of her teeth.

"As I said before, I should fire you," Conner said.

"You can't do that to my family." Dallas inhaled sharply. "Besides, we have a written contract. Even you can't break the law just because it suits you."

"You'll find I can do a lot of things if it suits me," Conner drawled.

"I don't think you've got a choice."

"There was no mention of a woman driver to the new owners."

"Maybe they didn't ask."

Conner gave a disdainful snort. "I'm sure it never occurred to them that a woman with no sense would be driving a stage."

"Makes more sense to have a woman who knows her job than to bring in a man who knows nothing about the route."

"When it comes to you, I doubt anything makes sense."

"All you need to know is that my family has a binding contract to run this station."

He wore a faintly menacing look, as if he was holding his aggravation in check. "Well, don't think I'm going to be easy on you."

"You haven't been easy on me since I laid eyes on you."

He ignored her remark and said, "I'm going to be your shotgun."

"What about Waco?"

"You know as well as I do that he can't do his job with his hand like it is."

How on earth would she be able to tolerate such an insufferable, unbending—handsome—man at such close proximity?

"I don't want you riding with me," she said.

His eyes, hard and speculative, locked on her face. "You didn't hear me. I'm your new rider."

"The hell you are!" At the tightening of his mouth, some of her confidence eroded, but she refused to give an inch.

"You're the most stubborn female I've ever had the misfortune to come across." A note of dry amusement colored his voice. "Must be the Irish in you."

His irritating words and bold stare grated on her nerves. Incensed, she started to give him another piece of her mind, but she knew it was useless and snapped her mouth shut.

His expression grew more somber. "You'll find out quick enough that you can't win against me. So don't try."

Dallas inhaled deeply, then slowly released her breath. Damm temper, she thought with self-disgust. Why did she always allow her rash ways to get the better of her? But she couldn't change who she was, any more than a bird dog could change its spots.

Unable to stand the thick and uneasy silence, she said, "You won't like riding with me."

"Like it or not, I'm your new shotgun until further notice." Although he stood with negligent ease, the tautness about his mouth belied his indifference.

"A driver's got to trust her shotgun," Dallas reasoned. "I don't know the first thing about you."

"You know all you need to know."

Her body tensed. "I do things my way."

"That'll change, too."

She drew herself up to her full height of five feet seven inches. "You can't do this!"

"I can." His gaze raked her, and he said ever so slowly, with quiet emphasis, "And I have."

"You wouldn't take over if I were a man."

"It doesn't matter to me what you think," Conner said calmly but authoritatively. "Unless you want to lose your job, I suggest you concern yourself only with the driving of the stage. I'll see to the running of the line. I don't need," he added, his gaze lingering on her freshly scrubbed face, "or want a woman's advice."

Swallowing her pride, she struggled to remain calm. She was beginning to suspect that one had to remain unruffled when dealing with Trey Conner.

"You might not need my help now, but there'll come a time when you will," she said with icy detachment that demanded his attention and his respect.

"I doubt it."

She'd rather be snakebit than betray the knot of trepidation in her stomach. With frosty contempt she channeled all her energies into keeping her features composed. "So all I have to do is follow orders, is that it?"

Conner's gaze took in her set face and rigid stance with open speculation. "I expect my orders to be followed." He stepped closer until their bodies nearly touched. For a moment she was subjected to a thorough and unnerving appraisal. "Do you understand?"

She didn't like the heat and tension behind his words, the energy in his quiet stance. "Oh, I understand, all right." Her voice dropped a degree with disdain. "I'm not supposed to think for myself, but blindly follow instructions."

"From what I've seen, I can't imagine you ever blindly doing anything, *Miss* O'Neal." His breath fell on her cheek.

"You might be surprised at just what I'm capable of."

"Surprised? No." Conner shrugged. "Interested? Maybe."

Dallas wanted to crack his hard shell. "Are you always so sure of yourself?" she asked, eyebrows lifted in speculation.

"Confidence is a quality I admire."

"Well, you certainly aren't lacking in it."

"Women have never found me lacking." He assessed her with a disruptive mixture of purpose and amusement. "In anything."

Anger and humiliation blotched her neck and cheeks. She drew a burning breath, but words failed her.

At her lack of response, Conner drawled, "What? Nothing to say?" He laughed dryly.

"Oh, I have plenty to say, but not if I want to keep my job."

"You'll find that I'm the type of man who lets nothing get in my way when my mind is set on something." His gaze trapped hers, a dark indulgence shining from his eyes. "Or someone."

Tension was hot upon the air.

She ground her teeth, reining in her frustration with more patience than she knew she possessed. Every minute she lingered here—with him—brought her closer to disaster.

Annoyed that she had allowed her thoughts to focus so sharply on Trey Conner, she redirected her contemplation to those who mattered most to her. "What about my sisters and brother? Will they be able to keep their jobs?"

"I see no reason why not, as long as they follow orders."

Dallas realized how much her job and her family's welfare depended on him, however exasperating she found his overbearing manner. She had no choice but to endure. For the time being.

"Why don't you approve of me?" she asked simply.

Her gaze, glowing green with challenge, met his, smoldering blue with warning.

"Not you. Just what you do." He spoke dispassionately, but an unnerving fire burned beneath his words. "I'm damned sure you shouldn't be driving a stage, but it seems that I don't have much choice right now. After all, you do have a signed contract. But I'll be watching you. Sooner or later, you'll give me a reason to fire you. It's only a matter of time."

Dallas compressed her lips. Well, she had asked. And he had bluntly answered. But it still hurt that she had to prove herself to yet another man. Not because she wanted to. But because she had no choice if she wanted to keep her job and her home.

She felt a twinge of apprehension. What did he expect from her? She had no experience with men. And she had no experience in dealing with the feelings Trey Conner evoked within her. The unknown was frightening. She masked her fear with anger.

"I may have to work with you, but I don't have to tolerate your attentions," she said heatedly, protecting herself with a childish outburst.

"Meaning?"

Indignation filled Dallas. He knew perfectly well what she meant. "Just stay away from me."

Conner released his breath slowly. "Don't worry on that account. All I'm concerned about is doing my job, and that's what I'm going to do." No traces of doubt softened his features. "Besides, what makes you think I'd have anything to do with such a cantankerous female as you?"

His words stung. "Cantankerous, maybe. But smart enough to know your kind when I see him. Stay out of my way."

He moved closer. His face loomed near hers, and his breath whispered across her face as he spoke. "If you know what's good for you, you'll stay out of mine."

Conner was a brooding presence, dark and languid. She was sharing space with him, fighting for every breath she drew. She noticed how broad his shoulders were, how muscular his thighs, how indolent his stance.

She noticed all these things.

And more . . . Too much more.

She watched his gaze shift to her lips and linger there, making her extremely uncomfortable, making her tingle all over. He was so tall and muscular, so alluringly handsome, so close . . . still so close. For one wild moment, she thought he meant to kiss her. And shamelessly, Dallas hoped he would.

Trey watched the color rise in Dallas's cheeks. Despite his irritation, he had to admit that not only was Dallas O'Neal obstinate, impulsive, and direct—she was a very attractive young woman. He admired the blond hair that framed her temples and emphasized the richness of her thickly lashed green eyes. Her face was pleasingly oval, with prominent cheekbones, a slender straight nose, and a delicately round chin. But it was her lips, tantalizingly full yet firm, that held his interest. They invited a man's kiss. Trey reined in his thoughts. He seldom allowed himself to feel any emotion, and he was surprised that he felt such a strong attraction to this woman.

Common sense told him that he should fire her, but his instincts told him that she didn't have a common bone in her body. He saw her dispatch him to the devil with her snapping gaze. He thought he saw something of himself within that look. He guessed that spirit could never be conquered, but the right man could subdue it. Her direct speech and actions piqued his curiosity. But he sensed she was all woman underneath her forceful exterior. Perhaps too much woman for the average man. But then, he wasn't average. His taste in females usually ran to women who never had a complicated thought in their heads, seeking pleasure for pleasure's sake, instead of females like Dallas who defied convention and considered themselves to be a man's equal. He disapproved of a woman driver, but he couldn't resist a mysterious challenge. He'd allow her to continue driving—for now.

"You'd better go back to the house," he said tersely.

Dallas's steps were angry and brisk as she walked to the house. Maybe Trey Conner had saved her and Waco's lives, and maybe he had temporarily saved her job. Maybe—but maybe not. But that didn't mean she had to tolerate his insults.

She found her older sister in the kitchen.

When she heard footsteps, Abbey looked up from washing dishes. She eyed Dallas shrewdly as she jerked a chair from the table and plopped herself down in it. Dallas had something on her mind. Abbey could always tell when something was bothering her.

"You going to tell me who's put a burr under your saddle?" Abbey asked.

"Who do you think?" Dallas replied, her tone laden with exasperation.

Abbey rinsed off a clean plate with warm water and set it down to drain. "What is it that bothers you about Trey?"

"Everything."

Abbey looked sharply at Dallas. "It can't be that bad, can it?"

"It can. And it is. He's the most arrogant, egotistical man I've ever met," Dallas responded heatedly, annoyed with herself for finding him attractive.

She had no business thinking such things.

She had no business thinking about Trey Conner at all.

"There's something about him that I don't care for," Dallas said.

"Maybe you're not as uninterested in men as you claim to be."

"What would I want with a man?" Dallas's words came out in a harsh rasp of denial and hope.

What indeed? her mind whispered.

But her body knew precisely.

Abbey laughed knowingly as she continued to wash dishes. "Sounds to me like you've finally met your match." She raised a sudsy hand when Dallas opened her mouth to dispute her. "Don't bother denying what's written all over your face. You don't like it because you've met a man you can't control."

"I suppose it doesn't matter that he wants to tell me what to do?"

"It might be good for you."

"You can't be serious!" Dallas cried, aghast that her sister should suggest such a thing.

"You might just learn something."

Dallas raised a brow. "Such as?" Her tone was dubious. "If I thought he might know something, then I might be inclined to take orders, but I doubt that he knows more than I do."

"About what?"

"You're trying my patience, Abbey."

"You don't have any patience." Abbey grinned. "Just answer my question."

"Why, driving a stagecoach."

"And what else?"

"Surviving in a man's world."

"Aha, now we're getting somewhere," Abbey said, her eyes lit with purpose. "But what do you know about men?"

"What do you mean?" Dallas didn't like where

this conversation was headed, and her tone said so.

"Do you know how a man thinks when it comes to women?"

"No."

"That's my point," Abbey said with satisfaction. "You've put the needs of this family ahead of your own. Instead of worrying about keeping this family together, you should give some thought to your own happiness."

"Who says I'm not happy? I've got everything I want."

"Do you, Dallas? Be honest with yourself."

"I have enough to think of."

"You've got to learn to quit trying to control every aspect of your life. Some things, you just have to put your trust in," Abbey said gently.

"Like bossy, overbearing men."

"I'm not worried about you. No man will ever be able to force you to do anything you don't want to do."

"When I came in, y'all certainly seemed to be having a good time." Dallas stared pointedly at Abbey, her words equally sharp.

Abbey stopped and regarded her sister. "Don't look at me like that. I know what you're thinking."

"And what's that?" Dallas asked with feigned innocence.

"That if you don't like him, I shouldn't like him. Well, I'm sorry, but I'm not going to be rude to him just because he ruffles your tail feathers."

"And I guess you're going to tell me that I shouldn't be worried about the possibility we might lose the station?"

"No. With all the strange things going on, all of us have to pull together. Which includes helping Trey get to the bottom of what's been going on lately."

Dallas rose. "I know better than anyone about the trouble going on. Someone doesn't want this line to succeed. There's not enough business to support two lines. If Trey Conner is here to troubleshoot, he's got his hands full. There's only one of him, and lots of miles between stations."

"That's why we've got to help, Dallas."

"Of course I'm going to help. Do you think I've worked as long and as hard as I have to see this line fall apart now? But I don't have to make it easy on Conner. He told me plainly that he didn't want a woman's help. And he certainly hasn't made my life any easier since I met him."

"What exactly did you say to him?"

"What did he tell you?" Dallas countered.

"Nothing, other than what he said in front of all of us at supper." Abbey's eyes widened as understanding dawned on her. "You didn't?"

Dallas nodded. "Once again, my temper got the better of me."

Abbey shook her head. "And he got the worse of it."

"Afraid so."

Dallas shared her sister's laughter, but she knew working alongside Trey Conner would be no laughing matter. It would be the hardest thing she'd ever done.

When it came to him, she'd have to learn to keep her emotions under control.

Even if it killed her.

Which it probably would.

Chapter 3

The smell of coffee and frying bacon heralded the coming of a new day and teased Trey into awareness. He tossed back the covers and rolled out of bed. Pouring water into the basin, he washed and shaved.

As he dressed, he recalled lying awake last night, remembering how pretty Dallas had looked in the barn. Despite her manly attire and job, she tempted him in ways he hadn't expected, and he had nearly surrendered to that temptation and kissed her.

Oh, she was stubborn and headstrong. And her temper was like a brushfire, needing only a spark to blaze out of control. A man would have to risk the heat in order to contain the fiery woman—if he could get close enough to her without being consumed.

He'd been thankful he had the ability to keep his emotions hidden, otherwise she would have seen the hunger in the deepest part of his eyes, and that would have been disastrous. For both of them.

He couldn't afford to succumb to his emotions. He'd spent most of his life acquiring power and authority, and he'd learned a painful lesson: Power and strength ruled. In order to survive, a man couldn't betray any weakness to his enemies, or allies. And Trey wasn't sure in which camp Dallas belonged.

She posed a threat to him unlike any other woman he'd known. He couldn't afford to feel anything for her. No, Dallas O'Neal was strictly off limits. He had a job to do; and he couldn't allow anything to interfere with fulfilling that obligation. He finished dressing and went downstairs to breakfast.

Trey entered the kitchen. Conversation abounded as the four O'Neal family members, along with Miguel, sat at the table, eating.

Dallas sat toward the end of the table, enjoying strips of crispy bacon between two flaky biscuit halves. She looked up from her meal. Their gazes met and held.

The warm atmosphere turned chilly.

Several seconds passed as they silently assessed each other. Trey felt an upcoming confrontation brewing like the coffee boiling on the stove. Dallas looked away first.

Even resentful and tense, Dallas O'Neal was beautiful. He would have to watch himself around her. Very closely.

Tyler's voice brought Trey out of his musings. "Good morning, Trey," she said cheerfully between bites of food.

"Good morning," Trey replied, seating himself next to Waco, two places down from Dallas. He reached for a biscuit. "How's your hand, Waco?"

"Better. But it hurt like a son of a—" Waco said, then finished, "Well, you know."

"It looks much better today," Tyler interjected. "Miguel's a healer. There isn't much that he can't fix."

Waco and Tyler were fraternal twins, each having the same golden skin as their sisters, Abilene and Dallas, the same blond hair and sparkling green eyes.

"I only do what the Old Ones allow me," Miguel said between sips of coffee.

Abbey wrapped the end of her apron around the coffeepot handle and lifted it to pour Trey a cup of the steaming dark brew.

Trey gave Abbey a smile. "Thanks."

Abbey pulled another pan of hot biscuits from the oven and dropped some onto a plate. She then served up a bowl of fried potatoes and onions, followed by a platter of eggs and bacon. With a bowl in each hand, Abbey made her way to the dining room to serve the three women who had stayed the night.

Inadvertently Trey's gaze found Dallas again. She was so close that he could reach out and touch her.

What did he want from Dallas O'Neal? Her obedience as an employee? Her compliance as a woman? His grip on his cup tightened. He had to keep the matter of Dallas O'Neal in the proper perspective. But what the hell was that?

Abruptly Dallas stood and headed for the back door. "Time's wasting."

Miguel finished his coffee and followed.

"Don't mind Dallas." Tyler wiped her mouth

on her napkin. "She cares more about them horses than she does most folks."

"That one has a mind of her own." Waco reached for the coffeepot, careful not to bump his bandaged hand against the table. "But then, you already know that." He grinned.

Though Waco was only nineteen, and thirteen years his junior, Trey found himself liking the young man. He smiled.

"Good breakfast," Trey said to Abbey when she returned to the kitchen. He rose, took one last sip of coffee, then headed outside.

He stepped into the cool air, ripe with the scent of honeysuckle. A mourning dove cooed its sweet morning song.

At the corral he leaned against the railing and peered over the holding pen. Miguel had cut out four horses for the morning run. Two were already harnessed.

Dallas had a gelding bridled and tied to a rail. With her back turned to him, Trey treated himself to an unhurried view of her. Hatless, her blond head caught snatches of sunshine like golden rays of the sun itself. She was dressed in her tight pants and a shirt tucked in at the waist, and the soft movement of her long, thick braid drew attention to the roundness of her hips and bottom. Trey stifled a smile, sure she was unaware of the effect.

When she bent over to fasten the bellyband around the horse, Trey's breathing quickened. Her pleasing bottom pointed in his direction. His palms grew moist. God, what sweet agony. He wanted her.

But he couldn't have her. So he might as well

quit torturing himself with such thoughts.

"Dammit!" Trey turned on his heel.

The saloon girl entered the private room and saw a lithe, good-looking man sitting at the table in the center of the room. He had crystal blue eyes and a strong, clean-shaven face. His hair was an unusual shade of blond, so pale it almost appeared white. His tailored suit was in stark contrast to the garb of the cowboys who frequented the saloon.

Jenny placed a bottle of whiskey and two glasses on the table. "Will your friend be here soon?"

"Should be."

"Maybe you could ask for me later."

"Maybe," the man drawled.

"I'll wait for you," Jenny offered in a soft, throaty tone, and she leaned over the table, giving him a clear view of her ample breasts.

She smiled and wet her lips in anticipation. She had heard talk from some of the other girls about this man. His fierceness in bed was fast becoming legend.

Jonas Webb dipped his hand into the whore's plunging neckline and squeezed one fleshy globe. "I'll see what I can do."

He enjoyed women who appreciated him. Life was made to be enjoyed, with all it had to offer. He liked people to pay attention to him. Power. Plain and simple. A powerful man controlled those around him. And he liked being in control—completely and totally.

Just then a man entered the room, and Jonas patted the brunette's bottom. "You go on now. Keep your bed warm."

With a smile on her painted lips, Jenny left the room, providing the men with privacy.

Frowning, Jonas splashed some whiskey into one of the glasses. "I don't like being kept waiting." He tossed back the drink, his lips pulled back from the liquor's bite.

The second man, an older, stately looking gentleman with silver hair, sat at the table. "You're getting paid well enough." He pulled an envelope from his inside suit pocket and slid it over to Jonas. "What I've got to say won't take long."

Jonas eyed the envelope. "I'm listening."

"There are those who are unhappy that it's taking so long for you to accomplish your goal. Remember, certain men have a great deal of money invested in this venture."

"You don't have to remind me." Jonas gave him an urbane smile and added smoothly, "These things have to be planned carefully."

"Were you successful in the robbery attempt?"

"No. Someone acted without orders." Jonas's smile thinned at the question. "But he isn't a problem any longer. I've decided to take over operations personally."

"What are you going to do?"

Jonas checked his irritation; his cold smile deepened.

"I'll take care of this matter. The Texas Overland Stage Company will be out of business as scheduled." His eyes narrowed. "No pun intended."

"I'll take your word that you'll get things done."

"Good, because I don't like interference." Jonas

brushed a bit of lint from his coat sleeve. "It creates problems."

The older man smiled uneasily and slowly rose. "I'll inform the others of our conversation."

Jonas leaned back in his chair and draped an arm over the back. "You do that."

The older man left by the alley door.

Jonas poured himself another drink. As long as there were gutless men, he'd always have a job. They came to him when they didn't have the stomach for their dirty work. The anticipation of excitement and danger sharpened his mind. He raised his glass in silent salute and drank deeply.

Jonas then strolled out front, located the whore, Jenny, and went upstairs, intent on enjoying himself, even if it was early in the day.

Momentarily Jonas stared at the whore's reflection in the mirror as she began to undress. Slowly, plying her practiced act, she unlaced her shoes and stepped out of them. Next she peeled away her black stockings, bending over to give him an unrestricted view of her breasts, pushed up high by her tight camisole and corset.

Jonas smiled and sat down on the edge of the bed. He delighted in women like Jenny. He didn't have to hide behind a tawdry show of morals. Whores were to be used. He knew what he was getting and how much it cost. That's why he liked them.

He met her eyes in the mirror. She gave him a saucy smile and untied the ribbon of her camisole, baring her breasts. She then slowly removed the pins from her hair and shook out her brown mane.

Jonas pressed his palms against the mattress as he felt his manhood press achingly against his trousers. "The clothes. Now," he commanded, suddenly growing tired of her game.

She slipped out of her clothes and knelt on the bed, pressing her nude, voluptuous body against Jonas's shirtless back.

"I'm glad you decided you had the time." She traced the edge of his ear with a fingertip. "Tell me what you like."

Jenny ran her tongue lightly along Jonas's spine. She slid her arms around his lean waist and ran her hands over his muscular chest. She pressed her body closer to him.

Her hands moved to the waistband of his pants, and slowly, one by one, her fingers undid the buttons. He growled and sucked in his breath as she freed his hard readiness.

Jonas stood and undressed. He then turned Jenny around, her soft bottom pressed against his front.

"Bend over," he said raggedly, near bursting at the thought of spending himself on her in such a licentious manner. "I want it from the back."

Sometime later, Jonas emerged from the Troubadour Saloon. His mouth twisted as he thought of his earlier entertainment with Jenny. When he had become rougher than she liked, the bitch had bitten him and screamed a stream of foul language. He knew the other clients had heard through the paper-thin walls.

He had made it painfully, unforgettably clear to the whore that no one treated Jonas Webb in that manner without suffering for it. No one. Jenny had paid the price for her thoughtless transgression.

For the hundredth time, Dallas wished the box weren't so small and Trey Conner weren't sitting so close to her. Each bump and sway of the coach pushed her against him. The weight and feel of his thigh brushing against hers was altogether too warm—and disturbing. She felt suffocated by his nearness. Thank goodness they were only a few miles out from their first stop at Lockhart.

She tried to concentrate on the road ahead and the handling of her four-horse team, but despite her efforts, her attention kept returning to the man beside her. She felt his gaze on her. The uncomfortable feeling grew.

Dallas looked askance at Conner. Her irritation rose a notch at the frank speculation on his face as he regarded her openly. Damn him! Had the circumstances leading to her job been different, she would have told him, plainly, what she thought of his rudeness. Even now she had to fight the urge. Taking orders from him chapped her hide. In less than two days, her normally uncomplicated life was suddenly complicated and disconcerting.

After what seemed an intolerably long time, Dallas halted the team at the station in Lockhart.

Trey climbed down and opened the stagecoach door. "You folks should stretch your legs. It'll take a few minutes to change teams."

Mailbag in hand, Dallas stood on the sidewalk and watched Conner as he helped two women from the coach. He seemed so self-assured, as if he'd done this a thousand times. It rankled Dallas that he fit into the routine so easily.

As she continued to watch him, she felt skittish. She wanted nothing more than to be on her way, doing what she did best—driving the stage. And she wanted to put as much distance between herself and Trey Conner as she could. If she wasn't careful, she could grow accustomed to his presence. Feeling comfortable around a man like Conner would be a mistake. He wasn't the kind who gave a woman a second chance. Only a fool would get involved with a man like him. She didn't intend to be one.

While the team was being changed and the passengers walked around, Dallas unloaded mail and newspapers for the local people.

Trey came around the boot, making sure the luggage was secure. He heard someone calling him, and he glanced in the direction from which the voice came.

A man of similar height and build, but with fair coloring, approached, a ready smile on his face.

Distant memory nagged at Trey. The man looked familiar. Slowly a name surfaced. Jonas Webb. They had been fellow officers during the war.

"Trey Conner." Webb said, shaking his head in surprise. "Well I'll be damned."

"Webb. I never expected to see you here."

The two men shook hands.

"I might say the same for you," Webb said tightly. "What brings you to these parts?"

"I'm the new line boss for the Texas Overland Stage Company."

"Is that so?" Webb's gaze cut to the coach, to Dallas, where it lingered briefly, then returned to Trey. "Who's the girl dressed in pants?"

"My driver, Miss Dallas O'Neal."

"I have to admit that not much shocks me anymore, but this does. Introduce me, will you?"

"Miss Dallas O'Neal, Mr. Jonas Webb. We served in the same cavalry unit during the war." Trey added beneath his breath, "Although we weren't always on the same side."

Webb's mischievous gaze passed over her, lingering almost imperceptibly at her breasts and her narrow waist. When he looked again at her face, there was an appreciative glint in his blue eyes.

"I've never seen a woman driver before."

Dallas felt swift, fierce color surge into her face, but she willed herself to remain calm. "Most people haven't."

Webb turned to Trey. "I bet that makes your job real interesting."

Trey's jaw tensed. "You think so?"

"Hmm," Jonas murmured, then to Dallas's utter amazement, he cupped her chin with his hand, turning her head ever so slightly. "You know, despite the men's clothing, you're very beautiful."

Dallas jerked away from Webb as if she'd been stung by a bee. "Don't talk about me like that." Her chest heaved with indignation. "And keep your hands off me."

"Why? Hasn't anyone ever told you how attractive you are?" Webb laughed softly. "If they haven't, it's a shame. With your beauty, any man would be happy to have you. Married or not."

Dallas's temper exploded. "I might have something to say about that." Turning a cold shoulder on the two men, she climbed aboard the stage, amid a creaking of springs and a huff of resentment.

With visible effort, Trey clamped down his anger. Why should he care if Webb appreciated Dallas? But he did.

"What sort of business keeps you here?" Trey asked, controlling the emotion in his voice.

"I'm afraid I run the line for your competitor."

An almost tangible aura of alertness surrounded Trey. "I guess we're in different camps for this war, then." He kept his expression unreadable.

"I suppose we are." Webb's tone was also carefully couched. "Can I offer you some advice?" He leaned closer. "Save yourself the trouble. You can't possibly win against me this time."

Trey read the dare within Webb's stare. Instinct told him that Webb's words held no idle threat.

"I'm sorry it's come to this between us. I'll try to remember that we were once friends."

"Have it your way," Webb conceded. "But I won't hold any hard feelings toward you."

"We both know we're going to do what we have to." Trey's voice crackled with intensity.

"May the best man win." Webb gave a mocking bow, then turned on his heel. In the past, Trey had gotten the best of him. Not this time. Never again.

He continued back to his hotel. He smiled as he thought of the wildcat, Dallas O'Neal. Now, there was a woman worth taming.

He recalled her wide, green eyes darkening

with fury, remembered the way her breasts had strained against the taut material of her shirt. His lower regions tightened.

He wanted her. And he always got what he wanted.

Jonas's lips curved as he envisioned his mouth suckling at those deliciously tempting breasts. He sighed in anticipation.

All good things come to those who wait.

He had plenty of time. And patience to spare.

He wondered how much of either Trey Conner had.

Dallas gritted her teeth as Conner hauled himself up and settled down beside her on the driver's seat. Unable to swallow the lump of anger in her throat, she remained silent as she released the brake and nodded to the man holding the lead horses' heads to step away. She signaled the team by pulling gently up on the lines until she felt the horses' mouths, then she loosened the lines. Harness jingled in the still air as the coach pulled away.

Attempting unsuccessfully to concentrate on the passing landscape, her mind replayed Jonas Webb's humiliating appraisal and the unspeakable suggestion of his words. She wore britches, but she wasn't trash. Color pounded in her cheeks.

Frowning, she felt an odd mixture of rage and hurt as she thought of Conner's apparent indifference to the incident. His lack of respect for her pricked her pride. How could she work for someone who thought no more of her than to allow another man to insult her in public? At that moment, in her painful frustration, she didn't give a parson's prayer if the stage line failed or succeeded.

Contriteness washed over her. That wasn't true. She couldn't help but care. Whether he approved of her or not, she would do her job.

Dallas glanced at Conner. By his grim expression, one would think he'd been insulted instead of her. Men! Lord save her.

Dark thoughts swirled around inside Trey—thoughts that grew blacker by the second. Hell! He should have punched Jonas Webb in the gut for his treatment of Dallas. But being so muleheaded and independent, she probably would have been angry had he come to her defense.

Trey ground his teeth. He couldn't blame Webb for enjoying the sight of Dallas's figure. What man didn't enjoy seeing a woman dressed in tight britches that molded her small, rounded bottom like a second skin? And what man didn't want to peel away that skin to expose the tempting fruit beneath? A man could go crazy thinking such things.

He recalled his days together with Webb during the war; he remembered Webb's taste in women. Webb was a man who used women for self-gratification and nothing more. However irritating Dallas O'Neal might be, she didn't deserve a man like Jonas Webb.

He wondered just what plans Webb had for Dallas. He had been too appreciative of her for comfort. The notion of Webb getting anywhere near her rankled him more than he cared to admit.

His thoughts dwelled too long and too hard on Dallas's charms—until something other than his musings grew hard. A sheen of perspiration covered his brow.

As Dallas moved her arms, the fabric of her shirt stretched tautly across her breasts, clearly outlining their soft curves. Oh, Lord! Trey groaned.

This stage was bound for more places than between Lockhart, Austin, and San Antonio.

This stage was bound for trouble.

At the swing station on the outskirts of New Braunfels, Trey watched Dallas climb down from the stage. She strode toward the porch, mailbag swinging briskly at her side. His gaze focused on her gently swaying hips. The soft buckskin clearly defined the male-teasing, heart-pounding perfection of her buttocks. His irritation sharpened. Damn those britches!

No. Damn her for having such a tempting ass to put in them. He liked what he saw. Very much.

And so would other men.

Spurred on by his frustration, Trey went after Dallas. He grabbed her upper arm, stopping her short of the door.

"I've got something to say to you." His fingers locked about her arm.

Dallas glared at him. "Well, I've got nothing to say to you."

Her dismissal irritated him further. "By God, you're going to listen to me—"

She cocked her stubborn little chin at him. "Or what?"

He wanted to take her over his knee and spank some sense into her. "You'll be sorrier than you ever have been in your life."

"That happened the day I met you."

She drew an indignant breath, and as she did so, the tempting rise and fall of her chest drove Trey nearly to distraction. He couldn't stand much more. Steering her away from the porch, he pulled her to a halt behind a thick growth of brush at the rear of the station house.

Seizing both her arms, Trey hauled Dallas to him. The mailbag lay forgotten at their feet.

He quickly realized his mistake as her nearness stroked his heightened senses. Rational thought proved difficult. The pads of his fingertips registered her body heat through the material of her shirt. His own body heat rose.

He watched a blush creep up her neck and spread to her face. The quickening of her breath and the slight flare of her nostrils proved to him that she, too, was aware of how their bodies touched.

He was no saint. He had to stop this foolishness.

And soon.

"Don't wear these clothes anymore," he ground out.

"What?" she demanded, raising her brows.

"You heard me."

Narrowing her eyes, she retorted, "Why?" Anger and frustration simmered in her voice.

"After what happened with Webb, I'd think that would be obvious."

"I'll be damned if you're going to tell me what to wear."

"And I'll be damned if you're going to sashay around in those pants anymore."

"Just what would you have me wear?" She laughed dryly. "I can just see myself driving the stage in a dress."

Anything was better than her wearing those irritating, eye-pleasing pants day after day. "You can wear britches. Only not so tight."

"Who are you to pass judgment?"

His jaw tightened. "Your boss."

"That doesn't give you the right to order me around. Besides, you didn't object before."

But neither had he been so painfully aware of her. He'd have to exercise authority on Dallas until she complied.

He lowered his face closer to hers to emphasize his words. "Just do what I tell you."

"I've always dressed like this. I'm not going to change for you now."

"Oh, yes you will, or you'll be fired. I have enough problems with the stage line without worrying about men gawking at you."

"Don't worry yourself on my account."

Trey started to reply, but the words tangled in his throat as he lowered his gaze. He swallowed. Her breasts were so temptingly close to his chest that he could almost feel their softness. His loins tightened along with his grasp on her arm.

He felt her breath softly strike his face, and he raised his eyes to her. He stared at the teasing display of her shapely lips. And the pleasing curve of her cheek. And the alluring green of her eyes.

His mind dully repeated her words. *Don't worry yourself on my account.*

"I have a feeling my worries are only just beginning." Irritation and painful desire roughened Trey's voice. "I don't want what happened today to be repeated."

"As if I do?" He heard the incredulity in her words.

"I don't know what goes on inside that brain of yours."

"You—"

Before she could get started, Conner leveled a chilling gaze on her. "I've said all I'm going to say."

Oh, but Dallas obviously had plenty to say. "What I wear is none of your business." She drew a deep breath. "Ever since you arrived at the station, you've done nothing but criticize my every move. I'm sick of it. Tyler wears pants, and I'll bet you haven't said anything to her."

"Finished?"

"No. I want to know why you treat me differently from the others."

"The others don't give me the trouble you do."

"Trouble? I should know about trouble. It's been tagging after me ever since I met you. I bet your middle name is trouble."

"You're wrong," Trey said slowly, evenly. "Trouble is spelled D-A-L-L-A-S."

She tried to pull away. "Let me go."

"Not until you get a few things straight. You're not wearing those pants anymore."

She huffed her annoyance. "And if I do?"

"You'll regret it."

"I'll have to take that chance then, won't I?"

"That's your choice. I've warned you." He lowered his voice, but the intensity remained. "I'll force you, but it won't be my fault."

"Why do you care so much?"

Why did he care? he thought briefly.

Because she was beautiful.

Damn!

Because he wanted her.

His neck and shoulder muscles tightened in aggravation. "My job doesn't include keeping half the men in this county from sniffing after you."

"They don't sniff after me."

"The hell they don't. I know Jonas Webb and his kind. More will notice you."

"Like you?"

"What man with eyes wouldn't notice you? I'm just trying to save myself some misery down the road."

Her green eyes glowed brighter. "Really?"

"What type of woman dresses like you?"

"You tell me."

"A woman who wants something."

"But we're not talking about another woman. We're talking about me."

"Exactly."

"So exactly what is it I want?"

What her defiance demanded. What his persistence dictated. "Something I figure you've needed badly for a long time."

And then he did the unthinkable. And the irresistible. His mouth slashed across hers in a punishing kiss that drove the air from Dallas's lungs.

Chapter 4

Dallas couldn't see straight. She couldn't hear anything above the pounding of her heart. She couldn't feel the ground beneath her feet. But oh, how she felt his lips on hers, consuming, devouring. Dark and wicked. Dear Lord, she had never been kissed like this. Her blood raced through her veins.

Trey tightened his hold on her, pressing his lean body hard against hers with overwhelming, threatening persistence. His tongue parted her lips and teeth and teased the recesses of her mouth with the sweet promise of something Dallas couldn't name.

She should have been angry, but she couldn't find the voice, or strength, to fight him. The heat of his kiss penetrated her, urging her to surrender to the honeyed, enticing seduction. She fleetingly wondered if this was what she'd unknowingly sought.

He continued to kiss her, his tongue tempting and beckoning—and defying her to resist. She couldn't have turned away if her life had depended on it. Her soul was lost in the raw, untried sensations—the warmth and texture of his clothing and his body against hers, and the heat and moistness of his kiss. She leaned into him. Reckless, secretive longings stampeded her thoughts and feelings.

Yet, despite the compliance his persuasive mouth demanded, she felt like a green-broke filly saddled by overwhelming sensations. Instinctively she knew she had to fight him.

She twisted her head away and glared into his glittering, hard eyes. "Let go of me!"

He captured her face between his strong, callused hands and outlined her moist, parted lips with his thumbs. "No, never."

Her limbs tightened, then quivered. Oh, God. Did he realize what he was doing to her already overworked senses?

The huskiness of his voice told her that he did. "Remember? I don't take orders. I give them."

His body commanded hers to melt against him and surrender to his heated embrace. Energy as intense and charged as summer lightning seemed to surround him, ready to strike with lethal accuracy at her vulnerability. Shoving futilely against the rock-hard wall of his chest, Dallas felt the corded movement of his muscles beneath her hands. The virility of his well-defined body threatened her way beyond a kiss. She had to stop him.

"Take your hands off me, you low-down skunk!" she rasped against his mouth.

Trey released her suddenly, and she stumbled backward. Glancing at the ground, she stood on wobbly legs, feeling disoriented, her sense of decency confused. What were those funny feelings? Her stomach was jumping like a grasshopper on a hot griddle. She struggled for breath.

Dallas looked up. Too late she realized her mistake. The silky seduction of his blue gaze promised sweet, beguiling answers to her secretive, womanly questions.

"Only because I wanted to." His voice stroked her senses like warm, soft velvet. "Don't fool yourself. You had that coming."

It took the span of several erratic heartbeats to untangle her thoughts and understand what he'd said. And when she did, her trampled pride brought a sputter of outrage to her lips. "I *what*!"

"You heard me." His gaze raked her with determination, conviction—and something deeply disturbing.

She should have blushed to kingdom come. She should have let out a yell that would have brought the station occupants running. She should have connected her fist to his arrogant chin. But the sense of danger and excitement rippling through her demanded that she stand her ground, not respond like some panic-stricken ninny.

Dallas anchored her hands on her hips. "You're about as wanted as a tick on a hound dog."

"You're too kind."

"Well, you're not my kind. So keep your hands to yourself."

Conner stepped closer. His voice seemed to reach out and wrap silky fingers of mockery about her. "Is that a threat?"

She didn't quite understand the message in

his eyes, but her breath hardened in her throat. "What if it is?"

His gaze darkened ominously with warning, then lit with amusement. "I wouldn't advise it."

"You wouldn't dare touch me again." Her tone dipped with defiance.

He caressed her cheek with the backs of his fingers. "I thought you'd figured out by now that I never back down from a challenge."

"Is that what I am?"

"One I could easily win, if you were my type." His voice turned low and husky. "Which you're not."

His insult was as hard to swallow as a dose of castor oil. So she wasn't good enough for him!

His gaze drifted uncomfortably close to her bosom. She felt herself grow warm. Very warm.

"I don't keep a woman for long. Makes things easier that way."

"Who'd want you?"

"I've never been turned away." Confidence coated his words.

His arrogance beat all, yet even now the heat of his kiss burned on her lips. Her breath caught. Her heart thundered. He was irresistibly exciting.

Dallas couldn't stand any more. She had to do something.

"Only a foolish woman would keep company with you for long," Dallas said.

"If I choose to stick around a woman, I always leave her very well satisfied."

Dallas's mouth dropped like ripened fruit from a tree. His frame, with its perfect proportions, underscored his words. Apprehension telegraphed along her nerve endings to every cell of her body. She knew she shouldn't look into his eyes, but she did. His intense gaze stripped her bare, leaving her a shivering heap of goose bumps.

She scrambled to recover a small measure of composure. She knotted her fingers into fists. At that moment, if someone had ridden up and offered to hang Trey Conner from the nearest tree, Dallas would have gladly handed him over. Hell, no! She would have swatted his horse from beneath him. He could have dangled from his own conceit.

Conner's widening grin dared her to respond.

Dad-durn it! She despised him with a passion so intense, it made her knees feel watery. It was her anger that made her weak, she told herself, not his seductive, disarming smile. Not his lips, which touched and parted hers, not his sweet, openmouthed kiss, which fired hotter and hotter.

Her mind and senses began to reel. How could she think such things after his insults? She neither needed nor wanted a man in her life. If she did, she could certainly do better than Trey Conner! And she definitely didn't have to stand here and be insulted by him.

Disdainfully she turned her back on him, only to feel his hand on her shoulder as he spun her around to face him.

"You wanted that kiss as much as I did." His mouth thinned into a hard line.

Blast his cantankerous hide! She'd nearly surrendered to him, and he had sensed it. Well, she'd sleep with a polecat before she'd ever admit it.

Dallas glowered at him, her chin raised, her temper soaring, her voice quivering. "A kiss from you is the last thing I'd ever want."

She spun on her heel and started for the station when Trey's sharp, biting voice stopped her. "Tomorrow you get looser-fitting britches."

She whirled and shot him full of holes with a lethal stare. His arrogance didn't sit well with her. Or his proximity to her traitorous body.

"Aren't you forgetting something?" He tossed the mailbag at her. "Remember what I said." The gleam in his eyes promised swift retaliation if she didn't follow his order.

Grabbing the pouch, Dallas stomped to the station. Breathing hard, she entered the cavernous room, angry and wary, not wanting to talk to anyone. She heard the door open and close behind her and felt Trey's gaze boring into her back. She hesitated a moment and then continued to stomp across the room, with her boot heels marking her way along the dusty floor.

Dallas set the mailbag down on a counter. With wooden movements, she began sorting newspapers and correspondence, stuffing the pieces in the appropriate boxes. Her surroundings blended into a drone of undistinguished details.

A woman's low, throaty laugh, followed by Trey Conner's rumbling chuckle, pierced Dallas's thoughts like a Comanche arrow. Curiosity made Dallas look up from her task.

Trey sat at a table near the door. The steam rising from the coffee cup he held was no more heated than the look the pretty brunette sitting next to him gave him. Dark, almond-shaped eyes sparkled with provocative admiration as she gazed into his face. Her white-gloved hand rested on his forearm as she leaned closer to catch his words.

The beginnings of stubble shadowed his strongly carved jaw and cheeks. His shoulder-length black hair fell with riotous abandon across his forehead. The harsh lines of his mouth had softened with his obvious amusement. His cryptic blue eyes gave full attention to the woman.

The hardness of his masculine features was enhanced by his seasoned ruggedness. At that moment, he seemed more ruthless, more dangerous, than ever to Dallas. Her palms began to sweat beneath her gloves.

She hadn't moved since her attention had been distracted from the mail, but suddenly she felt the weight of Trey's scrutiny touch her as surely as if he had literally reached out. Shaken by the vividness of the impression, Dallas curled her hands into balls atop the counter.

As if she hadn't suffered enough, Dallas then caught the attractive brunette's contemptuous gaze. She seethed in anger as she watched the woman cup Trey's strong chin with her fingers and forced his attention back to her. Laughter passed her lips as she gestured disapprovingly toward Dallas. Trey chuckled, which seemed to satisfy the brunette but did nothing to spare Dallas's feelings.

Unconsciously Dallas's lips tightened at the hurt . . . and yes, jealousy. Her stomach twisted into knots, the skin at the back of her neck prickled, while confusion flowed through her. He was a womanizer. He couldn't be trusted. He was insensitive, selfish, caring only about his own needs. Love was a trap, devised by man to enslave woman to his will. Dallas vowed to have no part of it. So why did it hurt so much to know what Trey truly thought of her?

Dallas could not, would not, admit to another living soul just how much it hurt to know Trey Conner had only been playing with her.

A surge of restlessness claimed Dallas, agitating her into movement. Her pulse thrummed a little at the base of her throat, but her chin was high as ever as she stepped forward, burying her pain beneath layers of anger.

"Stage is leaving in five minutes," she announced to no one in particular.

How the hell they hadn't killed each other on the return trip to the home station, Dallas didn't know. Considering their sullen moods and the number of terse words and stinging looks they had shared, anything short of murder was miraculous. And Dallas's ability to tolerate that fawning brunette, Miss Serena Crowley, was no less impressive. At every stop on the route, Miss Crowley took the opportunity to seek out Trey's attention. Dallas had wanted to scream every time she witnessed Miss Crowley rubbing her ample figure against Trey.

Dallas mentally thanked the Old Ones for providing her with the astonishing strength to keep her composure in front of the other passengers while she helped Miguel and Tyler put away the tired team in the barn.

As the sun dipped on the western horizon, so did Dallas's spirits. She had thought nothing could make her despise Trey Conner more. She had been wrong. She hated him for what he had done—no, what he did—to her. He criticized her every move. He barked orders at every turn. He watched her every minute. He made her feel things she shouldn't feel.

A vague, nameless response bit into Dallas's consciousness. She hated not being in control.

With a horse in tow, she walked toward a stall. Dallas tried her dead-level best to keep her thoughts from Trey Conner, for all the good it did her. She couldn't do anything *but* think about him. And remember how she had enjoyed his kiss. Warmth trickled down her spine as she recalled in vibrant, sparkling detail how it felt to have his arms locked around her, to feel his lips against hers.

She shook her head. How could one kiss trigger such unfamiliar, forbidden feelings in her? She must be touched in the head to allow one man to affect her so.

Her thoughts came to a stop, along with her steps.

Now, hold up, she admonished silently. He's just a man.

Dallas groaned. Didn't she know it? Too well, in fact. That was the whole problem.

She kicked dirt and straw with a booted toe. Any fool knew the difficult, if not impossible, thing about a man wasn't being around him—it was tolerating him.

Damn if Trey Conner didn't stick in her craw. . . .

Damn, if she wasn't beautiful even when mad. . . .

Trey's eyes narrowed and his fingers tightened

about his coffee cup as he watched Dallas sit down to supper. They were the only ones in the kitchen. Her mouth and brow were puckered like dill pickles.

Dallas had done everything within her power to avoid him on their return trip from New Braunfels. That suited him just fine. He'd been annoyed by what he would have done—or by what he wanted to do—if she had opened that little mouth of hers just once more.

She was an irritating yet refreshing change from the other women he had known. From the beginning, she had met him stare for stare, stood toe to toe with him, and traded him word for word. She was bolder and had more gumption than most men. Dallas O'Neal was some woman.

She drove a stagecoach, dressed in men's clothing, and didn't give a tinker's damn about what people thought, while trying to earn a living, surviving against the odds. He admired her grit. She had taken upon herself more than most in the name of family and pride. But at what price? Was she lonely?

He knew as much about loneliness as he did women—which was considerable. His kind didn't invite anyone to stay around long, nor did the type of women he preferred give him a reason for fidelity. He knew the gnawing pang of desire, the ecstasy of release, the satisfaction of being an accomplished lover—beyond that, he allowed himself to feel nothing.

Trey fought the unaccustomed twinge of sentimental emotion and turned his attention from the one woman he shouldn't want. He studied the dark coffee in his cup. Strong like Dallas. Just as bitter to take at times.

To take to bed . . . Would she be as wild and unpredictable as her temper? Or would she be tame and clinging? On the outside she was tough, but inside was she soft and melting?

Looking up from his coffee, he watched Dallas serve herself a portion of chicken and dumplings. She glanced across the table at him. Tight-lipped, eyes flashing, she attacked her food. But he knew she would have liked nothing better than to heave fluffy flour dumplings over his head.

Dallas brought out the worst in him—his conscience. He fought against it every time he looked at her. Damn her hide! He wanted every soft, tempting inch of her. Dallas, he reflected, with her fiery green eyes. Dallas, in heated argument with him, breasts rising in breathless agitation, with passionate tenacity lighting her lovely face. His mouth went dry. He couldn't logically say why he was attracted to Dallas. Yet she made him feel something he hadn't experienced in a long time. And she didn't even have the vaguest idea what she stirred within him, or what he wanted from her.

But he could tell by her mutinous expression and the glum set to her jaw that Dallas wanted to give him nothing but pure hell. If he weren't so damned irritated by the situation, he'd laugh.

But this was no laughing matter. She was too pleasing to the eye. And she felt as good as she looked. How was a man supposed to go about his work with a woman like her around, knowing he shouldn't touch her? He knew she'd never take his orders lying down. A wry smile touched his lips. That's precisely where he wanted her, lying beneath him, her flesh soft, yielding, trembling.

His gaze moved from the delicate blue veins etching her beautiful face, to her small, perfect nose, to . . . dear God, her seductive, pouting mouth.

His gaze, burning with blue heat, locked with hers, flashing emerald defiance. A man could surrender to the challenge in those eyes.

But he wouldn't. He couldn't.

Trey diverted the perilous course of his thoughts. "Let's call a truce."

Dallas glanced up from her meal. "Why should we?" Suspicion lurked behind the words.

"Because life's too short to be miserable." Because she had already made his existence a living hell. Because if they didn't do something, he would end up taking her across his knee and taking out his frustration on her tempting bottom.

She made a sour face as if she had been turned inside out and hung to dry. "My life's been that way ever since you came into it."

Trey clenched his teeth. Temperamental female! He bore down on his patience. "I don't think it does any good to find fault. Let's just try to get along."

"Why this sudden interest in making the best of things?"

"There's no telling how long we're going to be working together."

"You mean until you manage to get rid of me?"

"That's not what I said. Don't put words in my mouth, Dallas."

"Oh, but I know what you meant."

"You don't know anything about me."

"Don't I?"

"No."

She stiffened her back. "I know enough."

"Perhaps there's a side of me that you'd like."

"I doubt it."

"I'll be damned."

"Probably."

He lifted one corner of his mouth, slowly, confidently, arrogantly, so aggressively male. "Most women find me appealing."

"Well, I'm not most women!"

"I've never made that mistake with you."

"This conversation is leading to no good."

Trey raised a brow. "Because you don't want it to."

"That's not true."

"Afraid to try to get along? Scared you might actually like me?"

Like him? Never. "I'm not scared of that impossibility at all."

His look confirmed his response. "You should be."

Dallas tried to ignore the twisting in her stomach at his slightest suggestion. "Why all the questions anyway?"

"I want to know more about you."

"You know everything you need to about me, and I certainly know more than I care to about you!"

Despite her words, at that moment, Dallas wanted to know him—very much. She wanted to know him better than anyone else in the world knew him. She wanted to feel him put his arms around her and hold her close again. But she was afraid—she didn't know why—of the emotions she read in his eyes, in his manner. Her feelings frightened her.

None of this mattered, she told herself. It couldn't matter.

But it did.

"Do I know the real you?" he asked in a lazy drawl.

"Yes."

"I don't think so."

She was furious with him, she reminded herself, and she had to remain furious at him. Anger was the only way to sidestep his silken threat.

"No matter to me," Dallas said.

"So you say."

"I know what you're doing."

"Oh?"

"You're trying to find some weakness to use against me later."

"If I wanted to fire you, or if I wanted anything else from you, nothing would stop me," he said smoothly.

"Don't pretend to take an interest in me. I won't fall for your tricks." she said, annoyed with herself and him.

He must know damned well by now that she would obey him only when necessary. He didn't own her. He had no right to her.

They weren't . . . married.

For one brief, traitorous instant, the thought taunted her . . . teased her . . . stroked her into imagining what life would be like as his wife.

Her mind wandered; her body warmed.

Conner smiled. "My interest is sincere. Besides, I'm certain you can spot a lie a mile off."

His expression touched her deep inside. For the moment, his potent virility calmed the twisting emotions inside her.

Dallas returned his smile. "I can, so don't push your luck with me."

"I like that."

"What?" she asked, disconcerted by his statement.

"Your smile. You're even more beautiful when you do."

"I don't have much to smile about."

"Why won't you let anyone close to you?" Trey asked, putting Dallas uncomfortably on the spot.

She chewed her bottom lip. "So I can't be hurt."

"You mean so no one can hurt you again."

"Yes."

"Who hurt you?"

"The women in town make fun of me, talk about me behind my back." She raised her chin. "But I don't care. The nosy old biddies can just stay away. Doesn't make any difference to me."

"Don't tell me it doesn't matter. I can see the pain in your eyes. You look so vulnerable."

"Can't we talk about something else?" she pleaded.

Leaning back in his chair, he rested the heel of his boot on the rung of the chair beside him. "Tell me about your parents."

Her natural tendency toward rebellion made her want to counter with a demand that Conner tell her about himself first, but she was tired of fighting. For the moment anyway.

Dallas dared to look at him, his face softly illuminated by several kitchen lamps. The sharp curves and harsh angles of his face were too handsome. Too handsome for his own good. And hers.

The man puzzled her, and she didn't know why. It wasn't because of his good looks, or even his aggressive masculinity. The inner man held her interest.

"I don't talk much about my parents. Not since they died."

"But they helped to make you who you are. Isn't that worth talking about?"

Dallas instinctively knew Conner wouldn't give up until he got what he wanted. "I suppose so."

"Well?"

"We moved from place to place before I turned ten. Papa drove for different stage lines until he was offered a chance to buy this station." Breathing deeply, Dallas brightened, hugging happy memories close to her heart. "We had good times here. Papa taught me I could do anything I wanted, including driving a stage. He also taught me to respect the land and to have a love for horses."

"What about your mother?"

Dallas swallowed the lump of emotion in her throat. "She taught me to read and write. But more importantly, she always told us girls that we were just as special as boys and not to let anyone tell us different."

"That's why you're used to getting your way."

His voice conveyed a mixture of gravity and amusement.

"I don't call it getting my way. It's just being as good as the next person, man or woman." Dallas tilted her head. "What about your parents?"

"My father's dead." His voice grew distant, and the intensity of his gaze faded. "My mother's remarried and lives in Fort Worth."

"Any brothers or sisters?"

"No."

"I'm sorry—"

Trey cut her off. "Don't be."

As Trey sipped his coffee, Dallas studied his deeply tanned fingers wrapped around the cup. She imagined those same fingers curled about a pistol. She reminded herself that from what she knew of him, Trey Conner was a dangerous man. But the idea of what made a man choose a gunman's life intrigued her.

"What does it take for a man to kill?"

"Can't answer that."

Oh, no, Trey Conner, Dallas thought. *You're not going to sidestep me so easily.* "Then how can you make your living by the gun?"

Trey didn't blink. "Is that what you think?"

"Well, don't you?" she persisted.

"Being a line boss involves more than troubleshooting. You know that."

"I know about most men. I don't know about you."

"I use my gun when I have to."

"But you have killed men before in your line of work, haven't you?"

"Yes."

"How many?"

Trey shrugged. "Never counted."

"Or is it that you don't stay in one place long enough to count?"

"I stay until the job is done."

Dallas leaned forward, her elbows on the table. "Until someone's dead."

"Until things run smoothly."

"Like a well-oiled machine?"

"Like an efficient, profitable stage line."

"I've heard about how some owners hire ruthless men to handle their affairs. So why did the Overland owners hire you? Are you dangerous?"

"You asking me if I'm a wanted man?"

Conner's words rang with challenge, but she refused to back down. "Are you?"

"Why can't you just accept that I'm here to help you?"

"I have no reason to trust you."

"Look, I'm the best friend you've got right now. Besides, I've got a personal interest in the outcome."

Although he offered no other comment to further their conversation, Dallas felt the strong compulsion to continue.

"So are you running from the law or not?"

"No. But I'm not walking toward it either."

"Then, what are you walking toward?"

"What answer you looking for?"

Conner's gaze burned brightly with something Dallas couldn't name. But then, she wasn't sure she wanted to name it if she could.

"An honest one."

"I'm being as honest with you as I can."

The one question she had long wanted to ask

burned on the tip of her tongue. "Why do you resent me?"

She drew a long breath, then expelled it slowly as she awaited his answer. And in that same breath, she chided herself for caring what he thought at all.

"I don't resent you. I just consider you to be in the way."

"Of what?"

"There's no sense in going over this again."

His stern look told Dallas that the subject was closed, but she couldn't help but fire one last shot. "Don't go thinking that I've given in just because I asked."

"You're always quick to cut people with that sharp tongue of yours."

Dallas raised her chin. "So much for our truce."

"We can still have a truce if you'll be sensible."

Doubt riddled her tone of voice. "You mean, do everything you tell me to?"

"Something like that."

"Well, I'll tell you what you can do." Her expression soured with dislike. *"Exactly."*

Trey grinned and reached for the coffeepot sitting on the table. Refilling his cup, he calmly advised, "You think about what I've said and give me your answer later." He dipped his spoon into the sugar bowl, and it clinked with the empty sound of metal against enamel.

Dallas stood. The amusement shining in his eyes rankled her, but she spoke sweetly. "Here, let me get you some more sugar." She picked up the bowl and turned her back to him, moving to the cupboard.

Momentarily she set the container in front of him. She then strolled toward the door. "Enjoy your coffee."

Halfway up the stairs, Dallas heard Trey's enraged bellow. She smiled. So he didn't like salt in his coffee. Well, he'd gotten his answer. The only one that made sense to her.

The sounds of a chair scraping across the floor and heavy footsteps broke into her thoughts. Not that she was a coward, but she quickened her pace in case he decided to be less than sensible with her.

Chapter 5

Needing fresh air to clear his angry thoughts, Trey left the kitchen and headed for the front porch. It irritated the blue blazes out of him that he allowed Dallas to get under his skin. She had the damndest way of needling him. The little witch had no intention of trying to get along. He was convinced she thrived on confrontation. Well, he'd give it to her.

This was war, and he intended to win.

Dallas thought she could do whatever the hell she wanted! Well, he intended to be in her face every time she turned around or even thought about disobeying him.

Trey pushed open the front door with more force than he intended, sending it banging against the wall. Dallas was putting him through nine kinds of hell with that body of hers. What flesh-and-blood man could resist such perfection? No, she was making this damned hard on him. Certain parts of him were feeling the strain.

A chuckle came from his right, breaking into

his thoughts. He whipped his head around. The moonlight illuminated a woman's figure. As he stepped forward, he discovered Abbey sitting in the porch swing, holding a guitar.

Abbey grinned. "I can tell you and Dallas just parted company."

Trey moved to the edge of the porch and leaned his broad shoulder against a pillar. He jammed his hands into his pants pockets. "More like good riddance."

"Dallas can have that effect on people."

"More often than not, I'm willing to bet," he said between clenched teeth.

Abbey chuckled again. "Believe it or not, only around certain people."

"And I'm one of those lucky souls."

"Seems so."

"Everyone else in your family is reasonable. Why isn't she?"

They couldn't go five minutes without fighting. They were determined, single-minded, and prideful. They were an explosive combination.

"I could answer that, but I won't. You and my sister have to learn to work out your own differences."

"If that's possible."

"You've got to have patience."

"Believe me, I'm finding I have more than I thought," Trey said, releasing a sigh into the night air.

He allowed his gaze to wander over the landscape. The moon's soft glow cast the surroundings in silver highlights and velvet shadows. He breathed in the still air, rich with honeysuckle. Above the sounds of crickets, he heard soft strains of gently strummed music as Abbey once more played her guitar.

He sighed. The tranquillity of the moment and Abbey's soothing song helped to calm his ragged nerves. He had needed this reprieve from his anger, or else he would have marched upstairs to Dallas's room and wrung her lovely neck.

Displaying none of the agitation he felt, Trey pushed off the pillar and faced Abbey. "It's late. I'd best be turning in."

"Goodnight," Abbey returned.

Just what the hell was so good about tonight? Trey wondered. Not a damned thing.

The raucous laughter and noise from the saloon grew muted as the door closed behind Zeke Roberts. Lantern light cast ominous shadows across the back-room office. Zeke, hat in hand, cursed his luck. He'd seen that menacing look before on the boss's face. Somebody's head was going to roll. He just hoped to God it wasn't his.

Somebody hadn't done his job. Why else would the boss have called him to the office this late at night? The boss always expected his orders to be carried out, without question. When angry, the boss wouldn't think before he acted. The number of men he'd killed spoke to the fact. No man stood in the boss's way. No man—dead or alive.

Zeke studied his boss's austere countenance. Glowering at him from where he stood behind the ornately carved desk, the boss looked every bit the intimidating man he was. His mouth was a thin line chiseled in a face of stone, and his knuckles were white as he drummed his fingers atop the oak desk.

Jonas's deliberate words sliced through the silence, cutting into Zeke's thoughts. "I don't like being made a fool."

"What do ya mean, boss?"

"Why wasn't I told about Trey Conner?" Jonas's voice was smooth and silky, dangerous because of the lack of fire behind his words.

Zeke frowned. "You mean that new man out at the O'Neal place?"

"Hell yes!"

Zeke shrugged. "He didn't look special to me. Didn't figure a new shotgun made any difference."

"I don't pay you to think. I pay you to follow orders."

"Yes, sir." Zeke knew when not to buck his boss. He knew what happened to men who did. They weren't around long.

"He's not just a shotgun. He's a troubleshooter. That means problems for us."

"None I can't handle."

"I hope so for your sake."

"When have I let you down?"

"You haven't, yet."

"Then I'll handle this."

"You'd better." Jonas stopped drumming his fingers and leaned forward on the desk. "I don't like failure."

"Figure it done, Mr. Webb."

"Who was watching the O'Neal place?"

"Nate."

"I want another man to watch the O'Neal place from now on, night and day. I want to know everything that goes on." Jonas raised a brow. "Do I make myself clear?"

"Clear as rainwater."

"Good." Jonas walked around the desk and leaned back against it, crossing his feet at the ankles, his arms against his chest. He looked Roberts directly in the eye. "There are other matters I wanted to talk to you about."

"Such as?"

"I've decided now's the time to put pressure on the station owners to go with my company. I want their contracts bought up. They're no longer to serve Texas Overland."

"What if they don't want to sell?"

"I'm sure you can make them see things my way." He paused, then said, "Any way necessary."

Zeke smiled. "My Colt talks pretty loud."

"Just so long as it talks convincingly."

"I get you. You want me to keep making payments to the others?"

"Yes. Can't have Conner get too suspicious if all of a sudden he loses all his contracts." Jonas smiled. "Every line should have dishonest workers to keep their competition informed, don't you think?" Jonas laughed. "Everybody's got a price."

Zeke threw his head back, his deep laughter joining his boss's. "Whatever you say."

"That's why you're my right-hand man."

Zeke sobered and regarded his boss. "I've worked for you a long time now, and I haven't seen anyone interest you this much. What makes this Trey Conner so different?"

"That's my business." Jonas's gaze burned

brighter. "I intend to take care of Conner in my own way, in my own good time. No one's to touch him but me. Understand?"

Zeke nodded. "I'll pass the word along to the boys."

"I also don't want a hand laid on Dallas O'Neal. I've got plans for her."

Jonas stood and walked around his desk. He opened a drawer, retrieved something from inside, then walked back around, uncoiling a whip as he went.

Zeke's insides went cold. He knew what the boss had in mind for Nate. Jonas Webb rewarded his men well when a job had been done right, gave his men a free hand in most cases with no questions asked, but Webb was also quick to punish when disappointed.

Jonas caused the whip to dance across the floor with a deft flick of his wrist. "Send someone for Nate."

Zeke rose and went to the door leading to the alley. He opened it and said something to someone on the other side.

Moments later, a knock came at the back door. Zeke stepped aside as two men entered, dragging a third by his upper arms.

"Mr. Webb, what's this all about?" asked Nate in a thin voice. He paled beneath his tanned complexion, and his eyes kept darting nervously to the whip Jonas held.

"You let me down, Nate. I can't have men who don't do what's expected."

Sweat drenched Nate's face and neck, and he trembled. Looking at the cowering man, Zeke felt a small measure of compassion, but revealed nothing by his expression. He wasn't sticking his neck out for Nate. No, sirree. Not this cowboy.

"Zeke, stand at the front door and make sure no one interferes," Jonas ordered.

Zeke moved to comply, but kept his back to the door and his face toward the men.

At a nod from Jonas, the two men led Nate to a wall. Positioning him between them, they tied his arms with a rope, then tossed the rope over an overhead beam. They slowly stretched Nate from the ceiling. As Nate hung in the vulnerable position, his toes barely touching the floor, they tore his shirt up the back.

Jonas lifted his arm. "In the future, Nate, you'll do your job. And you'll do it right."

"Oh, God, Mr. Webb, please don't," Nate cried.

"You're a wanted man, Nate." Jonas rubbed Nate's cheek with a section of the whip. "How many other men would give you work knowing that?"

"Nobody, Mr. Webb."

"You do understand how important following orders is, don't you, Nate?"

Nate nodded, perspiration pouring off his body and face.

"And why punishment must be carried out?" Jonas asked smoothly. "How will I know you won't disappoint me again, Nate?"

With deft wrist action, Jonas directed the whip at Nate. The rawhide whistled past Nate's ear.

"Please, Mr. Webb. Don't!" Nate strained at his bonds, then lost muscle control. The stench of urine and fear permeated the air.

Jonas lowered the whip. He reached inside his

inner coat pocket and retrieved a handkerchief and mopped the sweat from his brow.

"Cut him down," Jonas ordered. "I think Nate's learned his lesson."

A second man walked over to Nate, a knife gleaming in his hand. The blade sawed through the hemp, and Nate dropped to the wooden floor on his knees with a thud. He didn't move; he just cried like a baby.

"That'll be all, Zeke," were the only words Jonas spoke as his second-in-command turned and left the room.

Restless, Dallas threw off the sheet and rose. She padded barefoot to the window. She had lain in bed for the better part of two hours, staring at the ceiling. The fact that she hadn't been able to get Trey Conner off her mind didn't help her agitation. The past few days had been very unsettling and tense. Her nights were no better, filled with annoying dreams of Trey.

The breeze cooled the perspiration clinging damply to her body, but it did little to soothe her frayed nerves. The solitude of the barn suddenly called to her.

Shrugging into her wrapper, Dallas crept downstairs and quietly let herself out the door.

Inside the barn, she was greeted by the low nickering of a horse, the musty smell of hay, and the pungent odor of worn leather. As her eyesight adjusted to the interior, Dallas noticed the soft spill of lantern light coming from the end stall.

A woman's low, sultry voice violated Dallas's sanctuary. No one came to the barn late at night unless there was an emergency. Just who the devil was in here and what were they doing? Horse thieves weren't strangers to these parts.

Intent on learning the intruder's identity, Dallas grabbed a pitchfork and stealthily made her way to the end stall. Drawing near, she heard an unmistakably masculine voice mingle with the woman's.

When she peered around the corner, Dallas wished to God she hadn't. She saw Serena Crowley, lying against a pile of straw, clinging to the body of a lithe, muscular man who pleasured his partner beneath him with kiss after kiss.

Primitive, pulsating arousal charged the heated air.

Her head back and her eyes closed, Serena Crowley moaned and whimpered against the man's mouth, urging him to do more than kiss her.

Dallas's eyes widened. The man was Trey Conner.

She felt as if a crushing weight had been dropped on her chest, making it difficult to breathe. The shock—and strangely, the pain—of finding Conner kissing Miss Crowley rendered Dallas incapable of speech or movement. Holding the all-but-forgotten pitchfork, she remained frozen, hidden from the couple's view among the shadows and half-light of the barn.

Moments of sickening, seemingly endless moans of pleasure were strung together on a strand of eternity as Trey gave testimony to his ability to arouse a woman with only a kiss.

Dallas couldn't stem the flow of emotions. The intensity of her feelings thawed her paralysis.

She took a blind step back as tears blurred her vision.

But not before Trey sensed her presence and raised his head to stare at her, all the while reaching for the pistol that lay next to him in the hay.

His blue gaze collided and locked with Dallas's green one.

Time came to a standstill.

Her eyes wide and glittering with unshed tears, Dallas grasped the pitchfork so tightly, her knuckles were white from the tension.

Heated pain ceded to icy rage. To think, she had allowed him to kiss her. Worse, she had enjoyed his kiss! What a blackhearted varmint Trey Conner was! He proved he didn't have an honorable bone in his body, moving from one available woman to the next with practiced ease.

Her anger blazed. How dare he kiss some morally low-down white trash in her family's barn for anyone to see?

Trey stood, raking straw from his tousled hair. "Dallas?" He stepped toward her. "I—"

"Save your breath," Dallas interrupted him, replaying the scene of only moments ago and seeing again the way he had kissed that loose woman.

"Honey, if she doesn't want to listen, then don't bother," came Serena Crowley's low drawl.

Infuriated, yet strangely shaken, Trey whirled on Serena. Still reclining on the hay, she smiled up at him. Her lush lips were still moist and swollen from his kiss. Those lips had excited him just a short time ago, but now the sight of her lascivious grin made him sickeningly aware of his actions.

Serena lifted her arms in wanton invitation. "Why don't you tell her to leave so you and I can spend some more time together?"

Trey looked at the older woman. "I'm sorry, Serena. Maybe this wasn't such a good idea after all," he said in a flat tone.

"Well, I never!" Serena gasped.

"Seems like you have plenty of times, if you ask me," Dallas retorted as she glared at the woman. "Get out of my barn." Dallas took a menacing step forward, her fingers flexing on the handle of the pitchfork, which she wielded at chest level, poised to swing. "Now."

Serena rose and pouted at Trey. "You gonna let her talk to me like that? Why, to listen to her, you'd think she was the queen of Sheba, instead of poor folk who dresses in men's clothing."

Trey sighed heavily. "You'd better head back to the house, Serena."

Miss Crowley lifted her head, her nose even higher, and swept regally past Dallas.

Dallas watched the woman saunter out of the barn, then she turned her gaze on Trey.

A scowl darkened his features as he regarded her. Suddenly Dallas felt trapped by his intense gaze, and she didn't like the feeling one bit. At this moment she didn't need much of an excuse to justify skewering him with the pitchfork she held.

Unable to trust herself from gelding him where he stood, Dallas turned to leave.

"Dallas!" His voice rang with urgency.

She could be tarred and feathered before she'd

listen to him. Dallas didn't slow her steps; she didn't look back.

"Don't you dare walk away from me," Trey commanded.

Unafraid of the consequences, unconcerned with reprisal, unthinking of anything except her irrational, driving need to put this man in his place once and for all, Dallas turned on her heel. "You son of a bitch," she rasped in breathless contempt.

She threw the pitchfork at Trey.

It landed only inches from his feet, the handle quivering from the force of the impact.

Never had she seen such intemperate, scalding fury as she did in Trey Conner's eyes at that instant. Her own anger kept her backbone straight in the face of his mounting rage.

Dallas turned and continued toward the entrance. Reaching the door, she started to open it. His hand slammed it shut. The seasoned wood rattled ominously on its frame.

He grabbed her arm and spun her around. They glared at each other in the murky light.

Trey's nostrils flared. "No one walks away from me."

Dallas heard the masterful ring to his voice, but she ignored it. "There's a first time for everything."

"This won't be it."

"What makes you so certain?"

"Is there any doubt?" he countered.

"I've had enough of you for tonight. I want to go back to the house. Get out of my way."

Trey reached out and grasped her upper arms, pulling her gently, yet firmly, to him. "I don't want you to leave, not yet. Not until I—"

"Explain? There's no reason. You had a need, and you took care of it in the only way a man knows how. His own selfish interests."

She felt the heat of his hard flesh through her thin nightclothes. She placed her hands on his broad shoulders to put a fraction of space between them.

"And what if I did? Miss Crowley had made it plain, from the moment I met her, that she was interested in me. I took her at her word."

"And her deed," Dallas said pointedly.

"There's nothing wrong with my accepting what she so freely offered." He paused, his expression turning thoughtful. "Why do you care?"

"I don't!"

"You were too quick to answer, Dallas. I think you're hiding something. I think that my kissing Miss Crowley bothered you. Why?"

"I didn't like you bringing her in here."

"That's not all of it. Coward. Come out and say it."

Dallas tried to pull away, but he held her fast. "I hate you," she said in a harsh rasp.

"What do you want from me, Dallas? Do you want to hear that I was thinking of you while I was kissing Serena? That it was your face I saw, not hers?"

He released one arm and stroked her cheek with his knuckles. "That ever since I met you, I've wanted to kiss you until you were breathless? That I want you so much it hurts?" His voice grew thick and unsteady. "Is that what you want to hear?"

"I don't know what I want," she said with quiet urgency. "When you're near, I can't think, nothing makes any sense. I've never allowed a man to treat me the way you have."

Trey's mouth tightened. "I don't mean to hurt you. Stop fighting me so hard. Stop fighting yourself."

"I can't," she said in a soft drift of words.

Trey pulled her close again. "You could."

She flattened her palms against his chest, straining from contact with him. "Not without losing a part of myself."

Trey glanced down at her hands pressed against his chest. How warmly sensual the golden color of her skin looked against the blue of his shirt. His gaze traveled to her face, held prisoner in the shadows and half-light.

Jesus, Trey groaned inwardly as he saw the vulnerability shadow her features. Did she realize how tempting she looked with her lips parted and trembling, her hair falling in a thick, golden tumble over her shoulder, the steady rise and fall of her breasts beneath the thinness of her nightclothes, the telltale flush spreading across her cheeks? And those beguiling green eyes—eyes lit with an inner fire and passion matched only by her outer beauty. Beyond her physical loveliness, he saw the subtle, intriguing complexities of her nature, which no man could possibly understand.

God, he wanted her! Every organ from his brain to his gut started to buzz like a locust. Disturbed by his slipping control, he breathed deeply, knowing that if he surrendered to his desire, he jeopardized his plans.

Damn.

His body urged him to kiss her, while his common sense pleaded for restraint. Desire, hot and heavy, flowed through his passion-starved veins, making movement torturous. He had never wanted a woman as much as he did Dallas.

His eyes betrayed his feverish emotion. "I can't let you go."

His mouth tightened grimly, a muscle leaping convulsively in his jaw as the smoldering blue of his eyes bored into hers. Before she could draw another breath, he caught her face between his strong hands. He stroked the corners of her mouth with his thumbs.

The musky, male scent of him was heady and strong, intoxicating her senses with its potency. Her heart hammered in her chest.

Their labored breathing grated into the hushed air.

His gaze told her that he meant to lay claim to her, that he wanted to kiss her . . . as desperately as she wanted him to do it.

Trey leaned forward, his face, raw with desire, a mere inch from hers. "You know what I want, don't you?" His warm, moist breath stirred the tiny curling hairs about her face. He traced her lips with the tip of his tongue.

"I should leave," she mumbled, afraid of herself, afraid of him, afraid of the passion beating at her like hummingbird wings.

"Yes, you should." His words were heated velvet against the lushness of her mouth.

He caught her to him and savored the sensation of her breasts, a heavy softness pressing against his chest, her thighs, a lithe pressure against his, the silkiness of her maze-colored hair, a whisper across his exposed forearms.

He tilted her face up toward him, his callused palm at the base of her throat, feeling her pulse beating strongly. His own pulse beat a rapid tattoo through his veins.

Trey pressed his mouth to her forehead, then pulled away. His hold around her waist tightened as he traced her cheekbone with the roughened pad of his thumb. His finger moved to her lips, urging them open, and drifted across the ridges of her small, straight teeth, then dipped inside her bottom lip and tugged gently.

He brought his finger to his own lips and rubbed it over them, leaving a sheen of her moisture on his mouth. He ran his tongue across his lips. "I like the way you taste."

He placed his hands on her shoulders, feeling their rounded curves beneath his palms. "I'd like to taste more of you."

Trey watched with fascination as she ran her tongue over her lips. He could sense her struggle to control her natural reaction to his caress.

"You can't," she whispered raggedly.

"Give me a good reason why not."

"This is wrong."

"Only if it doesn't feel right."

He spread his fingers along both sides of her jawline and held her face gently between his hands, savoring the velvet smoothness of her flawless complexion.

Trey was powerless to control his desire, and for the first time in thirty-two years, he found himself ruled by emotion. He hadn't thought it possible. Until now.

He lowered his head, slowly, his breathing unsteady. Gently but firmly he molded his mouth to hers. Their lips met, broke, then met again. He kissed her until her breath came in tiny, punctuated gasps of pleasure.

Without breaking the kiss, Trey bent her body over his supporting arm until her back bowed slightly. He pushed aside the edges of her wrapper, untied her gown, and slipped his hand inside the garment to softly cup one of her breasts.

Dallas instinctively arched against the masterful hand. Somewhere, in the corner of her mind, she knew this was wrong, but her reason couldn't latch on to the indecency of the situation. Never would she have suspected that she would enjoy a man's touch so much, but then, never had she met a man like Trey Conner. His fingers moved skillfully, making the blood work harder through her veins. He pushed down the material until the cotton cradled her breast, exposing her flesh to his heated gaze.

The shock of his hot mouth on her warm skin gave Dallas the strength to push at his chest. "No, don't."

"Oh, yes. And more. We don't always have to be fighting."

He put action to his intention and pressed his palm against her breast, rubbing her sensitive skin in a slow, circular motion. Her nipple came to life, hard and pebbly, against his hand.

Trey touched her neck with his moist lips. "So soft, so sweet," he breathed against her flushed skin.

She closed her eyes. "Trey." His name floated past her lips in a ragged whisper.

"I know."

"I've dreamed of your touching me like this for such a long time."

"Not as long as I've wanted to feel you in my arms."

"Do you really mean that?"

"It seems I've waited my entire life for you."

His touch all but reduced her to a puddle of delicious, wicked sensation. His slow seduction was too powerful for her, storming her senses in sensual assault. A strange, curious feeling blossomed in the pit of her stomach—twining down her body. She didn't know or understand what was happening to her, but she didn't care. Her traitorous body craved his touch.

In a sublime span of heightened awareness, Dallas's and Trey's souls became one. They were joined briefly by a desire that shamed the one and plagued the other.

Trey sensed Dallas's near surrender. Relishing such an unfamiliarly strong desire, Trey had become lost in the moment, his thoughts only of burying himself deep within this desirable woman. The knowledge excited him, yet, at the same time, sobered him to the seriousness of the situation. What the hell was he doing? He had a job to do, and seducing Dallas wasn't part of it.

He never regretted taking what women freely offered, but Dallas was an innocent. She didn't deserve to be hurt.

At that same moment, Dallas realized her wanton actions and her disregard of normal restraints. She squeezed her eyes shut at the pain. How could she have allowed him such liberties?

Trey broke the contact first and raised his head.

His nostrils flared faintly with a suggestion of proud arrogance.

Trey gently pushed her away. "I think you've had enough kissing for one night," he said in a thick, oddly breathless voice.

"Yes, I think so." She paused, "But . . ."

"What?"

"I like the way you kiss," she said shyly as she turned from him and stepped to the door.

When Dallas had walked out of the barn, a black frown creased Trey's brow.

God, she drove him to distraction. She seemed to have no fear of him, and the thought both angered and amused Trey. He wasn't used to such a willful, proud female. And yet, he didn't want to hurt her, didn't want to continually manhandle her. She irritated him, he admitted, irritated . . . and enticed him. But he still had a problem. He'd have to do something about her inclination to defy him. She'd have to learn her place on this station . . . and how she figured into his life. There had to be a more persuasive way of handling her.

But what?

Chapter 6

Dawn peeked above the horizon and spilled sunshine onto the dewy ground, coating the landscape in a warm glow. Pearly sunlight filtered through the weathered planks of the barn as Dallas sat on the edge of a tack box, watching Miguel treat a young horse for ringworm.

"Is she going to be all right?" Dallas asked, peering over Miguel's shoulder as he rubbed iodine ointment into the circular patches of bare skin.

"She will be fine with rest. No need to worry, little one."

"I never worry when it comes to you, Miguel. You're the best."

"Only because the Old Ones have given me my gift. As always, they guide my hands." He finished applying the ointment, then wiped his hands on a bandanna. "What are you going to do today since you are not driving?"

Dallas's face darkened. She jumped down from the tack box and stepped to the end of the stall. "Stay as far away from Trey Conner as possible."

Miguel came to stand beside her and placed his hand on her shoulder. "*Niña*, why does he trouble you so?"

Why did he trouble her? Dallas wondered.

She remembered staring into his piercing blue eyes, and heat flashed through her. She moistened her suddenly dry lips. He had touched her as no other man had done. And God help her, she had wanted him to touch her. She had wanted his hands and mouth on her, touching and tasting her in secret places. She had started out hating him, but something had changed somewhere along the way. Her breath came in painful, short spurts.

No, she couldn't soften towards him. She must hate him. She must remain angry at him.

But whatever her feelings, they were explosive and frightening.

Dallas shook her head, desperate to dislodge him from her thoughts. "Isn't it enough that I don't like him?"

"What don't you like about him?"

"For one thing, the way he keeps staring at me. Every time I turn around, he's looking at me like I've grown two heads or something."

Miguel laughed knowingly. "Ah, that is a man who is interested in what he sees."

"How would you know?"

"*Niña*, I have not always been an old man. I, too, can appreciate a fine woman. That is all Mr. Conner is doing."

"Well, I wish to hell he wouldn't appreciate me so much. I could do with a little less appreciation and a lot more confidence in my ability to run this station."

Miguel's hand fell away. "Not everything can be done your way."

That was just it. She wanted her way, and Trey Conner wasn't cooperating. Damn him!

Dallas shrugged. How could she make Miguel understand what she was feeling when she wasn't sure herself? Was she attracted to Trey Conner? Maybe, maybe not. Her head ached just thinking about it. And her breasts . . . and her stomach . . . and oh, God, lower.

Thoughts of him, like quicksand, sucked greedily at her resolve. Hell's bells! Why should she care? He certainly didn't! He was playing with her, and she knew it. His kiss had told her so. His practiced, arrogant, masterful kiss had conveyed his opinion of women—they were to be enjoyed, nothing more. But no promises accompanied his seduction. What would it take to make Trey Conner desire one woman, and one woman alone?

But his seduction was hard to fight. She could still feel the warmth and texture of his mouth on hers. And it left her craving more. So much more.

She caught herself and unconsciously stiffened her spine. She was acting as silly as a calf gone crazy on clover. Wondering things about him would only get her in trouble. She had to stop this foolishness. Now. She didn't want her feelings for him to change. She wanted to continue finding him impossible, arrogant, rude. Life would be simpler that way. They had to work together. There must be nothing else between them. Absolutely nothing.

"Well, I can tell you are uncertain of your path, and it bothers you." He raised a hand to silence her when she opened her mouth to dispute him. "Do not deny it. I can see this thing in your eyes, *niña*."

Dallas released her breath slowly, softly. "What can you see?"

"That you are afraid to let yourself feel as a woman would."

Dallas went to the barn door and gazed out across the yard. Inside, she felt a strange combination of excitement and dread. Was what Miguel said true? Was she afraid of being a woman?

Miguel's voice behind her disrupted Dallas's thoughts. "I also feel that you are afraid to have a life with a man. That everything you have accomplished in your life will be for nothing if you share yourself with a man."

"Are you suggesting that I give myself to a man?"

"No, *niña*. Only marriage will satisfy you. But do not refuse happiness because of pride. Love and trust are special gifts for your happiness. You can give of yourself without feeling less than a man's equal. You can be soft without being weak. These things, you must learn."

"And I suppose Trey Conner is the man to teach me all that you say."

Miguel smiled and shrugged. "It is a beautiful day. Go and have yourself a swim." He gave her a gentle push. "It will make you feel better."

"You're probably right," Dallas sighed. When she saw his eyes brighten, she added in a tight voice, "About the swim."

She returned to the house, gathered her things, and set out for the creek.

As Dallas walked along the well-marked path, her boots stirring up tiny puffs of dust, her thoughts turned again to Trey. She laughed dryly. He would get the biggest kick out of knowing she couldn't get him off her mind. She continued along the cedar-lined path until she came to the creek.

Cottonwood, cypress, and pecan trees spread their limbs across the meandering water, creating a private world of beauty and tranquillity. She inhaled the sweet, soothing scent of morning. She lifted her face heavenward and relished the warm sunlight trickling through the leaves of the old cottonwood and across her features.

Her earlier frustration and anger forgotten, Dallas made her way down a small incline until she reached a large oak, its protective, low-lying branches reaching across and skimming the water's surface. She removed her boots and socks, rolled up her pants legs, then climbed out on a twisted, weathered branch.

Hidden within the secretive shade, she dangled her feet and ankles in the cool water. She sighed. The water felt wonderful. Breathing deeply, she felt her neck and shoulder muscles relax, tension gently ebbing from her body. She closed her eyes.

Then the tranquillity was broken. She opened her eyes and looked about her surroundings. Her eyes grew wide. Her mouth went dry. Her breath tangled in her throat. There on the opposite creekbank, against the dappling of sunlight filtering through the rich, thick greenery and twisted, coiled mustang grape vines, stood Trey Conner. In all his vividly highlighted, splendid, and naked glory.

Motionless, breathless, she stared, unable to pry her eyes from every delicious inch of his muscular torso, bare for her private, unhurried inspection. Her tongue felt as if it were glued to the top of her mouth. She had never seen a grown man without clothes. She had never seen Trey Conner without clothes.

Her gaze swept across his face, with its sun-bronzed skin, across the rugged angles of his chiseled cheeks and strong jaw, past his straight nose, lingering momentarily on his firm mouth.

Warmth, like thick, golden honey, flowed through her, coating her senses in sweet, agonizing awareness. Unwanted. Unavoidable.

She gazed with perfect clarity upon each and every rippling, corded detail of his body's perfection. His broad shoulders were bathed in sunlight, his smooth, bare chest rippled with every move he made. She was mesmerized by his dark nipples, his taut, flat stomach, and his thick, black hair.

His . . .

Dallas lost her hold on the tree branch and tumbled backward into the water. Emerging with a toss of her soaked hair, she pushed strands away from her face and darted for land. She waded onto the bank and headed down the path as quickly as her shaky legs would take her. She had to hurry. Any moment Trey might see her.

Despite her soggy clothes and chilled skin, she felt heat sting her cheeks. Did he know she had been spying on him?

She stopped and drew a burning breath. What did she care if he had seen her? It wasn't as if she had known he was going to be there. Besides, he hadn't tried to conceal himself. For heaven's sake, he had stood in the open for anyone to see! So what if it just happened to be her? She clenched her teeth. She had the right to go anywhere she damn well wanted.

Yet Dallas had to admit truthfully, Trey couldn't have intimidated her more had he intentionally tried. She hoped he hadn't seen her.

She cleared her throat. She wished she could clear her memory of Trey's vivid image as easily.

Chewing on a piece of straw, Dallas rolled onto her stomach, hands folded under her chin. She hadn't outgrown her need for the hayloft's solitude. Hidden from prying eyes, she could think clearly. And she certainly had a lot to think about.

All morning her mind had traveled in circles, drifting from depression to dismay and then to anger as she tried to make a decision about Trey Conner.

Tyler's voice broke into her thoughts. "Dallas, you up there?"

Begrudgingly Dallas answered, "Yeah."

She heard her younger sister climbing the ladder until she saw Tyler's face come into view over the top of the last rung.

"All right, what's bothering you? Nobody's seen you since breakfast." Tyler climbed over the ladder and sat cross-legged next to Dallas. "You haven't been yourself the last couple of days. Wanna talk about it?"

Usually Tyler just wanted to pester Dallas about her need for privacy, but this time Dallas sensed her sister really cared. Maybe it'd help to confide in someone.

"Trey Conner is a wart on my life," Dallas said with a loud sigh. After each confrontation with him, she felt tired and older, her emotions racing faster than a roadrunner.

Tyler nibbled on a piece of straw. "Is that all?"

"Isn't it enough?"

"When it comes to that man, I'd say he's more than enough for any woman." Tyler shrugged at Dallas's intense look. "Can't help it. He's a right handsome man."

"Not you, too. Why is it everybody around here likes him but me?"

"Because you're too hard on him."

"Me? What about the way he treats me?"

"That's only because you're letting him get away with it. Why's that?"

"I wish I knew."

"If it were any other man who treated you low, you would've had him strung up in the nearest tree by now." Tyler clucked her tongue. "Yes, sirree. You've never been one to take any guff off anyone, especially a man."

"I can't think when I'm around him. I'm not sure I know myself anymore. I say one thing, but I do something else. It's driving me crazy."

"You?" Tyler laughed. "I wish whatever you two started, you'd finish. There hasn't been a peaceful moment around here ever since y'all locked horns."

"That's just it. We're too much alike to get along. We're both—"

"Stubborn? Headstrong? Independent?" Tyler finished with a glint in her eye that Dallas wasn't sure she liked.

"But if y'all don't settle things, what's going to happen to the stage line? You've got to work together, not against each other."

Dallas wanted to laugh. She'd always considered herself mature for her age, encouraged by her parents to live up to her abilities. She had thrived on the challenge of being her own person and being successful. Perhaps she had more growing up to do than she thought.

"Don't you think I know that?" Dallas replied. "But nothing's going to keep me from doing my job. I'll drive the stage as long as I can, with or without his approval."

"You've never dodged your duty."

"Dammit, I just wish Trey Conner would go away. I don't want to think about him anymore. He's done enough already."

Tyler, with more intuitive insight than before, asked, "What's really eating you?"

"All right. I'll tell you, but you've got to promise me you won't breathe a word to anyone else."

"I—"

"Tyler, swear to me," Dallas insisted.

Tyler puckered her lips, her curiosity clearly piqued. "I promise."

"He kissed me. Worse, I liked it. Too much for it to have been proper. Even worse, I think about it—a lot."

Tyler smiled. "I would, too, if I'd been kissed by the likes of him. I can think of a whole lot worse things than that."

"Will you be serious?" Dallas returned, wide-eyed.

"I am. What's wrong with him kissing you? He's a good-looking man. There's nothing wrong with you being attracted to him like a woman would."

"But I don't want to be."

"Don't you? You wouldn't be talking about it if you didn't."

"But what made him kiss me?"

"If you can't answer that, then you're in deep trouble."

"What makes you such an expert?"

"Nothing. But it don't take much to figure out why a man kisses a woman." Tyler spit out her straw. "Why you so mad, though. That can't be all that's eating you."

"I caught him in the barn kissing that Crowley woman."

"You're jealous."

"Am not."

"Aren't you?"

Dallas stopped to recall the entire incident. One minute he had been furious at her, all but shouting at her, his words stinging like bull nettles. The next he had crushed her to him in an embrace she had been powerless to escape. And his kiss. Just remembering it caused her insides to churn with warm, soft sensations.

But nothing had been soft about what she had seen of Trey this morning.

"Why would I be jealous?"

"Because her kind's always looked down their noses at us. And because she makes you realize what you haven't been—a real woman."

"Where'd you get all this wisdom all of a sudden?"

"I can read what you're thinking by the look on your face."

"You always could," Dallas said.

"Quit denying you're attracted to Trey. It'll keep you from getting a nervous stomach."

Dallas spit out the straw and rested her cheek on her hands. Her whole body heated with the thought of them naked, her flesh pressed against his . . . of him touching her . . . of her touching him. But then, what did she know? Nothing. She knew nothing about men.

She frowned. "Why do thoughts of him haunt me? Why can't I forget what happened?"

"Why should you? You haven't done anything wrong. Our parents taught us not to be ashamed of passion. But remember, they also taught us to keep our passion curbed till we're married." Tyler shrugged. "Besides, why shouldn't you like being kissed, even if Trey had been the one doing the kissing? So you had wanted him to kiss you. Is that a hanging offense?"

Yes. No. Maybe, Dallas thought. When Trey did wonderfully wicked things to her, right and wrong blurred.

He was handsome as sin.

She knew it. He made her think of sin often enough.

"Every time he touches me, I want something more, but I don't know what—except that it's forbidden."

"I think you've done enough soul-searching for one day." Tyler rose to her knees and swung her legs over the ladder. Before she made her descent, she said, "By the way, Abbey wants you to go into town to the general store and get some supplies."

"Why can't you go?"

"Because I'm busy helping Miguel."

"Oh, all right."

Dallas climbed down the ladder and dusted off her clothes. Maybe a trip into town was just the thing to lift her spirits.

Moments later, she had saddled her horse, got Abbey's supply list, and was on her way to Lockhart.

McDowell's Dry Goods was located near the center of town. The two-story building had two huge display windows with a door in the center. One window showcased items of interest for women such as hats, sewing material, scissors, buttons, and dolls. In the other window, articles such as tools and shoes were displayed to catch men's eyes.

Dallas walked inside. In the center of the cluttered store was a wood-burning stove. Many a card game, checkers game, and great conversation had taken place around that big potbelly.

At the rear of the building were tubs of pickles, tobacco, and crackers, and closed barrels of vinegar and molasses. Along one wall was a long counter. Behind it, shelves ran from floor to ceiling. Along one wall built-in bins contained coffee, tea, peas, rice, dried fruit, and oatmeal. Small drawers held pepper, cinnamon, cloves, and other spices. On the counter stood a large brass scale, along with tin-covered glass containers of licorice, stick candy, and wax gums.

While the clerk, a pleasingly plump, bald man with a ruddy complexion, took items from the shelves and put them in saddlebags for her, Dallas sampled a peppermint stick and browsed.

A selection of books drew her attention. She tilted her head to read the titles. It had been so long since she had taken the time to read. Before she had the responsibility of running the station, she had spent many happy hours escaping to faraway places. Her parents had seen that all their children were well read and educated to the best of their abilities. Often, people just meeting her would be amazed at her vocabulary and how well she expressed herself. Of course, the last several years she had slipped somewhat and picked up colorful phrases and wording. Swearing being the worst.

Moments later, purchases in hand, she headed outside. She had just reached the front steps when Jonas Webb, who wore a preoccupied look on his face, bumped into her on the sidewalk. She was thrown off balance and knocked to her bottom, with her legs spread wide and her hat sitting crooked on her head. Canned goods spilled from her saddlebags and rolled off the wooden planks into the street. Her peppermint stick lay in two halves in the dust.

Jonas Webb stopped, and his dark expression lifted. He smiled and extended his hand. "I'm sorry."

"You should look where you're going," Dallas said, her sunny disposition as soiled as her peppermint.

His smiled widened, revealing straight white teeth. "I said I'm sorry. What more can I do?"

"Nothing at all."

"At least let me help you."

She accepted the assistance he offered and let herself be drawn to her feet. Color throbbed in her cheeks at the humiliating experience. It seemed whenever she ran into Mr. Webb, disaster wasn't far behind. Though this was only the second time she had encountered the man, it was enough.

Amusement flickered in Mr. Webb's blue eyes. "At the risk of being scolded by you again, I must say that you're still as beautiful as I remember."

Dallas swallowed back a retort, her previous humiliation at his hands not forgotten, and pivoted to leave.

She found her retreat cut off by a firm hand on her arm. Mr. Webb forced her to face him. "May I call you Dallas?"

"You may not!"

"Can't we be friends?"

He surprised Dallas with his persistence, and she stared wordlessly at him. He certainly had his nerve!

Her chin rose a notch, and he laughed.

Furious, Dallas pulled away, then gasped softly as Jonas Webb's hands caught her shoulders firmly. "I'm not letting you go while you're angry at me."

"You have no right to hold me."

"But I do. I'm the one who put you in this uncomfortable situation." He released her, bent, and picked up the scattered cans, packing them in her saddlebags. He turned his attention back to her. "Now, before you go and tell me what you think of my bold ways, I'd like to make up to you for your trouble. Let me buy you some refreshment."

Although stated as an invitation, his tone clearly conveyed his unwillingness to accept a refusal. His charm melted most of her anger. Oddly enough, Dallas couldn't think of anything to say, but she wondered what he wanted from her.

Jonas smiled once more, and his eyes sparkled. He correctly read her thoughts. "I only want to buy you some lemonade. Nothing more." His expression was warm and inviting.

Not certain why she was compelled to do so, Dallas agreed. "All right. But just a glass of lemonade."

However, when Mr. Webb held his arm out for her, Dallas wasn't prepared for the eruption of strange emotions she felt. No one had ever treated her like a lady, and she'd never realized she wanted to be treated like one.

Awkwardly she put her arm in his. And with her saddlebags on his other arm, they then made their way down the sidewalk to a nearby restaurant.

Dallas did her best to ignore the curious glances from local passersby. How odd it must look to see Dallas O'Neal, wearing men's clothing, on the arm of a gentleman such as Jonas Webb. If she hadn't felt so disconcerted, she would have laughed.

They were soon seated, sipping two glasses of lemonade.

Jonas chuckled. "Well, I never expected to see you again so soon. What brought you to Lockhart?"

"My sister needed some supplies. I didn't have a run today, so I came to do the errands."

"How'd you get away from Mr. Conner?"

Her expression darkened. She didn't want to think about Trey. "The company doesn't own me. I do what I want."

She knew it was a half lie, but she saw no need to tell Mr. Webb company business. After all, he ran the competing stage line.

Amusement curved his lips. "Interesting. I would have thought it would be different working for Trey, knowing him like I do."

"How do you know him?"

"We served together during the war. We were officers in the same calvary unit."

"Were you of the same rank?"

"No. Trey was a major." Jonas's fingers tightened around his glass. "I was only a captain. He certainly relished giving orders."

"He still does." The words were out of Dallas's mouth before she realized. She smiled to cover her uneasiness.

She had sensed an undercurrent from Webb when he spoke of Trey. Yet seeing Webb now, he looked kinder, more sincere, less offensive than during her previous encounter with him. His attitude was every bit the respectful gentleman. Despite her first impression of him, Dallas found herself liking him.

Jonas forced himself to concentrate on their conversation. He would have liked nothing better than simply to look upon the beautiful young woman before him. As his gaze scanned her, he set to memory the delicate shape of her neck, the sensual curve of her breasts outlined by her shirt, the gentle rounding of her hips highlighted by her pants. His fingers itched to touch her, and he longed to take her to his bed, but he knew he had to wait. He also instinctively knew she would be well worth his patience. What sweet torture to sit here and enjoy her loveliness without revealing his hunger for her. He had to win her trust, and so he must keep his distance. Dallas O'Neal would have to be seduced slowly, surely.

What would Miss O'Neal look like dressed as a lady? He pictured her in his mind's eye, wearing a gown with her hair arranged in attractive curls atop her head. In her men's clothing, she was beautiful. But in the proper attire, he knew she would be stunning.

He smiled as she continued to talk. When she smiled in return, he was struck by an intense feeling of affection. Something he hadn't allowed himself to feel in many years. It was an emotion he couldn't afford to experience. He trampled the emotion beneath the heel of steely determination.

The way the light in her eyes danced when she laughed made his lower regions ache until he felt himself grow hard.

It was all he could do to escort her back to her horse and not take her into his arms and kiss her. He wanted to taste her sweetness. He wanted to feel the fiery passion he sensed within her. He clamped down his body's response as he prepared to leave her.

He groaned to himself. Her charms went beyond dangerous. They bordered on lethal.

Dallas glanced at the poster inside the general store's window, then turned back to Jonas. "Will you be attending the upcoming dance?" she asked innocently.

"I will if you'll be coming," he said in a voice tight with control.

"My sisters and brother usually go. Maybe I'll see you there."

Jonas could feel his brow bead with perspiration at the effort to check the desire pulsating through him. He managed a smile. "I'll make it a point."

He groaned inwardly as his body painfully underscored that particular choice of words.

"I'd best be going," Dallas said, untying her horse from the hitching post. "Thank you for the refreshment."

"The pleasure's been all mine." With that, he turned and strode down the sidewalk, intent on reaching the hotel and relieving himself.

He intended to have a great deal more pleasure from Dallas O'Neal. The sweetest he'd ever known.

Chapter 7

If Trey thought yesterday had been trying, today was that much worse. Today Dallas had gone too far. He hadn't thought she had the gumption to defy him. But she had. The proof was before his eyes as he watched her dismount. Oh, she had changed her clothes, all right. The pants she wore today were tighter than those she'd worn yesterday. If that was possible.

But when it came to Dallas, Trey realized, you could expect not what was possible, but what was improbable.

The time of reckoning had come. He walked toward her, his intent obvious in his brisk stride and his balled hands.

Dallas, on the other hand, had seen Trey when she rode up to the barn. The grim set to his mouth meant trouble—trouble she wanted no part of.

Turning her back on him, she tied her horse to the fence, unfastened her saddlebags, tossed them over her shoulder, and headed for the house.

His bellow was loud, and harsh. "Stop!"

She ignored the command and continued

walking, keeping her steps even and unhurried. Behind her she heard his heavy footsteps, the heels of his boots crunching bits of dirt and rock in a rhythm that said he'd just as soon nail her to a fence post as take any guff off her.

"Dallas O'Neal, stop right there!"

The order rang out with unmistakable authority. She could almost feel his breath on her neck. Unease stirred in Dallas's blood, but her rage kept close company. She was sick to death of his overbearing behavior. She wasn't on company time. This was her day off, to do with as she pleased. And she was pleased to ignore him.

Suddenly a hand seized her arm, strong fingers biting into her tender flesh, stopping her short. Her head whipped around. Her gaze locked and clashed with Conner's.

At the intensity of emotion riding high across Conner's face, and the force of his character, her heart skipped a beat, then slammed hard against the wall of her chest.

"Why didn't you stop?" he asked.

She knew she was challenging him. "Maybe if you'd asked nicely, I would have."

"I don't have time for games."

Trey stared at her with compelling force—a magnetism that drew her to him. She leaned forward a fraction. "I'm not playing any."

His touch was too hot. His nearness too dangerous.

As dangerous as the energy that surrounded him. Energy that crackled between them.

"Where have you been?" Conner asked.

"That's none of your business."

"If I make it my business, it is."

His hold tightened, and Dallas flinched. "You're hurting me."

"Just answer my question."

"I went to town."

"Dressed like that?"

She hated that dangerously silky tone of voice, hated the way it seemed to stroke her, inside and out. "This is my day off. I'll wear what I want. Go where I want. See who I want."

"See? Who did you see in town?"

"Your old army friend Jonas Webb." If Dallas had any common sense, she would have refrained from baiting Trey. But common sense had never been one of her strong suits. "We spent some time together. And *he* didn't seem to mind what I wore."

She knew by the narrowing of his eyes that his anger was spreading faster than spilled water. But other than the glint in his eyes, he gave no hint of emotion. He arched a brow. As always, his control infuriated her.

His voice lowered even more ominously. She drew a ragged breath and her nostrils filled with the scent of him.

"You're not to talk to Jonas Webb again."

She felt his warmth and both the anger and the sensual timbre of his words. "You have no right to tell me that," she argued.

"As line boss, I do. He's the competition. Until further notice, I don't want you around him."

"Not only have you told me what to wear, now you're telling me who to see. Well, I won't have it!" She wanted to grind her heel on his instep. But contradictory to her boiling anger was the urge to have him hold her.

"You'll do as I say," he warned. "Or you'll be fired."

For a moment they were two fierce, indomitable wills locked in silent, heated combat. Tension riddled the air around them.

"You don't have the authority to do that."

"And who's going to stop me? Do what I tell you or I'll lock you in your room."

Trey Conner could go hang! "You wouldn't dare."

"Oh, wouldn't I?" His fingers tightened about her arm. "Do what I tell you. Now!"

"I will when the mood strikes me."

"You'd better before I strike you."

Dallas drew a ragged breath. "Oh really?"

"You and I are going to have a little talk," he informed her. "Alone."

Before she could react, Dallas found herself steered toward the barn. Thinking it wiser not to resist, she suffered Conner's manhandling as he pulled her to a halt inside. He maintained his hold on her arm.

She glowered at him. "You're hurting me again, or do you intend to break my arm?"

"Not unless you force me to do it."

Dallas felt her stomach clench in dread, but she kept her backbone straight. She could be thrown into a heap of prickly pear cacti before she'd admit she was afraid to be alone with him. Not only was she afraid of what he might do, she was afraid of what she might want him to do.

Why would she, the daredevil of Caldwell County, as she thought of herself, suddenly turn coward? Another glance at his hard face answered her question. His expression was intent, powerful, and readable for once. She swallowed hard. His gaze promised revenge. For a moment, she actually believed he intended to wring her neck.

"You should have listened to me," he scolded her.

She hated his heated nearness, the husky tenor of his voice, his male scent, his strength. She hated the way her traitorous body responded to him.

"I would listen to you if you had something relevant to say," she charged him.

At the narrowing of his eyes and the flaring of his nostrils, she knew that her usual lack of caution had once again gotten her chin-high in hot water.

How does one deal with a man who has been pushed past his limits? You run like hell! She attempted to pull away.

"I wouldn't try it."

Dallas moistened her lips. No, she wouldn't risk it. She wouldn't give him an excuse to throttle her. She ceased her struggles.

"What did I tell you yesterday?" Trey asked.

"About my clothes?"

"Hell yes, about your clothes."

Her survival instincts told her she'd better give him the right answer, but she couldn't open her mouth.

"I want you to repeat," he said, "exactly what I told you . . . only this time . . . I want you to look me in the eye."

She swallowed, but she still couldn't find her voice.

"I know you've got plenty to say," Trey said.

"You're always full of piss and vinegar."

His caustic words were like a slap in the face. Dallas found her voice. "I don't have to stand here and listen to you." She struggled to draw a calming breath.

"If you value that hide of yours, you do."

Staunch in her rebellious pride, Dallas stubbornly refused to say the words that promised salvation.

"Well, Miss O'Neal, I'm waiting."

Conner was good at intimidation, damned good, but he'd be sadly mistaken if he underestimated her mettle. "You can wait until eternity."

When reason failed, Trey did what any irritated male would do—he shook her. "I want answers from you."

"This is my station and my barn. I don't have to tell you a damned thing!"

Trey released his hold on her arms, caught her wrists, and held them at her sides. "I want to know why you disobeyed me. Don't you realize that every time you oppose me, you're forcing me to take action against you? You're only making this hard on yourself."

Damned if he didn't get her hackles up—because her attraction for him grew each time she saw him. She didn't know why, since he manhandled her at every turn. It made no sense. She tried to fight his frightening allure with fury.

"Why do you care?"

"Never mind that. You're not leaving here until you give me an answer."

"What if I don't?"

"I've got time to wait."

"We'll just see about that."

"Before today is over, you and I are going to see to a great many things," he replied in a cool, constrained voice. "How should I handle you, Dallas? So far being firm hasn't worked." His gaze burned brighter. "Perhaps I've gone about this all wrong. Perhaps I should be gentle with you. Very gentle."

"What?"

"You're a challenge, Dallas. The most interesting one I've ever had." He leaned closer. "But I promise you, one I will win."

Her senses throbbed, ached, peaked at his words and his softening expression. "Wouldn't you like to know what I'm going to teach you first?"

Shivering in anticipation, she didn't have long to wait as his warm lips caressed hers, whispered against the soft lushness of her mouth, parted her lips in a breathless command. The scent of him washed over her, then mingled with her own to fill the air with the heady fragrance of fire and anger. Passion.

He broke off the kiss and stared at her, his gaze fixed on her moist lips. With slow sensuality, he traced her jaw and mouth with his thumbs, his touch warm. Dallas's limbs felt like water. She couldn't move, speak . . . or think. She only had the ability to feel what Trey's touch did to her.

"Do you know how beautiful you are when you're angry? When I see the green fire in your eyes, I want to make love to you . . . all night." His hands slid down her throat and across her shoulders, gliding over the fabric of her shirt. "I always tell myself to leave you alone, but when

I'm near you, all I can think, feel, or want is to touch you."

Trey grasped her arms and, groaning deep in his throat, pulled her against him and sought her mouth once more. He kissed her, greedily, hungrily. He anchored one arm around her waist, while with his free hand, he undid her braid. Her hair tumbled about her face and down her back in golden waves.

Trey brought a handful of silky tresses to his nose and inhaled. "I like the sweet scent of your hair." He brought a strand to his mouth. "And I like the way it feels, soft and silky to the touch." He trailed a feathery kiss across her brow. "You should wear your hair loose more often. It reminds me of you, wild and free." He traced the side of her neck, his breath falling hotly against her flesh, causing her nerves to rise to the surface of her skin in heightened awareness. "God, I want to feel, taste, and know every inch of you."

At the frank intimacy of his words, Dallas became absolutely incensed and lost the fragile control she had maintained over her reactions. She struck at him with her booted foot, catching him on the shin with enough force to jam her toes inside her boot.

Trey reacted instinctively and forcefully, knocking Dallas to the ground on her back. The impact drove the air from her lungs.

She struggled to sit, but the crushing weight in her chest made it impossible. She rolled to her side and gasped as she fought for air.

Trey knelt beside Dallas. A stunned hiss escaped him. "Jesus!" His shaky fingers brushed her hair from her face. "I didn't mean to hurt you," he growled. He sat cross-legged beside her and pulled her head onto his lap.

Her throat worked and she tried to talk, but the effort proved too painful.

"Ssh. Can't you be quiet for once in your life?" Trey said, amusement lightly infusing his concern. He trailed his fingers across her brow. "Are you okay?"

Only minutes passed, but it seemed an eternity until Dallas felt air flow into her lungs in restorative currents.

"Get . . . away . . . from . . . me," she rasped as she slowly regained her strength and voice.

"I wouldn't dream of leaving you in your time of need."

"You've . . . done enough . . . already." She struggled to sit, turned, and rocked back on her heels.

"Where you're concerned, I've only just begun."

"This is all your fault."

"I already said I didn't mean to hurt you, Dallas."

"Are you trying to say that you're sorry?"

"Maybe."

"Then say it."

He heard her words, but he felt her voice as it drifted over him, passing across flesh and nerve, in shimmering waves. At that moment, he was hard-pressed to deny her anything.

"All right. I'm sorry," Trey said softly, a smile curling his lips at how easily she could turn the tables on him. They stood and faced each other.

"I suppose your conscience is clear now,"

Dallas said smugly. "But I'd say by the smile on your face that you're less than sincere."

Trey's anger flared when she so easily dismissed his apology. It had taken a great deal on his part to supplicate himself to her, and she had thrown his effort in his face.

"You'd almost made me forget why we're here. I warned you that I'd have an answer out of you, one way or the other," he retaliated in a harsh, clipped tone.

Before she could move out of range, Trey had again secured her wrists at her sides. She knew his touch. Even better, she knew the effect it had on her will. Straining against his hold, she stared at him, defiance darkening her wild and challenging eyes.

She was pure rebellion—and beauty. Her hair had come loose and spilled about her like a golden cloud, her lips were still red and moist from his kiss. Her coloring, even in the muted shades of the barn's interior, was glorious. Her flesh was radiant and beautiful. Heat cascaded from her in great waves that washed over him—to flow into his body, constrict his muscles, quicken his pulse. Heat penetrated his being, and he was stunned by the savage and desperate way in which he wanted her.

He clenched his teeth. Damn, he should walk away from her, but he couldn't!

"Let's try again," he ground out.

Dallas drew a bolstering gulp of air. "I told you that you're not going to tell me what to wear."

"Wrong."

The way he spoke that single word, his

voice lowering to a deceptive velvet smoothness, caused her to tremble inwardly.

"I know it goes against your grain to take orders from me. You and your female independence. Anything that puts you under a man's authority chafes your hide, doesn't it?"

She started to open her mouth, but he cut her off. "We both know that every damn time you fight me, you do it because you're scared."

"Scared? Of you?"

"Yes. Scared spitless because of what I make you feel. You've lived your whole life proving you're a man's equal, scared to death to show any female emotion whatsoever, until I came along. You've told yourself that you have to watch me because I have a way about me. That it would come to no good to get involved with a man like me. And you sure as hell won't admit that I might make you feel like a real woman, instead of one who hides in men's clothing. So you figure you're going to fight me for all you're worth because you won't have to feel anything if you're angry. Well, we both know your plan isn't working because you like what I do to you. Too much for your high-handed way of thinking."

"You'd say anything to justify your actions and take advantage of me."

"Admit it, Dallas. You're mad because you enjoy my touching you, kissing you."

"If I'm so much trouble, why bother with me? What do you want from me?"

"Nothing. Everything. What are you willing to give?"

"A woman doesn't give to a man like you. Your kind takes without asking."

"I'm asking now."

Dallas's nerves threatened to unravel and expose her confusion. He was the enemy in their private war. She couldn't surrender to him. Yet, despite herself, she looked into his eyes. His intense gaze pinned her to the spot.

"I didn't ask for trouble," she managed in a choked whisper.

Sincerity webbed his voice. "Neither did I."

Quickly she turned from him, asking, "Are you finished with me?" But his strong arm came out to gently encircle her waist.

"Do you want me to be?" he asked, studying the slender column of her neck, clearly etched with delicate blue veins, as she strained away from contact with him.

"I don't know." She couldn't keep the tremor from her voice. "I don't know how to act around you. You make me so angry when I don't want to be. I want . . ." Her words tumbled to a halt.

"You make me angry, too," he said softly, gently squeezing her arm beneath his fingers. "But I know what I want. You."

Trey studied her face as her unsteady heartbeat mingled with his sporadic breathing. Her cheeks flushed with deep color in response to the intimate look he gave her.

"Please leave me alone."

"That's the one thing I can't do," he said quietly, almost apologetically.

He trailed his hands down her arms to her elbows, to her wrists. His touch burned, and she felt the pressure of his wide palms and tapering fingers beneath her shirt.

"Couldn't we try to get along?"

"I . . . don't . . ." She couldn't force the words out. Her heartbeat seemed to change rhythm as his thumbs traced slow, circular patterns on the backs of her hands.

Dallas's arms had turned to water for all the strength she had as she tried to free herself from his gentle touch. This was a tender side to Trey Conner she never thought she'd see. Or feel.

Slowly he raised her palm to his mouth, and his tongue drew lazy, wet designs across her tingling flesh. His mouth found the tiny spurting pulse at her wrist, and he tenderly kissed the sensitive spot. Then his hand stole down to her waist, and he tugged her toward him.

"No, don't."

"Why not?" he whispered as strong hands closed over her shoulders and inexorably drew her near his chest.

"Because I hate—" He silenced her when his lips moved with hushed delicacy over her cheek, across her nose, down to her chin. Then his mouth brushed her trembling lips. His open kiss was deep, wet.

Dallas felt as if she were dying inch by agonizing inch before she managed to gasp, "We mustn't." His sensual assault was doing crazy things to her insides. "You've got your nerve."

"No, I've got you."

"This isn't fair."

"Didn't intend it to be."

He lowered his head a fraction, and he kissed her throat, nipping and laving her heated skin as he went. Her knees weakened and she leaned heavily against him.

Trey supported her with one strong arm as he whispered, his voice pure seduction, against her mouth. "Enjoy it, Dallas. . . . For once, let yourself go."

His hands positioned her hips to bring her intimately against him—and to feel how much more intimate he intended to be, to feel him through their clothing.

His maleness was rigid . . . and very insistent.

Sense intruded and she broke away, resisting, and said "Even Grant didn't fight this dirty."

"Doesn't matter how one fights the battles," he whispered, "as long as you win the war."

He lowered his face to her bosom and, through the fabric of her shirt, he pressed his wide-open mouth against one breast. Sensation blew hot through her.

"Oh, please . . . please stop." Panic kept apace of her pleasure, and she teetered on the precipice of the frightening unknown. Her body grew tense as her lower regions responded to the primitive message of his body.

He anchored his hands on her slender shoulders and pushed her until her back was to the barn wall. One hand came up and planted itself beside her left shoulder. Lazily his other hand rose and rested by her right ear.

He pressed himself against her and lowered his head in slow degrees until his mouth was only a whisper away from hers. "Don't fight it." His breath stirred the tiny hairs at her temples.

Mercilessly he tortured her lips with his persistent tongue, licking the corners of her mouth.

She couldn't stop him, but she could stop herself. With all her remaining determination, she willed her body to grow still, unresponsive.

Instead of angering him, her resistance drew a chuckle from him. His lips found the hollow of her neck, and he breathed against her tingling skin. "You're putting off the inevitable. I won't let you ignore me."

She clenched her teeth so tightly that her jaw hurt as he gave her his undivided, passionate attention.

He chuckled again, low in his throat, and she felt him smile against her lips. "Just give in and enjoy it."

Her heart shot to her throat, then slammed against her ribs. He nipped her nose, then her chin.

If possible, she felt him grow longer . . . and harder.

Overwhelmed and embarrassed, she knew she would die if anyone came across them, but she couldn't have stopped him even if he hadn't been holding her. Despite her effort to deny herself pleasure, the sensitive points of her body ached, throbbed, tingled. She was wildly alive with every fiber of her being. If she didn't stop him, Trey would take her beyond herself.

She moistened her lips and made one last feeble attempt to resist. "Don't. I mean it. I won't go through with this."

"Ssh."

His hand drifted to the buttons of her shirt, and slowly, one by one, he began unfastening them. Finished, he drew aside the edges of the material to reveal her breasts covered only by a thin cotton undergarment. His gaze fastened on the barely concealed display.

"Do you know how much I want you?" His husky voice fell softly against her ear. His hand cupped her flimsily clad breast, and her eyes flew open.

She felt him, oh how she felt him, everywhere he touched her. Everywhere he stroked and caressed.

With slow yet steady intent, he made short work of the buttons of her chemise, parting the edges of the garment to reveal first one breast, then the other.

Dallas felt delicious fire flare through her as his fingers brought her nipples to throbbing awareness. For a second time that day, Trey knocked the breath from her, but this time she yearned for more.

"Still want me to stop?" Trey asked softly, just before he tormented one nipple with his teeth and tongue.

Dallas thought she would die from pleasure. Her trembling legs felt hot and limp, unable to support her, and she sagged against Trey.

In a remote corner of her brain, Dallas realized she should stop her irrational surrender to this man. With burning cheeks, through moist, swollen lips, she whispered, "You've got to stop this."

Her soft, sweet voice reached out and touched him in all the right places, although she said all the wrong things. He stood still, his breath a hard knot of air. All he could think of was finding release in her sweet body.

Trey had always had his choice of women. Why he wanted this one was beyond him, but he desired her with a vengeance.

Hellfire, did she have any idea what she did to him?

He wasn't sure exactly what he wanted, and he wasn't sure himself just how far he meant to go with her. Maybe he had just intended to remind her who was boss.

But he couldn't quit touching her.

Beneath the crush of his body against hers, he was aware of every soft, sweet, sensual curve. He couldn't think anymore. Only feel.

Let her go! he warned himself.

It was too late. He had tasted her lips, held her in his arms. She was passionate when angry. Just think if she had been willing. . . .

Trey nudged her legs apart with a raised knee and wedged it between her thighs. He applied slight pressure against her most secret place at the juncture of her thighs.

Fear, outrage, and a strong moral upbringing doused her heated passion. "No!" She wedged her hands between their bodies and shoved hard against his chest.

"What the hell!" Trey stumbled back.

Free of his embrace, Dallas sidestepped him. With trembling fingers, she buttoned her chemise and shirt.

She then glared at him, her chest heaving, her hands balled at her sides. "How dare you!"

Trey scowled at her. His black hair was tousled; his lips were taut and thin. Never had he looked more dangerous. "What's the matter with you? You liked it well enough a few minutes ago."

Just thinking of how she had responded to his seduction made her cringe with mortification.

Did he have so much power over her that he could make her forget herself so easily?

"I didn't know what I was doing," Dallas defended.

"Then, by God, woman, you'd better learn," Trey grated. "And quick."

"What?"

"If you had responded that way with another man, you wouldn't be standing there spouting virginal outrage."

Color surged hotly across her face as she realized how close she'd come to losing her virginity—and to a gunman. "Why, you're nothing but a no-account, no-good varmint." She took a shuddering breath. "You're lower than a rattlesnake."

Trey's eyes narrowed. "And just as likely to strike when stepped on. Be careful where you walk."

"Don't act as if I wronged you." Dallas was so angry that she had to force the words past her tight throat. "You're the one who forced yourself on me."

A wicked smile curved his firm lips. "That's not the way I remember it."

"Seems my memory is better than yours."

"You'll find my strength lies in other areas."

Without replying, Dallas marshaled her dignity and spun on her heel. With her chin raised and her shoulders straight, she stormed from the barn.

Chapter 8

Trey walked to the rear of the main house with his hands curled into fists at his sides. He wanted to hit somebody, anybody. He wanted to pummel something the way anger pounded through his body with each strident step he took. Heaven help the poor bastard who crossed his path. Especially any O'Neal.

Especially Dallas O'Neal.

In his mind's eye her image lingered, half-naked and furious, sparks of indignation shooting from her eyes. He still felt the passion that shimmered from her heated body. He still tasted her sweetness on his lips. Her soft, fluttering sighs haunted him. The muskiness of her heated skin lingered in his nostrils. He still remained hard as he remembered every knee-weakening, gut-wrenching inch of her curvaceous, supple young body.

He had intended to put her in her place. Instead, she had put him in his—a state of pure agony. Agony that he instinctively knew only Dallas could ease.

Fool, he berated himself. He wanted her even now. Too damned much. So much it hurt. His body testified to the fact. After each encounter with Dallas, Trey found himself thinking of her more . . . desiring her more . . . punishing himself more. He must be loco. How else could he explain his behavior or his reaction to a thoroughly irritating, pigheaded, pain-in-the-ass—oh, hell, desirable female? He couldn't rationalize it any more than he could stop breathing.

Dallas would probably hate him until her dying day.

He'd make sure she did. He had to.

For both their sakes.

His steps grew shorter until he reached the rain barrel at the rear of the house. With a hand on either side of the rim, Trey looked down into the still, reflective water.

He didn't like what he saw—a man who had been wrestling with his baser nature . . . and had lost.

Needing to douse the raging fire within him and cool his overheated fantasies, he dunked his head in the water. He lingered a moment, hoping the water would rinse his thoughts clear of Dallas. Seconds later, he rose up and leaned over the barrel, strands of long, wet hair clinging to the sides of his face.

Trey took a deep breath, trying to fill his lungs with calm reason, then he slowly released the air. He should've felt better, but he didn't. Hell, no. He only felt the ache in his loins, washing over him like the water streaming down his face and neck, drenching his shirt.

He had to relieve the burning passion and disgust deep in his gut. He had to restore sanity to his overheated senses. He soaked his head again.

After several seconds, he lifted his head and shook it back, sending a shower of droplets in all directions. He took another deep breath and wiped the water from his eyes, then pushed damp strands of hair from his face. He still didn't feel better, and his irritation with the whole infernal situation rose another notch.

He headed for the kitchen, hoping he wouldn't run into anybody. He didn't want to bother with any display of civil manners. He didn't want anything but a drink. Or two. Tarnation, he needed an entire bottle! Heaven help him if Abbey was a prude about liquor and didn't have any in the house. He wasn't in the mood to ride into town and suffer unwelcome company in a saloon. He intended to do his drinking alone. And a hell of a lot of it too.

He hit the door with the heel of his hand and nearly ripped it off its hinges. His boots struck the floor with a resolute rap as he made his way to the kitchen.

He burst into the room, startling Abbey at her cooking. "You keep any liquor around?"

Abbey wisely said nothing, only pointed to a jelly safe.

Trey opened the cupboard, the tin inset of the door rattling in its frame, and prowled behind the rows of preserves with his hand, glass jars clinking, until he found the whiskey.

He offered no words of apology for his inconsiderate behavior, although he did feel a twinge of shame. Abbey didn't deserve to receive the brunt of his rudeness, but he was in no mood for explanations. Besides, what would he say? *Oh, excuse me, but I'm pissed because I nearly seduced your sister*? Or *I'm in a foul humor because I can't keep myself from lusting after your sister*? He nearly laughed. Abbey was sure to understand. In a pig's eye!

Wordlessly Trey took the bottle and a glass to his room upstairs. He set both objects on the table next to the bed, then sank down onto the mattress. He uncorked the bottle and splashed a liberal amount of the amber-colored liquid into the glass. Tilting his head back, he tossed his drink down, wincing at the fire that seared his throat.

The whiskey hit the bottom of his stomach, but did nothing to ease the pain in his groin or erase Dallas's image from his mind. There, painted on the walls of his memory in vivid color, glared every striking detail.

He continued to sit on the edge of the bed, staring into the bottom of his empty glass, wondering how he'd gotten himself into this infernal mess. He was damned because he should leave her alone. Damned because he couldn't. He'd thought his emotions were controlled, safe, indifferent, but what he felt for Dallas was far from detached. He became aroused just being near her. She was an infuriating, tempting piece of womanhood. And oh, how she tempted him—until he thought he'd burst. No, any feelings for Dallas were downright dangerous. More lethal than any six-gun he'd ever stared down the barrel of. And his barrel was still a might long and as hard as steel.

He exhaled on a long groan. He should have left her the hell alone. He should have never laid his hands on her . . . or kissed her . . . or feasted on her perfect breasts.

But damn if he didn't admire her for stopping him. No other woman could have stood up to him and gotten away with it. Hers was a fiery disposition and an iron will, and he'd wager a month's salary that she could never admit defeat.

He'd also wager she would be beyond his wildest dreams in bed. Within her gaze blazed a zest for life, a spark that couldn't, or wouldn't, be extinguished. Durn if she wasn't something!

But if Dallas O'Neal thought she could twist him around her little finger by swishing that enticing tail of hers without paying a price, she was wrong. Dead wrong. Her actions had serious repercussions. It was high time she faced the consequences of her stubborn nature.

His hold on the glass tightened as he envisioned touching Dallas all over until she screamed for mercy. She had no idea how serious her little games could be. Throwing his orders in his face. Doing what she damn well pleased. A trip into town, a morning's escapade, wearing those blasted tight pants of hers. Dallas was only interested in getting her own way and to hell with everyone else.

Not that he didn't understand what she'd put into the running of this station. He did. He appreciated her efforts. What he couldn't tolerate was her lack of respect for authority. To survive in this world, one had to follow orders. Well, apparently most of the O'Neals knew how to do that. He thought of Abbey, Tyler, and Waco.

He liked them. He had no problem with any of them.

It was the other O'Neal he longed to throttle.

Dallas!

Shit. Men followed battle plans, knew how to fight, knew when to withdraw, knew when to surrender. But Dallas only knew to advance, and she took no prisoners.

Thoughts of war gave his mind a new direction. Jonas Webb. When Dallas had said that she had spent time with Webb, Trey thought the top of his head would come off.

Piss and vinegar! He'd throttle Jonas if he ever laid a hand on Dallas—the way he himself had. He knew Jonas's reputation with women. Hell, Jonas had even told him about some of his wilder exploits. Dallas didn't know how dangerous Jonas could be. She needed protecting from Webb and his kind, from every man with an itchy prick. No man would touch her without killing him first.

He was surprised at the depth of his jealousy and the intensity of his possessiveness. He supposed it stemmed from the fact that she was an employee of the company, and had nothing to do with how responsive her mouth was, how sweetly she moved in his embrace, how good it would feel to be surrounded by her. Tight and warm and . . .

Damn. Will you get your mind off that?

The smart thing to do would be to get the hell out of this place, to saddle his horse and head out for one of the other stations until his job was done.

But he couldn't bring himself to do that.

He didn't want to leave a job unfinished.

He didn't want to leave Dallas. Lord o' mercy, she had the power to drive a man wild with longing.

Nor, Trey thought soberly, would Dallas ever be convinced that she wasn't the only one to feel she'd been treated unfairly. For a moment, the pain returned to him, harsh, brutal, tearing his heart. He thought that he had learned to suppress it a long, long time ago.

He rarely recalled his past, but he found himself doing a lot of that lately. It did no good to look back, but his thoughts repeatedly strayed to his childhood. It had been one thing to have a distant father. It had been entirely another to have a mother who had been totally submissive to his powerful, sometimes abusive father. Trey felt betrayed by his mother's weakness. She had failed to protect him from his father's domineering expectations, sarcasm, and humiliation. Even after his father's death and his mother's remarriage, he felt he'd strayed too far to remain in Fort Worth with her.

The last few years he had traveled alone. He didn't have much in the way of belongings, but then, he didn't need much. All he had ever needed—or could depend on—was the pistol strapped to his thigh and his horse.

He had never stayed in one place long, just long enough to do his job and make a few women happy. And then, as quickly as his job was done, he was gone. Whatever the circumstances, he always left. With no regrets.

He gritted his teeth. All of it had been good enough—until now. Until he had met Dallas. She was like him. She was a fighter; she had courage. She was beautiful. She was pure, larruping desire. Brewed strong and heady. Intoxicating.

He set his glass down, sobering. Texas was really no place for a woman, any woman, without a man to protect her.

Texas was wild, primitive, dangerous, savage. Like Dallas.

The next morning, as was her routine, Dallas walked around the coach, checking to see that everything was right before starting the stage run.

As she plucked up the lines and carefully arranged them in her hand to check for the proper amount of slack, thoughts of yesterday washed over her. Within the span of a heartbeat, she replayed the scene in the barn. Regardless of how hard she tried to erase it, the memory clung to her. Shamelessly she had ignored normal restraints when headlong urgent desire had taken hold. As she yielded to that driving need, issues of right and wrong had blurred.

She recalled how passion had defined the lines of Trey's face, how she had clearly read what had been in his eyes. He had wanted her. And, heaven help her, she had wanted him. Something inside her, a naughtiness she had never known she possessed, caused her to long for him. Even now she pondered the conflicting emotions whirling inside her, more violent than any twister.

What had happened was wrong, but being in his arms had felt so right. Shamefaced, she admitted that she had never before experienced such intense emotions—emotions that left her drained, but strangely wanting more.

Dallas felt cold—then hot—then cold again. Her body trembled with repressed emotions as she continued to check the lines. Oh, she knew she was headstrong and unpredictable, all right. But she had never in her life done anything so daring with a man.

She couldn't find any peace in her thoughts. What she had wanted from Trey went against everything she considered honorable. How could she look at Trey without remembering what had happened between them? She couldn't forget. No more than her body could.

Possibly she could have accepted his condition of running the station. But to live and work so close to him, knowing that every time he looked at her he would remember that incident in the barn? Never.

Her cheeks burned. She forced her thoughts to the task at hand.

Finished with her check of the stagecoach, Dallas climbed into the driver's box, trying to keep her thoughts anywhere but on Trey Conner. She succeeded until he climbed up beside her.

Blast his cantankerous hide! She'd be so glad when Waco could resume his duties. She'd didn't know how much more of Trey Conner she could take.

She glanced down at his legs, which were so dangerously close to hers. Every taut, developed muscle in his thighs was delineated through the fabric of his pants, in disturbing detail. His lusty maleness wafted to her, and her stomach clenched involuntarily. He was sinfully male, and Dallas was desperately trying not to care.

Trey's deep voice broke into her thoughts, washing over her in tingling awareness, heightening her distress. "Ready?" he asked.

"Ready," Dallas replied, trying to check her temper and control her emotions, which she was losing far too frequently since Mr. Conner's arrival.

"Then let's get going," he ordered.

His nearness, his enticing sensuality, troubled her. She desperately fought the memory of his intoxicating kiss, the feel of his strong arms around her, her near surrender to his potent virility.

She lost the struggle against the hot, sinful sensations that coiled around and through every muscle of her body.

Her irritation swelled, and she snapped, "I know my job."

He leaned closer to her, and she felt his breath like a cool caress on her heated cheek. "Then do it."

Her own breath came as a hard knot in her throat. "I will if you'll let me."

To her consternation, he drawled, "No one's stopping you."

For pride's sake, Dallas wouldn't reveal how disturbing his nearness was to her. She straightened, and with whip in hand, released the brake. Amid a jingling of harness and groaning of leather, the stage pulled out of the station.

For most of the run, Dallas maintained a marginal distance from Trey, both emotionally and physically. Her body ached from the strain of holding herself straight in the seat so as not to brush against him. Her head hurt from the concentrated effort it took not to think about him.

The tension between them was palpable. If the passengers or station people suspected anything, they kept it to themselves as the stage made its appointed stops.

Yesterday in the barn, she and Trey had ruined any chance of finding a peaceful coexistence. The memory of their intimacy was burned inside her head, charring the edges of her mind with anger and guilt. After all, she had nearly surrendered to the man.

She couldn't explain her actions, but she wouldn't be vulnerable. She refused to gamble years of hard work and sacrifice on what Trey intended to take from her.

Take? Her mind wandered along a dangerous course. What would it be like to be taken by him? To know how it felt to be a woman, totally, completely. Looking out over the heads of her team to the road beyond, she could still feel his lips and hands on her. Her mouth tightened. She had to be her own person. She could never belong to another.

As the day wore on, and her thoughts kept drifting back to Trey despite her will, Dallas felt her aggravation soar along with the temperature. The stagecoach's route lay over country that gently rolled to the horizon's end, crossing terrain broken by mesquite, cedar, and scrub brush, interspersed with cacti. Occasionally she caught sight of a coyote or deer.

Through the dust kicked up by the horses, Dallas glimpsed Trey. He cut a sharp figure with his hat pulled low on his brow and his rifle at the ready. He was making her slap-dab crazy.

Before noon, Trey blew on the bugle, announcing an approaching station. Fifteen minutes later, Dallas pulled on the lines, and the stage rolled to a stop. She stepped on the brake lever.

Frowning, she squinted beneath her hat and cast her gaze about. There were no signs of Jigger Riggins, the station attendant. No fresh team of horses waited. No smoke curled from the chimney. There were no signs of any life. The only sounds were those of the disgruntled passengers and the jingling of harness as the horses stomped their feet to rid themselves of pesky flies.

Dallas put the whip in the socket by the seat and wrapped the lines around the brake handle. "That's odd. Jigger's always waiting. I can't ever remember him not having a team ready."

Trey glanced at Dallas before climbing down. "I'll take a look." He disappeared around the back of the building.

Unease clasped the base of Dallas's neck. She kept alert to the slightest sound or movement.

Trey reappeared inside the doorway of the station. With a wave of his hand, he motioned to Dallas. She gained the ground and stepped inside.

She removed her hat and tucked renegade strands of hair into place. Pulling the perspiration-moistened material of her shirt away from her neck, she looked around. When her eyesight adjusted to the shadowy interior, she saw Jigger Riggins stretched out across a table, apparently passed out, an empty bottle dangling from one hand. She moved closer and leaned over. Whiskey fumes assailed her. He was drunk as a skunk. Flies buzzed around his mouth and nose, but he remained motionless.

Trey, his expression dark and forbidding, appeared from the kitchen. "There's nothing to eat. And there are no horses in the corral. Looks like we'll have to go on to the next station."

"We'll do fine. I wonder what happened to Jigger. He's one of the most reliable handlers around. I've never seen him like this."

"He didn't get this way by himself," Trey said.

"What d'you mean?"

"Look at the floor. See the marks in the dirt? My guess is three other people sat at this table. I'd say three men, judging by how deep the marks are. That and the cards I found." He tossed several cards onto the table near Riggins's head.

"But why would he be this far gone?"

Trey regarded her, his brow drawn, then he said irritably, "You can't be that naive. Think, Dallas. The cards. Whiskey. Riggins gambled with the station's livestock and lost."

Instantly Jonas Webb entered Dallas's mind, but then just as quickly she dismissed the idea. No proof pointed to Webb.

Trey's thoughts had gone the same way. "I don't know if Webb is behind this, but I intend to find out."

Dallas shivered at the grim tone of Trey's voice. She pitied any man who crossed his path. Including Jonas Webb. She knew how determined Trey could be.

Trey turned and gazed out the back door toward the empty corral. Dallas saw the tightening of his shoulders and the clenching of his fists at his sides. His right hand brushed the butt of his revolver, then fell away.

He faced her once more. "We'd best get going. We've got tired, hungry passengers to consider. We can still make the Lacey place in New Braunfels."

Nodding her agreement, Dallas resettled her hat on her head and followed Trey outside. She watched his tense, quick footsteps and his rigid back. Trouble for sure or her name wasn't Dallas O'Neal.

With a brief explanation to the anxious passengers, she took her place atop the stage and coaxed her weary team onto the road.

An hour later, they halted at the swing station on the outskirts of New Braunfels. This time they were greeted by signs of activity and a welcoming plume of smoke rising from the chimney. Tired and hungry, Dallas looked forward to the break and the chance to stretch her sore muscles.

Trey showed no signs of discomfort. He climbed down from the stage with loose, graceful movements. Dallas both admired and resented his body's resilience.

She sighed. She'd feel better after she had something to eat and a good, strong cup of coffee. She looked around for Trey.

When he reemerged from the facilities out back, Dallas said, "The passengers have already gone inside. I'm going too."

"Wait up," he said curtly. "Look toward the corral."

Dallas glimpsed the horses tied beside the barn. "So?"

"How many head would you say?"

"Twenty, give or take one or two. What are you driving at?"

"I don't know of any station contracted by the Overland Stage Company that keeps more than two teams at a time. There are at least eight reserve horses here."

Dallas's eyes widened in understanding. "Are they Riggins's?"

"Very well could be. Keep your eyes and ears open inside."

Broodingly Trey looked at the stock horses. Lacey could have recently bought more horses. Perhaps . . . but Trey doubted it. The company didn't pay the station keepers enough to afford that many horses.

Dallas's glance followed Trey's to the station house, but for a different reason. Her stomach grumbled its demand for food. She had to get something to eat. Without another word, Dallas walked past Trey, who was contemplating the corralled horses.

As he suspected, upon closer inspection, he saw that some of the horses had been driven hard and not rubbed down, crusty sweat still dusting their coats.

He had seen this kind of tactic before. A competitor puts in gambling along the routes, enticing attendants to play high-stakes poker and gamble with livestock, even coaches. Always with marked cards. Always to the competitor's advantage. His lips drew into a taut, unforgiving line. He'd find out the truth soon enough.

A motion at the edge of Trey's vision caught

his eye. It was Dallas's long legs. She was headed for the station building.

"Dallas!"

She didn't slow her steps.

Christ! The little fool, she was walking straight into a hornets' nest of trouble. Trey ran for his rifle.

Dallas had heard Trey calling her, but she was so hungry, she didn't stop to consider the possibility of real danger. Knowing Trey, he'd be right behind her. She entered, then closed the door with a glimpse over her shoulder. No Trey. She shrugged.

She turned to face the occupants of the one-room station. A group of men sat at a table to the rear. The passengers from the stage sat in another group closer to the stove. Lewis Lacey cast what seemed a nervous glance at her while he served the passengers plates of stew.

Odd. But not as odd as she felt when she realized she was being sized up by intimidating masculine stares from the strangers.

Cigar smoke hung in cloying clouds above the heads of the men. Whiskey and unwashed bodies—and trouble—permeated the air.

The one time she wanted Trey to be there, he was nowhere to be found. The first rule of driving stage was to handle all situations calmly. She'd handled trouble before Trey's arrival, and she steeled herself to face these men now.

A man who had been sitting apart from the others looked up from his plate of food. She felt his gaze slide over her. Thank God, she had complied a bit with Trey's request and had worn looser-fitting clothes today.

"What you want?" he asked unhappily.

"Nothing. I'm the driver of the stage." She forced her voice to sound level, unsuspecting. "I'll just join the other passengers and have something to eat."

She turned toward the station manager. He was an older man, with a shock of brown hair that looked as if he'd been struck by lightning, drooping jowls, and small eyes in a round face.

"Lewis, how are you? That stew sure smells good." Her stomach rumbled again, not from hunger this time, but from anxiousness as Lacey looked from her to the stranger behind her, then back to her.

"I'm fine, Miss Dallas."

She forced herself to smile, not realizing how inviting her strained gesture might be to these disreputable men.

Her apprehension deepened when she heard the stranger speak to her. "If you come over here, I just might have something you'd like to eat."

Raucous laughter came from the men sitting at the rear table. To the side, the stage passengers barely touched their food, clearly uncomfortable with the situation, but not one person came to her aid.

Trey Conner, where the hell are you? She inhaled deeply. *Don't be afraid.* She decided the best thing to do was to ignore the man. She took a step toward the passengers.

"Come here, missy," came the stranger's voice again.

Dallas forced herself to face him. In different circumstances she might have thought this man handsome. But at the moment, with his cold, empty eyes trained on her, she found him intimidating.

Dallas waited, struggling with her misgivings and the almost overwhelming desire to flee, but she couldn't abandon her passengers. "No time to spare. So if you don't mind, I'll just have something to eat, then get my stage under way."

"But I do mind. Now, come sit down."

Lewis Lacey stepped forward. "Zeke, she don't want to."

Zeke turned his predatory gaze on Lacey. "Stay out of this. It don't concern you."

Lacey dropped his gaze to the floor, then turned back to the stove, leaving Dallas to fend for herself again.

Zeke stood up, the legs of his chair leaving tiny furrows in the dirt floor, and walked toward her. "As I was saying, make time."

"I really can't," she replied calmly, although every nerve in her body screamed a warning.

"Sure you can." The stranger reached for Dallas's arm.

She pulled back.

The door behind Dallas opened, letting in a swirl of dust.

Trey stepped inside, his rifle resting in the crook of his arm. Although his stance was negligent, Dallas felt ripples of restrained outrage coming from him.

A frightening expression lurked in his eyes as he surveyed the men. "What's taking you so long?" Trey asked. He looked pointedly at the man Lacey had called Zeke.

For a moment, the two men took note of each other. Tension wrapped around the room.

Uneasiness pricked along Dallas's backbone, and the urge to flee again chased its way back down her spine. Yet reason prevailed, and she forced herself to remain still. Her gaze darted from Trey to Zeke, who didn't seem to recognize the danger signals in Trey's blue eyes.

"What you boys doing?" Trey asked casually.

"Minding our own business. Maybe you should do the same." Zeke's hand drifted to his gun, hovering above the handle.

"It just so happens I am. It's my business to see that the stage gets a fresh team. As soon as that's done, we'll be on our way." Trey's gaze burned brighter. "So long as there's no interference."

"There won't be," Roberts returned.

"This time," Trey said slowly.

Zeke smiled, a cold gesture, and hissed, "This time."

The two men stepped outside and watched as the stage pulled away from the station.

Zeke leaned his way back against the wall, with one booted foot propped up, and pulled tobacco makings from his pocket. However, his eyes never left the coach as it slowly disappeared over a ridge.

"That goddamn shotgun thinks he's something. And I don't much hold with that." Zeke finished rolling his smoke, lit it, and took a drag. He inhaled deeply, then slowly released the air from his lungs. Smoke coiled about his head like a snake. "Boss gave orders that Conner's not to be touched."

Toby regarded Zeke. "Never knew ya to back down before. I guess that's why."

"Don't you never mind." Zeke's eyes narrowed. "All you have to worry about is following orders."

"I know ya, Zeke." Toby scratched himself. "You ain't gonna let that fella get away with standing you down, are ya?" He grinned crookedly, revealing blackened, rotten teeth.

"I'll have a go at that cocky son of a bitch when the time's right." Zeke smirked. "Not before."

"Why do ya figure boss gives a fig anyway?"

"None of my business." Zeke's gaze sliced to Toby. "Or yours." Zeke finished his smoke, tossed the butt of his cigarette down, and ground it beneath his bootheel.

"You and the boys get them horses taken care of. We've got work to do."

Chapter 9

Pausing outside the private room, Jenny rested her forehead against the doorframe. She prayed her second time with Jonas Webb wouldn't be as bad as her first. She still had slight ringing in one ear from the beating he'd given her. Maybe Jonas would be in a good mood. . . . Oh, Lord, let him be in a good mood.

Jenny closed her eyes. Not for the first time in her short but eventful life, she found herself wishing that she had never seen the inside of a saloon.

She drew a deep breath. She held no place in decent society. She was a whore—and would die a whore. And for now, she was Jonas Webb's whore.

Jenny lifted her head. She knew her place. She also knew that somehow she would have to find a way to please Jonas.

She raised her trembling hand to knock. She couldn't risk avoiding Jonas any longer. The door swung open wide, startling Jenny. The gleam of fierce annoyance in Jonas's blue eyes heightened her anxiety. She forced herself to swallow the cold lump of fear in her throat.

"I sent for you over thirty minutes ago. I don't like to be kept waiting," he said.

Dread knotted her stomach. "I came as soon as I could," she lied. "I had another customer."

A slightly, mocking smile curved Jonas's lips. "It would be wise to remember that when I send for you, you're to drop everything else and come to me." His gaze burned brighter. "Immediately." He inclined his head sharply. "Now get in here." In his left hand, he held a small knife. In his right, he held an apple.

Jenny inched past him into the richly adorned room. Tension coiled her insides into a taut, quivering mass.

She faced him. "You won't hurt me again, will you?" Her voice spiraled upward with fear.

His knuckles whitened as he gripped his knife tighter. "You brought it on yourself. Behave properly and I won't have to discipline you."

Horror gripped Jenny's throat in a strangling hold. This time would be no better than the last.

She took a faltering step backward. "Jonas—please."

Jonas advanced on her with menacing strides. "Don't snivel," he growled. "I can't stand it."

"All right, Jonas." Jenny moistened her dry lips. "I'll do whatever you want me to."

Jenny hoped she had appeased Jonas. But he flung the apple he held across the room, its pulpy meat splattering against the wall.

His eyes were flat, expressionless. "Didn't you learn your lesson the first time, Jenny?" His voice was dangerously soft.

"Oh, please don't." Jenny felt the blood drain from her face. "You'll never have to wait again."

He brought the knife to her face and pressed the flat of the blade against her cheek. "I'm afraid that's not good enough."

Chills chased their way along her spine as he slowly, agonizingly, lowered the knife. She clutched her hands in front of her, trying desperately not to move.

He pressed the point to the base of her throat and pricked her skin, a drop of blood trickling down her chest. "What will it take for you to learn your place, sweet Jenny?"

Jenny flinched. She tried to speak, but her vocal cords wouldn't work.

"I'm going to make sure you remember who owns you, body and soul." Jonas cut open Jenny's dress from neckline to hem. He stepped back. "Take the rest off."

Willing her mind to go blank, Jenny removed her underclothes, stockings, and shoes and dropped them to the floor.

Jonas stared at her, his gaze sliding hotly over the creaminess of her body. She knew by the fierce gleam in his eyes that his possession of her would be savage.

"On your knees," he whispered hoarsely.

Jenny complied, and Jonas grabbed a handful of her hair, wrenching her head back.

He stared down into her wide eyes. "Is your memory improving?"

"Yes," she moaned.

Jonas released his hold and knelt beside her. "Good."

He pushed her down to the rug. Growling, he

threw himself on her like an animal, his hands punishing, his mouth degrading.

"Now, Jenny, honey. You're going to please me."

Jonas's eyes were glazed with desire. His forehead was damp with perspiration. His fingers worked at the buttons of his shirt.

The whore was a pleasure he indulged in frequently. He liked what money could buy—and Jonas always bought the best.

Jonas delighted in pushing Jenny to her limit. Her obvious fear of him fed his ego. He was shameless, without morals when it came to taking a woman. That's why women liked him. He gave them what they wanted—a good rutting. And what he gave them had nothing to do with love. The truth was, human beings were incapable of loving anyone but themselves. But they could give each other pleasure—or pain—depending on preference. That's just what he gave Jenny, pleasure and pain. These games they played aroused him until his poker was stiff as iron. He was a scoundrel, and he loved corrupting people.

Suddenly the face of another woman loomed in his mind. Dallas. He smiled. If he couldn't touch Dallas O'Neal, he'd think of her, picturing her wondrous expression as he took Jenny. He'd use the whore . . . until he could have Dallas.

He looked down at Jenny. "Touch yourself," he whispered hoarsely.

She laid her hands on her chest and lightly skimmed them down until each covered a breast.

"That's right," Jonas panted. He rose up, undid his pants, and spread them open. Rooted in the expensive fabric was his rampant desire. Jenny's eyes widened.

She pressed her hands over her breasts, and rubbed in a slow circular motion, closing her eyes and writhing sensually. Jonas's breathing quickened. To satisfy him, Jenny cupped her breasts and pushed them forward enticingly.

"Make them hard for me," Jonas said hoarsely as he knelt beside her.

Jenny's fingers fanned her nipples, slowly at first and then faster in rhythm to Jonas's uneven breathing. She pinched them between her thumbs and fingers, trying to entice him further.

At last, he leaned back on the balls of his feet and said, "Bring them to me now."

She raised herself to a kneeling position and scooted toward him. He clasped her around the waist and hauled her onto his lap as he came to a sitting position, stretching his legs out. His mouth covered one breast hotly. Jenny locked her arms around him, then impaled herself on him.

His mouth moved over her breasts, his teeth hard on the edges of her nipples. She grimaced against the pain and pressed her hands against his shoulders. His thrusting movements became more frenzied.

Jonas gripped her hips as he grunted his satisfaction, spilling himself deep inside her.

His lust slaked, he pushed Jenny off him.

"Finished?" she asked, afraid he would want a second coupling.

He toyed with her breast. "No. I have business to attend to. But since you pleased me so well, I'll tell you about it." He paused and fingered a strand of hair that curled above her breast. "Of course, if you talk, you'll be punished. So I'm assured your silent cooperation. You see, I'm making arrangements for a competitor of mine. I first bought up some of his contracts. Then I put gambling in some of his stations, and he's lost a number of horses. Now it's time to place a few of my men into certain places to make sure my competitor's stages don't run smoothly."

"Isn't tampering with them dangerous for the people traveling?"

"Only if they're riding on the Texas Overland Stage." Jonas laughed. "Of course, it'll be dangerous for people to trust their money on those routes. One never knows when a stage will be help up."

"Won't anyone suspect when *your* stages aren't bothered?"

"Not when you own the sheriff and every other lawman between here and San Antonio."

"I see."

Jonas stood and dressed. He gazed down at Jenny. "Get dressed. I want you gone before the men arrive. It wouldn't do for you to distract me or them."

Jenny came to her feet. "Whatever you say, Jonas." She would say anything to get away from him.

Jonas patted her cheek. "That's a good girl."

Trey pushed open the swinging doors, stepped inside the saloon, his spurs jingling, and slowly walked to the bar. He intended to have answers, and he knew Webb was the man to give them. He figured that sooner or later, Webb would show up here. Jonas always had a penchant for cards. Especially poker.

Trey dipped two fingers into his shirt pocket and fished out a coin. Tossing his money atop the smooth, worn walnut, he called to the bartender: "Whiskey."

As the bartender headed toward him, Trey noted his average height and build, balding pate, framed by strands of straggly, graying hair, and thick, bushy mustache that hid his upper lip. Trey had seen his type a hundred times before. As with most bartenders, he probably prayed that his expensive backdrop mirror would last another night without being shattered by stray bullets. No doubt he believed that the best defense against violence was a double-barrel cut-down shotgun hidden under the bar and close by.

The bartender uncorked a bottle, poured a shot, then served Trey the rotgut. Trey tossed down the contents in a fluid motion, then leaned forward on his elbows, his lips drawn back from the liquor's bite. He set the glass on the bar, fingering one corner of his mouth. Turning, he leaned nonchalantly against the bar's walnut edge, hooking a bootheel on the brass footrail, and studied the saloon's interior and occupants.

Hanging kerosene lamps illuminated the large room. Sporting women mixed with the cowboys, farmers, gamblers, and plain whiskey soaks who were bellied up to the bar for a few jolts of rotgut. These women of easy virtue were as much a part of saloon life as the colorful nude painting hanging above the mirror behind the bar. Trey watched them drink their watered-down tea with anyone who could afford their company and wished to hop the floor with a partner for a buck a dance.

Usually he sought this type of woman. Some would soon drift away, get married, and live a proper life, raising children and attending church. Others would die after a quick and short, fast life, remembered only by cowboys. Their names didn't matter, but for a cowpuncher who hadn't seen a white female in weeks, a painted face was never forgotten. At the end of an evening with one of these women, a cowboy was satisfied, but often broke and occasionally smitten.

But even as his eye roamed over several of the girls, he knew he wasn't interested. Dallas O'Neal had soured his taste for anyone but her. Damn her!

Trey casually turned his head toward the entrance when he heard the doors swing back on their hinges. Jonas Webb passed through the doorway, followed by several gunmen.

Webb slowed his steps when he saw Trey. He motioned for his hired hands to hang back as he approached Trey alone.

Jonas turned sideways, his hip against the bar, and said, "I didn't expect to see you here."

"I came to talk to you."

Jonas inclined his head to the bartender, signaling for his usual drink. "What about?"

"Don't give me that. You know exactly why I'm here."

"Yeah, I suppose I do."

"I'm warning you," Trey said.

"About what?"

"To stay away from my stage line."

"What would I want with your line when I

have my own?" Jonas asked offhandedly.

"To do everything you can to make sure mine goes belly-up. I know it's you behind the holdup attempts. I know you've been buying up contracts. I know about the gambling. And I'm warning you."

Jonas laughed. "Warning me?"

"I have unlimited authority to rid the line of trouble. Regardless of where it comes from. And I intend to do my job."

"I'm counting on it."

"Is this another contest?" Trey's mouth thinned. "Are you still playing the old game? Even in uniform you couldn't stand taking orders from me. You never could handle the fact that you came up second best to me and that I always ranked higher than you." He shook his head. "The only clear thing is that there's not enough business to support two stage lines. Trying to drive me out is a bad move."

Jonas's jaw tensed, and in a quick movement, his hand pushed back the edges of his jacket to reveal his gun.

"You interested in seeing this out right here?" Trey queried, his voice dead level.

Jonas's gaze burned with challenge; Trey's stare smoldered with warning.

An unnerving silence fell over them before Jonas relaxed, his arms slowly uncoiling to his sides. "No, I don't reckon I am." He flashed a crooked smile. "You're the only man I'd allow to get away with that."

"Don't do me any favors." Trey figured it must have been the look in his eyes—the look of a man who had confidence in his draw—that caused Jonas to back down.

"Believe me, I'm not. I'm only making this entertaining for myself. The others were too easy," Jonas said smoothly. "You're different."

"I'll stop you."

"You can try."

"Just how far do you intend to go, Jonas?"

"As far as necessary."

"Does that include hurting innocent people?"

"It includes anyone who gets in my way." Jonas's blue gaze burned brighter. "I have important people who depend on me and pay me a great deal of money to do my job. So, you see, we're not so very different."

"The difference is that your money is tainted with blood. My conscience is clear."

"Is it?" A taunt lay beneath the smoothly spoken words.

"Yes."

"We'll see." Jonas drank his whiskey, then smiled again. "Now that we've talked, I want to play some poker. Unless you're afraid of losing to me."

"I'm not afraid of you—or of losing."

Jonas motioned with his head toward a table at the back of the saloon. "I figured you'd say that."

Trey took a seat opposite Jonas. He waited for the game to begin.

With a deft wrist movement, Jonas dealt cards to the other three players in a clockwise motion. First an older gentleman, next Trey, followed by a cowboy, then himself.

One of the saloon girls brought a round of

drinks. The gentleman to Jonas's left placed a stake on the table in front of him.

Trey checked his hole cards and decided to play this hand. "I'm in." He tossed his ante onto the table.

The cowboy followed suit, as well as Jonas.

Time passed.

The older man, his weathered face revealing little of his hand, leaned forward and tossed more money onto the pile. "I reckon I've got something that'll beat the rest of ya."

Without glancing at his hole cards, Trey regarded the exposed ten and jack of spades before matching the man's bet. "I think you're bluffing."

The cowboy called.

His expression carefully blank, Jonas fingered his revealed seven and eight of hearts. He tossed in his bet. "I'll take you on." His gaze cut to Trey on the last word.

Trey read the challenge within Jonas's stare. Instinct told him that Jonas's words weren't idle, and that his competitor was biding his time. But for what? And when?

Be patient, Trey counseled himself. He'd have to wait Jonas out. His own gaze remained unwavering.

The tension thickened to match the cigar smoke snaking over the men's heads. It broke momentarily when the cowboy pitched his cards down. "I'm out."

"Let's see how far this goes." A strident challenge echoed through Trey's statement. He would play Jonas's cat-and-mouse game.

The older man folded. That left Trey and Jonas.

"You suppose Lady Luck will be good to you?" Jonas asked Trey.

"She always is, but I don't need luck to beat you." Trey grinned.

Jonas shifted in his position, fanning his cards atop the table face down, and draped one arm over the back of his chair. With his other hand he reached for the whiskey bottle. Glass clinking against glass, he poured himself a drink. He tilted his head and gulped it down.

He set his glass down with a rap. "Speaking of Lady Luck, I saw your driver, Miss O'Neal, the other day. She's a fine piece of woman."

Straightening, Jonas dragged the final card he'd been dealt to the table's edge to steal a look. He checked the cards close to his chest and gazed at the silent man.

Outwardly, Trey attempted to appear relaxed. Inside, his gut tensed, then twisted like a coiled rattlesnake. He refused to take Jonas's bait, but rather maintained his composure.

"What do you mean?"

"She was wearing men's pants again. And tight ones." Jonas clucked his tongue and shook his blond head. "Why, they were so tight, you could see those neat curves plain as day. I certainly did enjoy her company. And I think she enjoyed mine."

Trey had an instant vision of Dallas. He also had the urge to wrap his hands around Jonas's throat and squeeze.

Glancing up from his cards, Jonas smiled his obvious satisfaction, his mouth curling into an insolent grin. "I intend to see a great deal more of Miss O'Neal, and I always get what I want."

"Be careful what you wish for."

"In the case of Miss O'Neal, I'm certain she's *exactly* what I've wished for. But then, Trey, haven't you wished for something in your life?"

"Straightforward actions are more effective than wishing."

"Oh, I don't intend to be shy when it comes to Miss O'Neal. Rather the opposite." Jonas paused, his eyes sharp and assessing. "We're going to become very good friends." He spoke with the certainty of a man who could never be satisfied unless he got what—or *who*—he wanted.

Although his every muscle tensed, Trey replied in a voice devoid of emotion, "She's not your type."

"And she's yours?"

"She's under my protection."

"From me?" Jonas laughed shortly, then his gaze pinned Trey. "Who's going to protect her from you, my friend?"

"She's not for you," Trey repeated in an uninflected, flat tone.

"I find her very pleasing." Jonas raised an eyebrow as if he relished the notion. "Her innocence appeals to me."

"Something you lack."

"The only thing that matters is for Miss O'Neal not to find me lacking. In any way. But then, you don't have any interest in her other than as your driver, do you?" Nonchalantly Jonas tossed another bill on the growing pile. "It's your call."

His calm demeanor hid the burning anger raging in Trey's mind. Like seared parchment, his voice crackled. "Still feel lucky?"

"Lady Luck stays in my hip pocket."

"Does she?"

Jonas chuckled. "She hasn't deserted me yet."

"That may change."

Placing his cards facedown on the table, Jonas retrieved a cigar from his pocket. He sliced the end of it with his knife, then placed the stogie to his mouth to moisten the exposed end. He produced a match from his pocket and lit it on the sole of his boot.

Dragging slowly on the rolled tobacco, Jonas drawled, "It'd take more than a streak of bad luck for someone to get the best of me." He clamped the cigar between his teeth, the tip glowing red.

The mocking, self-assured thrust of Jonas's jaw caused Trey's hand to curl around his cards. Anger flared in his gaze for a raw five seconds before he tossed money onto the pile. "You want to find out?"

"Stakes are high," Jonas said. "Getting higher all the time."

"Don't play," Trey said in a temperate voice, his smile revealing none of his thoughts, "if you can't afford the risk."

"I'm always one to take a risk."

"I call you, then." Trey's eyes were like chips of blue ice. "Let's see if you're bluffing."

"You're about to be very sorry man."

"Don't be so sure." A current of steel flowed beneath Trey's words. "Winner take all."

Jonas laid down his cards. "Straight flush. Jack, ten, nine, eight, and seven of hearts." He smiled, certain he had won the hand, and reached for the money.

"Not so fast, Jonas. You haven't seen my cards yet."

Trey flipped over his hand. He recognized the anger that flared briefly in Jonas's eyes and knew a moment of grim satisfaction. There on the scarred, burned surface of the poker table lay a royal flush, ace of spades high.

"Seems you've won." Jonas removed his cigar, dropped it, and ground the tobacco under the heel of his boot. "For now." Jonas looked past Trey, a smile forming on his lips. "It seems we have company."

Trey whipped his head around. He nearly groaned aloud. Dallas was walking straight toward him. *Why in blue blazes was she here?*

Dallas stopped beside him. However, she addressed Jonas before she spoke to Trey, which did nothing to sweeten his sour mood. "Hello, Mr. Webb."

"Jonas, remember?"

Dallas smiled. "Jonas."

Trey tried to control his irrational anger at Dallas's friendly manner. *Too friendly if you asked him.* Silently he cursed himself and her for the unholy tangle their relationship was fast becoming. He cursed the desire for her that gripped him even now, his body responding to the one woman he should stay the hell away from.

"Had yourselves a good game, boys?" Dallas asked.

"Your boss won the first round." With a tilt of his head, Jonas saluted Trey.

"Imagine that," Dallas said offhandedly.

Trey stood suddenly, nearly knocking his chair over. "What on God's green earth are you doing here?"

"What's the matter with you?" Dallas countered.

"You shouldn't be—"

"In a place like this? Why is it all right for you, but not for me?"

"Because I'm a man and you're a woman."

Jonas rose and moved around to where Dallas stood. "A fact I'm most happily aware of." He smiled at her. "Could I possibly hope you came to see me?"

"No, I'm afraid not. This is business, not pleasure." Dallas rewarded Jonas with another smile. She then looked at Trey. "I need to talk to you."

At that moment, it wasn't what Trey wanted. He wanted to throttle her. Instead, he gritted his teeth and pulled her into a corner, away from Jonas.

"What's so important that you've come into a saloon to tell me?" he ground his teeth.

"There're problems at one of the other stations. A rider came looking for you this evening. I thought you'd want to know. But I can see my effort isn't appreciated."

In her agitation, a strand of hair had worked its way free of her braid. She reached up to tuck it behind her ear, obviously unaware that the action stretched the fabric of her shirt across her breasts.

But Trey was more than aware.

"What isn't appreciated is your acting like a little fool around Jonas Webb," he said, measuring his words, nearly biting them off.

"I am not acting like a fool," Dallas replied defensively.

"Oh, aren't you?"

"No, I'm not. I'm merely being civil. Which is more than I can say for you."

His mouth took on a distasteful slant. "Then don't say anything for me."

Dallas drew a deep breath, then let it out in a huff of exasperation. "I won't."

"Good."

"Fine," she muttered.

"Go on back to the station."

With hard-won composure, Dallas tamped down her annoyance at his authoritative tone. She took several steps, then turned. "Don't forget your money."

That's precisely what Trey had done.

His eyes darkened, and a curse hovered on the tip of his tongue. Damn if that woman didn't infuriate him.

She was dangerous—dangerous because of his attraction to her. Come hell or high water, once his job was done, he wouldn't—couldn't—stay near Dallas O'Neal one day longer.

Trey walked back to the poker table. He gathered up his money, folding the bills and placing them in his shirt pocket.

"You and Dallas have a difference of opinion?" Jonas inquired with a seemingly pleasant half smile on his lips. "Don't make matters easy for me. No challenge, no fun."

Trey leaned over and placed his hands on the table. "You stay away from Dallas, understand? Don't make me kill you."

"You so sure of yourself?"

"I wouldn't want to find out if I were you. You've never won against me." Trey's gaze pinned Jonas. "And you never will," he said brusquely, conviction vivid in each clipped word.

Jonas's features hardened, his anger evident in the grim slash of his mouth and the flare of his nostrils.

For several moments, the air was thick with challenge.

Trey straightened and pivoted on his heel. He headed for the bar and ordered one more drink. Out of the corner of his eye, he saw Zeke Roberts come to stand beside him in a challenging stance.

Trey's humor was blacker than the underbelly of a thundercloud. He was spoiling for a fight. If this son of a bitch wanted one, he'd give him one. But he wouldn't make the first move.

He brought the shot glass to his lips and threw back his head, swallowing the whiskey. He set the glass down atop the bar with a sharp rap, then turned to glare at Zeke Roberts.

"You want something?" Trey nearly bared his teeth in predatory fashion.

"I don't think you should've talked to the boss like that in front of all these people." Roberts rested his hands on his hips. "I reckon you owe him an apology."

"Well, you figured wrong."

"Guess we don't see eye to eye."

"If you push me, the only person you'll be seeing is the undertaker. Now, if I was you, I'd back off while you still can."

"Maybe I ain't the one who should be fretting about staying healthy."

"You're cocky. Worse, you're stupid. Feeling confident, with your boss watching, because you've got your friends to back you up. You're probably thinking that the odds don't suit me." His blue eyes narrowed, glinting like the cold, blue steel of his revolver barrel. "Well, they suit me fine. You in good with your Maker?"

Several men sitting closest had already stopped their drinking and card playing to watch the confrontation.

"That's bold talk from a man with his back in a corner," Roberts sneered. "You any good with that gun?"

"You thickheaded enough to find out?" Trey said in a deadly, low voice. "Or you just tired of living?"

The entire room quieted at the words.

Trey could tell by the way his neck reddened that Roberts didn't like being embarrassed in front of the men, especially not in front of his boss.

Roberts started backing up, posturing for the fight to come. "What I'm tired of is your mouth."

The bystanders began clearing an area around the two men.

Trey moved to face Roberts squarely. He held his hand slack, the butt of his pistol between his wrist and elbow. "I warned you. If you haven't got spit for brains, then draw."

Roberts went for his gun, but he had barely touched the handle when Trey had already cleared leather and had the barrel of his Peacemaker pointed directly at Webb's right-hand man.

"You're dumber than I thought," Trey ground out.

Trey came closer, jerked the gun from Roberts, and tossed it aside. In the blink of an eye, his knee crashed into the other man's crotch. Roberts howled and doubled over, clutching his offended parts. But before he dropped to the ground, Trey slammed his knee into Roberts's face. The sound of cartilage popping and breaking reverberated throughout the room and across the stunned onlookers, clearly astounded at the speed which with Trey had acted.

Roberts crumpled to the floor like parchment, gasping for breath, one hand holding his privates and the other cupping his injured nose. Trey knelt and rolled Roberts onto his back. Blood streamed from Roberts's nose across his features, and he stared wide-eyed at the pistol Trey held.

"Consider yourself lucky this time. My mood's not as bad as I thought, or I'd have splattered what little brains you have all over this room." Trey's voice dipped. "Don't cross me again, or I'll blow you to kingdom come."

Shoving the gun back into its holster, Trey stood and surveyed the room. He saw Jonas wave off the other hired guns.

He turned and walked out of the saloon, knowing he was a dead man if he didn't watch his back.

Chapter 10

The next morning after breakfast, Trey sat at the kitchen table, his revolver broken down into pieces before him. His scowl deepened. He couldn't believe he'd lost his head last night—all because of Dallas. Damn his jealousy!

The longer he was around Dallas, the more ornery he got . . . and most likely, the more dangerous he became.

Trey began swabbing out the bluesteel barrel of his single-action Peacemaker. He reasoned he'd best be on his way to the Gonzales station and settle the problem there, instead of thinking about Dallas. Maybe he was losing his mind. Or maybe he was at risk of losing something else. . . .

He sucked in his breath. He didn't have a heart.

Waco entered, tossing his hat on the back of a chair. "Man alive, the whole town's talking about how you squared off against Zeke Roberts last night."

Trey's glare followed Waco as the younger

man walked to the stove, poured himself a cup of coffee, then sat across the table from him.

Waco started to sip his coffee when he looked over the rim of his cup at Trey. "What?" he asked, his cup hovering near his mouth. "Why you looking at me like I put a snake in your bed?"

"What exactly did you hear?" Trey kept his voice low, detached.

"How you were playing poker with Jonas Webb. Then Dallas came in, and after she left, you and Webb had words over her. And that Roberts didn't take kindly to the way you handled his boss."

"Anything else?"

"You best be careful. Seems like Roberts also didn't cotton to having you rearrange his face." Waco grinned, despite his obvious concern, and gave a low whistle. "Bet that was something to see. Nobody's ever stood up to either of those men since they arrived in Lockhart."

Finished with the barrel, Trey turned his attention to the cylinder, cleaning all six chambers. He tried his best to ignore Waco's inquisitive stare, but durn, if all the O'Neals weren't stubborn and persistent. Waco was not to be put off.

"Never known you to lose your head. What happened?"

Trey raised the cylinder to the light and whirled it to check each chamber. "I wanted answers from Webb."

"About what?"

"His involvement in what's been going wrong with the line."

Waco shrugged, but his look was a knowing

one. "And maybe his interest in my sister?"

Trey vigorously rubbed his pistol with a rag. "Dallas shouldn't have come in the saloon."

"Or shouldn't have talked to Webb?" Waco countered.

"Either."

Both men sat in silence as Trey finished cleaning, oiling, and reassembling the Colt. Once done, Trey raised the gun straight out to his right and sighted down the barrel. He pulled the trigger. Click.

"You getting ready to head out?" Waco asked.

Trey whirled the chamber, then loaded the revolver. "Yeah. My gear's ready. I should've already been in Gonzales."

"My hand's almost mended. You want me to come with you?"

"No. Stay here and look after your sisters."

"Want me to tell any of them anything?"

"Nope."

Waco smiled to himself. Trey Conner had the look of a man who had plenty to say—to Dallas O'Neal.

As Trey approached the Gonzales station, he slowed his blue roan to a walk. He scanned the area, alert to the slightest danger. The vague message left for him at the O'Neals' had mentioned trouble, but not what kind. He had no idea what the hell he was getting himself into.

The station consisted of a small structure built from crude, weathered planks, an adjacent corral, holding eight horses, and a lean-to.

A bearded, scruffy-looking, middle-aged man with a large paunch stood at the woodpile, loading his arms with pieces of oak and mesquite. He glanced at Trey and gave a curt nod, but no greeting.

Trey nodded in return, feeling uneasy as he noticed two other men, dirty in dress and appearance, slouched on the porch steps, whittling on pieces of wood.

Three men visible outside the station, Trey thought. How many inside? It wasn't time for a scheduled stage stop. There would be no one to help should these men decide to jump him.

He started to dismount when another person walked outside. The man wore a pair of dirty trousers, one knee torn out, tightened by a rope belt. His ill-fitting jacket hung off his slight shoulders, the sleeves trailing past his fingers. A battered hat hung low over the man's eyes.

Trey didn't like it when he couldn't see a man's eyes. Something, other than these men, smelled to high heaven.

Careful, he cautioned himself. *Go real slow.*

The man wearing the battered hat leaned against the porch post. "What can we do fer ya, mister?"

Pulling his rifle with its boot, Trey dismounted and tied his horse to a tree. "Thought I'd rest my horse and get myself something to eat." His stomach churned at the thought, but he had to think of some lie.

The man took out a cigar and lit it. "Come on in and I'll fix ya somethin'." He stuck it in his mouth and took a long drag.

This fellow seemed too eager to get him inside the house. Trey hadn't missed the way the man's eyes had darted to his companions either.

Stepping closer, Trey studied the man. "I didn't catch your name."

"Charlie," came the smooth reply, between puffs on his cigar. The man tilted his head back to get a better look at Trey. "You're about the tallest man I ever did see. And I just bet ya know how to use them guns of yours. But ya won't be needing them around here." He smiled.

The situation was growing more uncomfortable by the second, but Trey was determined to get to the bottom of whatever was going on here.

"You said you had food," Trey said, forcing a smile.

The man laughed. "That ain't all I've got." He pulled aside his jacket and shirt to reveal a sagging breast. "I've got this."

The three other men hooted, obviously enjoying the turn of events.

Charlie took Trey's hand and placed it on her drooping piece of flesh. "Ya want some?"

Hiding his revulsion, Trey slowly but firmly withdrew his hand. "No, thanks. Just food."

Charlie's gaze flared briefly with hate at his rejection. "I ain't good enough for ya?"

"Just not in the mood."

Charlie motioned toward the station house. "Come on then."

Trey followed the whore inside. He looked around the single-room dwelling with its plank walls and dirt floor. A shelf with cooking and eating utensils hung on the back wall. To the right was an old black stove. An iron pot sat on one cooking plate, its lid rising and falling to the rhythm of some foul-smelling concoction boiling within. In the left corner was a crude, handmade table with a single lantern, and two rawhide-bottom chairs.

Trey walked to the table and picked up a forgotten, dirty plate. "I thought Matt Peters ran this place. Must have been wrong."

His gaze sliced over to Charlie. He didn't miss the worried look that crossed her face as she looked to her three friends, who were walking inside.

"Never heard of him," Charlie replied, turning her back on Trey and walking to the stove.

Trey figured she didn't want to look him in the eye and give herself away. Most likely, the four of them had killed Matt Peters and done away with his body.

"Ya interested in some day-old bread?" Charlie asked over her shoulder as she spooned some slop onto a plate.

"That'd be fine," Trey answered, turning to take inventory of her three cohorts. He looked back to Charlie, who busied herself with dishing up food.

Trey moved around so he could see all four of them. "Have you always run this station?" he asked no one in particular.

He watched the other three men tense, giving one another sidelong glances. Charlie had lowered her arm and set down the spoon.

She turned, holding a plate in her hand. "Not long."

Trey eyed all four people. "I figured as much."

One of the men shifted his weight from one foot to the other. "I don't see how that's any of yer business, mister."

"That's where you're wrong."

"Don't be sticking yer nose in something ya shouldn't," Charlie snapped.

Trey kept tight control over his anger. "Afraid I can't do that," he said, his voice low and threatening. "I know for a fact that Matt Peters runs this station. So why don't you tell me who you are and what you're doing here?"

No one spoke.

"All right, have it your way," Trey said.

Before any of them could move a muscle, Trey drew his Colt, hammer back, finger on the trigger. "Drop your guns."

Reluctantly the four complied.

Trey aimed the revolver at Charlie. "I want answers, and I want them now."

"Hold on, mister," one of the men said, his voice dangerously high. "We're just doing what we was told."

"And what was that?" Trey asked smoothly.

"Shut up, Jake!" Charlie hissed.

The man swallowed. "To get rid of that Peters feller."

"And?" Trey prompted.

The man's eyes widened. "To make sure this station didn't serve the Texas Overland Company no more."

One of the other men made a move for the derringer hidden up his sleeve. It was the last move he made. He was dead before he could fire, a bullet lodged between his eyes.

"The rest of you walk out of here real slow and get on your horses," Trey ordered. "And tell your boss that I'll shoot the next man I find on Texas Overland property who doesn't belong."

The three left and didn't look back as they hightailed it away from the station.

Weary, dirty, annoyed, and more than a bit distracted, Trey approached the O'Neals' place after two days' absence. After he left the Gonzales station, he'd been to see another station manager, and spent hours wrangling with the man for new terms on a station contract, but nothing had been accomplished. Trey's company had been outbid by Webb's outfit. Trey considered the possible numbers of renewal contracts he could lose. He considered where Jonas got his money.

He speculated on whether Dallas had seen Jonas again.

He cursed himself; it was no wonder he hadn't been able to achieve anything as far as negotiations were concerned—he'd been able to think of nothing but Dallas. She'd become an obsession.

Trey glanced at his hand resting atop his thigh and was surprised to find it clenched into a fist. No man, including Jonas, would touch her. He couldn't stand the thought of anyone's hands on her.

Except his.

Cursing, he gripped his reins tighter and tried to rid his mind of thoughts of them together, himself and Dallas.

Dallas, her hair and skin damp and smelling of lavender.

Dallas, her mouth responsive beneath his.

Dallas, her thighs bracketing his.

Dallas, her small hands lazily stroking his warm spine.

Dallas, her breasts melting against his tongue like sugar.

Trey lightly touched his spurs to his horse's flanks, quickening his pace.

Not until he had reined in his horse at the barn did he realize he had missed Dallas. Every succulent, ripe inch of her.

He had been trying to keep a safe distance from her. Instead, he had been drawn closer.

Even now he hardened.

It was too damn easy to imagine Dallas naked and trembling beneath him, her flesh moist and heated from spent energy—and it was hell.

Dallas was used to having her way.

But then, so was he.

This could be a long, costly siege.

Trey dismounted and strode up the path to the house, his spurs jingling. He entered the kitchen to find Tyler drinking a cup of coffee.

He released a weary sigh. "I hoped to find Dallas here. Have you seen her?"

"Out back mending a seat in the stagecoach," Tyler replied, between sips.

"I need to talk to Dallas privately. Please tell the others," he said, quitting the room.

Cranky from fitful sleep, Dallas had risen before dawn. She hadn't slept well for the last two nights. She had tossed and turned, unable to find any comfortable position, unable to get Trey Conner off her mind.

He made her feel things that she had never known before, with a potency that unnerved her. Now she knew what it was like to desire and long for a man. Because of her independence, she had told herself that she didn't need—or want—a man in her life. But since Trey Conner's arrival, she'd begun to doubt her previous resolution.

She laughed dryly. If he knew of her fascination with him, would he return her feelings or would he think her brazen? The thought of caring for a man spooked her.

Her mouth turned down in a frown. This was silly, she thought. He probably didn't find her attractive at all. Only available.

What was the point of torturing herself with such thoughts? She had to put things in perspective and get on with her life. She had the day off, but she had plenty to keep her busy. Just what she needed to take her mind off . . . She didn't finish the thought. She attacked her mending of the torn leather seat, lost in her task.

Dallas was so preoccupied that she never heard Trey approach.

His rich, masculine voice broke into her thoughts. "I want to talk to you."

Every muscle in Dallas's body tensed, suddenly and painfully. "Oh, no."

"Oh, yes."

She gathered her wits—and her courage—to look at him through the stage's window, hopefully with detachment.

No such luck as he stood just far enough away from the coach for Dallas to notice how he wore his gun strapped low against his much too masculine thigh, and how disturbingly well he filled out his snug pants.

She also noticed the exhaustion etching deep grooves along his mouth, and the day's growth of black stubble shading his face. Dust coated his clothes and hat. Compassion tugged at her heart.

Beneath the layers of dirt and fatigue, she recognized the man she knew, the same strong features, the same solid frame. He was as rugged as the land.

Their gazes met and held. Then, as violent as lightning, a jolt of realization struck her. She had missed him. More than she cared to admit.

"We need to clear up some things." With his hat, Trey dusted the dirt from his shirt and breeches.

Dallas squashed her tender feelings. Damn him! Why did he have to show up now? He was the last person she wanted to see.

"I'm busy. We can talk later."

"No, now."

"And I said later," she said between clenched teeth.

He opened the door and started to climb in. She huffed in frustration.

Her irritation expanded like yeast-risen bread. "What do you think you're doing?" she snapped.

"If you won't come out, then I'll have to come in. But one way or the other, we *will* talk."

Tossing his hat aside, he settled in the seat across from her, his long legs angled to accommodate his height in the cramped interior. A dangerous silence fell between them.

Didn't he understand that she didn't want to be around him? Couldn't he guess that his presence reinforced memories she was trying desperately to erase? She didn't want to recall his intoxicating kiss, nor the feel of his strong arms around her, nor her own near surrender.

Some rebellious internal demon prompted her to provoke Trey. He was like a thunderstorm about to happen. She was drought-ridden earth. She couldn't stand the dark, turbulent, sulfurous atmosphere between them any longer.

Dallas broke the impasse with her usual sharp tongue. "It's always what you want. Never what I want."

"This is not about what either of us wants, but rather what we need."

Dallas swore at his tendency to be downright cussed when he chose. "Can't you just leave me the hell alone?" Turning her back on him, she knelt in front of the seat and took up her mending once more. "Haven't you done enough already?"

"I've upset you."

"If you've come to apologize, don't concern yourself. I just want to forget what happened."

"Turn around so we can talk face-to-face. Like human beings."

She laughed shortly. "Since when have you behaved like a human being where I've been concerned?"

"My reaction to you has been only too human."

And I reacted only too wantonly, she thought darkly. Was it her imagination, or had the temperature in the coach risen suddenly?

"Say what you've got to say," she told him, "then get out."

"We need to talk about us."

This was the one conversation she had wanted to avoid. Yet a small part of her—that foolish, romantic part—had desperately hoped for this chance.

"There is *no* us. Whatever happened was a mistake."

"The mistake was my allowing you to continue driving this stage."

She stabbed herself with the needle, then whirled. Her chest rose and fell in marked agitation. "What are you saying?" she demanded as she lifted her finger to her mouth and sucked the drop of blood that glistened from the pinprick.

His manly scent, carried on the heat of his skin, wrapped around her senses. It was the scent of dust and horseflesh and the sweat of hard work done under the hot sun. His nearness more than disturbed her. It frightened her. She was painfully aware of how his gaze swept over her, taking in every inch. And she quivered at the way the hard, lean length of his body sent primitive signals to the softness of hers.

"You're more bothersome than any female I've ever known." He laughed dryly. "And working with you is more trouble than I've ever had to endure."

"Why?"

"Because you're in the way."

He gazed at her with a warmth in his blue eyes that made her entire body feel overheated. "You don't like me arguing with you," she said breathlessly.

Trey leaned forward, his face dangerously close to hers, his look purely sensual. Those funny feelings were kicking up in her stomach again.

"It doesn't matter," he said. "I've decided it won't work."

The arrogance in his voice sharpened her

senses. Sick of his high-handedness, she charged, "You've decided? On what basis?"

"On the basis that you're a distraction."

He didn't move a muscle, yet she felt a physical fondling as surely as if he had touched her.

Dallas fought the effect of his drugging nearness. "What about you? You're the one who forced yourself on me."

"I never forced you." His features hardened. "You wanted me as much as I wanted you."

"Of all the nerve," she fumed.

Trey reached out. She tried to avoid his touch, but the close confines of the coach made maneuvering difficult. She braced herself. He caressed her cheek with the back of his hand, and her resolve teetered dangerously on the brink of collapse.

"You've never known a man, so you can't possibly understand what you're missing. I, on the other hand, have known women, and you intrigue me more than anyone else has before. I want to know you very much. That's why this situation cannot continue." His silken tone shimmered across her in tantalizing waves. "I'll figure out something that will work with your family."

Oh, God. Not only did she have to fight him, but she had to battle her own traitorous responses. She didn't understand why her body reacted so forcefully to his, but she knew she couldn't ignore it.

Dallas mustered as much confidence in her voice as she was able. She had to convince him—and herself. "Don't bother firing me. I've got a contract, and I'm not going anywhere. You have no right to dismiss me on such shaky grounds."

He responded with unnerving silence.

She had to do something. "If you won't leave, then I'm getting out of here."

She reached for the door handle, but a firm hand on her arm stopped her. She tried for the other side, but a leg thrown across the seat blocked her exit.

Trey unfastened one curtain, covering the window. "You can make this hard or easy on yourself. It doesn't make any difference to me. But you're not going anywhere until I'm through with you. One way or the other."

His insinuation sent a shiver of dread—and anticipation—through her. "You can't keep me here against my will."

He reached to the other side and undid another curtain. The black leather dropped softly into place over the second rear window.

"Oh, you'll stay. Quite willingly before I'm finished."

With a deft motion, he drew down the door curtains. Dallas felt as if he were sealing her fate.

She moistened her suddenly dry lips. "What makes you so sure?"

"Because you like what I do to you."

"I do not!"

"If it makes your virginal pride feel better, then deny it. But your body tells me the truth." Trey leaned forward, his arm lightly brushing her breasts as he unfurled the fifth curtain, then the last. "No one will bother us now."

"All I have to do is give a yell and someone will come running."

"No, they won't."

Instantly she knew he had given orders not to be disturbed, and she experienced a sinking feeling in her stomach. She knew his determination and realized she was powerless to stop him. But she would not make it easy for him.

He reached out and captured her wrists. Slowly, inexorably he pulled her to her knees and settled her between his thighs. The intimate contact was immediate and shattering. She pinkened from the base of her neck to the tips of her ears. She knew he meant to kiss her and was convinced he didn't intend to stop there. She was too susceptible to him and too determined to fight her attraction to permit herself to be this responsive to his touch.

Her chest rose in rapid, shallow breaths, making it difficult to keep her voice steady. "Trey . . . can't we discuss this?"

"It's too late for that, Dallas."

Dallas's stability spun away as she tried to pull back. "You're making the rules again, and I won't bow to them. Now, let me go."

"That's the problem. I can't."

Her muscles were beginning to cramp from the strain. "Leave me alone."

"That's the second part of the problem."

"You're not making any sense."

He maintained his hold on her wrists with one hand, while he caressed her cheek with the back of his other hand. "When it comes to you, nothing makes any sense."

She shifted her body restlessly. "I'm not asking it to make sense to you. I just want to do my job."

"But if you truly expect to continue to driving

the stage, you're asking the impossible. You're expecting me to work alongside you in cramped conditions, and not react as any other man would when in such close quarters with a beautiful woman." His voice, rich as velvet, floated across her tingling body.

"Don't make fun of me. I know I'm not beautiful."

She inhaled raggedly as one of his fingertips lazily traced a path from the side of her neck to her collarbone. His touch then outlined her lips. Dallas's senses vibrated at his nearness.

"Then you know very little, because you're the loveliest, most desirable woman I've ever known."

"Stop saying that."

One side of his mouth turned up. "I wish I could."

Dallas fought her own desire. She wasn't wanton. She wasn't.

"What you can do, Trey Conner, is take your hands off me this instant."

"If it were only that simple."

His fingers drifted close. Dallas closed her eyes in anticipation of his touch and her breathing quickened.

Seconds ticked by, but nothing happened. Disappointment strangely mingled with frustration. She opened her eyes, fuming silently.

Trey raised one of her hands to his lips. He kissed her palm, each finger, then startled her by closing his lips around her little finger and sucking it into his mouth. His teeth gently grazed the skin of her pinky, which until now, she had never known was sensitive.

A jolt of need went through Dallas. With any other man that gesture would have been an affront—but this was Trey. For two seemingly endless days and torturous nights she'd ached for his voice, his touch, his kiss. The present reality of it, was setting off tiny explosions deep within her, was far better than any memory.

He kissed the inside of her wrist, and she felt the wet friskiness of his tongue. His teeth sank lightly into her tender flesh, and she groaned. Her breath was trapped in her throat by a mind-stealing kiss that started at her mouth and ended with a trail of fervent kisses down the column of her neck.

I want him—a pulsing rhythm repeated itself in her mind—*I want him*. But she knew he was too experienced, too seductive, too confident for her.

"Please." She forced the words past taut lips. "Let me go."

But it was blatantly clear to her that his intention wasn't to release her with only a kiss.

His hands performed a different task. He efficiently unbuttoned her shirt with one hand, and with the other he parted the material and stroked her thinly covered breast. She moaned, deep in her throat, as his forefinger and thumb commanded the nipple to life.

She couldn't let this happen here, in a stagecoach, in broad daylight! So said Dallas's mind, but her body was of a different opinion, a primitive opinion. It craved the luscious attentions Trey was giving it, and far more.

Suddenly his hands encased her hips and held her a heartbeat away from him. "We have to settle this, once and for all."

She opened her eyes and looked at him, understanding in her gaze, even as his hands pushed her shirt off her shoulders, down her arms, to her waist. She felt the erotic sensation of his silky hair against her skin as her camisole followed after her shirt and he bared her breasts.

"So beautiful," Trey murmured as he pressed his face to her chest. "I don't know what you do to me."

For Dallas, it wasn't a question of what she did to him, but rather what he did to her. And what he was doing was sinful and heavenly at the same time.

His hands cupped her ripe, beckoning breasts and gently kneaded the full, firm flesh until her nipples ached. The throbbing traveled lower . . . until it settled in her warm, vibrating center. Then, as if to lay claim to her flesh with his touch, he ran his splayed hands down her rib cage to her waist, across her flat stomach, and back up again.

Profound delight streaked through her when his mouth captured one breast, teasing her unmercifully. Her fingers curled reflexively in the richness of his shoulder-length hair. She pressed his face closer in wanton demand.

Her breath left her in a feathery sigh as Trey sought possession of the other breast. The sensation extracted a ragged, brazen plea from her moist, parted lips. Her legs became liquid; and she would have sagged to the floor had it not been for the support of Trey's strong hands at her waist.

Feeling as though she were being swept along by a powerful river current, she surrendered completely to the pleasure Trey was agonizingly orchestrating on her more than willing body.

Their labored breathing tangled, becoming one sound in the dim interior.

Between spurts of her erratic pulse, she felt Trey shift his attention. He pulled her fully against him, until their chests touched. An involuntary sigh escaped her as he wrapped his warm, strong arms about her. She didn't care that Trey Conner held her entirely too intimately in his arms. He was the first man for whom she had felt the sweet, melting female ache to yield, yet she knew to succumb to her desire would be weakness.

He cupped her chin and forced her to look up at him—into those damnable blue eyes. She knew he meant to kiss her again, but not even his first intoxicating contact prepared her for the effect of his lips on hers this time. She might have been able to resist if his kiss had been bruising and demanding, but this dizzying, lazy seduction undid her.

His hands moved to her breasts. The feel of his callused palms was sweet torture. She grew hot—then cold—then hot again.

Their bodies pressed closer. Her breasts rubbed against the fabric of his shirt. The heated crush of material bathed her in emotions so tantalizing that a shudder passed through her.

"I want you so badly," he said, his voice raw.

Trey, too, was caught in finely meshed emotions. Every fiber of his being yearned to make love to her. But he knew if he took her now, she would give herself to him body and soul. He wasn't sure he wanted the responsibility of that commitment. It took all his willpower not to make love to her there on the floor of the stage.

Her thighs were nestled intimately between his. Her breasts were pressed achingly close to his chest. She smelled too damn good. He could practically taste her breath as it mingled with his.

She moaned, and his breath caught somewhere between his lungs and his throat. How could he have ever wanted to stay away from this creature? He had been with whores who prided themselves on knowing how to get a man's blood to the boiling point. But no woman had ever had an impact on him the way this one did.

"Dallas," he whispered raggedly.

She sighed. Even the way he said her name, his voice low and husky, added to the erotic confusion of her senses. She climbed out of the recesses of passion and forced herself to think clearly. It was the hardest thing she had ever done.

"Let go," Dallas rasped against his mouth.

The kiss continued for a lingering moment, then Trey drew back, staring into her face. "If that's what you want."

With distressing design, his gaze slowly traveled up the slender curve of her neck. His carefully blank expression revealed nothing as he studied the graceful feminine line of her cheeks and jaw, her small, straight nose, before journeying over her long, lush lashes. Finally his gaze rested on her lips. All the while, he traced the satiny sweep of her shoulder and collarbone.

The combination of sensations assaulted Dallas, leaving in their wake a rapidly beating pulse. She struggled to find her voice. "I think you've done enough today."

"Not as much as I would have liked."

As fast as her trembling fingers would allow, she dressed. Maintaining a proud lift of her chin, she straightened her shoulders, left the coach, and walked toward the house.

She sensed they played a dangerous game. She had once called him handsome as sin. But he was the devil himself to make her want him with only a touch.

Chapter 11

Dawn found Trey hard at work helping Miguel with blacksmith duties. Heat coiled around the interior of the lean-to and settled as glistening sweat on his forehead and exposed forearms. Steam hissed from the water bucket, accompanied by a loud sizzling as Trey submerged glowing, red-hot horseshoes into the cooling water.

He didn't mind the physical labor. In fact, he welcomed the chance to exert himself. If he could stay busy enough, he wouldn't have time to think, and he didn't want to think about Dallas.

His conscience, however, would not cooperate. Slipping back to thoughts of their encounter in the stage, he couldn't believe he had nearly made love to her in broad daylight. Besides, she was a virgin, for Christ's sake! He was older, more experienced than she was; he knew better. He could have most any woman, but not her. Not Dallas. His mind knew to stay clear of Dallas, but his body didn't seem to listen to cool reason. Every time he touched her, held her close, or kissed her, he reacted hard . . . hot . . . hungry. At her nearness, he couldn't think clearly, feeling only delicious anticipation.

His whole body vibrated with pent-up frustration. He was surprised at the depth of his irritation. He supposed it stemmed from not having had a woman for so long, and convinced himself it had nothing to do with feelings of guilt. He wished he could get his mind off Dallas . . . off her pretty little mouth . . . off her tempting sweet bottom. . . .

He cursed beneath his breath. With Dallas, he felt an anticipated pleasure, a curious tantalizing of his senses, stronger than he'd ever experienced. Why did her touch leave him tense with wanting?

Whatever his reasons for craving Dallas, he was a damned fool for letting this go so far, for lusting after a soft, tempting piece of virginity. But he'd be doubly damned if she would run him off this station. He had a job to do, and he intended to do it. Of course, he'd have to be around Dallas, that was part of his job, but he sure as hell had no intentions of ever touching her again.

It would be hell if he didn't.

Trey looked up and saw the source of his torment. Dallas sat perfectly still on the top rail of the corral, staring out over the horses. Morning light bathed her figure in honey tones, highlighting her blond hair with a golden halo, and cast her in serenity. A gentle southerly breeze lifted and tugged loose strands of hair about her face like tiny kite tails.

Trey knew the picture was an illusion. There

was nothing serene about her nature—hers was fire and temper and heat. If only Dallas knew how his heart pounded, knew how his palms sweated, knew how his breath came hard and tight in his chest at the sight of her, she'd probably laugh.

His gaze returned to the thick golden braid of sun-streaked hair trailing halfway down her slender back . . . hair long enough, he thought with a surge of heated pleasure, to cover her breasts.

Against his will his gaze lowered to those same tempting breasts, rising and falling gently with each breath she took. His hands remembered the shape of them; his lips remembered the sweetness of them.

His gaze moved to her mouth. So innocent, yet so provocative. So lush and deliciously inviting.

He swallowed against the hard knot of desire coiling and twisting his insides.

"Fire and damnation," he breathed, struggling to gain a fingertip control on the ragged edges of his lust.

Trey jerked the glowing curved steel from the fire and placed it on the anvil and proceeded to pound out a rhythm as erratic as his breathing.

At noon, Dallas sat with the others at the kitchen table while Abbey served the meal. She was hungry, but she hadn't wanted to suffer sitting through the meal with Trey. She knew, though, if she had refused to eat, someone would have suspected something, and that was the last thing Dallas wanted.

She had successfully managed to avoid Trey

until now. He sat across from her, a brooding presence in the room. She was sharing space with him, fighting for every breath she drew. It was the first time she had seen him since . . . the stagecoach.

She didn't want to look into those eyes and see his satisfaction or ridicule. But she had no choice.

She felt a nervousness in her stomach, and it was difficult to stay where she was. She wanted to walk away from him and the feeling inside of her.

But still she had no choice.

Her pride demanded that she face him squarely. She was no coward, and she wouldn't give him the pleasure of thinking she was. She forced herself to look at him.

Her gaze met his. His face was implacable. His eyes were like blue smoke, concealing his thoughts. What was he thinking? Did he consider her no better than the common whore?

Did he remember how she had melted against him as she moaned at his kiss? She would certainly never forget the searing sensations of having his tongue on her skin, kissing her, tasting her.

Although guilt weighed heavily on her shoulders, she stiffened her spine with resolve. He could go ahead and think what he wanted. She couldn't stop him from doing that either. But she sure as hell wouldn't lower her head around him. Hadn't he forced himself on her? It hadn't been her fault. The blame rested on his shoulders.

Abbey spooned up large portions of lima beans

and thick-sliced ham, served with cornbread. Cups of steaming hot coffee finished the meal as usual.

"Well, that about does it. Y'all dig in," Abbey said, setting the last plate in front of Dallas.

Waco inhaled appreciatively. "Hmm. Sure smells good."

"I'm starved," Tyler added, giving serious attention to her food.

Trey swallowed a bite of beans, then said, "You're the best cook I know."

Abbey's face was wreathed in smiles. "One has to like what they do."

"It certainly shows," Trey said.

"If you're trying to get on my good side," she said, chuckling, "you just did."

Dallas looked daggers at Trey. Now he was trying to butter up Abbey, most probably so she'd take his side if any argument came up. As if he sensed her scrutiny, he glanced up. She felt like choking when he gave her a mock salute with his coffee cup.

She dropped her gaze. Suddenly she'd lost her appetite. She drew a breath to quell her agitated feelings, knowing she was only making herself miserable by fretting.

"Dallas, did you get that tear mended in the coach?" Abbey asked, between bites.

Dallas paled slightly, then flushed hotly, her mind racing over the intimate encounter with Trey.

Calm, she told herself. *Stay calm.*

She clutched her coffee cup. "Yes, it's been taken care of."

She cut her eyes to Trey, and their gazes clashed

in a silent tug-of-war. Who'd be the first to cross the line? In that silent test of wills, they relived the intimate moment in more detail than either wanted.

"Yes, everything's been taken care of," Dallas repeated slowly, with a resolute lift of her chin.

Trey wiped his mouth on his napkin, then rose. "Again, that was delicious, Abbey. Thanks. I'll be getting back to work now."

"You're welcome, Trey," Abbey returned, thoughtfully watching his departing figure.

Abbey hid a smile behind her napkin as she watched Dallas finish her coffee. She knew with certainty that her sister had finally met her match. Dallas's experience with men was, at best, limited. Most suitors had disapproved of her frank, tomboyish ways or been frightened by her beauty and independence. Whatever the circumstances, Dallas always sent them packing.

But Trey was different. He wasn't the type to be molded to Dallas's expectations, or to be put off by her radiance, her sharp mind, or her less than refined manners. The look in his eyes had been one of a man inexorably drawn to an irresistible woman. Although Abbey's experience with men was just as limited, she had recognized the stark look stamped plainly on his face. It pained her to see her sister deny her feelings and close herself off from affection.

Abbey's inner voice told her that Trey Conner was special. She approved. She only hoped that Dallas's stubborn pride wouldn't get in the way of her happiness.

* * *

Late that afternoon, Trey, hauling an armload of firewood into the kitchen, came upon Abbey preparing supper.

Her face smudged with flour, she looked up from the gravy she was making. "Thanks. I was getting low on wood. Just put it in the box."

"Tyler told Waco you needed some, but I told him I'd bring it."

Abbey paused, her inquisitive eyes keenly on Trey. "You always take on so much work in one day? Or is something bothering you?"

Trey returned her direct gaze with one of his own. "What would be bothering me?" he repeated.

"I wonder what." Abbey laughed in a low, throaty tone. "Or should I say I wonder who?" She waved him off with a hand dusted with flour. "Don't worry, I won't tell."

He sat down. "I'd rather not talk about Dallas."

Abbey smiled. "Did I mention any names?"

"You didn't have to. We both know who we're talking about."

"I just wanted to make sure you knew that." She kept stirring the drippings, milk, and flour in a large cast-iron skillet. "I couldn't help but notice at noon, the way you two were looking at each other."

"What do you think you saw?"

"You always answer a question with another question?"

"I learned early in life not to give away my thoughts. You never know when they could be used against you."

"You have nothing to fear from me."

"I know that." He caught the faint smile curling her generous mouth.

"And I know what I saw. Anyone looking close enough could have seen it. It's plain as day that you two are attracted to each other. You're a poor liar if you tell yourself otherwise."

"Is that so?"

"There you go again answering my questions with one of your own. And yes, that's so."

Trey didn't like the direction this conversation was taking. He especially didn't like the way thoughts of Dallas, which he had worked so hard to push aside, intruded upon his mind, more vividly than before. He tried to tell himself his attraction to Dallas was the result of denying himself something he wanted. A new experience for him. Women never found him lacking, and he never found them hard to snare. Until Dallas. She was the lone exception—to every woman he'd ever known. Which was considerable.

Despite his dark, contemplative mood, his expression softened slightly. "I know this is a question, but do you always try to fix people's lives?"

"If something needs repairs. Nothing worse than something being broke, if it could have been fixed easily."

"So what's broken?"

"For starters, communication. I don't think you two ever discuss anything in a calm manner. You're always arguing. And each one is trying so hard to convince the other that they're right, that neither of you really listens to what you're saying." Abbey removed the skillet from the heat and directed her full attention to Trey. "I know Dallas can be difficult at times."

Trey snorted loudly. "At times. Hah! When isn't she difficult? I've never known a woman to have such a temper."

"It's true. She's got to realize her temper will destroy her if she doesn't learn to control it." Abbey's tone turned more understanding. "And I know she can be stubborn."

"Your sister gives a whole new meaning to the word."

"But if she believes and trusts someone, there's no end to the love she's capable of. The way to win Dallas is to have a great deal of patience, and treat her with even more kindness." Her words took on a gentle emphasis. "I believe you're that man. She needs someone who, besides being gentle and patient, is strong enough to set her straight when she's wrong."

"If she would just learn to listen to instructions." Trey paused, then stood. "Oh, hell, forget it. She'll just have to get one thing straight. She'd better do what she's told. I've got enough to worry about without having to wonder about what kind of trouble she's brewing."

"Dallas needs to respect authority. But let me give you one last bit of advice. If you injure her pride, you could break her spirit."

"She's just so damned irritating." Trey ran his fingers through his hair in a distracted manner. "I've never met a woman like her."

"But isn't that why you're attracted to her?"

"Sometimes I'd like nothing better than to take her over my knee and give her the spanking she deserves. She's a spoiled brat."

"She's always gotten her way. Maybe it's good that she's learning that she can't always have it."

"If she gets nothing else through her brain, she'd best remember who's boss around here. I'll tell you this. I've got a job to do without having Dallas give me trouble every inch of the way. And she'd better get that in her head damned quick because I'm not going to put up with any foolishness."

Trey walked out, the back door slamming shut, making his point.

Abbey smiled. Yes, sir. Trey Conner had it bad.

Wearing a preoccupied expression, Jonas sat behind his desk, a pile of forgotten papers strewn across the oak surface. He wasn't thinking of business. He was thinking of pleasure . . . of Dallas O'Neal.

He smiled. He had been toying with the idea of hiring her away from Trey as his driver, but he knew what would happen if he did. Trey would come after her. Oh, Trey might not admit he cared for the girl, but he hated to surrender any possession.

A slow grin spread across Jonas's face. If Dallas accepted the position, she would be close at hand, and he'd have an opportunity to win her over. He'd court her, though he had no intentions of marrying her or any other woman, and he'd teach her the pleasures of a good man's bed.

More importantly by hiring Dallas, he would be striking a blow against Trey.

He decided to begin his pursuit in earnest by

asking Dallas to accompany him to the upcoming town dance. And he knew the way to a woman's heart—a new dress. Granted, circumstances were different with Dallas, but despite her tomboyish appearance, he sensed her to be all woman, a wildly seductive spitfire. She'd accept the dress and his offer to the dance.

Jonas's mind filled with an image of Dallas wearing a form-fitting dress trimmed in ruffles and lace, with a bodice cut just low enough for a glimpse of her breasts, but not too low to be considered indecent.

He'd teach her to be daring later.

Jonas picked up a pen and scribbled a note, then called for one of his men to have the invitation delivered to the O'Neals. He would send new dresses to all three sisters.

There was no way Dallas would turn down his more than kind consideration.

Leaning back in his chair, idly stroking his cheek with the tip of his pen, Jonas looked forward to Saturday with keen anticipation . . . and a keen appetite.

After supper dishes had been cleared, Waco walked into the kitchen with three boxes. He gave one to Abbey and a second to Tyler.

He handed the last parcel to Dallas. "This one's addressed to you."

Overcome with curiosity, she spared Trey only a glance before she tore away the twine and ripped open the package.

Dallas gasped. Inside the box was a lovely gown of lavender lawn. The sleeves were puffy, trimmed with the most delicate lace imaginable, and the neckline, while certainly within the bounds of propriety, was anything but demure.

Tucked in one corner of the box was a note.

"Don't keep us on pins and needles. Who are these from?" Tyler peeked over Dallas's shoulder. "What does the note say?"

"Jonas Webb sent the dresses."

Hesitating, Dallas chewed her bottom lip.

"That can't be all," Abbey pressed. "What else does he have to say?"

"He also asks me to accompany him to this Saturday's dance."

Dallas replaced the note in the envelope, then held the dress to her.

"It's nice. But what'd you do for him to send you a dress?" Waco asked curiously.

Trey's imagination ran wild. Just what the hell *had* Dallas done to earn the dress? Or what did Jonas want as payment for the gift?

Caught up in the spontaneity of the moment, Dallas didn't see the rigid set to Trey's shoulders, or the way his blue eyes snapped with anger.

Dallas couldn't have been more surprised.

Trey couldn't have been more furious. Staring grimly at the soft curve of her lips, he was enraged at her obvious pleasure over Webb's gift.

Jealousy licked at him, clawed at his insides like a raging mountain cat. Jonas was challenging his claim to Dallas—something Trey's pride would not tolerate. Both Jonas and Dallas would learn that, if threatened, like a scorpion, he could . . . and would . . . strike quickly with deadly precision.

"It looks like it'll fit you perfectly," Abbey said as she fingered the delicate lace. "It's nice to have a man show his appreciation." Her gaze cut to Trey for a brief moment, then back to Dallas.

Still holding the dress up to her body, Dallas whirled around the kitchen. She had never owned anything so beautiful, so feminine. So tempting.

She stopped. "I can't accept this."

"Why not?" Confusion wrinkled Tyler's brow. "I'm not sending mine back."

"I don't know if we should. Besides, it's been years since I last danced. Not since Mama and Papa died."

"Accepting gifts from a man is done all the time. There's nothing wrong, especially when he sends each of us one." Abbey shook her index finger at Dallas. "You're going to keep that lovely dress and accept his invitation." She laughed. "Since when do you care what folks say? For heaven's sake, all you're going to do is dance with him. It's not like you have anyone to answer to."

"What's that supposed to mean?" Dallas asked, puzzled by Abbey's straying glance toward Trey.

Trey. He'd told her to stay away from Jonas. He'd be madder than a hornet's nest if she were to accept Jonas's invitation. Well, she'd show Trey that she didn't give a fig for his overbearing manner.

She didn't need—or want—Trey Conner, but for some devilish reason, she intended to show him the woman he would never have.

Dallas gave a small shake of her blond head. "You're right, Abbey. I'll send word to Jonas and tell him how much we appreciate the dresses. And that I would be happy to accept his invitation."

Her defiant gaze and the rebellious lift to her chin blew the lid off Trey's anger with explosive brilliance.

He had no sympathy for Jonas.

He would show Dallas no mercy.

She had thrown his authority over one too many times.

"Like hell you will!" The hard-edged words ricocheted off the walls. Trey took two menacing steps toward Dallas until he stood nearly toe to toe, chest to chest, with her.

For a moment the two glared at each other, their gazes locked in silent combat, oblivious to the others present. Anger radiated off them in waves, and the already intolerable tension in the room grew to alarming proportions.

"I think they should be left alone," Waco said, beating a hasty retreat. Abbey and Tyler followed on his heels.

Trey leaned forward a fraction closer, his nose coming dangerously close to hers. "You've got some explaining to do."

Dallas wasn't about to explain anything. Anger burned like a raging fever in her cheeks and neck.

Tension built in the heated silence.

Several more seconds of pulsating stress passed, until Trey said in a menacingly soft voice, "You're not going with him."

Dallas felt the charge of his fury, but she refused to bow to his intimidation.

"Afraid of a little competition?" She raised a brow. "You're not the only rooster in the hen-house, you know."

"And neither am I a coyote licking his teeth, waiting for the kill."

"Maybe Jonas just enjoys my company."

"Oh, he intends to enjoy you, all right. If you're not careful, he'll take everything from you and give nothing in return."

"Are you any different? What did you give me?"

"I've been as honest with you as I can." He released his breath in a hard, grating sound. "And I sure as hell didn't plan on what happened between us."

"Are you saying Jonas is deliberately planning something?"

"Very damned carefully." Each word was brittle and cold. "And if memory serves me correctly you didn't like him from the first time you met him. Why the sudden change of heart?" His anger at himself and his anger at Dallas drove him to be punishing, hard, relentless.

"I was obviously wrong about him."

"First impressions are usually right. With my job, you learn to either live, or die, by your instincts."

Trey watched the rapid rise and fall of her breasts, noting her agitation. Let her be angry. He could deal with her anger more easily than with his desire for her.

"I have strong suspicions Jonas is behind the attempts to ruin the line."

"But you don't have proof."

"I'm never wrong about these things."

"But you've admitted to me just how human you are. People make mistakes."

"I'm human when it comes to you. I'm right about Jonas. You don't go through four years of hell with someone and not know them. Believe me, I know more than I want to about Jonas Webb."

"A person can change. Jonas could have."

"No more than a bull can give milk," he said his voice confident.

"Until you have proof, there's no reason why I shouldn't or can't see him."

"I certainly wasn't wrong about you. You're too muleheaded, too bent on saving your pride, for your own good. You can't have it both ways."

Just being so near this exasperating man made Dallas's rebellious flesh tingle with longing, but she hefted her chin another notch and stoked the fire in her eyes.

"I never have with you," she said.

"You've ignored a directive of mine for the last time," Trey responded with a raspy sigh of irritation.

"I have a right to be in anyone's company I want. My personal life is none of your business."

"Everything you do is my business." He pulled her close. "If Jonas wants you, he'll have to get past me."

Ah, he's jealous, she thought. *That's good. Let him be.*

However, Trey was behaving suspiciously possessive, and Dallas bucked against the notion. "You don't own me, so don't tell me what to do."

"You have no idea what you're getting yourself into."

Hell's bells! Why couldn't Trey stop meddling and let her work out her feelings for herself? Her restlessness was all his fault!

"Maybe not, but I seriously doubt that it would be any worse than having to tolerate you." Damn him! "Why do you care?"

"Why do you want to go to the dance?" Trey countered smoothly. "To give Jonas an opportunity to sniff around you?"

Dallas placed her hands on her hips and shook her head. "Don't be vulgar."

"I don't hear you denying it."

Unwilling to admit it on a conscious level, Dallas had secretly wanted Trey to look at her the same way he had Serena Crowley and treat her like . . . an attractive woman.

She raised her chin. "Because I'm not going to dignify your crude remark with an answer."

"You don't want to admit the truth."

She ground her teeth. "About what?"

"How I make you feel. How beneath all those layers of men's clothing beats the heart and soul of a woman. And that scares the hell out of you because I'm the one who made you feel that way."

Enraged by their argument, Dallas didn't notice the way the fabric of her shirt strained across her breasts with each deep, shuddering breath of anger she took.

But Trey did. The sensual display blew a fortifying breath into his own anger.

"If you just want male attention," he said in a rough drift of sensuality, "I'll give you all you can handle—and more."

"Maybe you don't like the idea that I won't give in to you," she said airily. "Or maybe your pride can't stand the fact that I get along with other men—just not you."

"What's that supposed to mean?"

Pleased to see, by the narrowing of his eyes, that she had obviously hit a nerve, Dallas replied, "Just what I said."

"You're not going to give another man the pleasure of seeing you in a dress. If you wear a dress for anyone, it'll be me. I'm the one who makes you feel like a woman."

"Funny, but if you feel that way, how come you aren't the one who gave me the dress?"

"This is getting us nowhere."

"What do you want me to do?"

"Not go."

"What would I tell the others?" She gave a toss of her head in a nonchalant manner. "Oh, I can't go because Trey doesn't trust me around Jonas. I don't think that would set very well with you because you won't admit you're jealous."

"It's Jonas who I don't trust," Trey said. "You're twisting my words around."

The same way he twisted her insides around, Dallas thought. Every time he came near her, he stirred up feelings that took forever to settle.

"So you're not jealous?" Dallas asked.

His grin was slow and molten. Damn him. His masculinity weakened her at times when she most needed strength.

"Answer this, then." He cupped her chin with his hand and lowered his voice to a silky, seductive whisper that set her pulse racing. "What did you do for the dress? Twitch your tail?"

Dallas was so outraged at his implication that she had been immoral, she couldn't find words. But she found a physical expression for her fury.

She slapped him with all her might. The sound echoed angrily in the air.

A heartbeat later, she froze from the raw violence radiating from Trey's eyes.

"Fine, Dallas. Have things your way . . . this time. But don't say I didn't warn you." He stepped closer, his breath striking her face. "But I intend to go to the dance, too. And have a very good time. I'm sure I can find a more than willing woman to share the evening with."

Dallas watched Trey spin on his heel and leave.

For once, she'd given Trey a taste of his own medicine. So why didn't she feel better?

Chapter 12

With a hand-rolled cigar between his teeth, Jonas sank into the tub. Neck-high in hot water, he leaned his head against the rim and released an appreciative groan as he felt his muscles relax.

Since he'd risen this morning, he found his thoughts wandering, drifting into soft visions of Dallas. Images of her silken glory of flaxen hair, her golden skin and vivid green eyes, the graceful lines of her supple body, lingered.

Jonas removed the cigar from his mouth and draped his arm over the tub's edge, the cigar scissored between two fingers. He closed his eyes.

Odd, but he had been as giddy as a schoolboy ever since Dallas had accepted his invitation to the dance and his gift of the dress.

He anticipated tonight would be one of the most enjoyable evenings of his life. He hardened at the thought of holding Dallas in his arms, escorting her across the dance floor.

To a degree, it annoyed him that Dallas had such power over him. He should take her soon.

Once he had gotten her out of his system and had satisfied his lust, he could keep his mind on business and his thoughts clear.

But he needed a bit of distraction now.

"Jenny!"

Within seconds, Jenny hurried through the doorway of the adjacent room and came to stand next to the tub. "Yes, Jonas?"

His gaze scanned her red dress. The low-cut, ruffled neckline revealed her tempting cleavage.

He gave her a lazy smile. "Scrub my back."

"Whatever you want, Jonas." Jenny leaned over the edge of the tub, fishing in the water for the cake of soap, giving Jonas an eyeful of her breasts.

"That's right." His predatory glance held hers. "Whatever I want."

"I can't find the soap," Jenny said.

"It's between my legs," he said in a deep, sensual rasp. Swallowing, Jenny inched her hand along Jonas's leg, up his muscular thigh, until her fingers brushed the thick nest of hair covering his manhood.

Nervously she licked her lips. "I don't feel . . . the soap."

"Oh, it's there," Jonas murmured. "Keep going."

Her fingers edged past him, settling on the soft underside of him—and the bar of soap.

"You have wonderful hands, Jenny." His smile deepened as his hand moved over hers—and he squeezed. "And you know what to do with them."

Jenny bit her lower lip. "Don't you want me to scrub your back before the water gets cold?"

Jonas laughed and released her hand. "Yes." He inched forward in the tub. "I do."

With circular motions, Jenny lathered Jonas's neck and back.

"Hmm," Jonas sighed, and bent his head forward, his chin nearly touching his chest. "That feels so good."

A sharp rap interrupted the moment, and Jonas looked toward the door. "Who is it?"

"I need to talk to you, boss," came Zeke Roberts's voice.

"Come in." Jonas half growled in irritation.

A disgruntled Roberts walked in.

Jonas scowled. "This had better be important."

"Just got word from one of the boys." Roberts sounded slightly winded as he breathed through his mouth. "Somebody tipped Conner off about the Gonzales station. He went down there, cleaned our people out, and hired himself a new man."

Jonas tensed. "Find out who leaked the word and take care of him." His gaze burned with reproach, but he kept his voice level in spite of his anger. "How much does Conner know?"

"He didn't find Matt Peters's body, if that's what you're aiming at, boss."

"I don't want anything pointing to me. He's only got his suspicions to go on right now. I want to keep it that way."

"You have nothing to worry about."

Jonas pulled one of Jenny's arms over his shoulder and down his chest, placing her palm against his breastbone. "How can you be sure your friends won't talk?"

"They've been taken care of."

"Good." Jonas idly ran his finger up and down her arm. "What else has Conner found out?"

"Only that you've been buying up contracts."

"There's nothing illegal about that."

"I paid the two handlers on the north route, like you said." Roberts winced, gingerly touching his bandaged nose when he tried to smile. "If anybody asks, they still work for Texas Overland, but they know who to be grateful to."

"They understand what to do?"

"Told 'em not to make things look too plain when accidents start happenin'."

Jonas raised Jenny's hand to his mouth, sucking on a fingertip. "Good job. There'll be something extra for you next payday."

"Speaking of? When you want the boys to start after those stages again? It's been a while since they pulled their last job."

"Soon. But you can't rush these matters. How would it look if all of a sudden, everything started going wrong?"

Roberts shrugged, looking at his boss with discolored, bloodshot eyes. "Yes, boss."

"Whatever happens tonight, I don't want any trouble." Jonas's jaw tensed noticeably. "No one's to touch Conner." His thoughts brushed on Dallas. "I don't want my plans ruined."

Sensing the rage that burned in Roberts, Jonas assured him, "Revenge is sweeter when it's been savored awhile." He nodded toward the door. "Get going."

Jonas balled his hand into a fist. He forced his muscles to relax by the strength of his will. He'd waited a long time for satisfaction. Trey Conner was in for some unpleasant surprises.

* * *

That evening, in a big metal tub in the center of the kitchen, Dallas sat in her bath, lost in thoughts as tepid as the water. Earlier she had washed her hair with rainwater from the collection barrel out back and rinsed her blond tresses with lemon juice. Now the heavy mass was coiled and pinned atop her head. She had needed a hot bath to relax and ease her concerns.

Although a fun-filled evening teased her, she discovered she couldn't raise any enthusiasm.

Trey had been the devil himself. All week he hadn't spoken to her unless it was absolutely necessary. He had even taken to eating his meals on the back door steps, alone. His actions made it perfectly clear that he couldn't stand the sight of her.

For the most part, Dallas had occupied her time doing chores and driving the stage. She kept her distance from Trey, not wanting another violent confrontation. More especially, she had no desire to confront her feelings for him.

As for the others, they kept their concerns and opinions about the thick, brooding tension between herself and Trey to themselves. No one had much to smile about.

Sighing, Dallas knew it would soon be time to go into town. She also knew she had to face the consequences of her handiwork.

With her bottom pointed toward the door, she rose in the tub, water sparkling on her creamy skin, and reached for the towel draped on the back of a chair.

"Jesus Christ, woman!"

Gasping, Dallas snatched the towel to her and

whirled around, knocking over the chair and sloshing water onto the floor in her haste.

Trey stood in the doorway, staring at her long and hard, his firm lips drawn in a taut line. "What the deuce do you think you're doing?"

"I would think that's obvious," she replied in a small, tenuous voice.

Although he knew he should get the hell away—and pronto—Trey found himself mesmerized, unable to move.

Her eyes were wide, her face flushed, her embarrassment evident in the glow of lantern light. She clutched the inadequate towel to her breasts and waist. Her long, sleek legs, and the hint of curving hip and soft, shapely thigh, were bared to his heated gaze. His heart slammed against his rib cage. His breathing quickened.

Trey took a step back, closing his mind to the innocent temptation before him. "Why didn't you lock the door?"

"I thought I did."

His senses were reeling from the heady atmosphere in the room. The fragrance of soap, the scent of lemons, along with the lingering aroma of peach and cinnamon from freshly baked pies, mingled in the air.

"For godsakes, put some clothes on." His voice was thick with longing. He turned and slammed the door behind him.

In the tub, Dallas thought of Trey's reaction to the sight of her half-naked, and hot, coiling sensations wove through her legs, twisted around her middle, threaded across her breasts. Her nipples ached with the remembrance of his touch—with her need for his touch.

As she recalled his naked image that day at the creek, her limbs trembled. She remembered in vivid, breath-stealing detail every inch of his tall, muscular frame.

Dallas caught herself and forced her thoughts back to the upcoming evening. She would go to town and have fun—even if it made her miserable.

By the time the O'Neal clan, along with Miguel and Trey, arrived in Lockhart, the dance had already begun.

No one within fifty miles ever missed one of these gatherings. Why, it was practically an unwritten law to attend. The citizens of Caldwell County knew how to put on a dance and a great feed.

Brightly colored lanterns hung in the trees above tables in the yard that were laden with food. Separate tables had been set up for refreshments. The delicious aroma of beef and pork roasted over mesquite wood, the dripping fat sizzling in the fire, caused more than one person's stomach to growl in anticipation.

Dallas couldn't remember seeing so many folks in attendance before. This was the biggest dance ever. People were everywhere, standing in groups, milling about, dancing.

Raucous laughter drifted on the cool evening air. Conversation grew lively; the music became spirited. A banjo, guitar, fiddle, and harmonica kept most folks up and dancing.

Trey pulled the wagon to a halt, and everyone stepped down. Abbey, Tyler, Waco, and

Miguel needed no encouragement to join the merrymakers.

Trey hadn't said a word to Dallas since intruding on her bath, that afternoon but then, they'd hardly spoken for several days. Her inability to read his thoughts frustrated her. A highly charged aura surrounded him, like a storm gathering strength.

Her own feelings weren't difficult to discern. A part of her felt awkward, out of step without her accustomed men's clothing. Security in familiarity, she'd heard somewhere. Yet a part of her, as she had pulled on her dress, had been aware of how the soft material glided over every inch of her skin. The dress made her feel wonderfully different, made her tingle in sensitive places.

Trey finished tying the team, then turned toward her. His gaze flicked over her.

The lantern light must be playing tricks on her, Dallas thought. She could have sworn his eyes held a glint of admiration. Would he say anything about her appearance? She waited. His lips settled into a grim line. He turned and stepped forward, blending into the crowd.

His indifference hurt more than she had thought possible. Dallas had no sooner lost sight of Trey than Jonas Webb appeared at her side. "I've been looking for you."

"Sorry." Dallas did her best to smile brightly. "We got a late start."

She blushed under his appreciative gaze.

"How beautiful you look," Jonas breathed as he openly admired the lavender lawn dress and her blond tresses pulled back with a matching ribbon, wisps of hair curling at her temples. "But then, I knew you would."

His compliment gave her confidence. Trey certainly hadn't commented on how she looked. She plucked up her spirits. "It's lovely. And so were the dresses you sent my sisters. Thank you."

"You are most welcome." He inclined his head. "Shall we?"

"We've wasted enough time already." Dallas accepted Jonas's proffered arm, allowing him to maneuver her through the crowd.

Dallas nodded, aware of the curious stares being directed her way as Jonas exchanged pleasantries with numerous people. She forced herself to maintain her smile, hoping everyone, and one person in particular, would notice what a good time she was having.

In the background, the band played a lively tune.

Jonas stopped and bent his head so Dallas could hear him over the music. "Care to dance?"

His breath struck her softly on the face. It wasn't an unpleasant experience, but Jonas didn't make her feel the same way Trey did. The comparison disturbed her. Was she going to compare every man she met to Trey Conner?

She wouldn't give Trey the satisfaction of searching for him in the crowd. And in case he was watching her—well, she'd give him something to look at. Let him think she was having the best time of her life . . . without him.

She raised on tiptoe, speaking near Jonas's ear. "I'd like that."

Smiling at her, Jonas swept Dallas into his arms and onto the dance floor. Despite previous reservations, she found herself enjoying Jonas's company, and she soon lost herself in the evening's fun.

Across the way, Trey glowered. He wasn't having fun. Far from it! He didn't—couldn't—miss the bright smile Dallas wore for Jonas's benefit. The little witch! A muscle twitched in his cheek from his clenched jaw.

She never smiled at him that way, he thought. His logical mind wouldn't examine the reasons why not.

As he continued to watch Dallas, Trey was caught off guard by his savage envy at the vision of her in another man's arms. He didn't know when, but he had come to think of her as his. He had no intention of letting her out of his sight or out of his grasp.

His jealousy soared like the noonday temperature. Damn! He had to stop torturing himself, or he'd do something stupid like walk up to Jonas Webb and strangle him. Webb wasn't worth hanging for. Trey spun on his heel, knowing it was in his best interest to leave and cursing the fact that Dallas remained in Jonas Webb's arms.

Needing a diversion from his tumultuous thoughts, Trey walked toward Waco, who stood chatting with some friends near a beer keg.

Trey picked up a mug and drew himself a beer. "None of you have moved from this spot since you got here." He lifted the brew to his lips. "Don't tell me you three came to a dance to stand around."

"We haven't picked out our partners yet," Waco remarked.

Trey raised a brow. "None of them pretty

enough for you or what?" He took a sip of beer.

"Naw. There are a couple who are real lookers," Drew Reynolds, the shorter of Waco's two friends, said. "We've been weighing their finer points." He cupped his hands as if he held two large melons.

Suddenly Drew stopped, his jaw going slack, and stared across the dance area. "My God, Waco, is that your sister Dallas?"

Waco glimpsed Dallas across the way and shrugged. "Yep."

"What happened to her?" Drew grinned. "I've never seen her look that way 'fore."

"She does look pretty," Waco returned.

"Pretty ain't the word." Drew whistled. "Never seen a woman dressed up so fine."

Wordlessly Trey continued to drink his beer, the whitening of his knuckles the only sign of his aggravation.

"I guess she never had a good enough reason before," Waco commented offhandedly, looking at Trey.

"I wish I was that reason," Drew said.

Waco cut him a look.

Drew threw up his hands. "Can't help it, even if she is your sister."

"No offense taken." Waco smiled slowly. "You're just stating fact."

Waco glanced at Trey. "You're looking mighty pale, Trey. What's the matter? Don't that beer agree with you?" He winked at his two companions.

Trey drained the mug, then wiped his mouth on his sleeve. "I like the beer just fine," he said in a slow, even voice.

"Then what ails you?" Waco's eyes glowed with amusement as he paused thoughtfully. "Maybe you don't like Webb sparking Dallas?"

Trey let the empty mug dangle from two fingers.

"Meaning?" Irritation packed the single word.

"Nothing." Waco dropped his gaze and kicked the dirt at his feet, but the smile on his lips lingered. "Why, nothing at all."

No one spoke for several minutes.

Waco then nudged his other friend, Rusty Williams, in the ribs and nodded in the direction of a pretty brunette. "What about her?"

Across the way, the gazes of all four men locked on the attractive woman with ginger-colored hair, her shapely figure revealed by the snug cut of a gown the color of new spring grass.

Glad to have his thoughts steered away from Dallas briefly, Trey asked with mild interest, "Who is she?"

"I think her name's Rose," Rusty answered.

"Know anything about her?" he pressed, while his gaze remained on the brunette, who was talking to another woman at the refreshment table.

"She's only got one thing on her mind—getting married." Drew's brow wrinkled. "And her ma's real mean."

Trey grimaced. That wasn't the kind of gal he needed tonight—one with strings attached. He wasn't the marrying kind. "I think I'll find someone to dance with."

Waco sobered. "What about Dallas?"

Trey's grim expression fell back into place. "She made her choice."

He left them. As he walked across the dance

area, he spotted another attractive brunette standing on the area's perimeter.

Jenny drew in an appreciative breath at the sight of the man coming toward her. In the lantern light, his black hair shone like dark velvet, his sun-bronzed skin a rich contrast against his white cotton shirt. And his eyes—she'd never seen eyes so blue, so compelling.

She admired the way he held himself, the way he moved. She liked everything she saw—and more.

Jenny wet her lips and glanced nervously at Jonas. He hadn't seen her. She knew her kind was not welcome to socialize with the locals, but the lure of the music had drawn her.

Her gaze returned to the intriguing cowboy. What would it hurt to have a little fun? Maybe he wouldn't know who she was. Jonas hadn't said she couldn't enjoy another man's company. She'd be crazy to turn down this handsome stranger.

At that moment, Dallas was berating herself for being nine kinds of a fool. Try as she might, she hadn't been able to ignore Trey. From time to time she found herself looking for him among the dancers, chancing to see if he was with someone.

Sipping a glass of lemonade while Jonas engaged another man in conversation, Dallas caught sight of Trey as he made his way toward a pretty little brown-haired gal.

She only saw his back, but she knew him by the cut of his white shirt, tapering from his broad shoulders to his slim waist, and the fit of his tight pants, outlining the narrowness of his hips. He strolled with his usual predatory gait.

Trey refused to look in Dallas's direction as he kept walking toward the brunette. He had told Dallas that he intended to enjoy himself, and he meant it. If she chose to dance with a polecat like Webb, he'd find his own company. Dallas wasn't the only woman in the world.

He stopped next to the woman. "Evening, ma'am."

"Evening."

He inclined his head toward the dancers. "Care to?"

The woman chewed her lip. "Why don't we dance here?"

"In the shadows?"

"Why not?"

Trey answered with a sensual, slow, devastating smile, his teeth showing white against the brown of his tanned skin. "Why not?" He took her in his arms, and they began their own private dance.

Dallas had moved to the refreshment table on the edge of the dance area. Trey's and the woman's laughter drifted to her on the night air.

She felt as if someone had reached inside her and robbed her lungs of their last breath of air. Why couldn't he laugh with her? Why hadn't he looked at her at all?

His early words came rushing back. *I intend to go to the dance, too. And have a very good time. I'm sure I can find a more than willing woman to share the evening with.*

The only real surprise to her was that it had taken him this long . . . and how much it hurt to watch.

Fine! Why should she care? She had the attention of an attractive man. What more could she want?

She wanted the man who held another woman.

Dallas walked back over to Jonas. "Jonas, I'd like to dance again," Dallas said with forced brightness.

Jonas smiled in return. "All right."

His smile didn't ease the hurt inside, but she'd die before she'd show Trey how unhappy she was.

The dance was a slow tune, and Jonas held Dallas close, intimately guiding her through the motions. She should have felt some stirring of attraction. She didn't. However, she continued to wear a bright smile, laughing gaily, convincing Jonas that he had her full attention.

But Dallas cataloged every move, inventoried every expression, itemized every gesture the brunette and Trey made to each other. She died a tiny bit when Trey pulled the woman closer to him, and the woman answered with a knowing smile on her face. When the woman pulled his dark head toward her and kissed him full on the mouth, Dallas learned how painful living could be.

This was the second time he had betrayed her with another woman. She was certain he had no heart—she knew hers had stopped beating.

As soon as the woman's lips touched his, Trey silently flayed himself alive for being the biggest fool of all. Instead of her kiss tasting sweet, it soured his stomach. He looked down into his partner's face and forced himself to reveal none of his revulsion. After all, it wasn't the girl's fault. He recognized her from the saloon. She might be a whore, but he sensed she was a gentle woman at heart. She didn't deserve to be hurt.

Dallas had ruined his appetite for other women. He had intended to teach Dallas a lesson. Instead, he had learned a valuable one himself. No other woman would satisfy him. It was pointless to try.

Trey pulled the woman off to the side. He set her at arm's length. "I'm sorry ma'am—"

"Don't be." She smiled. "I'm not. I enjoyed the dance."

"Wish I could've been better company is all."

She peered up into his face. "I don't even know your name."

"Trey Conner, ma'am."

Her expression clouded for a couple of beats, then brightened. "Mine's Jenny Hargraves."

"A pleasure to meet you, Miss Hargraves."

"There's no need for you to be nice to me." Jenny chewed her lower lip. "I could tell by your eyes that you recognized me."

Trey started to open his mouth, but she silenced him. "No need. I've worked my trade long enough to be able to read what's in a man's eyes."

"Makes no difference to me." He touched her cheek. "None at all." And he meant it.

Jenny sighed. "I wish I'd known you before you belonged to someone else."

Trey frowned. "Who says I belong to someone?"

"If there's one thing I know, it's men." She toyed with one of his shirt buttons. "You got all the signs of being taken, not that it pleasures me to say so."

He wanted to laugh. Was he so obvious? He hadn't been honest with this woman—or himself. What a joke. Since when had the skirt chaser Trey Conner started concerning himself with honesty? With women, no less?

Every time he thought of Dallas O'Neal—which he did at least a thousand times a day—he wanted to touch her.

He kindly took Jenny's arm. "Someday a man's going to see what a treasure he's found in you, Jenny Hargraves."

Tears brightened Jenny's eyes. "Someday," she whispered.

After he had escorted her back to her friend, Trey excused himself and went to get another beer. He needed something to cool his heated thoughts of Dallas. He took a long drink just as Waco walked up to him.

"Well?" Waco asked.

"I changed my mind."

Waco smiled. "Glad to hear it."

As the festivities wound down, Trey spent time with Miguel. The two men sat beneath an oak tree on the outskirts of the dance.

Trey lost track of time and how much beer he drank. He raised the mug to his mouth, curled his lips back, and took a deliberate drink. The beer blunted the edges of his irritation.

"Miguel, do you understand women?"

The elderly Mexican laughed shortly. "What man truly understands a woman?"

Holding the mug between both hands, Trey stared into the bottom of the cup as if he searched for answers. "Have you ever been married?"

"*Sí*, a long time ago."

Trey rubbed his forehead. "What happened?"

Miguel finished his own beer, then drew his hand across his mouth, smacking his appreciation. After several seconds, he replied, "She left with another man."

Trey fingered the glass rim. "You didn't get mad?"

"In the beginning, but after a while, I gave it up. Such things destroy a man." Miguel paused, looking at Trey. "I finally forgave her."

"What's forgiveness got to do with anything?"

"The Old Ones teach us that forgiveness and love are the medicines for the pain that we carry inside."

"And just how do you know when you've found this forgiveness?" Skepticism lurked behind Trey's expression and his words.

"When you stop punishing yourself and others, *amigo*." Miguel pointed to his heart with a thumb. "And when you feel peace in here."

Trey looked dubious.

"I can see the denial in your eyes, *amigo*." Miguel's voice was calm, his gaze steady. "Open yourself and allow the Old Ones to talk to you. Stop holding grudges. Forgive the people in your life. The Old Ones tell me of your painful childhood. If you hold on to feelings of hurt and pain, you only punish yourself."

"I don't know that I can do that," Trey admitted honestly, not trying to rationalize Miguel's knowledge of his past.

"If not, you'll only carry the painful memories in your resentment, and it will make you bitter inside." Miguel shrugged. "How can you truly love another if you are hostile?"

Trey remembered his childhood and a sad little boy looking for a corner in which to console himself because he yearned for his domineering father's approval, which never came.

"I learned at an early age not to show my feelings or emotions." Tension lined Trey's voice.

"You learned this thing to protect yourself from being hurt. But you must ask yourself why you are trying to protect yourself from love," Miguel said with quiet assurance. "When the lover is complete and whole, the mate will appear." His face was full of strength, shining with a steadfast and serene peace.

Trey wished he could find peace. Years of using his gun and traveling from place to place had left him weary. He gave a humorless laugh. "Who said I was looking for a mate?"

"We are all looking for love." Miguel's eyes glowed with inner knowledge. "Learn to forgive and heal yourself."

"It's too late for me," Trey responded with level certainty.

"You are wrong, *amigo.* Let me tell you what the Old Ones have revealed to me." Miguel readjusted his cross-legged position. "Dallas will teach you that love is innocence, and she will learn from you that love is trust."

"I doubt—" Trey began.

Miguel held up a hand. "You will teach her that love is passion, and you will learn from her that love is surrender."

"What?"

"All things will become clear in time, *amigo.*"

Trey tried to analyze their conversation, but his eyes strayed to Dallas. She was dancing with Jonas. Again! And obviously having a damned good time, too, judging by her smile.

Did she have to be so irresistibly beautiful? Did she have to laugh at everything Jonas said? Why didn't she dress him down for holding her too close? Wasn't she tired yet?

Trey's eyes narrowed as he watched Jonas pull Dallas over to one side. He took her hand, raising it to his lips, and planted a light kiss on it. A red haze settled over Trey. He wanted to yank out Webb's tonsils and strangle him with them.

By the time the dance ended and Trey made his way to their waiting wagon, his gut was coiled so tight, he was ready to hit something.

Abbey and the others made their good-byes.

Waco looked toward the west. In the distance, swollen, ripe thunderclouds banked the night sky. His gaze passed over Trey, then Dallas.

He whistled through his teeth. "Storm's coming."

Chapter 13

Trey cursed his misfortune. Beside him sat Dallas, temptation in the flesh for the return trip. Instead of focusing on the road, his gaze strayed to the creamy sweep of satiny skin exposed by the dipping neckline of her dress. He experienced the incredible urge to kiss the spot where her slender throat connected with her delicate collarbone and taste her warmth again. He imagined freeing her hair and burying his hands in its glorious wealth, feeling the silky tendrils beneath his fingertips, feeling it against his chest, his cheek, his mouth.

Feeling . . . more than he damned well should. He wanted to make love to her with frightening intensity.

How could he look at her sensual, provocative face without desiring her? And that tempting, sensuous mouth of hers, her ripe lips so lusciously lined? She was trouble for sure.

What flesh-and-blood sinner wouldn't want to feel her slender body pressed next to his, wouldn't want to tangle intimately with those long, shapely legs? What man wouldn't make love to her with his eyes? What man wouldn't want to fill his hands with those tempting breasts? Hell, he was guilty on all counts. Damned good thing that a healthy appetite wasn't a hanging offense.

He hardened with desire at the assault on his overburdened senses. On the warm night air, he could smell the tantalizing fresh lemon fragrance of her hair. He imagined hearing the soft beating of her heart. His body clamored for release.

Furious with himself and his eroding control, he brought the reins down across the horses' backs with a snap. The swelling in his tight pants never abated. Overhead, the sky darkened with sullen rain clouds. A hot, heavy, brooding feeling wafted in the air.

Once at the station, Dallas bid everyone a hasty and cool good-night, not caring if anyone wondered who had put a burr under her saddle. She trudged up the stairs, feeling overwhelmingly depressed.

Trey, on the other hand, remained locked in silent combat with his baser instincts, waiting impatiently for the others to go inside. Only after they left did he put away the team.

Angry and perturbed, he stepped slowly from the barn, intent on countering his agitation with a sedate and steady pace. The night pulsed with the sound of crickets. The air was sultry and fragrant with promised rain; the sky overhead appeared a ripe, heavy black, streaked with silver shards of lightning. Almost immediately it started to drizzle—which did nothing for his volatile mood. Already getting wet, he decided the barn was closer and turned, heading back the way he'd just come.

In a matter of seconds, gusts of wind whipped the heavens into a froth and thunderheads burst with the impending storm. As soon as he reached the safety of the barn, a drenching downpour fell.

Standing at the open door, Trey watched slivers of lightning cut across the sky in vivid bursts. Thunder rattled the heavens. The whole world seemed to tremble with the storm's mighty fury. A primitive response drew him forward. The rain trailed down his face and neck with cold, watery fingers.

Unsettled and agitated by the turbulent storm raging outside, Dallas kicked off the bedcovers and sat up in bed. She drew her legs up to her chest and wrapped her slender arms around them. Resting her chin on her knees, she listened to blasts of thunderous cannons. Her windowpane rattled with each turbulent shelling.

The storm's fury called to her. Her heartbeat grew stronger . . . louder . . . building apace with the charged atmosphere. She wanted to taste the raindrops on her lips, smell the rain's sweet scent, and feel the wind in her hair and the rain's cool kiss against her heated skin. Rising, clad only in her nightgown, she raced barefooted downstairs.

Hesitating on the back porch, she reasoned she could dry off and wait out the storm in the familiar comfort and warmth of the barn. She ran out of the house.

Just as she crossed the yard, thunder boomed overhead, followed by milk white fireworks. Alabaster flares highlighted a figure in the middle of the barnyard.

Surprised, Dallas stopped in midstride. It was Trey, his back to her, captivated by the storm.

A crack of thunder reverberated, startling even the windblown trees. Trey whirled, but showed no surprise at seeing her. For several tenuous moments, they stared at one another, each bathed in ghostly light.

With his face ravaged by the storm, Trey appeared a predator, stalking the night. His eyes stayed on her, luring her with a dangerous attraction. Dallas couldn't distinguish the pounding of her heart over the pounding of Nature's watery fists pummeling the earth.

Frightened by the tug of his raw virility, Dallas took a tentative step backward, but Trey acted with a hunter's agility and quickness and pulled her into the barn.

Fear turned into anger as she thought of him in the shadows with that other woman at the dance. He had his nerve. If he wanted a confrontation, she'd give him one. "I would've thought you'd had enough of women for one night."

"I enjoyed myself," he drawled.

"You certainly did!" Jealousy tainted her thoughts and sharpened her tongue. "As much as I did. Jonas was a wonderful partner."

"So was Jenny."

She sniffed. "I'm surprised you got around to asking her name."

He laughed shortly. "Got around to more than that."

"You're just the type to brag."

"You know I don't." His voice lowered. "Don't you, Dallas?"

She bristled with shame and indignation. "I saw you kissing her under the oak trees."

"Didn't think you cared enough to watch."

"I-I—d-d-on't," she stammered.

"Then why bring it up?"

She couldn't answer.

Several breathless, dissolving moments ensued before he released her and lit a lantern. She pressed into the shadows in feverish hope of escaping.

The smell of sulfur lingered in the motionless air as he struck a match. A luminous ribbon unfurled slowly in the darkness, then warm buttered light spilled softly around them. She stood stock-still, her widening eyes gathering the light.

The heavy atmosphere ripened with his footfalls on the straw-strewn floor as he came to her. With his approach, his gaze held her as surely as he meant to hold her. . . . Her blood sluiced through her veins in thick waves. Her heavy limbs ignored her mind's shout to run.

Wordlessly Trey captured Dallas's waist with both hands and pulled her into the circle of light. He looked down at her. Rain plastered the nightgown to her body, outlining every curve, angle, and plane of her frame. Her hair hung down her back like a waterfall. The flame twined a wreath of gold about her head and face. Anticipation tightened her features, casting her in a feverish radiance that made her large green eyes all the more expressive. She was the most alluring female he had ever known. He appreciated the shape and texture and smell . . . and fiery spirit that made her so beautiful. His sporadic breathing reverberated through him like the thunderstorm outside.

Her chest rose and fell with her own tangled breath. Her breasts were temptingly alive beneath her wet nightgown, her dusky nipples pebble-hard, and her rounded hips and curving thighs gave the lower section of the soaked garment a sharp, sensual angularity. As he looked deeply into her green eyes, which were like fine-cut glass in the flicker of lantern light, he longed for her, desired her. Surely his heart would burst from the beauty of her form and essence.

Trey didn't want to hurt her, yet he wanted her. He couldn't look at her without wanting to see all of her. The more he tried to close off his senses, the more keenly he could taste her silken, petal pink skin and her moist, hot mouth; feel the golden shower of her damp hair against his skin. The harder he attempted to pull away, the tighter he held her to him.

He tried to tell himself that it would be best if he left Dallas the hell alone. It would be best if he quit lying to himself.

He did the honest thing and kissed her.

Lured, yet terrified, Dallas struggled against her desires and Trey's actions. She couldn't fight his hot, seductive kiss, nor his innate magnetism. Her nerves were knotted cords of agonized excitement and urgency, threading from one sensitive body point to the next.

Outside, the storm raged. Inside, raw need ignited. Turbulent, driving emotions held in check too long erupted with violent, compelling urgency. She sensed the same within him by the feel of his mouth on hers, his hands gripping her.

He groaned softly as he parted her lips with his tongue and dipped inside the moist recesses of her mouth, nibbling, stroking, caressing in a primitive, sensual dance. His mouth and tongue cavorted and twined with hers . . . sanguine . . . confident . . . possessive. The kiss was a passionate blending of lips—fire and passion—heat and desire. Their breaths mingled, then escaped in feathery exhalations.

His hands slowly moved with a hushed delicacy to her breasts. The feel of his callused palms through the wet cotton of her gown was sweet torture. His kiss, his touch, mesmerized her. The feel and taste of the man soothed the clamoring of her resistance. Her heartbeat mingled with his until only one beat resounded in every fiber of her being. He bent his head, nipping the sensitive skin along her throat as his thumbs and forefingers teased her covered nipples into aching eagerness.

She had every intention of pulling away, but she had no will to act. He wrapped her in a heated embrace. An involuntary sigh escaped her. Her mind reeled. Trey Conner held her practically naked in his arms, but she offered no protest. He was the first man for whom she had felt the delicious, melting female ache to yield.

"Dallas, I need you." He cradled her face between his hands. "Make me whole." His tone sounded rough, but his hold felt so soft—so right.

His blistering touch, and his equally vehement words, caused a smoldering spark to flare, igniting her. Even the low, husky resonance of her name on his lips caused her erratic senses to blaze.

How could she fight something she wanted as much as he? She couldn't.

Trey felt a tightening as passion, molten and thick, blazed through him.

Sensing her surrender, he stared intently into her eyes. He saw his own desires reflected tremulously back at him in her passion-lit gaze. He couldn't deny himself or her.

He saw the ginger circles of her nipples with each unsteady breath she drew, saw the shadowy patch between her thighs. He moistened his lips at the thought of those soft curls against his hot, eager mouth.

A groan, part delectable longing, part bittersweet anticipation, escaped him. He gently pushed her damp hair from the sides of her face, lifted it over her shoulders, and settled the mass down her back. He stroked her enticing lips and soft cheeks with the back of a hand, memorizing the feel and contour of her.

He ached to bury himself, regardless of the consequences, in that sweet, tempting body of hers. He imagined her taut with longing, every inch of her smooth skin bathed in readiness. He lost himself in the feel, scent, and taste of her. Only her soft, acquiescent womanhood would cradle his full and heavy manhood.

He slowly unbuttoned her nightgown to the waist. The fabric gaped open, and Dallas clasped it, only to have Trey take her wrists and pull them to her sides.

"Don't," he said in a strained voice. "I want to look at you."

He parted the material with his large, strong hands and reached inside the nightgown, feeling her bare flesh. His palms moved with gentle reverence over her breasts.

He moaned as he raised his hands to her softly rounded shoulders and eased the material down her arms, revealing the tiny budded nipples and pale, flawless flesh pulsing with her heartbeat.

Her scent wrapped around him and clung to his awareness. His hand slid down the warm, silky play of skin at her throat, over the soft swell of one breast, down the perfect ridges of her rib cage, across the gentle curve of her hip. The material slipped over her hips, over the darker gleam of the downy curls of hair between her legs, until the nightgown dropped into a wet crush at her feet.

Humid night air rippled over her in rich, tingling swells.

Their eyes met. Although she flushed, Dallas didn't move beneath Trey's sensual, hypnotic stare. It was not her nature to submit, but she could find no resistance within herself. His fervent gaze caressed and stroked her in her most secret places. He opened the closed door to her heart.

She longed for him to touch her—wanting him as badly as he wanted her. She gazed at his broad shoulders, the corded muscles of his arms flexing against the sodden wrinkle of his shirt sleeves, and his large, strong hands. He smelled of rain and man. His firm, sensual mouth drew her gaze.

She raised a hand and outlined his damp, warm lips with a fingertip. "What is it about you that fascinates me so?"

She stared deep into his eyes and saw her reflection there. Odd, she could see herself so clearly. Suddenly, sharply, a strange, raw vitality twisted and tangled inside her. She experienced incredible longing within the shaky framework of her emotions.

She felt as if she were viewing herself through his eyes . . . Blue steel. Forged by desire.

Suddenly, unsure of herself, she tried to step back, but his hand prevented her retreat. He watched her intently. Even his eyes had the ability to ask questions, seek answers.

"Can you read my mind?" Confusion dusted her voice.

"Your responses tell me," he replied.

"You know what I'm thinking?" she asked in a haunted whisper.

"And feeling."

She licked her lips. "What *do* I want?"

"Us." His eyes became incandescent blue flames. "Together."

She inhaled, then exhaled on a feathery breath of air. "Is that what you want?" Danger had always lured her.

"God help me, yes," Trey avowed.

He didn't sound scornful or mocking, only begrudgingly honest. Suddenly he seized her hand and brought her fingers to his mouth. He guided her fingertips back and forth across his lips and the ridges of his teeth.

She went still, her breath a hard knot in her throat.

He took her face between his callused hands and maneuvered it near his. His mouth drifted close to hers; his lips brushed her parted ones with velvet heat. Warm, delectable sensations swirled within her, curling her insides with ribbons of delicious longing. Every inch of her tingled. Aware. Alert. She relaxed against him.

The kiss deepened, hardened, as he urged her lips apart with his persuasive tongue. Instinctively she opened her mouth wider, and he plunged his tongue in farther. He tasted faintly of salt, but most deliciously of man, a taste that she craved. Her mind ceased to function, but her senses exploded in a prism of colorful, explicit sensations. She was acutely aware of her body, taut and pulsing with desire, yet soft and willing. She felt his body, the flesh-and-blood texture of his hard persistence. She burned from the heat of her need. Her hair flowed over his arms in damp waves as his hands traveled lower and pressed against the small of her back, molding her to his eagerness.

The kiss continued until she would faint from breathlessness. She pulled her mouth free and gasped for air.

He looked down into her face. "That's only a sample, sweet Dallas."

His touch pleaded . . . promised . . . to instruct her on the enticing subject of sensuality. It was a terrifying, provocative notion.

She forced her gaze from his mouth, but she made the mistake of looking into the limpid blueness of his eyes. They held her with all the heat and intensity she felt radiating from him.

For Trey, he lived neither in the future nor the past, but in the present. Desire racked his body like a fever. He wanted this woman. He wanted to know Dallas as no man had ever known her, to familiarize himself with the feel of her skin, to dip his tongue into her womanly honeycomb and taste her chamber dripping with intoxicating sweetness.

A wave of equally powerful emotion—tenderness and compassion—broke over him. He had to steady his hands as he reached out for her, reminding himself of her innocence. His hands glided across her slender, satiny shoulders, feeling the delicate framework of bone and tissue and warmth. Her wide, liquid eyes drew his attention, lured him into her soul.

The walls of the barn receded into the gossamer circle of lantern light. Her scent sweetened the close, hot air. His world narrowed to those bewitching green eyes. The fever of desire rose in him, a knot of hunger in his gut, a throbbing in his temples, a white-hot passion filling his veins.

He lowered his head and his lips brushed her temples, the sensitive, tingling skin beneath her ear, the hollow of her throat. He lightly ran splayed fingers down her sides to her breasts, where the swollen weight filled his hands as he stroked and kneaded. When she moaned and arched her back, he smiled at the proof of the pleasure he was bestowing upon her.

He traveled the sensuous line of her spine until his hands rested on the soft curve of her backside.

He pulled her closer, lifting her until she stood on tiptoe.

When she trembled in his embrace, the tension inside Trey threatened to spill over, making his body seethe with suppressed urgency. Seeing the rapid pulse at the base of her throat, he knew she felt the strain simmering between them.

Trey struggled inwardly between two equally strong but conflicting emotions. He longed to make love to her, to make her his completely, to see her eyes soft with passion. Yet, at the same time, he knew that if he wanted to protect his heart by keeping her out of his life, he had to turn away now.

Surrendering to the overpowering urges of his body, he bent his head and covered her mouth this time with more certainty and fierce hunger.

Stunning sensations whirled inside Dallas. His mouth against hers conveyed his burning thirst as her lips opened to him eagerly.

Moments passed in a sensual blur until Trey broke off the kiss and shrugged out of his clothes.

He entwined his fingers about her delicate wrist and pulled her to him. Their bodies pressed together. The feel of him, large and pulsating, cascaded over Dallas.

His flagrant manhood pressed into her stomach. She placed her palm against his chest and felt his heart beating like a drum beneath it. His muscular body, unyielding and powerful, was solid beneath her touch. Her aching breasts longed for his touch, and the hollow feeling of wanting deepened inside her.

He pressed his mouth to hers and sought to lay claim to her with the consuming persistence of his lips alone.

Time became suspended on wings of desire until he ended the kiss. He pressed her into half shadows and backward onto a tack box on the floor.

"Trey . . ." she rasped as he knelt between her knees and began kissing her upper thighs. "Stop . . ." Her muscles and flesh quivered.

"I haven't even begun to teach you what I know about giving pleasure," he told her between flicks of his tongue and nips with his teeth that testified to his considerable expertise.

She gasped in shock and delight as his fingers buried themselves in her downy mound of hair. "Trey." Her voice tangled in her throat. "You're torturing me."

"Not as much as you do me."

"I can't think."

"Don't want you to."

He kneaded her inner thighs as he enjoyed her.

Intense, hot, stabbing pleasure began growing in Dallas, and she clasped his head in her hands, her leg muscles quivering uncontrollably.

Suddenly Trey rose and positioned her so that she stood on the tack trunk above him, her feet straddling his hips. He parted her folds of sensitive flesh with the fingers of one hand and guided her down onto his mouth and he thrust his tongue deep into her quivering warmth.

Her eyes widening, her body taut as a drawn bow, she gasped as she tried to pull away from his sinful mouth. "Oh, Trey, no . . ." She drew a ragged breath. "Please . . . I can't . . ."

She swayed, her knees threatening to buckle beneath her. Her hands gripped the back of the stall railing in a desperate attempt to balance herself as Trey continued to taste her.

Of their own shameful volition, her hips undulated against him, and her body became sleek and damp with heated passion.

Her breath came tight and fast as enjoyment built inside her to alarming, unfamiliar proportions. She tried one last feeble attempt to pull away, but determined, yet gentle, hands imprisoned her hips.

Tiny, punctuated gasps came from low in her throat as the sinfully delicious urgency built to a fevered pitch. The muscles in her legs and buttocks and stomach clenched and unclenched in delicious spasms.

As a brilliant sunburst of sensation streaked through her, she flung her head back and gave a raw, strangled cry of fulfillment and writhed wantonly against his mouth.

He continued to sample her, and helplessly she convulsed with release. Against a backdrop of wispy images of lantern light and half shadows, and the raging thunderstorm outside, she surrendered her passion, then collapsed against the stall railing, spent and breathless.

But he wasn't finished. "Now you'll be able to take all of me in," he informed her in a sensual rush of words as he stood, gathered her in his arms, and carried her with him to a pile of sweet hay.

Her release had been so all-consuming that her body was still quivering when he laid her down in the straw. Looking up at him, she struggled to draw breath as he settled himself beside her on the fresh straw.

His liquid blue eyes burned into her, and her old fears resurfaced. She'd fought her attraction for him, denying her vulnerability and need for a close relationship. But now, as she gazed into the face of this flesh-and-blood man who burned for her, she was more frightened than ever to think of giving so much of herself to him. . . .

He must have sensed her inner turmoil, for he reached out and offered reassurance by lightly stroking her cheek with his fingertips. "There's nothing to fear."

Delicately he skimmed downward until his palm caressed her taut nipples. He watched the enjoyment on her face as his hand moved back and forth.

Lowering his head, he moved his mouth over her swollen nipples, his tongue playfully flicking, then circling. Suddenly his lips closed tightly over one, drawing hard, and Dallas moaned against the sensual assault. Warmth rushed downward from her sensitive breasts to her stomach, then lower.

Her trepidation gone, she felt a necessity that was almost frantic, a hunger for him that held all the intensity of the storm raging outside. She felt as if she had wanted him forever.

"Please," she whispered, all her senses once more focused on the overwhelming contact of their naked bodies.

"Not yet." His hands urgently fondled, massaged, caressed her breasts, her buttocks.

Her skin burned from the onslaught of her emotions. She throbbed with the anticipation of drawing Trey deep within her and holding him tightly.

Trey's feverish mind thought of nothing save having her slender legs wrapped around him in agonizing delight. He was heavy and full.

He settled between her legs. Leaning over her, kissing her again and again, he touched her silken stomach and felt it quiver, then slid his hand up to cup her breast.

He hesitated at her opening. His body ached for release, but his concern for Dallas demanded he proceed slowly. He had never known desire could be like this, so overpowering, and he experienced a joyous sense of freedom and gratitude.

Only Dallas could make him feel this way. The heated velvet of her skin, the naked hunger in her eyes, and her tiny cries of pleasure fed his senses and made him feel wildly alive.

Only Trey had the power to make her traitorous body surrender itself to him with abandonment. But before reason could displace emotion, he eased into her tight passage. She gasped, breathless and startled, as the thin barrier of her virginity gave way to his insistent manhood.

Pleasure mingled with pain. She threaded her fingers in his black hair and pressed her lips to his, signaling her acquiescence. His tongue invaded her as did his velvet and steel manhood, sliding in and out of her with sure, determined strokes of living fire.

The essence of their mating flowed throughout her pleasure-heightened body, and hoarse, ragged cries spilled from her.

Flesh against heated flesh.

Soft and yielding femininity cradled hard and insistent masculinity.

A stairway to pleasure, each step covered with silk and fire until . . . they passed through its doorway.

Chapter 14

Lying beside Dallas on the straw, Trey stared at the rafters, listening to the rasp of her breath and the background sounds of the storm. God, why couldn't he have kept his emotions locked up? Why couldn't he have stayed away from her?

He sighed. He prided himself on not allowing others to know the depth of his needs. Tonight he had revealed too much of himself to Dallas, a mistake he'd make sure didn't return to haunt him. There couldn't be anything between them. His first priority had to be the running of the line. Dallas was a private concern.

Trey sat up. His gut twisted in self-disgust. In the faint lantern light, he saw the pain that flickered in her wide, soulful eyes. His kisses had left her lips swollen. His searching hands had left her hair in wild disarray. More important, he had left her tainted.

Tension clasped the back of his neck. *Damn you, Trey Conner.*

His jaw tightened. He had to make her hate

him, he thought as he established rigid control of his features.

Trey kept his voice void of sentiment. "Dallas."

She refused to look at him and threw an arm across her eyes. "Just leave."

He knew she didn't want to talk, and he knew better than to argue with her. Rising, Trey dressed and strode out of the barn.

As soon as he was gone, Dallas sat up and forced herself to breathe deeply. She wondered if he had made love to her simply because she'd been willing. His gentle and patient attention to her inexperience had been a kind gesture, but hadn't been meant to forge a lasting bond between them. Trey had entered her life, changed it dramatically, and soon would be gone.

Don't just sit here like a ninny, she told herself irritably. *Stand up and walk out of here with your head held high.*

With trembling fingers she plucked the hay from her tangled hair. She found her nightgown and slipped it on, then rose on shaky legs. She bit her lip when she saw the bloodstain on the hay. Damn her traitorous body and her passion! Were a few moments of pleasure worth the price she'd have to pay? Shame and mortification blotched her cheeks scarlet. This barn had been her sanctuary from daily troubles. Now it imprisoned her with tormented thoughts of the beautiful but brief moment Trey was hers—a moment others would call disgraceful.

She slowly walked outside.

The storm had subsided, and the fresh, moist air cooled her feverish skin. All she had left was her pride. She'd look to the future, not to the past, although this night would be forever branded in her memory . . . and her heart.

With the rising of the sun, Dallas felt her shame more keenly. She sat up in bed with a shudder. Today she would have to face her family.

She massaged her throbbing temples with her fingertips. Why had she allowed Trey to make love to her? She didn't know herself anymore.

She couldn't hide from her family; she couldn't hide from Trey.

Her thoughts snagged on his name. Trey. What would he think of her?

Would he have a good laugh at her expense, knowing she was no better than that Crowley woman? The memory of the ease with which she had surrendered to his charms made her headache worse.

Guilt stung her as she thought of their shared intimacy. She had responded with wild, reckless abandon. He would think of her as no better than a whore, just another one of his conquests. She deserved no respect because she had shown none for herself by her actions.

"Dallas?" came Abbey's voice through the closed door.

She pushed stray hair from her face. Did she look different? Would Abbey be able to detect what she had done? Thank goodness she wasn't wearing the same nightgown as last night. Nightgown! Her mind seized on the word. What had she done with it? If her sister came in and saw the dirty garment, she'd know something had happened for sure.

"Dallas, are you all right?"

Dallas leaped from the bed, then froze, caught by the discomfort between her legs. She moistened her lips. "Just a minute."

She looked frantically about the room until her gaze settled on the soiled gown tossed to one side. She rushed over to the corner, snatched the garment up, and stuffed it behind her clothes in the wardrobe.

Dallas hurried to the door and opened it. "What's the matter?" She projected a note of nonchalance in her voice she didn't feel.

"I was beginning to get worried." Abbey's brow wrinkled. "It's not like you to sleep this late."

Abbey's loving concern brought on a fresh wave of self-recrimination. What would Abbey, or Tyler, or Waco think of her now if they had witnessed her behavior last night? Shame washed over her face like a scarlet tide.

"I have a headache and didn't realize what time it was," Dallas said evasively. The words weren't a lie. Her temples did pound.

"What's the matter? Didn't sleep well?" Abbey looked at her closely. "Storm keep you up?"

No, she hadn't slept well, but no thunderstorm had kept her up.

Trey Conner was the tempest that had plagued her night. However, she couldn't place all the blame on his shoulders. Her willingness last night forced her to carry a share of the burden. She had gotten exactly what she had allowed.

Dallas's throat knotted with guilt, and she

turned from her sister and headed, with no small amount of discomfort, for the washbasin so Abbey wouldn't see the remorse Dallas knew must be stamped across her face.

"You want me to fix you a cup of tea for your headache?" Abbey asked.

"Don't bother." Dallas turned her head a fraction and forced a smile for her sister's benefit. "I'll be fine."

Abbey's eyes narrowed. "If you say so."

"I do." Dallas motioned with a wave of her hand. "Now, get going so I can dress."

When Abbey left, Dallas removed her gown, letting it slide down her body to the floor, and poured water into the bowl. She filled her cupped hands with the cool water and splashed her burning cheeks.

She glanced up and caught her reflection in the mirror. Funny, she saw her same green eyes, same blond hair, same mouth, same nose, same chin. She didn't look any different, though she felt like her insides had been stirred up and still hadn't settled.

She was the same person, but she wasn't. . . .

She raised trembling fingers to her lips as she recalled Trey's fiery kiss. Other parts of her tingled in vivid remembrance.

Had last night been a dream? No, her body responded.

Her breathing grew raspy as she recalled the feel of his moist breath on her skin, the feel of his hot mouth on hers, the feel of his velvet steel deep inside her. No matter how she longed to erase last night's memory of him from her mind, she couldn't. Her body and her mind wouldn't give up their recollection of his lovemaking.

* * *

Trey, his body as high-strung as his temper, stalked into the kitchen and headed for the stove, where Abbey always kept a pot of hot coffee.

"Where've you been keeping yourself?" Waco asked.

Trey poured himself a cup of the strong brew. "What do you want?" he growled.

Waco raised his eyebrows at Trey's brusque tone, but replied smoothly, "Thought you might help Miguel and me with some of the horses."

The cup hovered near Trey's lips. "Can't you handle things?"

"My hand isn't quite healed." Waco scowled. "Didn't think you'd mind."

Trey felt a twinge of guilt at the baffled look on Waco's face. It wasn't the kid's fault that his sister made him so mad.

Trey took a seat at the long table and sipped the scalding drink. "Let me finish my coffee first," he said, sounding contrite—almost.

After leaving the barn, he hadn't closed his eyes the remainder of the night. Remorse had hammered at him for what he'd done to Dallas.

Abbey entered the kitchen and smiled at the two men, obviously unaware of the tension slowly dissipating like so much smoke.

"Where's Dallas?" Waco asked. "I haven't seen her all morning. It's practically noon."

"Says the storm kept her up last night, and she's got a headache." Abbey walked to the stove and fed pieces of oak into the fire chamber. "She'll be down in a minute."

Nodding his response, Waco picked up a leftover biscuit from breakfast and took a bite. Abbey continued to build a steady hot fire for baking.

Trey looked first at Abbey, then at Waco. Neither one knew about last night. If they did, Trey would have already been in a pack of trouble. Not even his position as line boss would have spared him their protective fury.

But how in hell could he look these two, or Tyler, or Miguel, straight in the eye after what he'd done to Dallas? How could he justify his abuse of their trust?

Self-disgust almost caused him to choke on his coffee. The damage he had inflicted on Dallas was permanent. He'd ruined her for any other man.

He should have known better. He was older, more experienced in the ways of the world. She had been willing, but he had seduced her with his persistence and expertise. She had been naive and susceptible to his determined pursuit, and he had wrongfully initiated her into womanhood. All in the name of passion, he had toyed with a young woman's passion and had severed his friendship with this family.

God, how Dallas must hate him. Hadn't she hated the sight of him last night? He had seen the pain in her eyes. Why, for once in his selfish life, couldn't he have considered her feelings before his desire? For Christ's sake, she'd been a virgin! She had deserved tenderness and understanding. He had given her none. What kind of unfeeling bastard was he?

Damn! The sooner he was out of her life, the better. After this job, he would clear out.

So why did it hurt so much to think of not having Dallas in his life?

Trey left his unfinished coffee on the table and walked outside.

"Jenny, get that drink, pronto!" Roberts snarled from the end of the bar. "Boss don't like waiting."

You don't have to remind me, Jenny thought. *How well I know.*

She trembled inwardly at the hostility in Roberts's voice, but she carefully hid her aversion. If Roberts thought he intimidated her, he'd be pleased—and she refused to give that mangy dog the satisfaction.

Picking up a glass and bottle of whiskey, Jenny followed Jonas's right-hand man out the rear of the saloon, across the alley, and into another building cast in shadows by the afternoon sun.

Inside, the smells of sweat and unwashed bodies, tobacco, and whiskey saturated the hot, close air. Along with excitement at the prospect of bloodletting. She took in the loose-knit ring of men, heard their coarse shouts of encouragement to the two fighters. Between brief lapses of conversation, she also heard the unmistakable thud of flesh striking flesh.

With shirt sleeves rolled up to his elbows, his fists raised, Jonas stood in the center of the human fence. He circled his opponent like a predator moving in for the kill.

Jenny's insides grew cold. Jonas fought for the thrill alone. And he meant to win—at any cost. He thrived on violence and bloodshed. The use of his fists made him feel like a man.

She prayed the poor bastard who fought Jonas survived, but she had her doubts as she stared at the man's battered condition. One eye was swollen shut. Blood streamed down his chin and neck from a severely cut lip. With an arm pressed protectively to the left side of his rib cage, he grew increasingly weak with each staggering step he took. He wouldn't last another two minutes.

The man lasted one, then pitched forward, facedown, his body thudding heavily against the floor. Out cold, he didn't twitch a muscle.

A roar of approval rose as money exchanged hands and the circle of men dispersed. By twos and threes, they filed out the door, commenting with surprise that Jonas's opponent had lasted as long as he had.

Jonas wiped his forehead with a handkerchief as he walked over to Jenny. She uncorked the bottle, poured a shot of whiskey, and handed him the glass.

Always in a good mood when he won, Jonas smiled his thanks and downed the drink in one gulp. His lips drew back from the liquor's bite. His speculative gaze roamed over her. "Well, how much of the fight did you see, Jenny darling?"

"Enough," she answered evasively, knowing he wanted her to appreciate his prowess with his fists. He was a brave man when the odds were in his favor.

Jonas draped an arm about her shoulder. "Why don't you and I go back to my private room and entertain each other."

Jenny swallowed her revulsion. When Jonas drank, his mood darkened and his handling of her became rougher and more abusive than usual. She forced a smile, not wanting to incur his anger. "Sure, Jonas." Maybe things would be all right if she said what he wanted to hear, did what he asked.

"That's my girl." He guided her out the door and toward the saloon.

Jenny concentrated on keeping her smile in place, but she didn't relax. She couldn't. She knew from Jonas's expression that the afternoon would require all her energy and clear thinking.

Upstairs in Jonas's private room, she had no appetite for the late lunch served by one of the other girls, but she went through the motions of pushing food around her plate to look as if she were eating. She didn't raise her eyes, afraid of what she'd see in his.

Jenny had learned not to speak unless Jonas spoke first. He didn't. He only watched. His gaze, steady and speculative, rested on her. His earlier, lighter mood evaporated with each drink he took. The silence hung as heavy and oppressive as the heat, squeezing the hope from her.

With whiskey bottle and glass in hand, Jonas rose from the table. "What did you do last night?"

He'd never asked her how she spent her time before. Clasping her hands in her lap, she sat in stunned disbelief, thinking of the dance, until she realized he had settled into a chair near the window waiting for her to respond.

Rising on trembling legs, she walked over to him and sat near his feet, her legs curled beneath her. "Not much." The calm in her voice belied the turmoil she felt.

"What kind of answer is that?"

"I don't know what you mean, Jonas," she mumbled. *Stay calm.*

Her mind flooded with memories from last night, and her dance with Trey Conner replayed in her mind. She hadn't planned to meet Conner, or anyone else. She had wanted only to enjoy the music.

"Were you with anyone?" he pressed.

She busied her hands with smoothing the skirt of her dress. "I didn't have any customers," she replied defensively.

Jonas poured the last of the whiskey into his glass, drained the amber liquid, and set the bottle and glass on the table beside the chair. "So you weren't with any men last night?" His words were framed carefully, like everything else Jonas did.

She went cold inside. Oh, God, he knew. He knew about her dance with Trey Conner. She should've known. Jonas had spies everywhere.

"I-I-I," Jenny stammered despite her effort to keep her voice even.

"I think we've put this off long enough, don't you?" He swayed slightly as he rose from the chair, assisted her from the floor, and, with a cruel grip on her arm, guided her toward the bed.

The slanting rays of the afternoon sun angled through the window and cast the room in light and dim patches. His actions threw a shadow of dread across her heart.

Jonas clamped his hands on her shoulders and pushed her down on the edge of the bed. "I intend for you to give me a great deal of pleasure." He bent his head close to hers, his breath reeking of whiskey. "After all, isn't that what a whore's supposed to do? Give pleasure?"

Jenny's eyes closed against his degradation and his punishing kiss. Emotionally she escaped into the memory of the dance, her partner, and his kindness toward her.

She endured Jonas's embrace until he pressed her onto her back on the bed, her legs dangling over the side. She stared up at him as he towered above her and mocked her with his cruel blue eyes.

"You didn't answer me, sweet Jenny." He paused thoughtfully, then added, "Are you telling me everything?"

Involuntarily, against her better judgment, she defended herself. "I did nothing wrong!"

"Shut up," he told her. "I want to see you. I want to look at every lying inch of you." Jonas reached out and jerked Jenny to her feet.

Jenny stood rigidly before him, her vision fixed on the rug.

He buried his hands in her hair and snatched the pins from it. Her eyes watered at the pain of her smarting scalp. She felt the mahogany mass tumble about her, the soft tresses cascading below her waist.

"I keep what belongs to me until I decide otherwise." The chill of his words penetrated her to the bone. "And that includes whores. Do you understand?" When she failed to raise her eyes, he clenched his hand in her hair and yanked her head up. "Look at me!"

He stared long and hard into her eyes, his lips compressed into a taut, thin line. "Don't you know that I won't tolerate my property being handled by someone else?"

Her eyes locked with his and she remained

silent, knowing any further dispute would go badly for her.

"Everyone knows you're my whore." Jonas spoke evenly now, although his grasp on her hair never eased. "Most women in your position would be happy for my attention. But you have to be ungrateful. Why?" He tugged her face closer.

She closed her eyes against the anger radiating from his. "It was just one dance."

"One dance, you say?" His body seemed to sing with tension. "Only one dance with Trey Conner. Maybe you're the one who's been giving him information."

Jenny's eyes snapped open. "I never talked to him before the dance. I swear."

"Too late, sweet Jenny. Too late." He shook his head. "No one lies to me and gets away with it."

He delivered a stunning blow to the side of her face. Her head snapped back on her slender neck, and she swayed in his hold.

"I've been patient with you." His lips peeled back in a snarl as he crushed her to him. "But not anymore." His mouth closed on hers, and she tasted the warmth and saltiness of her own blood as he bit her lower lip. "You've gone too far this time," he muttered as he tore at her clothes.

Through a haze of pain, Jenny gathered her senses. She knew she shouldn't struggle. Without a contest, he would quickly mete out his punishment and grow tired of her. But something inside her rebelled against his touch. She struggled in his embrace until she worked free of his hold. Her feet tangled in the rug, and she sprawled on the floor.

He stalked her slowly, and deliberately, with

a look she had never before seen in his eyes. He bent over her but did not touch her. Instead, he pulled out his pocket knife.

"Why didn't you tell me you saw Trey Conner?"

She fought the panic clawing at her throat and forced herself to look up at him. "I didn't think you'd care."

"Even a whore like you isn't that stupid."

Her voice caught in her throat, but she forced the words out past cold lips. "I didn't do anything but dance with him."

"Perhaps I made the mistake of not clearly marking you as mine." His voice dropped a degree. "Something I'll amend now. After I'm through with you, sweet Jenny, no one will ever question to whom you belong."

He knelt beside her. She watched in horror as the knife blade came closer and closer. She threw her arm up to protect her face. The steel sliced down her arm, leaving a trail of blood and pain from wrist to elbow.

She waited for the next assault, but he stood transfixed, staring at her arm. "A shame to ruin such beauty, but I'm afraid you've left me with no choice."

"Jonas, please," Jenny pleaded, her breath as ragged as her cut flesh.

"You shouldn't have gone to that dance, Jenny."

She screamed as he cut her face from cheek to jaw before she fainted.

"Tyler! Waco!" Abbey called from the back door. "Everybody come on. Food's getting cold."

Dallas sat at the far end of the table. She had managed to avoid Trey all day, but her stomach clenched with hunger. If she didn't eat with the family, suspicions would be raised, and she didn't want that.

The back door slammed several times in succession as the others filed into the kitchen.

"What's for supper?" Waco asked, plopping himself down in his usual spot. Miguel sat beside him.

Abbey wiped the perspiration from her brow with the corner of her apron. "Stew and cornbread."

Tyler found her seat. "Hmm. Smells good."

As Trey settled into his place across from Dallas, she suddenly felt shy and nervous. Would he look at her with censure in his eyes?

Abbey placed a large cast-iron pot on the table and began ladling the aromatic stew onto their plates.

Miguel shoved a huge spoonful into his mouth and nodded his appreciation. "Delicious," he complimented.

Abbey brought a plate stacked with golden, grainy cornbread to the table.

Trey said nothing, but chewed a mouthful of stew.

Soon Waco had everyone chuckling heartily over his troubles with a stubborn mule. Dallas joined in the merriment, forgetting for a time her own troubles with Trey. Laughter was the medicine she needed, and she swallowed a generous portion.

Abbey gained control of herself long enough

to suggest, "If anyone's interested, I've got peach pie."

"I was wondering when you were going to get around to those pies," Tyler said. "Smelling them all day just about drove me crazy."

Abbey returned from the pie safe with the anticipated treat and cut generous slices for everyone.

Declining a piece with a shake of her head, Dallas scooted her plate aside and leaned back in her chair.

"It's not like you to pass on my peach pie," Abbey remarked.

"Sorry, Abbey, no room," Dallas said, feeling Trey's gaze on her.

She grew uneasy, but she wasn't a coward. She met his eyes squarely for the first time.

"Waco, do you think you're up to riding shotgun with Dallas tomorrow?" Trey asked, in between bites of pie.

Both Dallas and Waco spoke in unison. "Why?"

Without moving a muscle in his body, Trey slid his gaze back to Dallas. "Because I'm going to San Antonio for some new horses."

Dallas returned his regard with eyes just as resolved as the blue ones they met. "That's my job," she proclaimed.

A muscle ticked in Trey's jaw. Otherwise, he remained perfectly still. "It used to be."

Dallas's voice had a definite edge to it. "It still is."

"You're not going."

"Oh, yes, I am."

"Maybe next time."

"I choose to go this time."

"Well, uh," Waco said. "We'll let you two work things out." He jumped from his chair so quickly that he nearly tipped it over. He motioned for the others to follow.

Dallas and Trey were left alone at the table, like two prizefighters in opposing corners of a ring.

"Don't try to bully me," Dallas stated.

He gritted his teeth. "I'm not doing anything but giving you the facts."

Her chin rose. "The fact is, I'm going."

"You're not going; that's the way it is."

She shot out of her chair as straight as a Comanche arrow. "Well, we'll just see about that."

Trey lept to his feet likewise. "Don't act childish."

"Is that what you call my behavior when I stand up to you?"

Trey shoved his chair away. "I'm warning you, Dallas."

"You can warn me all you want." Her eyes narrowed. "I'm going."

They faced each other indignantly, chests heaving so hard, they almost touched.

"You've got another job to do," Trey reasoned. "Who'll drive the stage?"

"Tyler can. She's done it before."

Trey needed to make Dallas feel guilty about abandoning her responsibility as driver, and make her so angry, she wouldn't consider bearing his company. He could deal with her anger better than his feelings for her. "So you'd go to San Antonio with me and leave your little sister to deal with the danger we've faced on the line?"

"Don't think I don't know what you're doing. You're trying to make me mad so I won't go." Dallas laughed shortly. "Well, it won't work. It's just as dangerous going to San Antonio as driving for the line."

"I'm not covering my back and yours."

"You don't have to."

The tension mushroomed to an unbearable level.

Dallas knew Trey was ready to explode, but instead of pressing his argument, he gave her an exasperated look more barbed than a verbal insult. He spun on his heel and stalked from the room.

Chapter 15

Through the open window, a rooster's crow signaled the morning. Dallas snuggled between the bedcovers. Her eyes snapped open. Jumpin' Jehoshaphat! She'd overslept. She bolted out of bed, hastily splashed cold water on her face, and dressed. With her packed saddlebags slung over a shoulder, she rushed downstairs.

As she reached the kitchen, the aroma of sizzling pork and fresh-baked biscuits welcomed her. Her stomach growled.

Abbey stood at the stove, frying ham. She turned her head and smiled. "Morning."

Dallas walked to the table and dropped her saddlebags on the floor beside her. "Morning." She picked up a warm biscuit and sliced it in two, then lathered butter on the fluffy pieces. "I've only got time for a quick bite."

Abbey speared a portion of ham and laid it on a flaky section. "Where you off to so early?" She thoughtfully regarded Dallas's saddlebags. "Must be important."

Dallas poured a glass of milk from a blue-speckled crockery pitcher. "San Antonio."

Abbey's gaze cut to Dallas's face. "Oh?"

Dallas took a bite of her breakfast and chewed. Her sister's knowing expression caught her off guard, and she swallowed the suddenly tasteless fare. Color sprang to her cheeks. "Don't look at me like that!" How much did Abbey know? "It's my job to see to buying horses for the station, and I intend to do just that."

Abbey shrugged. "Have it your way."

"What's that supposed to mean?" Dallas demanded, her dander up.

"Does Trey want you along?"

"I'm going."

Abbey cut more ham and laid the thick slices in the cast-iron skillet. "You didn't answer my question."

"What do you think?"

"What I already know." Abbey chuckled. "He's going to skin you alive."

"I can handle myself."

"Uh-huh. But can you handle him?" Abbey smiled broadly. "You'd better finish your breakfast. You'll need your strength for the long ride ahead."

"I've seen that look before." Dallas gritted her teeth. "Go ahead and say it. I'll need my strength for the *confrontation* to come."

"Would it do me any good to try to talk you out of going?"

"No." Dallas washed down the last bite with a swallow of milk and wiped her mouth on her sleeve. "I better get going. If I give him half an excuse, he'll leave me." She picked up her saddlebags and slung them again over a shoulder. "He's taking me with him, whether he likes it or not."

Abbey's brow furrowed. "He's already gone."

"*What?*"

"He left about two hours ago." Abbey's scowl deepened. "I thought you knew."

Dallas slapped her thigh with her hat. "Damn him!"

Spinning on her heel, she marched out the door. She didn't slow her pace until she reached the barn.

She stepped inside, and to her consternation, found it a lonely, empty place . . . without Trey. In the silence she could almost hear the echo of her heartbeat.

Perhaps she missed him, her body taunted.

Never! her mind denied. But her body spoke louder. She remembered the hard strength of his muscular form lying beside her and the practiced caress of his hands arousing her flesh, the exquisite feeling as his mouth took hers.

More vividly, she recalled that sensual moment when he'd branded her with his white-hot possession. The intense images set a fierce hunger gnawing at her loins. Suddenly, poignantly, she ached for the sight of him.

She had cursed him. But wasn't she also damned, longing for the physical gratification he gave her? Dallas lifted a hand to run trembling fingers through her hair. Would any other man ever satisfy this lusting of her flesh?

Her motions brisk and angry, Dallas saddled her mount. She led the horse out of the barn and swung herself onto its back. Trey had a two-hour head start on her, she remembered angrily.

Kicking the mare into a canter, she struck out to find his trail.

She knew only one thing: If she couldn't forget him, she'd make damned sure that he didn't forget her.

That night, with his back propped against his upended saddle, Trey stretched his legs out. He stared into the campfire, his attention focused on the blue-tipped flames, but he remained alert to every sound.

His instincts told him that someone had been following his trail for the better part of the day. He hadn't seen any physical evidence of pursuit, but nevertheless, he felt it in every bone of his body.

Had Jonas sent someone to even the score?

Years of conditioning allowed Trey to stay calm; he had continued to ride at a steady pace as if he didn't suspect anything unusual. As soon as the sun had set, he'd decided to make camp for the night. He planned to give the son of a bitch following him a surprise—a very unpleasant one.

He stared more intently at the flames. The warmth on his skin reminded him of Dallas's fiery beauty and her passion. Why had he been foolish enough to touch Dallas? If he allowed himself to get used to her, she could become a habit. A hard-to-break one. Then where would he be?

The fire made a soft hissing sound as the ashes settled against the red glow of the embers. A breeze swept past, fanning the coal bed white-yellow. He tossed a few more pieces of wood on the fire and watched the flames leap heavenward with the indomitable spirit of one determined woman.

Dallas . . .

He clenched his jaw. No, he might have made love to her, but he wouldn't fall in love with her.

A sudden noise rudely intruded on Trey's musings, and his attention was immediately snapped back to the present. There. Straight ahead. He eased his hand to his holster and drew out his pistol.

The sound came again. Only closer this time. The crunch of rocks and earth beneath bootheels. He cocked his pistol; he brushed the trigger with his finger. He strained to peer through the night shadows.

A figure emerged from the darkness. It was little more than a shadow at the perimeter of firelight.

Trey's gaze sliced over the intruder, taking in every detail. The only aggression he saw was a variety he'd become all too familiar with. He eased his finger off the trigger and holstered the gun.

"Took you long enough to catch up with me," he said, wondering why he hadn't considered earlier that it could be his own stubborn stage driver tracking him.

"Why did you leave without me?"

"Walking up to me like that, I could have shot you," Trey said through his teeth as he stood.

"But you didn't." Dallas tied her horse to a nearby tree and moved closer to the circle of light. "Answer me. Why did you leave me behind?"

"I thought I made that clear." Trey moved next to her, closing his hand around her upper arm. "Why the hell did you sneak up on me like that?"

"Sneak up on you? Hardly." She wrenched her arm free. "A blind man could have joined you in your bedroll before you'd have noticed."

Trey forced a lid on his anger. Grudgingly he admired Dallas's abilities. No other female he knew could track the way she did, or ride the way she did.

Nevertheless, she had disobeyed him—again. White lines framed Trey's mouth. "What do you think you're doing?"

"What I said I would."

"Dallas." Irritation simmered in his voice. His temper was like steam, hissing and seething. "I told you that you weren't coming with me."

"And I told you that I was."

A muscle worked in Trey's jaw. "You think you're pretty smart, don't you?"

"I found you, didn't I?"

Tension crackled between them as they glared at each other.

"An Indian or outlaw could have found you, or didn't you think of that?" Trey said, a hard edge to his voice.

Frustration rankled Dallas. "Nothing happened."

"It could have."

"But it didn't."

"That's not the point," he said scathingly.

"Then what is?" she demanded curtly.

"Of all the half-witted things to do."

"Who are you calling half-witted?" she shot back.

His lip curled derisively. "If the shoe fits."

She smiled tightly, her malice evident in each sugar-coated word she uttered. "I know where I'd like to put my boot."

"As soon as it's daylight, I want you on your horse, headed back to the station."

She groaned her frustration. Damn him and his infernal ways! "I'm going to San Antonio."

"How will it look to others, an unmarried woman traveling with a man?"

"Since when do you care about my reputation?"

"Somebody's got to."

Mentally Dallas dug in her heels. He wasn't going to bully her. "You place such importance on doing your job." Her chin jutted at a stubborn angle. "Well, I'm simply doing mine."

Trey's senses sharpened and his pulse raced. God, he was aware . . . all too aware . . . of her nearness, her heated scent, the flawless perfection of her beauty, and his desire for her.

"You're not a man." The lines framing his mouth deepened. "Quit trying to prove you're as tough as one."

"I never claimed to be as tough as a man, and I certainly don't have to prove anything to you."

"Admit what you will, but why can't you just let yourself be the woman you are? It's no disgrace."

"It's my choice how I want to act. I don't need your approval."

But she very much had his approval.

Damn, he wanted to kiss that tempting, pouting mouth of hers.

He wanted to do more.

To want Dallas with such intensity was dangerous, because longing and affection stripped a man of his defenses. Most alarming of all, he knew he was in jeopardy of losing his heart.

"Oh hell, just stay out of my way," he finished in a heated rush of words, furious with himself and his attraction to her.

He moved to his spot near the fire and stretched out on the ground, resettling himself with his back to his saddle. He pulled his hat down over his face and crossed his arms on his chest.

Undeterred by his brusque dismissal, Dallas saw to her horse, then spread her bedroll across the firebed from him. She pulled her blanket to her chin and settled down for a night's rest. She was sure he'd see things differently in the morning.

He didn't.

When he shook her awake, he looked as surly and sullen as he had last night. "Time's a-wasting."

Rubbing the sleep from her eyes, she uncurled herself and stood, first shaking out her long legs, then stretching her arms. Every stiff muscle of her body reminded Dallas that it had been a while since she had slept beneath the stars on an unyielding bed of earth and rock. She tackled the task of combing and braiding her hair. Next, she brushed her teeth, using water from her canteen to rinse. Having finished with her limited grooming, she felt more confident to meet the challenge of a new day—and a disgruntled man.

As she tied her bedroll to her saddle, he approached her. She peered at him from beneath the concealing sweep of her lashes. A day's growth of black stubble emphasized the strong, masculine lines of his jaw and chin.

She must be crazy to insist on traveling with him.

Was he trouble? Probably.

Was he a threat? Definitely.

"We're pulling out of here in five minutes," he groused. "If you want breakfast, you'd better hurry."

She squatted beside the fire's remains and wolfed down a cold biscuit, then chased the hard lump with a cup of strong coffee so hot, it practically scalded her throat.

Maybe, albeit reluctantly and tacitly, he had agreed to let her ride with him to San Antonio, but that didn't give him the right to treat her like a slave. After all, she had a job to do. Didn't she?

Across the clearing, she watched him saddle his horse. She sensed a tension in his movements, and she was gripped by a numbing ache of dread. His distant behavior confirmed what she'd suspected: He thought her no better than a common whore.

The creaking of saddle leather and the jingling of spurs broke into Dallas's misery. She raised her head. Briefly their gazes met. He stared at her as if he could penetrate her soul. He did. She looked away first and stared down at her coffee cup. She heard him ride off a short distance.

She sat fingering the rim of her cup for a long moment, staring into the dark dredges at the bottom. She didn't need a man in her life, she reminded herself. So why could one look from him leave her feeling empty inside? She tossed the remains of her coffee into the ashes.

She swung herself into the saddle and adjusted the reins between gloved fingers. As Trey rode up beside her, she gritted her teeth.

"Keep up or you're on your own," he warned. "I want to make San Antonio day after tomorrow." With that he spurred his blue roan forward, leaving Dallas to glare at his back.

Several miles later, Dallas rode past Trey and took the lead.

Just as well, he thought. He could keep an eye on her this way. With Dallas, he was learning not to turn his back too quickly. He never knew what she might do next.

Last night he'd wanted to wrap his hands around that slender neck of hers and squeeze. But despite his anger, she had foolishly followed him.

His heart knocked against his ribs at her impulsiveness. She thought she could take care of herself, but she had no idea of the danger on the trail. She was still a woman. With a woman's body. A strong, healthy woman, but nonetheless a woman.

Headstrong and rash, Dallas acted without thought to the possible consequences. One of these days she was going to find herself neck-high in hot water.

He wanted to take her over his knee and . . . Damn, if she didn't have the cutest bottom this side of the Mason-Dixon.

He gritted his teeth. This trip was going to be as hard as he was.

In the waning hours of daylight, they stopped and camped alongside a creek. A warm southerly breeze sighed through the pecan and oak trees, their leaves making soft night music. The whispering of the wind through tall grass, accompanied by crackling firewood, chirping crickets, and bellowing bullfrogs, added harmony to the night.

After they had eaten a supper of scorched beans and hard biscuits, washed down with hot, strong coffee, they sat near the fire, but on opposite sides.

Coffee cup in hand, Trey settled back against his saddle. Taking a sip, he looked over the flames at Dallas. He nearly choked.

She sat with her back to him. She had undone her braid. She was pulling a hairbrush through her thick, blond mane, the reflection of the flames catching on the honey tresses. As Trey watched, she lifted the heavy strands off her neck. Her skin looked creamy and pale in the firelight. He wanted to plant his lips along that tempting flesh.

Apparently oblivious to him, she rebraided her hair, then rolled her shoulders to relieve the tension from the day's ride. Standing and turning slightly, she stretched her arms above her head and bowed her back slightly, her breasts straining against the material of her shirt.

God, she was beautiful. Trey's reaction to her was immediate and intense. Irritated with his response, he turned away. She was too damned beautiful for her own good—and his.

He rose to his feet, needing to put some distance between them.

Dallas watched from the corner of her eye as his retreating figure blended into the darkness. Knowing her luck, he'd be in a bad mood all the way to San Antonio. Why? Because she refused to be left behind. He would never acknowledge her abilities. She could help him, *if* he would just let her. But oh, no, his manly pride wouldn't dare allow him to take the advice or help of a mere woman. That'd be too much to ask. Men!

Sighing, she put her hairbrush in the saddlebags. Her skin felt gritty and sticky from trail dust and heat. A bath would be nice right about now. She lay down on her blanket.

Minutes passed. *Where was he?* Well, if he liked brooding in the dark, it was none of her concern. She rested her cheek atop her folded hands and sighed into the night air.

She had no idea how much time had elapsed when Trey returned to the fire, but it seemed an eternity.

She sat up. "Where have you been?"

"I went for a walk."

"In the middle of nowhere?"

Cursing, Trey sat down on his bedroll. "I don't see that it's any of your business."

"You're right." Dallas rolled to her side and propped herself up by one elbow to see him better. "It's none of my business."

"Remember that."

His thoughts skidded to a halt. Through the darkness of the trees, he'd glimpsed moonlight striking something. He tensed. A few seconds later, he saw another wink of silver reflected off . . . his instincts kicked in . . . perhaps a spur or buckle. Rider coming.

"What's the matter?" Dallas asked, her eyes wide.

Springing to his feet, he grabbed his saddle,

blanket, and rifle and strode toward his tethered horse.

"Answer me!" Dallas came to her feet and hurried after him. "Where are you going?"

He ignored her question. "I want you to stay put." His words were fraught with tension.

He tossed the blanket over the gelding's back, then swung the heavy saddle into place. He raised the stirrup, buckled the cinch, then let the stirrup down.

Drawing his Colt from its holster, he spun the chamber, counting his bullets. He then checked his lever-action rifle for ammunition.

Dallas swallowed as she watched his determined, practiced motions. "I'll go with you."

Untying his horse, Trey grabbed the reins and a fistful of mane and hauled himself into the saddle. He looked down at her. "You stay right where you are; that's an order."

"But—"

"I don't have time to argue, Dallas," he said sternly. "Do what I tell you." He spurred his horse and rode into the darkness.

Trey sat his saddle with fluid, practiced ease, yet his features tightened with apprehension. Who the hell was out there?

He hoped his imagination had been playing tricks on him.

But he knew it hadn't.

A short distance later, he reined in his horse, pulled his rifle from its scabbard, and slid from his saddle with one lithe movement. His gaze penetrated the darkness.

Tension clasped his neck and shoulders. He kept his rifle close. And waited.

Soon a horse and rider came into view, bathed in the light of a full moon. The man pulled his horse to a stop and dismounted. Dropping to one knee, he studied the ground momentarily, ran his fingers across the earth, then remounted.

Trey's breath hissed through his teeth. This was no cowboy, but a professional tracker—sent by Webb. Jonas wouldn't stop until he controlled the stage lines, wouldn't quit until Trey was out of the way.

He weighed his options. He had the advantage of surprise and could get the drop on the stranger. If he didn't deal with the rider now, he'd have to deal with him later.

His mind flashed a warning: Dallas. He squeezed his eyes shut and cursed. His eyes snapped open. The rider was gone. His mind screamed into the darkness. Dallas! What if the tracker found her? Only his pounding heart answered.

He vaulted onto his horse's back and rode toward camp. His pulse accelerated; his breathing grew ragged.

Trey always approached the enemy with cool intent, never allowing his emotions to show. But not now. Fear rode high across his features, drawing his skin into tight lines of dread.

What if that goddamned tracker had taken Dallas by surprise . . . ?

Trey remembered every cruel thing he had ever said to her. He regretted the times he had deliberately hurt her. Self-loathing tasted vile in his mouth. He would never forgive himself if something happened to her. Never.

He rode into camp and dismounted. No sign of her.

"Dallas," he called, seeing her tethered mare off to the side. *"Dallas."*

Nothing. Fear singed the edges of his heart.

Then he saw her emerge from her hiding place behind a large oak tree. He sorted through his tangled emotions until he found a safe one: anger. "Saddle your goddamned horse!"

"What?"

"We're being followed," he bit off.

"You fool," she huffed. "I'm the one who was following you."

He flexed his hands as if he wanted to strangle her. "Shut up, Dallas. And just do what I tell you."

Whirling, he strode to the campfire and viciously kicked dirt onto the flames, smothering the fire. He gathered supplies and stuffed the articles into his saddlebags, which he had left beside the campfire.

"Mount up."

"But—"

"Either you put that sweet little ass of yours in your saddle or I'll throw you, facedown, across the front of mine."

Dallas snapped her mouth shut. His threat left no room for argument.

They mounted their horses and rode out into the darkness.

Miles later, Trey stopped. Dallas slid off her horse, her legs weary from the hard ride. She walked stiffly to a nearby cottonwood tree, sat, and leaned against the trunk.

Through tired eyes she watched Trey strip the saddles from their mounts. He showed no signs of fatigue. How did he do it?

After he had tended the horses, Trey knelt beside her. "Can't take a chance on building another fire."

She stripped off her gloves and accepted her bedroll from him. "You want to tell me what all that was about back there?"

"No."

"I think I deserve an explanation why you yelled at me like you did."

"Fine, have it your way. You always do. There's someone on our back trail. I thought you might have been in danger."

She met his gaze and saw not only his fury but his fear. Understanding displaced her irritation. "You weren't angry, you were afraid for me. Afraid something might have happened to me." No longer weary, she reached out and touched his cheek.

He started to turn his face from her, but her hand stopped him. "Don't. Please look at me." Sensuality dusted her words. "How long have you cared, Trey?"

He gazed at her. He didn't move a muscle, but she felt a physical fondling as surely as if he had touched her. Her nerves and muscles tensed.

"God, for too long. I've tried so hard not to, but I can't fight you—or my feelings—anymore."

Inhaling sharply, she raised her hands and pushed his hat from his head. "Then don't." As she sank her fingers into the black velvet of his hair that hung around his lean, rugged face, her senses vibrated, down to her nerve endings.

Nothing had prepared Trey for the effect her words had on him. He might have been able to resist her if she had maintained her own anger, but this understanding undid him. His mouth swooped down on hers. Low, guttural sounds came from deep inside his throat. In that timeless moment, he was like the wolf, driven by instinct and need to claim his partner, to protect, to mate.

But when she moaned and whimpered with her own need to bond, he froze. *Don't do this if you can't offer her love.* He lifted his mouth from hers and stared into the darkness, breathing hard. *Don't cause her any more pain.*

He pulled away and sat beside her. He raked his fingers through his hair. "Damn!"

"Trey, what is it?" The words and air staggered from her lungs. "What have I done wrong?"

"It's not you, it's me."

"Don't you like kissing me?"

"Too much." His jaw knotted. "I can't stop."

Silence, tense and thick, hung over them.

"What's wrong with that?" Dallas whispered.

"Plenty. I'm . . ." His breath escaped on a long, disgusted sigh. "I'm not the man you need."

"But you're the man I want."

He gave a harsh, short laugh. "You don't know what you're saying."

"Yes, I do."

"You're so innocent, and I'm—"

"What?" she interrupted.

The words were torn from him. "Not good enough for you."

"Let me be the judge of that."

"I can't. Our being together is all wrong. Nothing can ever come of it."

She sat straighter. "What you mean is that you don't want me." Her words rang with bitterness. "Why pursue something you've already had?"

His head whipped around and his gaze pinned her to the spot. "Lord help me, if I were to make love to you a thousand times, I'd still want you. Even now I want you—even though I know it's wrong. I want you so badly . . . oh, God." He stood and walked away.

He couldn't look back, couldn't bear to see the pain in Dallas's eyes that he had surely placed there.

Never had he hated himself more than at this moment.

Chapter 16

Kneeling down, Trey regarded Dallas's sleeping profile. As he drew a raspy breath, her scent invaded his senses. His fingertips whispered across her pale cheek and along her delicate jaw.

He listened to the slow rhythm of her breathing and despised himself for causing her pain earlier. He never meant—never wanted—to hurt her. In the past, he'd always been damned sure of what he wanted. Now he wasn't so certain. He had no right to want her. He wasn't capable of giving her the love she deserved.

A stray shaft of muted silver light illuminated her face, and Trey felt a sharp pain stab his chest. In the unguarded moment of sleep, she appeared as a china doll, so beautiful, so fragile.

He was caught in finely meshed emotions. Her beauty and purity of spirit bound him to her as securely as any rope. Every fiber, every nerve, every muscle of his body yearned to be joined with her. But he knew that if he were to openly declare his feelings, she would give herself to him body, mind, and spirit.

What could he give her? Not what she needed. Certainly not love. Never love.

He settled down atop his bedroll, his rifle nestled in the crook of one arm. At that moment, getting her safely to San Antonio was the only thing that mattered.

In his office, Jonas sat at his desk and read the scant lines of the telegraph.

Not pleased with progress. Must have controlling interest soon. Do what is needed.

Frowning, he crumpled the message in his hand and tossed the wadded paper into a nearby wastebasket. He brought his hands together, his fingers forming a steeple, and pondered his options. Aggravated, he muttered a curse. These things couldn't be rushed, not if they were to be done right. He prided himself on doing a job thoroughly.

Pushing the chair back, he rose and began pacing about the room. He considered his next move. He hadn't wanted to act this quickly, but he had no choice. The investors wanted their money. And if they didn't get their share, he wouldn't get his. He'd worked too long and hard to allow this project to go up in smoke.

Jonas stopped his pacing, smiled, and opened the door. "Zeke, get in here." Why hadn't he thought of it before? It was perfect for what he needed to accomplish.

He walked to his desk and scrawled a note,

then folded it and put the paper in an envelope. He turned and leaned the backs of his thighs against the oak piece, folded his arms against his chest, and crossed his ankles.

His second-in-command sauntered into the room. "Yeah, boss?" He hooked his thumbs in his gun belt.

Jonas's eyes gleamed. "Here's what I want you and the boys to do." He handed Roberts the message. "Take care of it right away."

Roberts tucked the envelope inside his vest pocket. "Right, boss." He pivoted and left.

Jonas's thoughts pounced on Jenny. He frowned. He hadn't been able to control his rage at the thought of her being with Trey Conner. She was his, a possession like anything else he owned, to do with as he liked until he grew tired of her.

He'd beaten the girl a bit too thoroughly, and he had been forced to summon the doctor. Now the whore could die. The thought stalked Jonas like a mountain cat.

He pushed away from the desk and stepped to the window, staring out, his reflection catching in the glass pane. Although influential, he would undoubtedly stand trial if the bitch died. He might even hang. All because of a worthless whore. He gave a dry, short laugh.

He crossed the room to the liquor cabinet and poured himself a generous measure of Kentucky bourbon. He raised the glass and pressed the cool crystal against his warm forehead. He just hoped that damned country bumpkin of a doctor was good enough to keep the whore alive. He didn't relish having his neck stretched, not for a piece of white trash.

And not when victory seemed so close at hand.

Soon, and after all these years, he'd have Trey Conner exactly where he wanted him. Revenge was best served cold.

He intended to see that Trey choked on it.

The sun had not yet reached its zenith when Trey and Dallas arrived in San Antonio, a settlement of rich contrasts. Spanish and Mexican influences were found in the old adobe and stone buildings and ancient squares, which juxtaposed against typically American wooden structures and more elegant homes and hotels. The Bexar County seat boasted a variety of interests for the sporting man, from gaudy saloons to sleepy cantinas to rowdy gambling halls.

Heat reflected off the dusty street in shimmering waves that rode on the hot, still air. Horses, tethered to the hitching posts that lined the road, hung their heads and swished their tails at nagging flies. With hats pulled low across their faces, several men leaned back in their chairs, propped up against a building, the heels of their boots hooked on the railing.

Trey and Dallas crossed the main, tree-shaded plaza, stopped in front of the Menger Hotel, and dismounted, tying their horses to the hitching post.

Trey pulled his rifle from its scabbard and tossed his saddlebags over his shoulder. Dallas fetched her own belongings and stepped onto the sidewalk. With the lever-action weapon under his arm, Trey motioned for Dallas to precede him into the hotel's shadowy interior.

Dallas took in the richly adorned lobby and

wondered how Trey could afford this place. She never dreamed she'd be staying in the finest establishment in San Antonio.

When he finished registering at the desk and turned toward her, she said, "I'm surprised you brought me here."

He gave her that lazy, sensual smile she'd come to know so well. "I could hardly take you where I normally stay."

She was left speechless for once, only a telltale blush giving evidence she'd heard him.

As they ascended the stairs, Dallas turned to look at Trey. "Are we going to see about the string of horses this afternoon?"

"Yes. I don't want to have to stay any longer than necessary." He moved beside her as they walked down the hall to their rooms. "I'll meet you in the lobby in half an hour."

Late that afternoon, the sun rode low on the horizon, casting its molten-red mantle over the landscape and buildings. The peaking temperature toasted the air.

Dallas sat on the top rail of the corral and viewed the horses. She batted away the flies and groaned. Blast the infernal insects! They were almost as intolerable as Trey. He had allowed her to have her say on the best animals, then told her to wait for him while he wrangled over the price with the owner.

She removed her hat and wiped her forehead on her sleeve. Loose tendrils of hair stuck to her face and neck. The smell of manure and sweat permeated the air. Dust kicked up by hooves coated her clothes, crept down her collar and into intimate places, and gritted against her teeth. Stifled by it, Dallas longed for a bath and fresh change of clothes.

Across the way, Trey and the Mexican owner completed their transaction.

Shortly Trey joined her. For the first time in two days, he grinned. "Made a good deal with the old bandit."

The smile that teased at the corners of his mouth caused her heart to pound. She gripped the railing, her knuckles whitening. "He's a tough one." With effort she maintained a level voice. "How'd you manage?"

"Told him that I knew he got those horses from raids into Mexico."

His dazzling smile was doing crazy things to her insides. She unhooked her bootheels from a lower railing and started to push away. He lifted his arms to assist her down. Her heart beat faster as she clung to the hard muscles of his broad shoulders.

Momentarily he held her suspended, her breasts brushing his chest. Their gazes locked.

Her muscles contracted at the searingly intimate touch of his hands on her waist, her breathing shallow and sporadic. She barely noticed the wagons, horses, and people. She imagined how it would be if Trey touched her bare flesh again, and prayed he hadn't felt her quiver.

His hands remained firmly on her waist as he set her on her feet.

"Let's celebrate our good fortune tonight." The corners of his mouth turned up in a devilish grin. "I want to buy you a dress and take you out to supper."

How handsome he looked with his features softened by his lighthearted mood.

Recklessly and good-naturedly, caught in the spontaneity of the moment, she giggled. "What about the cost?"

"I can afford it."

She glanced up to his face in time to see an indulgent gleam in his blue eyes. "All right."

Her pulse accelerated upon seeing his self-assured smile. She realized how relaxed she had become with him and immediately stiffened, pulling her arm from the light grip of his hand.

Moments later, they walked inside the mercantile. The store was filled with a wonderful blend of aromas: molasses, coffee beans, fruit, vinegar, spices, and aging cheese.

With splayed fingers over the small of her back, Trey steered Dallas toward the back of the store. They passed a set of large brass scales and the black iron wheel of the coffee grinder. Tin-covered glass containers, filled with assorted stick candy, lined the counter.

Along the other side of the store ran a long bare counter for dry goods. Behind the counter, one could find combs, pins, buttons, shoes, and mirrors. Tucked into the corner was a nook for a visiting dressmaker.

"May I help you?" the proprietress asked.

"Yes," Trey said. "We're interested in purchasing a ready-made dress."

The woman's eyebrows shot up in surprise as her gaze swept Dallas's attire of men's clothing. She cleared her throat. "I'm not sure I can help you."

Dallas turned her head to hide her discomfort over the woman's disapproving perusal.

"Well, if you'd rather I spent my money somewhere else," Trey drawled slowly, belying the tension Dallas felt in his touch.

"You misunderstand me, sir." She paused to purse her lips. "I wasn't sure what type of dress you were looking for."

"An evening gown."

"I do have one dress you might be interested in. It was fashioned for a young woman just about your wife's size and coloring."

Dallas tensed at the woman's reference to her as Trey's wife. What would it be like to wake up every morning with him at her side? To love him to the point of distraction? To bear his children? She trembled as heat shimmied down her spine at the thought of her naked skin pressed intimately, hotly, against his.

The proprietress clucked her tongue, unaware of Dallas's distress as she continued, "Unfortunately, the young woman grew too fat to fit into it, and I haven't been able to sell the gown to anyone else. No one's been small enough to wear it."

She disappeared, then reappeared with a gown draped over her arms. She held it up for Trey's endorsement.

He nodded and gave Dallas a gentle push. "Try it on."

She followed the woman into a back dressing room. The proprietress chattered incessantly while she assisted Dallas with wiping the grime from her body, then slipping on the gown. Never had anything felt so heavenly as the coral faille silk and white taffeta creation sliding down her body.

Once dressed, Dallas reemerged for Trey's inspection. Suddenly she felt very awkward and shifted her weight from one foot to the other. She desperately wanted Trey's approval.

With disturbing, yet exciting, scrutiny, his gaze traveled slowly over the revealing lines of the gown. No words were necessary as pure appreciation gleamed from the depths of his eyes. The almost physical possession of his gaze sent her pulse pounding.

"I'll take it," he said in a soft drift of words, his tone implying his desire for something more than the gown.

She would have stopped with the dress, being overwhelmed at the cost, but Trey insisted that she buy white slippers, black ribbed stockings, and perfumed soap. He gave the clerk instructions on having the purchases delivered to the hotel.

Having emerged from a luxurious bath, Dallas felt renewed and excited for the evening ahead. She looked at herself in the mirror. She gazed at the silk and taffeta gown, with its jaconet underskirt and train, fitted waist, small puffed sleeves, and ribbon-trimmed neckline. Her waist-length hair was pulled back with a single matching ribbon.

Her cambric chemise and drawers, trimmed in delicate lace alternating with tucks and frills, combined with the softness of her black stockings, created a sensuous feeling down to her toes. She felt delightfully, wonderfully, wicked. Her gown and accessories were perfect. She hoped the evening would be just as perfect.

A knock interrupted her musings. Taking a deep breath, she opened the door. Trey stood in the hall. His freshly washed hair curled in dark waves about the collar of his tailored white shirt, brushing the soft leather of his black vest. He wore form-hugging pants tucked into shining black boots, emphasizing his lean hips and long, hard legs. Never had she thought him more handsome.

His eyes were alight, startlingly blue. He smiled at her, his lips curling slowly, seductively. She could imagine being a part of his world.

No, for the way that her heart leaped, it seemed that he was her world for the moment.

His gaze wandered over her. "You're beautiful," he whispered, tucking her arm into the crook of his. "Are you ready, Dallas?"

Her name was a song on his lips, his touch gentle at her waist.

Much to Dallas's delighted surprise, Trey had reserved an intimate table in the dining room downstairs. The hotel boasted a Continental chef and superb French wines.

As they entered the restaurant, Dallas was spellbound by the elegance of the subtle lantern light that bathed the room in soft, golden tones. She noticed that the tables were lavishly draped with snowy linen tablecloths and set with heavy china and silverware.

Dallas trailed her finger over the tabletop and hesitated slightly as she was seated to savor the elegance that surrounded her. She felt as if she were dreaming and desperately hoped she wouldn't wake too soon.

Dallas sat quietly as Trey ordered from the waiter who had been hovering nearby, and traced the intricate design on the tablecloth. "Would you call our trip a success?" she asked, once the waiter had left them alone.

He eyed her speculatively. "In many ways."

"Do you frequent San Antonio?"

"I'm here often enough."

"On business?" She paused, fighting down a pang of jealousy. "Or pleasure?"

"Yes."

"Which one?"

"Both."

Her lips formed the single word "Oh."

Soon food and wine were served. A violin played a sad but beautiful piece somewhere in the background, and the silhouettes of dancing couples were visible through the room's walls of frosted glass.

After the waiter filled their plates, they spoke of ordinary things and enjoyed the delicious food.

Trey leaned forward. How handsome he looked, Dallas thought, watching the soft lantern light on his rugged face. How striking. Quite unlike other men. Definitely different from other men.

Did it matter?

He threatened to steal her heart.

For so long, she had lived from day to day with meager anticipation of what tomorrow would bring.

And when he touched her . . .

She wanted to feel alive. She wanted him.

He didn't move. Not for the longest time. Compelling blue eyes touched hers, searching for something. She wasn't sure what.

"Do you like it here?" he asked at last.

"Oh, yes . . ." Dallas's entire being felt warmed by the magic of this evening. "I've never been to a place like this."

Her companion's eyes, startling blue, gleamed as he smiled. "I wanted to show you a fine time."

"Did you?" she said, her voice low and dreamy. Taking a sip of wine, she studied him over the rim of the delicate crystal glass.

"Yes." The look in his eyes matched the rich promise in his voice. "I'm glad I'm the one to show you."

"Why me?" she asked softly.

"You're the one woman I've always looked for, longed for."

"I don't deserve all this."

"Yes, you do. And more."

"Are you the man I've been looking for?"

"I hope so."

Embarrassment and confusion at his intimate confession washed over her. She desperately sought to change the direction of the conversation.

"I wonder what it's like to have a great deal of money," she said abruptly.

"Why?"

She closed her eyes—for just a moment. From the darkness behind her lids, she whispered, "I suppose because my family's never had much."

"You have love."

She slowly opened her eyes. "Yes, we do."

"You're fortunate." His voice, low and husky, hung in the air. "Some people never know the closeness of a caring family."

"Did you?"

"No." She saw a brief flash of vulnerability before he shadowed it. "But I didn't need anybody." A tinge of pain edged his words.

"Everyone needs someone."

"Do you?" His voice, though low and hushed, bordered on urgency.

She moistened her lips with the tip of her tongue. "Yes."

Her gaze met his, and she became aware of the prolonged contact. Then, suddenly, he moved beside her. His right hand touched her throat, fingers gently but firmly tracing, caressing. Quite possessively, as if it were the most natural thing in all the world. . . .

A giddy laugh burst from her lips. Something made her rise, breaking the physical contact, as if she knew she would fall hopelessly under his spell if she didn't escape now. . . .

Out of her disjointed thoughts came a question. "Why don't you ever talk about your family?"

In an unguarded moment, Dallas glimpsed the specter of anguish in Trey's eyes. "My family is a closed subject." He stood and extended his hand. "Let's dance."

The music and the wine sang through Dallas's blood as she laid her hand in his, and he swept her into his arms.

Chapter 17

When they returned upstairs, Trey unlocked the door to Dallas's room and crossed the threshold to escort her within.

"How can I thank you for such a wonderful evening?" she asked.

The warmth of her voice cascaded over him. She looked so beautiful, framed in the doorway and limned in the golden pool of lamplight from the hallway. He wanted to touch the cool silk of her dress. And her soft hair. And her smooth cheek. And her sweet mouth.

Yet his desire for her went beyond the physical. He ached to possess her in all ways, to know her thoughts and dreams, to glimpse inside her soul.

He placed his hand on the small of her back and ushered her inside. Dallas turned as he reached behind him and gently pushed the door shut with a soft, ominous click.

Trey battled with himself, caught in a churning muddle of conflicting emotions. If he took her in his arms and kissed her, really kissed her, he wouldn't let her go. How could he take the chance of hurting her again?

His passionate side won. "Will you kiss me, Dallas?" His lips curled in a faint smile.

His words, silky and soothing, seeped through her wine-induced calmness. He advanced on Dallas like Sherman on Atlanta! And she felt just as defenseless. He halted a fraction of an inch before her, their chests practically touching. His eyes had darkened to the color of still, deep water, and his gaze remained steadily upon her. Her breath caught in her throat at the intensity she saw there.

His fingers drifted close. Dallas closed her eyes in anticipation of his touch, and her stomach knotted. His warm, halting breath stole across her lips and nose. Seconds ticked by, but nothing happened. Disappointment mingled with frustration. She opened her eyes.

She found herself staring into the damnable blue depths.

"A kiss?" Her breath came too quickly and, she feared, revealed too much of her response to his request.

His smile deepened. "Just one."

With every tingling inch of her she felt his nearness, the heat, the tension. She moistened her lips with the tip of her tongue. "You want me to kiss you?"

"Yes." He reached out and touched her cheek, his hand moving downward, his fingers stroking the sensitive skin of her neck. Induced by the hot, fluid magic of his touch, sweet sensations streaked through her, and she swayed toward him.

She couldn't protest. She could only feel the power of his presence.

His lips hovered near hers. "Well, do I get my kiss?"

Seconds passed as Dallas fought for reason, for words. The wine in her blood worked against her. "I don't suppose I can deny such a modest request."

She knew, though, that a kiss from this man was downright dangerous, but she was hopelessly pulled in by the disarming combination of power and tenderness in his eyes. Her gaze dropped to his hands. Strong hands. He could inflict pain or bring pleasure.

She was being foolish. He only wanted a kiss.

Or did he?

He reached out to take hold of her arm in a firm, yet gentle, grip. His mouth inched closer to her own; his lips brushed her cheek. She couldn't fight the raw, seductive power of his masculinity. His eyes entered into her naked soul. She leaned into him, wanting more.

"Not just any kiss," he said. "But a long, slow one."

She should resist the sinful temptation of his proposal but she trembled with the powerful need to savor him. She felt his breath, soft, light, subtle, on her face, and knew that, sin or not, she would kiss him.

She wanted just a taste. . . .

His left hand slid around the small of her back and urged her closer. Her lips parted and she inhaled a shattering breath. He was so warm and hard with his muscled body supporting hers, and he held her so close that she felt the buttons of his shirt pressing into her breast. His belt buckle dug into her abdomen, and his strong thighs rubbed against hers through the fabric of her skirt and underskirt.

His strong hands caressed her spine . . .

In the shadows and half-light of a private room . . .

Male, powerful and tall, pressed against female, soft and fragrant. Their bodies spoke louder, clearer, than any words of their desire possibly could.

Dallas closed her eyes. Each slow pass of his hands skimming over her body, his fingers stroking and kneading her heated flesh, worked magic on her.

Her desire grew. She wished desperately that she could stem the passion flowing through her, yet she couldn't. She surrendered to the moment and raised her hands to his chest, her senses registering the hard sinew and muscle beneath her touch. Every gossamer fiber of sensation in her feverish body hummed at the feel of such raw, sensual vigor.

If she had good sense, she would have demanded he leave her room that instant.

Yet, at the moment, good sense wasn't her strong suit.

In a whisper of silk and taffeta, she rose on tiptoe, tilted her chin upward, his breath falling warmly on her cheek, and pressed her lips to his. She tasted wine and the warmth of his mouth. What she had begun, he finished. Her knees grew weak as his tongue intimately explored the inside of her mouth.

Before she could resist, he swept her into his

arms and carried her to the bed. His hands and his mouth worshiped her as he slowly undressed her. Never had she burned with such longing, been more attuned to every strand and fiber of sensation in her quivering body.

She lay naked to his view.

His gaze grew darker.

He left her briefly when he rose to undress. His discarded clothing joined the tumble of silk and taffeta on the floor. She regarded the distinctive contours of his wickedly sculpted physique. Unable to breathe, Dallas could focus on nothing but the man who stood before her.

By day, Trey was stirringly handsome: the enticing angles, the play of bronze skin and black hair. By night, his appearance was even more devastatingly arousing: the buttery glow from the lamp danced across his body, defining in light and shadows every rippling plane of hard, graceful muscle.

He settled himself between her legs. While he kissed her eyes, her nose, her cheeks, her chin, Trey teased her aching bud with his throbbing length until Dallas grew moist and eager for him. Arching her back, her puckered nipples pressed against his chest, she captured his face with her hands and kissed him with feverish abandon.

Never had any man frightened, yet excited, her with every inch of his hard, flowing muscles.

He slipped his hands beneath her and raised her buttocks. Mesmerized by his passion-glazed eyes shimmering in the smoky light, she moved to meet him as he slid, molten and rigid, into her pulsating depths.

The pounding of her heart echoed in her ears. She clung to Trey, melted against him, and undulated her slender hips to draw him deeper. The aching sweetness of his possession thundered through her, encompassed her entire being.

Dallas cried out wildly, surging against him, her eyes wide with raging passion. Her strong inner muscles tightened around him in spasms of pleasure, and Trey shuddered, groaning, as that shattering caress sent him over the edge.

And even then, even in a moment so primitive and overwhelming that it completely blocked coherent thought, she nearly whispered that she loved him, but instead she cried out, trembling from the force of her deliverance, and basked in the aftermath.

Withdrawing from her, he rolled onto his back, bringing her with him. Breathing deeply, he cradled her against his side, gently pushed passion-dampened strands of hair from her face, and tenderly kissed her forehead. She felt his light, caressing breath bathe her heated skin as he brushed an earlobe with his tongue. With one hand, he massaged the back of her neck until she laid her cheek against his chest.

For a small slice of eternity, they were at peace.

At last, Trey stirred and sat up on the edge of the bed, his long legs dangling over the side. Lantern light capped his dark hair in a smoky hue, the rugged angles of his face shaded.

"I'd better go to my room." His voice was heavy with emotion, and perhaps shame. "It wouldn't be good for you if anyone saw me leaving." He stood and dressed.

Dallas scooted up against the headboard and tucked the sheet beneath her armpits. Her eyes were downcast. She couldn't meet his gaze; she didn't want to see the condemnation there. Too much had happened between them to try to express any regrets. She wanted to remember her lovemaking with Trey with tenderness and joy, not with poignant remorse.

They'd have to live with the consequences of their actions.

Trey buckled his gun belt around his lean hips, then tied the holster down against his muscular thigh. He paused beside the bed and looked down at her.

His nearness compelled her to lift her gaze. His eyes were like smoke, concealing his thoughts. She sensed he wanted to reach out to her, yet he kept his arms stiffly at his sides.

"What happened was my fault," he said softly. "But I won't make promises I can't keep."

"I haven't asked you to make promises to me." Her voice wavered like a flickering candle.

"I'm sorry." Shaking his head wearily, he whispered, "I wish I could offer you more."

She nodded. She should have admired his honesty, but secretly she had hoped that he would give her the one thing she desperately wanted and needed from him: commitment. Her heart was heavy with dashed expectations.

Trey strode out of the room, softly closing the door behind him without so much as a backward glance. She stared at the now empty space where he had been. With the same certainty that she knew she loved him, Dallas knew that Trey couldn't—wouldn't—return her love.

In the whole of her life, never had she been so lonely. Silence throbbed where only moments ago Trey's vitality had shimmered in the room.

Although he hadn't been gone but a few moments, she already missed him.

She wished she could spend her life with him.

Life with Trey . . .

Shivers of remembrance bit into her thoughts. She discovered what a bittersweet experience it was to live with pain and pleasure as she relived each delicious, savoring moment. She raised trembling fingertips to her passion-swollen lips and still felt the heat of his tempestuous kiss.

She placed a hand on her flat stomach.

Her trembling sigh played like a haunting melody in the stillness of the room.

As Trey walked down the dimly lit hallway, thoughts of Dallas struck a nerve he hadn't wanted to feel. An unanticipated, overwhelming need reverberated through him. Dallas.

He didn't need her in his life, he reminded himself. He had to ride away and leave her, and not look back.

Who was he fooling? He frowned. Rather, what was it that scared him?

One answer came to mind with stark clarity—love.

He would never be able to lock away memories of Dallas, or to forget the silky softness of her skin beneath his hands, beneath his mouth.

He could never forget her hair, rippling like wheat over her breasts, demanding the harvest of his touch. Nor could he ever forget the springtime green of her eyes.

In his mind's eye, he could still see her face, sweet with pride and passion. She was a Texan, and Texans didn't know the meaning of surrender.

He knew surrender. He had wanted to reach out to her and say the comforting words that he knew she longed to hear.

Trey walked around the corner of the hallway on his way to his room. With his thoughts centered on Dallas, he never saw the pistol that smashed against the side of his head. The impact forced his head back and drove him to his knees.

Dazed, he started to rise, his body directed by involuntary reflexes. Another glancing blow caught the back of his head. Groaning, he dropped again to his knees, rocking back on his heels. He held his head between his hands. Squinting, he tried to clear his blurred vision, to see his attacker. Slowly the figure of the man came into focus.

The stranger laughed harshly. "That was too easy. Jonas said you'd be tougher. Thought you'd give me a better fight than that." The man spat to the side and cocked his gun.

Trey found the strength to rise suddenly, without warning, and charge his assailant, catching the stranger in the midsection, sending them both crashing against the wood-paneled wall. The man's head snapped back forcefully, and he sagged down the wall to slump on the floor, his pistol clattering down beside him.

The man struggled to draw a breath, his eyes wild in a white face. "You bastard." He grabbed for his gun.

But Trey was quicker and he seized the man's

pistol. He fired. The bullet punched a hole in the stranger's chest and slammed him backward. His eyes, already glazing, were full of hate as he slid sideways to the floor.

With hammer cocked again, Trey kept his gaze trained on the man on the floor. If the bastard so much as raised an eyebrow, Trey would give him more of the same.

With his last breath, the man's lungs emptied and he lay still.

Trey forced himself to ease his grip and release the hammer down on the six-shooter. He breathed deeply against the pain in his head.

"Oh, my God," came Dallas's tormented whisper in the ensuing silence.

Trey turned his aching head, blood streaming down the side of his face, and looked at Dallas, who stood in the middle of the hallway, clutching her robe about her.

Their eyes met, his hard and pain-filled, hers wide with shock. No matter how many times they saw death, most folks never got used to it. Dallas was no exception.

They had no time to say anything. Running, booted feet sounded on the stairs, and a crowd of men spilled over the landing and into the narrow hall. Trey dropped the dead man's pistol and composed himself before people crowded around the body. A spate of questions and comments riddled the air.

One man nudged the gunman's boot with his own. "Who the hell was he?"

"A hired gun who picked the wrong target," Trey commented calmly, although his head hurt like hell. "Someone better fetch the sheriff."

He walked over to Dallas, and she lifted a trembling hand to his cheek. "You need a doctor."

"No argument there." He grimaced at the pain when he attempted a smile to reassure her.

She struggled with her voice. "Is that the man who was tracking us?"

"I'm almost certain." The lines framing his mouth deepened. "And now I know who sent him."

"You don't mean Jonas Webb?"

"When are you going to get it through your head that Webb is no good and will stop at nothing to get his way? What he wants is to put the Texas Overland Stage Company out of business. And he wants you."

"Let's don't talk anymore about Jonas Webb." Torment eclipsed her eyes. "You could have been killed."

Tension rode high across his features as he touched her cheek. "Would you have cared?"

"How can you ask such a thing?"

For what seemed an eternity, he stared at her. "Would it have mattered?" His ragged whisper tumbled hauntingly past his lips.

She did not pause to think or reason, her reply spilling from her soul. "Yes, damn you!"

Opaque blackness blanketed Jenny. An occasional garbled sound penetrated her darkness.

Where was she? Was she dead?

Her head lolled to one side. Pain sliced through her. Pain meant she was alive.

She sensed movement around her, and she

heard voices. But whose? She couldn't tell.

Gradually the darkness lifted.

Beneath her hands, Jenny felt sheets instead of flooring. The softness of a mattress supported her back, instead of wooden planks. Tears of relief spiked her lashes, and her breath trembled past her lips.

She tried to raise her head from the pillow, but the effort was too much. Pain streaked through her body, and she moaned.

"Jenny."

She opened her eyes, seeking the source of the kind voice, and saw Dr. Crenshaw's benign face floating above her.

Her throat felt parched, raw. She attempted to speak, but no sound came out. Moistening her dry lips, she tried again. "Water—" she croaked.

"Yes, yes, my dear."

The doctor held a glass to her mouth, and she parted her lips enough to allow a dribble of water to seep past her lips.

She moaned when the glass was taken away. "Can't have you drinking too much," he warned. Pulling his bag beside him, he leaned toward Jenny and gingerly said, "Let's have a look at you."

While Dr. Crenshaw checked her injuries, Jenny's mind wandered.

Her breath knotted in her throat. *Jonas*. He had done this to her. Rage struck her as she recalled the blow he'd given her, then the flash of the knife blade as he laid open her cheek.

So you'll remember who you belong to, he had tormented.

How could God have created such a monster?

Somewhere within her tangled thoughts, she vowed that Jonas would never harm her, or any other woman, ever again.

Chapter 18

As the first pale fingers of dawn stretched across the landscape, Trey and Dallas mounted their horses. Amid the soft thud of hooves, the jingle of bit chains and spurs, and the creak of leather, they rode out of San Antonio, with a string of horses in tow.

Silent, tense minutes passed into hours as horses and riders kept up a brisk pace.

Dallas didn't try to draw Trey out of his deep preoccupation, but instead, kept her eyes trained on the trail ahead. As she rode, she tried to justify his silent brooding. No doubt he was attempting to exorcise his demons by maintaining a bracing gait.

She had fought a few demons of her own. How could she have allowed Trey to make love to her? Again strange things were happening to her, and she didn't know how to stop them. She couldn't lie to herself and say she hadn't wanted him to hold her and to kiss her. Since the day Trey Conner arrived, she'd been dishonest with herself, denying her fascination with him. Funny thing, though, she doubted she had fooled anyone except herself. But more sobering, she had secretly hungered for, and surrendered to, a taste of his passion.

She wondered if Trey would take her with him when his job was done, and within the same breath, she knew the answer. He would ride away—alone.

She swallowed. He *would* leave. And she had to let him go. They had no future. Even if she could stop him, she wouldn't.

But she'd never be sorry that he had come to the station . . . had come to her.

Miles later, they halted beside a small creek. Its banks were lined with cottonwood and pecan trees. A peacefulness surrounded the area. Trees spread their shadows across the water, creating a serenity that smoothed the rough edges of her nerves.

Trey dismounted and led his gelding, along with the string of horses, to water. He looked at Dallas but said nothing. His gaze, however, stayed on her, probing, searching. For what?

"Are we camping here for the night?" she asked.

He nodded.

Dismounting, Dallas led her mare to water. She removed her hat and hung it on the saddle horn, then retrieved her canteen. A gentle breeze drifted across the water. Sighing, she bent and filled the canteen.

As she straightened and capped the container, Dallas sensed Trey's scrutiny upon her. Their gazes locked. She read the desire she had come to know so well in his compelling eyes. Joy surged through her at the knowledge that he still wanted her. Then his look became distant, and his mouth hardened into sullen, stubborn lines. He led the string of horses to a stand of trees and secured them to a rope line strung between two oaks.

She watched him as he pitched camp. Part of her longed for him to stay with her—forever—yearned for his touch, craved his kisses. The part of her that dangerously, hopelessly, loved a gunman.

She chewed her lower lip. She had made up her mind early in life not to marry. She'd been afraid, still was, to trust her feelings. She was afraid of falling in love. Wasn't it better not to love at all than to know your love was doomed from the start?

Too late. Even if he didn't love her, she loved him. No power in heaven or on earth would change that, she thought miserably.

She wasted no further time in analyzing feelings that could never be resolved. After gathering wood, she built a small fire. The aroma of beans and boiling coffee soon wafted through the air. When the food was ready, she dug into the burlap sack and pulled out two tin plates and spoons. She spooned beans onto both plates and handed one to Trey.

Sitting on opposite sides of the fire, they ate in silence. Each strained not to look at the other, yet each was drawn by the force of unsated passion to watch the other.

After supper, Dallas needed time alone. Wordlessly she tossed the remains of her coffee into the fire and set her plate on a nearby rock. She rose and walked to the creek.

She strolled along the creek bed until the campfire was only a faint glow behind her. The sounds of water gurgling and grass rustling in the darkness as she passed were comforting against the frustration churning inside her. She picked up a pebble and tossed it into the water.

The turmoil of the last few days left Dallas drained of all emotions except one: confusion. True, Trey had never said in words that he loved her, but he had said he cared, and his actions spoke louder than his words. Harboring a lingering hope that she could soften him, she vowed she wouldn't give up. Not now. Not when she sensed she was so close.

Dallas felt a presence and whirled. She came face-to-face with Trey. His warmth seemed to penetrate her. She could feel his strength, feel his heat.

He touched her chin with his thumb and forefinger, raising it gently. "We need to talk."

Dallas met the steady blue light of his eyes. "All right."

Suddenly, with a glimmer of hope, she remembered something Miguel had told her once. One had to believe to keep magic from vanishing.

Magic. Oh yes, Trey's touch was magic. . . .

His knuckles moved over her cheek. "What I've got to say isn't easy for me."

Her heart sank. "Oh?"

"What were you thinking when you followed me to San Antonio?"

"I had to be with you," she replied honestly.

"Why?"

"Because I needed to be with you."

He caught her by the shoulders. Blue eyes

touched hers, searching for something. . . . She couldn't keep her longing for him from escaping as she returned his gaze.

"You shouldn't have followed me."

His cold words settled like a dead weight in her chest. She wanted him to tell her that everything would be all right.

"Why don't you want to be with me? What's wrong with me?" she cried.

"It's not you," he said wearily. "It's me. I can't give you the lifelong commitment that I know you want."

"I'm not asking for marriage," she responded.

"I've told you that I care, but we're two different people." He paused, shrugging, "We can't even go a day without fighting. It would never work."

Dallas drew strength from his impassioned words. "It would if you gave us a chance. We're both trying to make a life for ourselves. Why can't we make one together?"

"I'd only wind up hurting you."

"I'm willing to take the risk."

"But I'm not willing to cause you any more pain."

"Let me decide what's best for me."

"We can't continue the way we've been going. I don't want to do anything more to endanger your reputation."

"You're not. I know what I want, and I don't care about propriety." She leaned closer. Her heart pounded against her rib cage. "I want to be with you."

"You can't know what you're saying."

"I *do* know what I'm saying." She moistened

her lips. "What I feel for you isn't some youthful infatuation. What I feel is what a woman feels."

"There's no place in my life for a woman right now. I've got a job to do."

"Is that all you can think about?"

"No, dammit! I'm trying to think about what's best for you."

"Give of yourself what you can," she implored.

"And what would that be?" He gave a short laugh. "I don't stay in one place long enough to settle down. I make my living with a gun. What kind of life would that be for you?"

"I don't care."

"You say that now. But in time, you'd change your mind."

"You don't know that!"

"It's no good, Dallas. We've got to put an end to this."

"How can you just give up like that?"

"How can I go on making love to you, knowing I'm abusing your family's trust?"

"My family is not of concern here. What matters is that we care for each other."

"I'm not capable of the marrying kind of love. I don't know *how* to love anyone."

"Why? Because you had a rotten family life? I don't care."

"Yes, you do. Honor, pride and trust mean a great deal to you."

"Not if I don't have you."

"Oh, Dallas—"

He drew her into his arms and kissed her. It was a kiss born of slow seduction and the pure passion that made her yearn for him above all else. His masculine scent filled her, along with the penetrating warmth of his kiss. She wanted him to make love to her, and his ardent embrace assured her that he desired the same.

When he touched her . . .

She was vibrantly alive—more than at any time in her life.

Her heart opened. For his bearing, his character, his energy, caressed her as surely as any touch.

He pressed her down against the cushion of thick grass. His tongue moved, exploring, delving deeper into her mouth, stoking the fires of her passion. The stars, bright and clear, applauded them from above; the ground, rough and hard, cradled them from below. Allowing the magic to embrace her, she tasted, sampled, relished the feel of the rugged terrain of his body and the sensation of his mouth hot against hers.

She basked in his kiss, and when he broke away, he stopped and looked at her. His ardent gaze sparked heated sensations within her core. The universe became a blur of sensuous, mystical images of Trey, the warmth of him, the scent of him, the feel of him.

He rose and stripped. Dallas stared at his magnificent form, muscular and bronzed from head to toe. And boldly, flagrantly aroused.

He knelt before her and pulled her into his embrace. She held him momentarily with her eyes. Then he lowered his head and took her lips once more in fiery possession, his tongue like a sword of living heat within her mouth.

She clung to him, feeling a wild, sweet craving infuse her. She matched his fevered kiss with equal passion, her tongue twining, mating with his. She wound her fingers into his hair, reveling in the softness beneath her touch.

He broke off the kiss once again. His gaze encompassed her being like a warm caress. "How could we have ever fought this?" wondered Trey, the gunman, the man, the lover, his breath a warm huskiness whispering across her cheek.

She shook her head, at a loss. "I don't know."

"All I know is how wonderful you feel in my arms," he swore vehemently.

She cupped his face with her hands and drew him back to her. Sweet, intoxicating surrender swept through her. She wanted to touch his hot flesh, feel his power and strength. Her fingers wove themselves into the velvet thickness of his hair. She kissed him again, eagerly, wantonly, passionately.

Somewhere within the swirl of sensation, she became aware of his fingers on her shirt, then his knuckles brushing her flesh as he unfastened each button. Fire licked at her limbs, toasting her nerves and senses with sweet, aching desire. The garment fell away.

His fingers then began their conquest of the ribbon and buttons of her chemise. Everywhere he touched her, she felt as if her skin burned. She melted against him, and he enfolded her in his embrace. She rested her head against his chest.

"I don't know what to do with you," he whispered huskily.

"You certainly had me fooled." Grinning, she idly rubbed his chest with a fingertip. "Now, let me show what I can do for you."

Rising to her knees, she captured his face between her hands and softly brushed his lips with hers once . . . twice. Yet another time. Her tongue drew lazy patterns across his mouth.

She felt the anticipation coursing through his body and she inwardly rejoiced when he pulled her into his arms, held her, cherished her. He eased her to the ground with fingers moving sensuously over her cheek, down her neck, across her rib cage. He pressed his mouth, hot and eager, to the pulse at the base of her throat and ringed the sensitive area with the tip of his tongue.

Their ragged breathing blended together; their heartbeats became one vibrant tattoo.

She grew impatient with longing as he lazily lowered himself down beside her and undid the ribbon of her chemise, freeing her breasts to his heated gaze and even more heated touch. His palm cupped one satiny melon, lush, ripe, succulent. She writhed with pleasure when his mouth latched on to the precious fruit, and liquid fire swirled in a tight spiral in her womanly center.

"Oh, God, Trey . . . please," she panted in a sultry cascade of words, knowing precisely what would satisfy her craving.

She arched her hips, and he guided her out of her pants and underclothes, and tossed the garments aside. He anchored his hands on her hips and pulled her toward him. He pressed his face, his mouth, his tongue, against the concave plane of her stomach, and she sucked in her breath. His fingers caressed her hips; his knuckles brushed the sensitive flesh of her inner thighs.

He settled his body against the feminine cradle of hers, and she felt his hot, protruding manhood throbbing against her sex. She nearly swooned and closed her eyes at the intense pleasure. He fitted his form tighter to hers, and she felt the velvet and steel of him thrust into the silky petals of her womanhood. She cried out and clutched at his back with curled fingers. She felt the ebb and flow of muscle as he moved. Slowly, deeply, possessively. Her inner core erupted into a volcanic flow of hot, molten sensation. His lovemaking was pure magic—ancient as time itself.

She sensed Trey's attempt to be the patient, seductive lover. She also felt the hunger driving him, propelling his body to find ecstasy within her as he thrust hard, determined, deeply. He brought her to ecstasy with shuddering, violent release and baptized her womanly core with living fire. They grew still, their rapid breathing mingling in ragged exhalation.

Slowly, ever so slowly, her fragmented self came together and she became aware of the world around her as she knew it.

Sleek and moist, the aura of their lovemaking lingering on his damp skin, he eased himself from her and, as she snuggled into his warmth, he circled her in his arms and kissed her.

A soft breeze rippled across them—lightly, gently—anointing the lovers with utter contentment.

Trey and Dallas approached the station by nightfall the following day. Gusts of wind among the trees and tall grass carried a peculiar odor. She couldn't quite place it. Odd. And the sky's unnatural glow. Very odd.

She rubbed her eyes. She was tired, that's all. Despite what she told herself, apprehension gripped her.

Within minutes the horses grew skittish, dancing sideways, pulling against their restricting bridles and halters. Dallas's mount suddenly whinnied, then reared. Another gust of wind whipped her, the air filled with a pungent odor. The horse reared again, fighting the bit in its mouth.

Trey came alongside her. "I don't like this." His low voice carried his own sense of unease. "Something's wrong."

"What's that smell?" Even as she asked the question, her mind delivered the reeling answer: fire! Her eyes widened in horror. "Oh, my God, Trey. Fire. And it's coming from the station."

Simultaneously they spurred their mounts forward, leaving the string of coach horses safely behind.

Her heart in her throat, Dallas bent low over her mare's neck, riding with every ounce of skill she possessed. Dear Lord! They had to be safe.

Reaching the station, Dallas saw the flames. The barn was on fire. Oblivious to all else, she dismounted and ran across the yard. Roaring sheets of flame and crackling, popping wood nearly deafened her.

A pall of thick, black smoke filled the air, and Dallas felt as if she were suffocating. She coughed, then gasped for breath, but the hot air singed her throat and lungs.

She spotted the others, who had formed a bucket brigade extending from the trough to the barn, and ran to join them. Repeatedly she passed container after container to the men fighting the inferno.

In those long, terrifying minutes, Dallas ignored

her muscles, which were screaming in agony. She barely acknowledged that her labored breath grated in her lungs and the perspiration trickling into her eyes was salty and stinging. Despite the pain, Dallas refused to quit and doggedly continued to pass buckets of water.

She stopped once to look for Trey. Out of the swirling confusion of smoke, she caught sight of his soot-covered figure at the far end of the line. Nearest the danger, he threw water on the flames.

Suddenly the barn moaned—a low, ominous sound that drew all eyes and momentarily stilled all hands. Then, having sounded its warning, the wall buckled, showering those nearest with sparks and burning cinders.

Stunned, defeated, horrified, the small band of scrappers stood and watched the structure collapse. Silence stole over them as the fire roared in victory.

Trey disappeared around the back of the fallen building.

"What happened?" Dallas asked, perilously close to tears.

"I heard the horses and came to check on them." Miguel wiped the soot from his face with a handkerchief. "Already the fire burned."

"Did we lose any horses?"

"No, thank the Old Ones." His eyes reflected firelight. "They were all in the corral."

"I don't understand how the fire started," Tyler bemoaned, her voice shimmering with anger and pain. "No storm or lightning. None of us had even been in the barn since this morning." She sniffed back her tears of fury.

"It makes no sense," Waco added, his face lined with fatigue and bitterness. "Why did it have to happen to us? What'll we do now?"

Abbey stepped between the two and put one arm around Tyler and one around Waco, hugging them. "We'll rebuild is what we'll do. We're O'Neals, and O'Neals don't quit when the going gets tough."

Reality came as a raw, tremulous sigh for Dallas, and her soul ached. "We'll come back from this. It won't get the better of us."

"Let's go inside and I'll make a pot of strong, hot coffee," Abbey said. "I'm sure we could all use a cup."

Dallas nodded, but her eyes searched the shadows for Trey.

Nearing the saloon, Trey stopped for several minutes and scanned the buildings and surroundings for any signs of Jonas's men. Satisfied at last that no one was waiting for him, he carefully moved into the deepest shadows and stealthily made his way up the back steps to the second floor.

He strode down the hall toward Jonas's room, his right hand gripping a kerosene can. Rage pounded inside him, keeping time with his brisk steps. He should've dealt with Jonas a long time ago.

Trey eased the door open and stepped inside the room. Jonas, from his chair near the fireplace, shot Trey a startled look. With satisfaction, Trey closed the door behind him.

"Surprised to see me, Jonas?" Trey moved farther into the room.

Jonas pinned Trey with an insulting glare. "Not at all."

"Good, then we both know why I'm here."

"The way I figure it, someone must be pressuring you to take care of business, and you gave the order to burn the O'Neals' barn," Trey said in a voice level with conviction. "But your men got a little careless." He tossed the kerosene can at Jonas. "They left something behind."

Jonas caught the can and briefly looked at it. "This doesn't prove my involvement." He rose, his rigid carriage evidence of his annoyance. "I'm afraid you'll have a hard time trying to convince the sheriff of my culpability on the strength of this."

"Who said anything about the sheriff? I intend to take care of this in my own way."

Jonas's lips twisted with derision. "I would be disappointed if you didn't try."

For the breadth of a second, their gazes locked—Trey's determined, Jonas's hostile. The silence in the room was thick with ripening tension and charged emotions. Then the moment shattered.

"You know me, Jonas. I don't start anything that I can't finish."

Jonas's nostrils tightened. "Are you threatening me?"

"No threat, just fact."

Jonas's jaw grew taut, his mouth hardened into a cruel, menacing line, and his expression darkened with cold contempt. "You always did think you were better than me, but this is one time you aren't going to win. Before this is finished, I'll have your stage line," he taunted. "I did some checking on you, Trey. I know you're not just the line boss, but the owner."

"So?"

"So you have more at stake here than just your job." Jonas's features were animated with his rising excitement. "I intend to ruin you. When I'm through, you'll have lost everything. Including Dallas O'Neal."

Trey listened to Jonas's words with volatile emotion equally as explosive as Jonas's anger—but far more dangerous because of its lack of fire.

A muscle worked in Trey's jaw. "I'll tell you this once, and only once. Stay away from what's mine. And that includes Dallas O'Neal." Intent hardened his features. "If any harm comes to Dallas or her family, I'll hold you personally responsible and I vow I'll come after you."

White lines framed Jonas's mouth. "Not if I find you first."

"You'll make a mistake," Trey said, a hard edge to his voice. "You never could keep a cool head."

"You're no better than me." Jonas's voice rumbled with anger. "And I'm finally going to prove it."

"Claims and facts are two different things. We'll see when the time comes."

"When the time comes, I'll kill you. And with you out of the way, Dallas O'Neal will be mine. If she's as good in bed as she looks, she'll be worth the wait."

Rage shot through Trey and struck his tenuous control with deadly aim. His anger was loosed like a hunter's arrow as a vision of Dallas came to the foreground of his mind. An enraged bellow ripped from his throat and tore past his lips, and he lashed out with a punishing fist at Jonas's midsection.

The wind rushed from Jonas's lungs in a harsh rasp of air. He remained doubled over for several long moments, until he finally straightened. Hatred, like hot coals, burned in his eyes as he scowled at Trey.

Then Jonas did something that surprised Trey and inflamed his anger. He laughed.

"So the mighty Trey Conner cares about someone other than himself." His mouth curled insidiously. "Taking Dallas from you will be all the more sweet."

Trey reacted blindly and without forethought. He charged Jonas. They crashed to the ground in a tangle of fists and limbs. Only after he had inflicted sobering and crippling pain on Jonas did his anger lift.

Drawing a burning breath, then another, and flexing his bruised hands, Trey dispassionately viewed Jonas as he lay sprawled unconscious on his back on the floor. Blood trickled from cuts above his brow and under his eye, from his nose and a split bottom lip.

Trey felt a moment of intense, deeply gratifying satisfaction. Jonas had gotten what he deserved. In aces.

Trey wrenched the door open, sending it crashing back on its hinges, and stalked out.

Jonas's head jerked from side to side on the sweat-drenched pillow, his features contorting, his eyeballs rapidly moving back and forth beneath his closed lids.

He'd spent himself on the bitch, Jenny, and had pulled his withered manhood from the whore's perspiration-covered body when a black-hooded figure sprang at him from the murky shadows. Jonas wrestled with the figure, vainly trying to dodge the intruder's fists, but the intruder pummeled Jonas's face and body with bone-jarring impact.

With his hands twitching, Jonas tried to raise himself from his pillows but failed miserably. Time and again, the hooded figure landed blow after blow, and Jonas cringed at the sickening crunch of broken cartilage and bones. He opened his mouth to scream, but his vocal cords were paralyzed. The intruder continued to rain punches on him until he whimpered cowardly for mercy.

The black-clad figure stopped his assault and snatched the hood from his head. Trey Conner.

Then, strangely, Conner shifted shape and became Jenny. A gun materialized in her hand and she took aim at Jonas. Her finger brushed the trigger . . .

He saw his own death in her wide, crazed eyes.

No, no. Jonas's mouth worked silently as his mind screamed. No.

Jonas came awake with a jerk, his eyes flying open as he stared in terror around the dark room, expecting to see Trey Conner materialize from the shadows. He couldn't move. He was unable to protect himself from Conner's anger. Jonas's heart raced and the stench of fear filled his nostrils. His labored breathing reverberated in the silence, as he desperately searched for a means of escape.

Pain, sharpened by the slightest movement, ripped through him. This was no dream. This was agonizing reality.

Jonas lifted swollen eyes to the bedroom windows and saw the deep darkness. His breath burned in his lungs and parched his throat.

Conner.

Rage pounded in his temples as he recalled the beating he'd taken. As God was his witness, Conner would pay for what he'd done. Jonas spat a harsh curse.

Suddenly the door nearest Jonas's bed swung open, letting the half-light of a kerosene lantern flow into the room.

Roberts.

"Mercy, boss, are you all right?" Roberts rushed to the bedside. "I'm going to fetch the doc."

Jonas closed his eyes against the dizziness, swallowed. "Go." Pain swept over him in excruciating waves, swamping him with nausea.

He hung his head over the side of the bed and heaved. Once. Twice.

Spent and empty, Jonas collapsed against his pillows. His breathing was shallow and his face pale. Before he surrendered to the pain-induced darkness again, Jonas swore he'd see Trey Conner in hell for this!

Chapter 19

After the others had found their beds, Dallas sat at the kitchen table, her hands curled around a glass of buttermilk, and gazed about the familiar, comfortable surroundings.

For several long, numbing moments she actually made herself believe that the barn hadn't burned and stood untouched.

Yes, she could still see each weathered, wind- and rain-beaten plank. She could still sit in the hayloft and draw the familiar smells of sweet hay, oiled leather, and horses to her. She inhaled.

The odor, dreadful and acrid, of charred wood, and the pain, raw and scraping, of her throat and lungs sent Dallas tumbling back to reality.

She squeezed her eyes shut against the memory. Still, she saw every devastating detail. Only a blackened, smoldering mound remained where the barn had been.

Where would they find the money to rebuild? She opened her eyes resolutely. *Somehow they would find a way.*

She looked about the kitchen. *Thank God, the*

house hadn't burned. She felt as though the house itself had drawn her to its heart, to comfort and strengthen her. The sun would rise soon as it did every day. Life would go on as always. They would survive this tragedy. They still had one another.

The opening and closing of the back door, followed by footsteps, brought Dallas out of her reflections. She glanced up to see Trey standing in the kitchen doorway.

As she took in his appearance, Dallas felt overwhelming compassion. He stood a foot inside the room, regarding her with opaque, troubled eyes. Fatigue painted deep grooves near his mouth, and his bottom lip was split and bleeding. His features were drawn and tight, and a muscle ticked in his visibly bruised jaw. He flexed his hand and grimaced, drawing her attention to his reddened, scraped knuckles.

She wanted to go to him and wrap her arms around him, comfort him, but she knew his pride wouldn't allow it. "Where have you been? What happened?"

"It's a long story and I don't feel like going into it now." He paused and then asked, "Is there any coffee?"

"No, but I'll make some." She knew it wasn't worth pressing him for more information now.

He walked to the table and dropped wearily into a chair opposite her. "Don't bother."

"You've hurt your hand." Dallas rose. "Let me look at it for you. I can bandage it, at the very least."

"It's nothing."

"Don't be ridiculous." Her lips tightened in

concern and aggravation. "Those knuckles need to be seen to."

Ignoring his scowl, she fetched a cloth, a bowl of water, and salve. She came to stand beside Trey and set the articles on the table.

She wet the cloth. "Give me your hand."

"I'll see to it myself."

Ignoring his stubborn reply, Dallas stuck out her hand. "I said give me your hand."

Reluctantly Trey complied.

While she cleaned the bruised flesh, Dallas asked the one question foremost on her mind. "What do we do now?"

"Keep on as we have been."

"What about the horses?"

"We'll use the lean-to until another barn can be raised."

She dabbed the knuckles dry. "We don't have the money to rebuild."

She saw the compassion playing softly across his face and heard the soothing tone to his voice. "You let me worry about that."

His concern tugged at her heartstrings. "But it's not your problem."

"Keeping this line running is." He paused, as if struggling with himself, and then said slowly, "I care what happens to this family." His voice ripened with conviction. "All of us have come too far and worked too hard to let this line go under now."

As their eyes met, Dallas felt his determination reach out and touch her spirit with confidence. "So we make the San Antonio run tomorrow?"

"We've got to. Payroll has to go out. I'll need Waco to ride second shotgun."

Nodding, she applied salve to the scrapes. "This should take the soreness out."

He stood and gazed deeply into her eyes. "Thank you."

His gentle words were like balm to her bruised soul. "You're welcome."

Dallas waited as Trey hauled himself up and settled beside her on the driver's seat. Her gaze strayed to his scraped knuckles, curled around his rifle, then traveled to his bruised face. Her throat knotted with emotion.

He hadn't revealed where he'd been last night, or what had happened, although she'd tried to get answers from him. He still kept a part of himself locked away from her.

Waco climbed atop the coach as the second shotgun. He gave Dallas the go-ahead signal with a nod of his head.

Dallas released the brake and spoke to her team through the lines. The stage rolled out of the station, bound for San Antonio, carrying passengers and payroll.

She frowned. Hurt, and a dash of anger, pricked her at Trey's unwillingness to talk, to confide in her. After all they had shared, he still couldn't let down his guard. What would it take for him to trust her? She cared about him. She would never betray him or his feelings.

She glanced at Trey. By his grim expression, she knew he was aching, outside and inside. She wanted to ease his pain, but he wouldn't let her. She needed him to ease hers.

While Dallas concentrated on the road, whirling thoughts gathered like a twister inside Trey.

He clenched his jaw. He welcomed the pain of his scrapes and bruises—pain kept his hatred for Jonas Webb alive. His fury over what Jonas had done to Dallas and her family was fresh and raging.

But he hated himself, too, for what he had done to Dallas. He knew his silence hurt her, but the less she knew, the better for her. He didn't want her involved in this ugliness with Jonas any more than necessary. He had to protect her, even if it meant upsetting her. He wouldn't be able to live with himself if something happened to Dallas.

He couldn't live without her. . . .

He'd made up his mind. This would be Dallas's last run, no matter how much she protested.

Zeke Roberts leaned on the saddle horn, his view hindered by the fading light, and wiped one sleeve across his sweaty brow. Like the men with him, he grew impatient, his neck craned, his gaze fixed on the ribbon of road below.

"Zeke," the rider next to him drawled, shifting a wad of tobacco in his mouth, "you shore you got it right about that payroll bein' on that there stage?"

"Boss is never wrong." Zeke scratched his stubbled chin. "It'll be here soon enough."

Another outlaw spat a stream of tobacco juice on the ground, then wiped a bit of yellow-stained drool from his whiskers. "Zeke, I heard your older brother got hisself another gang. That right?"

"Yeah, he's running in Colorado." Zeke leered. "All that gold out there is nice pickings."

"He'd be one to team up with. Ain't no one

would cross him. He's the meanest outlaw I ever knowed."

The other outlaws murmured their agreement.

"Shut up!" Zeke barked. "Here she comes!"

The outlaws covered their lower faces with their bandannas, drew their pistols, and galloped after the stagecoach.

Dallas felt her neck muscles tighten. Danger. She could feel it.

As the stage continued at a steady pace, she weighed the possibilities of stopping now to survey the territory and then negotiating the road to San Antonio in the ever-encroaching darkness, which was a dreaded prospect. Even in the light of day, this route, with its long stretches of hazardous trail and its ample cover for outlaws lying in ambush, was one of the bloodiest stretches of stage road in the state. But she had six passengers and payroll on board and a schedule to keep. They couldn't waste time now. Maybe her instincts were wrong.

As she navigated the stage around a turn in the road, she shuddered.

Outlaws were upon them before anyone realized it.

Shots rang out from behind them. Crack! Crack!

The reverberation bit into Dallas's consciousness like the claws of a mountain cat.

Shouts and curses rose from the men inside the coach.

Return fire was launched by the passengers, Waco, and Trey as Dallas braced herself and whipped the team into a frenzied gallop.

The outlaws bore down on the coach, gaining ground.

The stage bucked and swayed, accelerating over the rut-strewn road. Driving in the dusk with the coach lanterns yet unlit, Dallas needed to hone her skills if there was any chance to keep the coach from taking a spill. Suddenly one of the steel-rimmed wheels hit a hole and lurched precariously. The vibration set Dallas's teeth on edge, but she held on to the lines.

Her heart pounded. Her mouth went dry. She gripped the lines tighter.

Trey moved to join Waco atop the stage.

The air reverberated with cracking pistol shots and rattling wheels, and the earth shook with hammering hooves. Dallas couldn't tell where the thundering ended and where her heartbeat began. Sharp needles of dread pricked her spine.

Nostrils flaring wide with exertion, muscles straining and bunching against the harness, the team maintained their breakneck speed.

Dallas squinted her eyes against the stinging bits of rock and dirt flying up from the driving hooves, and concentrated on the road beyond. The opaque outline of a building came into view. If she could reach it, there might be hope for them.

A bullet whined past her ear—so close she imagined she felt the heat. She heard Waco and Trey lay down thick fire, shell casings littering the top of the stage.

Suddenly one of the lead horses staggered, breaking its stride, and nearly went down to its knees.

Dallas pitched forward in the driver's seat, but

quickly righted herself. Using her command of the lines, she kept the coach from rolling as the horse regained its footing.

She didn't slow the team until the stage pulled into the abandoned station's corral. Along with the passengers, Waco, and Trey, she scrambled from the coach and took shelter within the crumbling stone walls.

The group quickly took up defensive positions near the gaping windows whose shutters had long since rotted and fallen off.

Squatting beneath one window, Trey checked his rifle's firing mechanism and then reloaded. Finished, he stood and settled the lever-action weapon in the crook of his arm as his gaze swept the surrounding terrain.

Dallas eased over beside Trey, hugging the wall beside the window. "Can you see anything?" Her voice trembled.

He glanced at her. "Nothing yet." His attention returned to the landscape.

She drew several deep breaths, trying to steady her heartbeat and her nerves. "How'd they know about the payroll?"

"Don't know."

Suddenly he tensed, cursing beneath his breath.

Dallas's eyes grew wide in alarm. "What is it?"

"Get down."

"But you need my gun. I can shoot as well as the next man."

"I'm not taking any chances with you. Now, get down!"

She dropped to her knees, her shoulder pressed against the decaying wall.

The seconds stretched into agonizing minutes as the defenders waited and watched.

Up a rocky slope, a horse snorted.

Trey swore violently. He raised his rifle, the tip of it sticking out the window. "The outlaws are staked out behind that incline," he whispered while sighting down the barrel.

Several more torturous minutes passed. Dallas felt every muscle in her body begin to burn from the strain of her crouched position.

Trey levered a shell into the rifle's firing chamber. "Don't anyone shoot unless you've got a clear shot. Can't waste the ammunition."

Dallas maintained fingertip control over her strained emotions and forced herself to remain in her kneeling posture.

Suddenly gunshots erupted from the rock formation beyond. Bullets ricocheted about the room. Particles of stone and wood showered Dallas.

Waco and the other male passengers followed Trey's instructions, carefully aiming and firing.

Trey squeezed off a shot, the rifle recoiling slightly against his shoulder. In the blink of an eye, he fired again.

In the distance an outlaw howled in pain.

Momentarily the outlaws' firing ceased.

"What do you think they're up to?" Waco whispered from his place beside another window.

"They know we're not going anywhere," Trey said levelly. "They'll wait us out."

"So what now?" Waco asked.

"We'll hole up in here until morning," Trey said, "and take turns on watch." He motioned to a couple of the men. "You two, go first. One near the corral. The other closer to the station."

Moving over to Waco and putting his hand on the younger man's shoulder, Trey said, "Watch the rear."

Waco nodded and went to the back room of the station.

Trey went to Dallas and looked deeply into her eyes. "I want you to find a spot and lie down." Concern warmed his gaze and his words. "There's nothing you can do at the moment."

"I want to help."

"You will, later." He tapped her chin with his index finger. "I need you to be rested to drive the stage. You're no good to me, or any of us, if you're dog-tired."

She moistened her lips. "Trey, are we—"

"It'll be all right, Dallas." His tone was low, reassuring.

Dallas discovered a room that miraculously housed a bed of sorts. She took her hat and beat the corners of the room and the bed for any lurking scorpions, rattlesnakes, or rats. She sank down on the rope springs and gratefully stretched out on the bed.

Darkness filled the room, except for a sliver of moonlight on the floor, as Dallas lay awake, listening. The silence throbbed in her ears. Exhausted, emotionally drained, she closed her eyes and tried to sleep.

Her efforts proved futile. Anger and apprehension made poor bedfellows. Would any of them come away from here alive?

She had a lot of life left to experience. She wanted the chance to live it. And now that she knew what it was to love, she knew how full life could be.

She had thought she didn't need a husband. Too many men she knew used women solely for their own pleasure.

She closed her eyes. Immediately Trey's face filled the void behind her lids. She couldn't disregard her feelings for him.

Yet she swore that no man would ever again take her love without giving his devotion in return—if she survived. Trey was the only man she had ever wanted to marry.

Tears trickled down Dallas's cheeks. She furiously brushed them away. Trey Conner had made her cry for the last time! She would face him from this moment on with strength and courage . . . and control.

The wind swirling over the crumbling windowsill chilled Trey despite its warmth. Somewhere in the distance, a coyote cried—a lonely, despairing sound.

With his back propped against stone, he stretched his legs out, thinking longingly of holding Dallas, breathing in her fragrance, caressing her soft skin. He wanted her with him, beneath him, crying out softly in hunger.

He felt the involuntary tightening of his muscles, and the accompanying pain that sliced through him. He might not have the chance to hold her again, to experience her intensity, her spirit, her passion for life itself.

Life . . . Their chances of leaving here alive were slim.

Trey closed his eyes tightly, squeezing dire

images from his mind. Fatigue hammered at him, but he steeled himself for the fight to come. He knew their attackers were after more than just the payroll.

Morning's first light didn't wake Dallas—gunfire did. More specifically, the unmistakable sound of a bullet thudding into the bedroom wall. Sharp cracks pierced the cool gray morning, and Dallas sprang from the bed, her eyes wide, her hair mussed from sleep.

She collided with Trey in the doorway. He caught her as she rebounded off the muscular wall of his chest. "Are you all right?"

"Yes." Through the open window she could see the fire of reporting guns from a rock outcropping several yards away. "What's happening?"

"It seems our friends haven't given up." Anger rode high across his features. "During the night, they killed the two lookouts and drove off the horses."

She clutched at his sleeve, afraid to ask, "Waco?"

"He's fine." Trey retrieved a pistol and handed it to her. "Just in case. But you should be safe if you stay here, away from the window."

There was another explosion, followed by the whine of bullets. One whistled past her face and slammed into the wall behind her. Stunned, she whirled, her features pale and drawn.

The bullet had barely lodged in a splintering of wood and mud before it was followed by more shots. A second bullet grazed her cheek. A third barely missed her.

"Damn it, get down!"

Trey threw her to the floor, protecting her with his body. He crouched by the window, taking careful aim before firing. He squeezed off several deafening shots. The acrid smell of gunpowder burned in her nostrils.

He turned to her. "You weren't hit, were you?" His voice held an odd catch.

She shook her head, her throat tight from fear. "They're not going to give up, are they?"

Trey scowled. "No."

"How much longer . . . before they . . . before we . . . ?" She couldn't force the words out.

"Before we run out of ammunition?" Trey finished. "We've got about six rounds each. Got to make every shot count." He grinned suddenly. "Where's my stubborn Dallas? If you can put me in my place, you can handle a few outlaws."

Despite her anxiety, she returned his smile. "You're certainly worse than one."

"You got that right. Listen, one of the passengers was shot," he said, the moment of levity gone. "He's in the back room with Waco. Would you check on him?"

"Yes, of course."

Grateful to have something to occupy her time, she headed to the back room, where she found Waco staring out the window. The passenger, covered by a blanket, reclined in a corner. His eyes were closed and his breathing came in shallow drifts. For one chilling moment, she wondered if he might be dead.

She knelt beside him, pulled back the blanket, and checked the makeshift bloodied bandage that bound his ravaged abdomen.

At her soft probing touch, he opened his weary, red-rimmed eyes. "Thank you." He smiled weakly at her. "I reckon at a time like this, a man doesn't want to be alone."

"I'm glad I can help." She forced a smile of her own, although she noted his face was etched with pain and his skin was a disheartening sallow color. "Don't talk too much. You need your rest."

She reached for a nearby canteen and raised it to his mouth. He managed to swallow a small amount of water. She pressed her hand to his forehead, the skin hot to her touch. Infection had already set in.

His eyes closed; his chin dropped to his chest.

She cast Waco a despairing glance. "I don't think I can do much for him."

Waco encouraged Dallas. "Do what you can."

She hated waste, and that's what senseless killing was—sheer waste. In the West, a man's horse held more value than a man's life, she thought bitterly.

She glanced at her patient. Periodically she moistened her bandanna from the canteen and wiped his feverish brow, although he had slipped into unconsciousness.

Time passed as she kept watch over the man.

Rising, she stretched her sore, cramped muscles and joined Waco at the window.

The sun rode low on the western horizon, casting the clouds in shades of lilac, gold, and crimson.

"Beautiful, isn't it?" Waco said softly.

"Yes." She rested her head against his shoulder.

Neither spoke of the possibility that they were admiring their last sunset.

Dallas looked toward the rock formation. Although she couldn't see the outlaws, she felt certain they were there.

Guessing her thoughts, Waco said, "I don't think they'll attack past dark. They want the money, but they want their fun, too. Just like shooting fish in a barrel. They want to be able to see us squirm." He hissed through his teeth. "Bastards."

"Waco? Can we make it out alive?"

"Don't know."

Again they fell silent.

Waco moved from the window and pulled some jerky from a sack. He handed her some. "You'd better eat something."

She took the food from him. "Thanks." She bit off a piece and chewed. Swallowing, she said, "I sure miss Abbey's cooking at times like this."

"Yeah, I know, but let's don't tell her." Waco gave her a crooked smile. "Don't want her thinking she's special."

Dallas uncapped the canteen and took a sip. The tepid water slid down her dusty, parched throat. Wiping her mouth on her sleeve, she passed the container to Waco.

"I'm going to see if I can get some rest," Dallas groaned, fatigued. "Call if you need me."

"I will."

She slipped back to her room and sank down onto the bed. She tossed and turned, until at last she drifted into an exhausted sleep.

The rattling of a wind-whipped shutter awakened her.

Movement near the bed caught her eye.

She wasn't alone.

Someone was watching her.

She held her breath and waited.

"I came to check on you." Trey stood beside the bed, watching her. "I didn't mean to wake you."

She released the pent-up air from her lungs and replied, "You didn't wake me." She gestured toward the window. "The banging shutter did."

"Try to go back to sleep." He started to turn away.

She stopped him with a hand on his arm. "Don't go," she whispered. "I'd rather have the company than the sleep."

He looked at her. Her eyes were wide, her lips trembling.

"Are they still there?" she whispered.

He heard her words, but he felt her silken voice shimmer across him and wrap around his soul.

"Yes," he replied thickly.

As an officer during the war, later as a gunman, he'd lived too long with death as a constant companion. He didn't fear dying, but seeing the evidence of Dallas's fear tore at him. Even harder for him to endure was the guilt he felt for her being here, trapped in this abandoned station with those bastards outside moving in for the kill.

"Please, hold me," she whispered.

With a low, anguished moan, Trey pulled her to her feet and into his arms. She twined her arms about his neck and clung to him.

He pressed his mouth to hers and kissed her

passionately. Hungrily, impatiently, she returned his kiss and deepened the gesture when her tongue darted inside his mouth.

He wrapped his fingers in her hair. Strands the color of sun-ripened wheat streamed past her slender shoulders as his lips trailed across her soft cheek. She whimpered low in her throat while his mouth sought her eyelids and temples to brand her as his.

"I didn't think I was afraid of anything," she said in a low, haunting voice. "I was wrong. I'm afraid we'll never get out of here. I'm afraid of never knowing what I've lost. I'm afraid of dying."

He smoothed her hair, then cupped her face, her skin cool in his hands as he lifted her mouth to his. "I'm here," he said gently before his mouth descended upon hers again.

He brushed her lips with languorous, feather-soft strokes, and his hands moved down the graceful line of her spine and cupped her soft bottom, molding her body closer against the hardness and detail of him. Urgently, demandingly, he claimed her with his mouth, and her lips parted with a sigh. Her tongue darted past his pliant lips and filled him with desire, while his hands, still tangled in her mane of thick hair, gripped her tighter. She writhed in his embrace.

With great effort, he restrained his almost overwhelming desire for fulfillment, causing him to tremble with the depth and scope of his need.

"I'm so afraid, Trey."

"Shh."

"I'm afraid of losing you, afraid of losing myself to you. Suddenly I'm such a coward."

"I've never known you to be a coward. It takes courage to face the things you have. I admire your strength."

"Where is my strength now?"

"In my arms, Dallas," he said thickly. "My love."

"I love you, too." Her voice conveyed all heartfelt emotion.

For several moments they remained in each other's arms, as if neither could bear to part.

Then he took her hand in his and led her to a corner of the room. There he sat down with his back against the wall, his legs stretched out, and pulled her down beside him, where she rested her head in his lap.

He idly stroked her hair.

"Won't you tell me something about yourself?" she asked.

For a moment she thought he wasn't going to answer her, then he said, "My parents didn't know anything about love."

"Where are your parents?"

His hand stopped its slow, drifting strokes of her hair. "Father died when I was young. Mother remarried."

Her heart ached at the sadness she discerned in his voice. For the neglected, lonely boy in Trey, she offered her compassion. "I'm so sorry."

"Don't be."

Dallas wanted to wipe the painful memories from his mind . . . and his heart.

She raised herself up on her elbow and kissed

his lips. "I would never hurt you," she whispered. "I love you." Her words were adrift with sensuality.

"And I love you," came his heated reply. "God help me, I do."

His confession flowed over her like golden honey, sweet and delectable. Oh, how long she'd prayed to hear those words. She pulled them to her heart.

"Then God help us both," she replied.

"Now that we've found each other, I wish I had all the time in the world to love you."

"Tell me how you'd love me."

"I'd make sure that you were well satisfied, so you'd never look at another man."

"And?"

"I'd kiss you all over, slowly, until your body trembled. I'd taste every sweet inch of you, knowing I hungered for you only."

"Go on," she whispered.

"I'd watch you grow fat with each one of the babies I'd want and love to give you. Every evening I'd want to sit on the front porch of our house and watch the sunset with you." He hesitated. "What about you?"

"I'd lie next to you at night and watch you sleep, knowing how much I loved you, knowing you belonged to me. I'd sit before the fire with your arms wrapped around me and know how safe and loved I was." She paused momentarily, then her voice dropped. "Any regrets?"

"If I hadn't allowed you to drive, you wouldn't be in this mess."

"You couldn't have stopped me."

"Do you have any regrets?" he asked.

"That I didn't tell you sooner about how you've changed my life. Forever."

They remained in each other's arms for a long time.

Miguel and Tyler walked into the tiny office, illuminated in smoky, hissing lantern light, and closed the door behind them. Sheriff Jeffrey looked up from his supper of fried chicken.

Harlan Jeffrey was a bear of a man, with hands as big as a grizzly and a grip to match. He sported a thick brown mustache, bushy brown eyebrows, and a head full of unruly brown hair.

He wiped his mouth on the corner of a red and white gingham napkin tucked inside his shirtfront and rose. "Miss Tyler, Miguel. What can I do for you?" he asked, his voice a low rumble.

"We have an urgent matter to discuss with you." With his hat in hand and his features pinched and drawn, Miguel came to stand beside the desk. "The Old Ones have shown me a vision. Dallas and Waco are in trouble."

"We've got to hurry." Tyler's words were clipped.

"What kind of trouble?"

"Outlaws. You must get a posse together. We must help." Anxiety peppered Miguel's voice. "The outlaws have too many guns. I am afraid for the people on the stage."

"But I don't know where to look."

"The Old Ones have shown me. We will lead you." Miguel gripped his hat tighter. "Please hurry. I do not think they can last much longer."

Sheriff Jeffrey dropped the half-eaten chicken leg, and his chair screeched back. "I've known you too long to question your visions, Miguel. Let's get going."

He snatched his napkin from his shirt and tossed it down. Plucking his hat off the wall hook, he crossed the room and jerked open the door.

Tyler rushed out, Miguel after her, jamming his sombrero atop his graying head, and Sheriff Jeffrey followed close behind.

Like the previous morning, gunshots woke Dallas. This time, however, she expected it. Rising, she washed her face and neck sparingly with water from her canteen.

Somehow the gunfire sounded different. It seemed closer. She hazarded a glance out the window. Her eyes widened in surprise as she caught sight of the outlaws galloping in retreat across the hills while other riders bore down on them.

Her heart pounding with joyful relief, she whirled and raced out the door to find the others. Trey met her in the hallway.

"It seems we've been saved," he said.

Dallas stared at him. The strain in his voice, the weariness in his features, made her uneasy. "What's wrong? There's something you're not telling me." Her pulse thumped, filling her throat.

"It's Waco."

Her blood seemed to freeze in her veins. "What about him?"

"I'm sorry."

She blinked in confusion. "What do you mean?" Her breath tangled in her lungs. "He's not . . ."

No denial came from Trey.

She stared at him for a long moment, then the light in her eyes dimmed and her lips trembled. "He's dead?"

Trey nodded.

Her voice was raspy with disbelief and pain. "What happened?"

"He was shot."

"Who?" The fury in that word tore at her heart.

"Zeke Roberts."

"How do you know?"

"The outlaws made a rush at us. One rider came closer and fired in Waco's direction. I saw Roberts."

"Where is my brother's body?" she asked, stumbling over her words.

"In the back room."

She brushed past him.

Trey watched her run down the hallway and disappear into the room. Closing his eyes, he drew one shaky breath, then another. He couldn't separate his suffering from hers. He would have done anything to spare her the pain. Never had he felt so helpless.

A moment later, her wail of grief reverberated through him like gunfire. His temples throbbed.

He walked to the front of the station and stared out the door. He saw Tyler and Miguel dismount and stride toward him.

"Is everyone all right?" Tyler asked breathlessly.

Trey felt so tired. "Your sister needs you. She's in the back."

Tyler hurried to be with Dallas.

Trey's stormy gaze swung to Miguel. No words were necessary. Miguel sagely nodded, then followed Tyler.

After what seemed an eternity to Trey, Dallas emerged. She walked toward him, her complexion pale, her green eyes overly large and bright against her ashen skin. Her tangible grief mingled with his own.

She looked up at him. "Where the hell were you when Waco needed you?"

Taken aback by her rage, he could only look at her, unable to find words.

"You bastard!" Dallas drew back her hand and slapped Trey with all her might, her stinging blow leaving the mark of her fingers blazing crimson on his face.

He swayed, then straightened. Stunned, he stared at her, taking in her pinched, furious expression.

Slowly, understanding dawned on Trey. He pulled her to him and cradled the cap of her head with a large hand as she sobbed her grief into his shoulder.

Chapter 20

When Dallas opened her tear-swollen eyes, she felt an odd detachment. Yesterday she had cried until she thought she had no tears left. Today she felt empty inside. Curiously, though, a strange tranquillity fell over her, as if her soul had been purged. She felt no grief for her departed brother, no anger at Trey. She had learned to survive by never looking back. Now she could only gaze straight ahead and keep putting one foot in front of the other.

The station was cool and quiet, incredibly normal, as she made her way downstairs to the kitchen. Abbey pulled pans of cornbread from the stove as if nothing out of the ordinary had happened. To look at Abbey's composed features and to witness Dallas's detachment, one certainly wouldn't know that today they would bury their beloved brother.

Walking past her sister, Dallas smiled wanly at Abbey. Dallas didn't bother heating water for a bath. Instead, she grabbed a few things and went to the creek.

Mindlessly she went through the routine of washing her hair, then bathing. She didn't want to think. Thinking made you feel. And she didn't want to feel anything—not today.

Several hours later, Trey and Miguel drove the three sisters to the cemetery on the outskirts of Lockhart. Dallas felt only an odd sense of unreality. As if it were all a bad dream. Any minute she'd wake up and find Waco safe and sound and weaving stories about the trip to San Antonio.

Buggies, buckboards, and single mounts tethered to the fence surrounded the cemetery. Folks always said a great many mourners came for those who died young. They had certainly turned out in droves to pay their last respects to Waco.

Trey assisted Dallas down from the wagon. Despite no words being said, the solid strength of his arms comforted her, shoring up her fortitude for what lay ahead.

With leaden steps Dallas walked to the grave site. With dry eyes she listened to the minister say a few words over Waco's simple pine coffin.

Dallas wondered if anyone else shared the detachment that allowed her to endure the ceremony. She noticed that Abbey's back was ramrod-straight, her eyes unblinkingly focused on the coffin. Tyler, her shoulders squared and her arms hanging at her sides with clenched fists, gritted her teeth. Frequently Dallas saw her lift her eyes from the pine box to stare off into the distance. Miguel's shoulders hunched under his sorrow.

Pain throbbed behind her eyes and hammered

in her throat as the ceremony came to a close and the coffin was lowered into the ground.

Waco wouldn't have wanted them to grieve long. They would do their best by him to remember a kind, loving brother, alive with generosity and compassion. Waco would've wanted it that way.

Dallas lifted her gaze to the vast blue sky in a final farewell to her brother. Finally she turned and followed Tyler, Abbey, and Miguel to the wagon. Silently they made their way home. Women from the Baptist church followed them to the station, and served lunch to the mourners. Other neighbors also brought food and expressed their sympathy.

Funny, Dallas thought, looking at all the food on the kitchen table, who could eat at a time like this?

Needing to be alone, she made her way through the crowded house to the front porch. She sat in the swing and looked out across the yard. Tears she didn't think she had in her streamed down her cheeks. She would never hear her brother's sweet voice or see his handsome face again.

Trey sat back in the parlor chair, his fingers curled around the drink he'd just poured himself. He felt as if someone had reached inside his chest and squeezed his heart mercilessly as he recalled Dallas's eyes—so wide, so troubled. She had looked so vulnerable. And so alone.

He felt her pain as if it were his own.

"Amigo?"

Trey looked up to see Miguel standing in the

doorway, watching him. "Would you care to join me?" Trey asked in a brittle tone.

"I will sit with you for a while." Miguel regarded the glass of whiskey in Trey's hand as he settled into a nearby chair. "That will not cure what ails you."

"But it might help me forget, if only for a short while." Trey raised the glass to his lips, tilted his head back, and swallowed. The whiskey burned a fiery path down his throat and into his stomach. "If I could change things, I would."

"I know, *amigo.*" Miguel sighed. "But you must not blame yourself."

"It's my fault." Trey fingered the rim of the glass. "I insisted Waco ride shotgun."

There was a short, tense silence.

"You cannot be responsible for another man's path." Miguel's voice was firm with conviction. "There is nothing to be gained by blaming yourself for something you cannot control."

Trey glared at the older man. "I'm the boss. It was my decision to carry that large a payroll. It was my decision to drive through the night."

Normally a patient, understanding man, Miguel raised his voice to Trey. "Your concern should be to the living. Waco is beyond your help. Dallas needs you now."

Tension etched deep furrows in Trey's face. "I'm the last person Dallas needs."

"*Amigo,* listen to me. Remember what I told you before. Open your heart. Do not keep your heart closed and deny yourself happiness."

Trey pushed the whiskey bottle away from

him. "What could I give her?" For once in his life, he had trouble meeting another man's gaze.

"Love. That is all she wants, all anyone needs."

"I wish it were that simple," Trey snapped.

"Why make matters hard?" Miguel countered.

"I could never make Dallas happy."

"How do you know this?"

"Because I've never loved anyone." Trey's voice was fraught with regret. "I don't know how. I don't want to hurt her."

Miguel came to his feet and placed a hand on Trey's shoulder. "It would hurt her more for you to walk out of her life."

"It would save her a lot of pain in the long run." Trey's frustration, anger, and pain blended into one implacable thought. "I'm no good for her."

"Why don't you let her be the judge of that?"

Trey massaged his temples in a vain attempt to relieve the pain throbbing there. "After everything that's happened between us, I'm sure she hates me. You can't build a marriage on hate."

Miguel sighed. "How do you know her feelings? Has she told you?"

"No."

"Give her the chance to tell you what is in her heart," Miguel urged.

Trey felt restless. He stood and declared, "I can't allow her to throw her life away for me."

"Listen to your heart, *amigo*, and follow what it tells you to do."

Trey balled his hands into fists at his sides. "It's telling me the wrong thing. Can't you understand that?"

"Face your emotions." Miguel's voice was low,

forceful, his message persistent. "Once you have done that, you will know they do not mislead you."

The impact of those words battered Trey's resolve like physical blows. He tried to answer but failed.

Miguel was suddenly beside him. Trey knew Miguel could read in his face all the things that he so desperately wanted to hide.

"Do you love her?"

Trey tried to swallow back the truth, but he couldn't. "Yes," he confessed.

Miguel's voice was gentle. "Does she know this?"

"Yes."

"Has she spoken to you of her feelings?"

"Yes."

"Have you considered the possibility of a child?"

Trey's head snapped up. His gaze burned with intensity. "What has Dallas told you?"

"You know that is not her way. I may be old, but I am not blind. I have seen the knowing looks that pass between you."

Trey straightened his weary, aching shoulders. "I've thought of little else."

"Would you want Dallas to go through such a thing alone?"

Trey looked away. "God, no, but I don't know what to do."

Miguel smiled gently, reassuringly. "The Old Ones have shown me the happiness that awaits you and Dallas. You have wasted enough time because of pride."

Trey nodded, then watched as Miguel turned

and walked out. He had never run from anything before. He would honor his love for Dallas. He couldn't bear the thought of a life without her.

She was his life.

His mood dark, brooding, and volatile, Jonas sat stiffly in the chair behind his desk, his breath short and labored. He had not known it was possible to live with such hatred—hatred for Trey Conner for besting him—and not go mad.

A cautious knock sounded at the closed door.

"Come in," Jonas said flatly.

Zeke Roberts strode into the room. "You sent for me, boss?"

"Yep," Jonas affirmed curtly. He opened a drawer, pulled out an envelope, and tossed it across the desk at Roberts. "There's enough money in there for you to leave Texas."

"Why?" Roberts asked, clearly surprised. "I followed your orders."

The very reminder of Roberts's stupidity rankled Jonas anew, prodded the raw wounds within him. Jonas didn't tolerate fools. "You idiot, don't you realize what you've done? By killing Waco O'Neal, you've caused me a great deal of trouble." Not to mention jeopardizing his plans for Dallas.

If she were ever to discover his part in her brother's murder . . .

"I don't want to have to answer any questions about you," Jonas said. "You're finished working for me."

"But, boss—"

"You heard me." Jonas's decision was absolute. "This place is going to be hot for a while.

I don't want the law snooping around and interfering with my business."

His voice dropped, the tone menacing. "You've given Trey Conner the perfect opportunity and reason to come after me. If I'm not careful, all my plans could be ruined."

He gave a brittle laugh, stemming from his hatred and his fervent desire to see Trey Conner brought low at long last. Little else mattered.

Roberts opened the envelope and counted the money inside. "What about the rest that's owed me?"

The gunman's question broke into Jonas's thoughts. Jonas frowned. "You'll get it. A man with your talents for murder and robbery won't have trouble finding a job." Jonas gave a curt nod toward the door. "Now, get going."

Trey found Dallas on the front porch. She sat in the swing, staring out across the landscape, lost in thought . . . or memories of Waco. Trey stood just inside the door, out of her line of vision. Giving her another moment of privacy, he steeled himself to face her.

Trey sensed her need to be alone, but the vulnerability he'd seen today in her eyes made him realize that Miguel was right. She needed him. He just wasn't sure if she knew it.

And if she was with child? The uncertainty rattled him.

He wondered how best to approach Dallas. Never had he felt so helpless as he noted the tracks of spent tears down her cheeks.

He considered how much he'd learned about her pride and strength. If he mentioned his suspicions about the baby, she would fight the idea of marriage, mistakenly thinking she was trapping him.

She must have sensed his presence, for she said, "I'm all right. You don't have to stand there."

Trey's lips tightened at the lingering anguish in her voice. He attempted to disguise his anxiety with a mask of calmness.

He joined her on the porch, choosing to sit on the steps. "I know this isn't the best time to talk, but I don't think we should wait."

"All right."

He cleared his throat uneasily. Oh, hell, there was no easy way to do this. "If you'll have me, I want to marry you."

She stilled her swinging motions, and her face grew paler. "Why this sudden change?"

"Let's just say I've seen the situation for what it is."

"Which is?"

"We need to get married. We're at our best together."

Dallas visibly trembled. Color flared in her cheeks. He could see that she was fighting her reaction to his words. "That's very noble of you, but it's not necessary."

"Now, hold on. I'm not trying to be noble."

"Then what are you doing?" Dallas asked, her words even and pronounced, her composure perfect.

"Look, I've never done this before. I'm sorry if my words aren't exactly what you want to hear."

"It's not what I want to hear because I'm certain you don't mean it."

"You know I never do or say anything I don't mean."

"Look, I can take care of myself. You don't have to hang around here for me."

"But I have an obligation to you I can't ignore. I've come to care about your family, and I can't knowingly ruin their good names."

"Not to mention my good name, is that it?" Her humiliation burned in her cheeks. "Since when do you care what others think?"

"I don't. But I can't ride away and leave you to deal with the possibility of a child, alone."

"You're making this harder than it has to be."

"Nothing's ever been easy when it comes to you." Trey gave a short laugh. "Since I met you, you've turned my life upside down."

"Well, if you think that knowing you is easy, you've got another think coming." Her voice tightened with exasperation. "I'll save you the trouble of having to face my family by refusing to marry you. Now you can ride away with a clear conscience."

"When will you stop acting childish?" His expression hardened. "I guess what I'm trying to say is that I want to marry you because I love you."

Myriad emotions played across her face. "And I love you," she whispered, after a long time.

He moved from the steps to join her on the swing.

He took her hand in his, and the tension ebbed from his face. "Believe me, I made a list of all the reasons I shouldn't marry you. I'm not sure I'll be a good husband. I may be incapable of loving you the way you deserve." He raised her hand to his mouth and kissed her knuckles. "But my heart told me I'd never be able to walk out of your life," he whispered against her skin. "Whatever we have to learn, we'll learn together."

Tears born of joy, not pain, trickled down her cheeks. "Oh, Trey, I love you so much." She threw her arms about his neck. "Yes, I'll marry you."

"Well, there's one thing for certain," he said against her hair. "Life with you will never be boring."

He pressed his mouth to hers and sealed their future with a kiss as tender as his feelings for Dallas.

At last, he broke contact and raised his head. His expression grew somber. "There's something else I've got to tell you."

Her previous joy turned into apprehension. "What?" Dread hung thick in her voice.

"I can't marry you until I finish my job."

A sick feeling of premonition rolled in the pit of her stomach. "Jonas?"

"Yes."

"What are you going to do?"

"I paid him a visit the night the barn burned, and I made him a promise that if he ever hurt you, or any of your family, he'd answer personally to me."

"But no one was hurt. And the barn can be rebuilt."

"You don't understand."

Then she did. "Waco?"

"Zeke Roberts didn't come after the stage without orders." He clenched his jaw. "Orders from Jonas."

"Let the sheriff take care of it." Her determination was palpable.

"Dallas, I can't begin a new life with you until I finish what I set out to do."

"But we won't have a life together at all if you get yourself killed."

"I promise to come back to you, very much alive."

"Oh, Trey, I'm frightened for you. If half of what you've told me about Jonas Webb is true, you don't know what he'll do." She clutched his sleeve. "Please, let the law handle Webb."

"There's no hard evidence connecting Webb to Roberts's shooting of Waco. But I know Jonas was behind it. Just as he was behind the gunman who jumped me in San Antonio."

Gently, yet firmly, Trey uncurled her fingers from his shirt. "I'm the only one who can settle this score. If for no other reason, I owe it to Waco." He stood. "I'll leave Roberts for the law, but Jonas is mine."

He kissed her forehead, then left her to stare at his retreating back. As soon as Trey was out of sight, Dallas sprang to her feet and raced to find Miguel.

Worry darkened Miguel's already coffee brown eyes as he watched Dallas saddle her horse beneath the lean-to. "I do not like what you are doing. Let me speak to the Old Ones before you go."

"There's no time for that. I've got to reach Jonas before Trey does," she said in a clipped tone. "I don't want any more bloodshed. I've got to try to keep them from killing each other."

"You do not know what Webb will do. Let me go with you. We have already buried one family member today. I do not wish to bury another."

"He's not going to hurt me. I'm not even going directly to him. I'll have somebody tell Jonas to meet me in the livery stable in town so I know he'll come alone. I only want to talk to him."

"This is dangerous," Miguel warned her sternly.

"I don't care. I can't stand by and do nothing, and take a chance that Webb might kill Trey." She swung herself into the saddle. "Try to stall Trey as long as you can." With that, Dallas kicked her mare into a dead run toward Lockhart.

Jonas opened his eyes and looked about the bedroom. Grimacing, he sat up slowly and propped himself against the ornately carved headboard.

His aching body, his slowly mending injuries, were reminders to him of his hatred for Trey Conner. Rage gripped Jonas and obliterated the pain from his mind.

Jonas was startled by a sharp rap on the closed door. "Come in," he said in a terse tone.

Jenny entered, carrying a tray of coffee and biscuits. With a slow, halting gait, she crossed the room and set the tray on the table adjacent to the bed.

Jonas watched her closely as she poured him a cup of the fresh brew. She had taken to styling her hair differently, wearing curls close to her face to hide the jagged scar.

She handed him the coffee. "Dallas O'Neal

gave me a message for you. She said it's mighty important that she see you right away."

Dallas. Jonas smiled at his good fortune. "Where is she?"

"She said for you to meet her in the livery stable."

"Why there?"

"She didn't say. And I didn't ask."

"All right." Jonas took one sip of the coffee, then set the cup and saucer down on the tray with a rattle.

Suspicion darkened his expression. What was Dallas up to? Why the smithy's? Perhaps she didn't want anyone to know about their rendezvous.

He thought about her brother's funeral earlier in the day. Had she connected him with Waco's murder? No, she wasn't the kind to take the law into her own hands.

He jerked back the bedcovers and swung his legs over the edge of the bed. "Get me some clothes, Jenny."

She brought him the requested garments. With careful, deliberate motions, he dressed.

A chill snaked down her spine as Jenny watched Jonas slide his knife into the belt sheath, a strange twist to his bruised features.

Something bad was going to happen. She felt it in her bones. Jonas dwelled too much on his hatred of Trey Conner. And wherever Dallas O'Neal went, Conner wasn't far behind.

Inside the livery stable, Dallas paced, straw rustling beneath her boots. What was taking Jonas so long? He should've been here by now. She prayed to God that Miguel had been able to stall Trey and buy her valuable time. But this delay was squandering precious minutes.

With brisk strides across the stable, she tried to reconcile her present actions with her hunger for vengeance against Jonas. If Jonas had ordered the robbery attempt, and had been ultimately responsible for Waco's death, how could she justify coming to plead with him?

Because she loved Trey more than she hated Jonas, her heart thundered.

She spun on her heel to pace in the other direction. A shadow fell across her and she saw Jonas standing in the doorway. When he moved farther into the dim interior, she gasped at the sight of his badly bruised, cut face.

Instantly she knew what had taken place between the two men. The revelation was written on her face.

"Don't tell me your boss didn't tell you of the visit he paid me?" Jonas gave a dry, brittle laugh. "I'll be ready for him next time."

Dallas took a step toward him. "That's why I'm here. Trey's coming for you."

Suspicion, and yes, surprise, darted across his discolored features. "Why are you telling me this?"

"Because there's been enough killing and bloodshed already."

"Sorry to disappoint you, but I've never backed down from a fight," he replied in an ominous whisper.

"I hoped I could reason with you."

His blue eyes glittered with savage intensity. "Why the sudden concern for Conner?"

"Because I love him," she said with gentle conviction. "We're going to be married."

"How could you betray me?" With menacing strides, Jonas advanced on her. "Surely you knew I cared for you."

Wide-eyed with disbelief and utterly speechless, Dallas stared at him.

"No woman throws me over for another man." He leered at her, vehemence pinching his features. "You know I can't let you go, don't you?"

Realizing the certain danger she faced, she whirled to run, but she wasn't quick enough.

An arm hooked about her middle and Dallas was jerked back against Jonas's solid frame. He whirled her around to face him and twisted his fingers into her loosely braided hair, cruelly yanking her head back. She cried out in pain, then froze in horror as she saw the faint glint of blue steel, then felt the finely honed point of a knife against her neck.

"You've left me with no other choice, Dallas."

He pressed the knife blade deeper into her flesh. She winced in pain, then froze as a tiny trickle of blood ran down her neck. He'd cut her!

"Please . . . Jonas," she whispered. "Don't hurt me."

She felt the blade lift, and she experienced a dizzying wave of relief.

"It's too late, Dallas."

The quiet threat in his words extinguished that faint, flickering hope. Then she felt the pain as he punishingly gripped her jaw and squeezed.

Mindless desperation caused her to struggle, but his hold tightened, his fingers digging into her soft skin. He brought the knife to her face, running the flat side of the blade across her cheekbone in a sadistic caress.

She squeezed her eyes shut and waited for him to cut her throat.

"Don't worry. I'm not going to kill you."

He lowered the knife. Her eyes flew open.

"Yet." He ran his knuckles down her cheek and across her jaw. "I'll wait until Conner arrives. Then I'll have the pleasure of killing you both."

In the ensuing silence, the distinct sound of a revolver's hammer being cocked could be heard. "Let her go, Jonas, or I'll kill you where you stand." Trey spoke in a deadly calm voice.

But Jonas was past sanity and he grabbed Dallas, jerking her in front of him as a human shield. "I don't think you want to risk firing a shot. You might hit Dallas." Keeping one arm clenched around her waist, he lifted a hand to wipe the blood from the tip of his blade against the fabric covering her breast. With obvious relish, he placed the honed edge to her throat. "Or make me nervous."

Hatred and dread roiled inside Trey at the sight of blood on her neck, at the sight of Dallas's eyes, large with stark terror. A muscle constricted in his jaw.

Trey had one chance to save Dallas. Although Jonas used her as a shield, Trey might be able to drop Jonas with a bullet between the eyes, knocking him backward.

Trey tensed. He had to act. Now. Or he would lose the woman he cherished and loved more than life itself.

Not without a fight!

On the count of three, he told himself.

One . . .

Suddenly a pistol shot shattered the taut silence.

Dallas screamed as Jonas slumped against her, his weight pressing her to the floor. He fell atop her. She frantically scrambled from beneath his sagging body.

In the split second of blurred confusion, Trey crouched and prepared to fire at the figure standing just inside the livery's rear door. His finger eased off the trigger as he recognized the woman from the dance.

Jenny stepped forward, the barrel of the pistol wobbling in her shaky grasp. She stopped and stared down at Jonas's lifeless body. "I couldn't let him hurt anyone else," she said in a reed-thin voice. The gun thudded to the ground beside her.

Trey didn't spare Jenny a second glance, but went to Dallas and gathered her in his arms. He touched her injury, reassuring himself it was only a minor cut, then he buried his face in her hair.

With joyful relief trembling on her lips, Dallas pressed her cheek against his broad chest. She reveled in the heat and strength of him, her pain forgotten within the safety of his embrace.

"Thank God, you're all right." His breath escaped in a raw, faltering sigh.

She heard his thundering heartbeat beneath her ear. "I am now." She pulled away and searched his eyes. "What's going to happen to that woman?"

"Nothing. She acted in self-defense."

"What about us?" she asked, her voice simmering with all her heartfelt hopes and desires.

"I intend to marry you as soon as possible and never let you leave my side" he answered, his words a testament to his love.

"Including driving the stage?"

"Yes, with me riding shotgun beside you." He gazed deeply into her eyes. "We're a team, and nothing or no one is ever going to split us up. You see, Dallas, I actually own the stage line. After you marry me, it becomes our line. And I don't ever want it any other way."

Taking a deep breath, she whispered, "I love you so much."

"I intend to spend the rest of my life showing you just how much I love you." He sealed his promise with a kiss.